WAITING FACE

L.J. PELTROP

SUMMERSET
BOOKS

WAITING FACE

Copyright © 2020 by L.J. Peltrop

Summerset Books a division of HOV, LLC.

www.summersetbooks.com

summersetbooks@gmail.com

Cover Design: Hope of Vision Designs

For further information regarding special discounts on bulk purchases, or to contact Author L.J. Peltrop, email ljpeltropauthor@gmail.com

ISBN Paperback: 978-1-7357761-0-1

eBook: 978-1-7357761-1-8

10 9 8 7 6 5 4 3 2 1

Printed in the United States of America

CONTENTS

Dedication

Dedicated to those who could never fit in. No matter what you may be going through, do what you love and pursue it at all costs; only then will you find where you belong.

To Pamela Thompson, I'm the writer you always knew I was meant be.

"I am what time, circumstance, history, have made of me, certainly, but I am also so much more than that. So are we all." – James Baldwin

Author Foreword

If you're reading this, thank you. This book was written in some of the most extreme and desperate circumstances imaginable. It was the story I needed to write in order free myself from the mental and sociological chains - I unwillingly inherited. It's funny, most people want to write a novel, but unfortunately most people can't. And who is to say I'm any different? Since childhood, I was profoundly moved by the power of words. In which, if they're formed in a particular fashion; sentences and paragraphs could inflict pain, object remorse, manifest love or my personal favorite—cultivate the magic to heal.

As the reader of this novel, although he's fictional; I need you to look at the character, Michael, as his own person. He and I have similar ways and traits yet, we're two completely different individuals. Please take the time to see him as his own, and not a mirror of myself. Unfortunately, in the beginning I didn't possess the strength or tenacity he has. But, through him, I was able to find my own. I needed Michael just as much as he needed me. Without him, I couldn't write and without me, he couldn't exist but together, we became liberated. In the countless and draining hours it took to tell his journey, I enjoyed every last minute spent with him and I hope you will too.

WELCOME TO SECOND HOUSE

A hot shower wasn't enough today. Usually, a good sneeze and steaming water removes all the coke boogers from the night before, but here I am once again plucking them away into the street. I'm counting the hours until I'm able to flop back onto my bed. I'm excited to start my new serving job tonight. It's partially the reason why I have any energy at all right now. The fact that I'm not riding on a piss-smelling bus to get there is the best part. Give or take, the seven-minute walk to Second House from my apartment is everything. Next to Billie, I have the shortest commute by far, and if my car wasn't sitting in my parent's driveway with a blown engine, I would still walk—especially on a gorgeous day such as this one.

It took till the third week of May for the weather to switch over from the bipolar climate of New England spring to the scorching days and cool nights of early summer. Living in the southern part of Connecticut, this particular location of State is also the sub-region of New York City. Occupying residency here has its perks. We get to experience the four seasons—with a twist. For example, in the middle of March, on some random day it might be sixty degrees, sunny, without a single cloud in the sky and before you know it, two feet of heavy snow on the ground the next morning. Safe to say summer is upon us now. You can tell by the lack of warm clothing by pedestrians. Unfortunately, that's when the open-toe sandals come out and the people who relax so effortlessly wearing them rear their hideous feet with reckless abandon.

My favorite part of the seasonal change is seeing the women who bust out their thigh-high shorts and sundresses. Speaking as a heterosexual young man, there's nothing sexier than a tight-waisted, thick-legged woman in a pair of 'whore' shorts that hug oh so close on a great set of freshly-shaven legs. What really causes a spike in the temperature during a July heatwave is a healthy layer of moisturizer to make those razor blade thighs and legs really shine. Oh God, let me stop before I give myself a chubby before walking into this damn restaurant. Speaking of chubby…rubbing one out before going in would've shaken off any 'first day on the job' jitters. Not that I've done it before. It's something my dad would always suggest when I started dating in college. I'm picturing him now, with his low-sunken voice followed by his goofy chuckle. "Make sure you rub one out before stepping out, Mike, you want to shake off any first date jitters." What a creep my dad is, but he means well.

At the end of my street facing the crosswalk, my analog watch reads a quarter-past five as I wait for the traffic lights to turn red on both sides of the two-way intersection. The city never made it their business to put a walking signal here, and it's nearly impossible to cross the street with ongoing traffic. It's not all that dangerous, but trying to get from one sidewalk to another is as hazardous as it is in any other neighboring town outside of Manhattan.

My apartment is no less than two hundred yards from this upscale apartment complex that happens to have a nice walking path that I can cut through to get to Second House. The walkway shadows a forty-foot wide stream. The body of water stretches over some length, but my house sits on a hill, which makes the tiny river nonexistent from my third-floor attic apartment. Whenever I get the chance to travel through the small passage, I take it in for the allotted brief moments I'm here for a walk or a morning jog along this river. This location alone revives the meaning of a 'new' day; probably when you catch the sunrise, I suppose, more so, I can barely imagine myself. Relishing in the landscape can be too much at times; I'll run the risk of becoming aloof. I'm never spared of the futile envy as I march past my blow dealer's fourth-floor balcony, which oversees the entire river and a panoramic view of the sunset. If you catch it at the right time, you can get a great snapshot of the city skyline.

"Hey, Michael," a faint feminine voice shouts. I glance back and there's no one there. What th—

"Hey, Michael up here…" I gaze up to the familiar fourth-floor patio and there goes Tracie's daughter, Cam.

I wave. "How's it going little lady, where's your mom?"

"She's in New York, I think. You wanna come up and play Barbies with me?"

"I can't today little lady. I start my new job tonight, remember?"

"Yeah, I remember. But Michael, that's boring, you should come up and play."

"Wish I could, Cam baby, but I got to work. How else am I going to afford the cab to take you ice skating? I need money to do that, and that's why I have to go to work."

Cam smiles. "You said this Sunday, right?"

"Little lady, have I ever lied to you?"

She giggles. "No."

"So, those ice-skates I got you for your birthday, you got them laced up right?"

"Uh-huh."

"Alright then, Sunday it is. When your mom gets back, tell her to shoot me a text, please. Wait a second, who's watching you right now?"

"Nana."

"Oh, tell her I said hello. Well, I gotta get going wish me luck."

She screams, "Luck!" and I smile.

"Alright, little lady see you later."

"Michael, wait!" Cam yells.

"Yeah?"

"I love you."

"And I love you back. If I don't see you later on, have a good night sweetie."

"You too."

When I reach the end of the path, it's as if coming back to the harsh realities of living in this miserable swamp ass of a town. Soon as I get to the end of the brick pavement, in my way stands a few crack dealers who loiter in the parking lot along with the junkies they sell too. To the right of the parking lot, there's the off-track betting building where all these scumbags dwell and splurge their social security and disabilities checks on whatever they choose to gamble on. It's been here for years, and I always found it to be despicable for the city to keep it ten-feet away from the local bus hub. Hard-working people have to pass by the sight of addiction and despair every day as they wait for their transport. Whenever I was doomed to endear the city bus- no doubt, I sulked. But, fuck them and those pissy shuttle traps – today's a new day and I have a new job.

On the other side of the off-betting track is the local bodega, ran by Arabs, and it always reeks of bad Halal (although very convenient for buying loose Newport cigarettes when I can't afford a pack). But, the wife and husband who run it, are great people, and they can make one hell of a steak and cheese. But they're never open past 6 pm. A few feet from the store's entrance, the transit busses line up along their designated spots. Usually, the out of town shuttles are always running behind schedule yet aside from winter snowstorms, the in-town bus drivers are on time for the most part. I guess that's just public transportation for you—take it at your own risk, I suppose. "You need a car, Michael," is what my mother has been screeching ever since the tower set my car in her driveway. But – today, I could care-less about anything that's runs on wheels and a motor.

The next street over is Second House; a restaurant and bar combo. Before making an entrance, I walk past the empty patio that's scattered with stacked up metal chairs and five blanketed round tables able to fit a party of four comfortably. There are three six-by-six blackboards. Etched in chalk are listings and prices of bottled and draft craft beer, whiskeys, and a lot of bourbons. Seems as if the owners know their booze as it's quite the drinking menu with bourbon and whiskeys I've never heard of. Looks like I'm going to learn a lot. What the fuck is Eagle Rare Whiskey? I have no fucking clue, but whatever it is, it sounds expensive. Expensive means tasteful and so working in this industry, the higher the taste, the higher the tips.

Once I arrive at the entrance, I turn the heavy brass handle, embracing the new opportunity I'm about to embark on. Inside, the aroma of homemade barbecue and fried chicken robs my senses. No host or hostess to be greeted by, and the front desk is overspread with plastic menus and what could be food specials. The country music coming over the speakers is a little hard on the ears, but the early 1900's cash register sitting on top of the wooden desk is welcoming, I guess. Underneath the wooden base is a glass case, and in it are neatly folded black shirts with white lettering printed in cursive spelling out 'Second House.' I'm assuming in a few days; I'll be wearing one of those shirts.

Over the music, a mix of guest banter and the voices of sportscasters coming from an NHL set the ambiance. From the looks of it, they do pretty well at the bar, especially given the time of day it is. And for the odd number of patrons who are occupying the table seating— they seem pleasantly confined. I then count out fourteen table tops which deem fit just for two- I assume they all can be conjoined for bigger parties. There's booth cushion that runs along the wall, it extends from the beginning of the bar to what looks as if it's the back entrance of the restaurant. I then count eighteen bar stools. Above the stocked bar are two big wide-screens. The atmosphere alone says, "easy" but the leisure seems highly sought after, this might be the go-to spot for happy hour.

Towards the back entrance, I spot a husky, four-eleven maybe or at best five-foot, short-haired blonde woman wearing one of the shirts from the inside case, with dark blue denim jeans, and a long black apron that almost touches the floor. She might be in her early to mid-thirties. She's tending to a couple seated a few feet from the back exit. By the way they're laughing and carrying on with her they appear to be regulars. The man tending the bar is about 6'3 with salt and pepper hair—fair enough to say, he was once in decent shape—an athlete even, but that ship has sailed. If I had to guess, he might be in his early forties, but you could tell how years of bad living diminished his boyish looks—which morphed him into a "washed up" neighborhood bartender—at least this occupation suits his overall appearance.

I watch aimlessly as the talkative bartender picks up a *Tito's Vodka* bottle, shuffles to the ice well, and scoops shaved ice then pours vodka into a rocks glass then halts two-thirds away from the top. He then takes the fountain gun, and presses the soda button. As the club soda rushes over the ice, he adds a little more *Tito's* and buries a miniature black straw then wedges a lime along the rim for the finishing touch. He slides the beverage in front of the customer he's been conversating with. "Yeah, Carl, you're right," the bartender says, "This might be the Rangers best year yet."

"And you know, Graham, there's no other team in the Eastern Conference with a better defense. We're looking too strong this year, brother, too strong. I swear it," the customer replies.

"If there's one thing we can agree on it's how we feel about the Rangers this season," Graham laughs. Assuming this is the perfect time to make my presence known; I take two paces to the end of the bar where Graham is. Exhaling my pent-up breath and then rubbing the sweat off my palms, I smile. "Hi, Graham, how are you? I'm Michael. I'm here to start my first day of training as a server."

Graham makes eye contact and continues to wipe down the bar counter then in a blink of an eye, he begins to size me up. The way he's studying my presence, it's almost as if I were a homeless person who just came into to ask to use the restroom. Suddenly, a drink ticket starts to print, the sound takes his attention off me. Graham, not even acknowledging I just asked him a question pertaining to my livelihood, snatches the ticket, places it on the bar, turns his back, and starts to prepare the order.

"Weathers, right?" Graham shouts.

"That is me, Sir…"

He turns. "Yeah. A.G. said you were starting today," he glances at his wristwatch. "You're about thirty minutes early, but I guess that's a good thing."

"Like my dad always says, if you're on time you're late," I joke.

"No offense kid, with a name like Michael Weathers... well, how can I put this... I was expecting somebody with not so much color if you catch my drift."

I chuckle. "I'm sorry, Sir, you'll have to forgive me, but I don't catch your drift."

"Well... I thought you'd be...and again, no disrespect kid, but your name sounds white as hell," he laughs. "A name like Jamal or Tyrone would have been less of a surprise, you know?"

"He's right, kid, your name sounds white as hell," Carl interjects.

"Ahh... I don't know what say, Graham. But my mother always said I had the element of surprise. So, I guess I have that going for me," I say around a forced grin.

"Yeah," he smirks. "That seems to be the case here. But alright, Mike, hope you don't mind me calling you Mike?"

"No, I don't mind at all. Mike is universal, right?"

"I guess so. I never thought of it like that. So yeah, if you wanna head over to the back of the bar where Tina is. You'll be training with her tonight."

"Alright. And that's the blonde woman back there?" I ask.

"You stand correct. I'll see you later," he replies.

"Nice meeting you Graham."

He waves. "You too, Mike, good luck."

As I approach, Tina's movement suddenly shifts towards the kitchen then she takes a sharp right. I follow her more closely now. Hopefully, she doesn't think I'm some weird creep. To my left, I catch her while putting an order into the Point of Sale system, POS for short. Before I can introduce myself, she blurts out in a Eastern European accent, "Can I help you?" Tina says.

I smile at her. "Hi, I'm Michael Weathers. I'm here to start my training as a server. Graham told me I would be shadowing you tonight."

She frowns back. "Oh, how nice for you. Nobody told me that I would be training anyone today. So, this is news to me. A.G. usually tells me about the new hires."

In order to calm the tension, I give a friendly chuckle. "Didn't mean to strike a nerve. Unfortunately, I need a job, but again I apologize if I made you feel uneasy, I'm just showing up."

"I guess it's not your fault, I just hate training new people 'cause there's a lot of shit I have to cover within a very small amount of time. I have five hours or less with you and I don't know how experienced you are—that ties into your training too. A.G. likes to hire people with no experience then they quit because it's too much or we can't keep them 'cause they keep fucking up. Tell you one thing, Newbie. Oh, by the way I know you have a name but I don't have the time to remember it or care to, so you're going to go by Newbie unless you prove you have what it takes to work here, let alone be a waiter. Got it?"

"Okay, got it. I see your point. To make things a little easier for you, Tina, or at least try too. I was in hospitality for about four to five years throughout college. I was referred to you guys by my former boss Dick Bailey. And is there a place I can put my backpack?"

She shuffles around the server station and kicks a tightly wrapped package of white cloth guest towels into the corner. "Yup, I'll show where you can put it in a bit. Follow me into the kitchen real quick." Tina moves with tremendous purpose out of the service station, continues through the back of the bar, and straight through the kitchen's heavy wooden doors. She walks up to the expediter station and takes three ten-ounce cheeseburgers plated with fries out of the heated window, separates three silver ramekins, fills them with ketchup, and finally places each one with a burger.

"Oh, Dick Bailey, I know him—he comes in here all the time. Sometimes when I finish my shift he'll pop up and buy me a round, really good guy to work for from what I hear. Why you'd leave?"

"A few years back before my corporate job, I was promoted to the head waiter position pretty quickly but then he closed down the restaurant that following February, and before you know it, I went from head waiter to working security with my dad. Shortly after graduating college; I found work as a copywriter at LBS the investment bank and I was with them for about three years almost. You need help running those burgers?"

"No, but thank you. One thing you'll learn about working here is the more you can run and drop food on your own, the better it looks not only to your table but to management too." She kicks the middle of the doors as she leads the way out onto the floor. She scurries over to the couple I saw her with moments prior. As she places the food in front of the guests and the third plate in front of an empty seat she says, "Hey, guys this is Michael." She smiles. "He'll be following me tonight. Michael this is Jill and her husband Robb. They're in here all the time, so get familiar with these lovely folks." The married couple both extend their hands for a formal greeting.

"Hi guys, I'm Michael, happy to make your acquaintance. Who's the third burger for? If you don't mind me asking."

Jill smiles, showing off her perfect white teeth. "Well, it's a pleasure to make your acquaintance as well, Michael. I wish our son was as well-mannered as you. Speaking of him, that burger is his, he's trying to find parking."

"And my wife is right, Michael, I sure wish John had your mannerisms. Take notice, this being your first day and all. Every time we come here to eat our son is always late, always." Robb says.

Jill begins to cut her sandwich in half saying, "I like to call it fashionably late."

Rob takes a sip of his beer. "You're too lenient on that boy and you know it. He wouldn't know what being on time was if it hit him on the head. No wonder he's a mama's boy," he laughs.

Tina and I both chuckle. I can't speak for her but over the years, working in this type of environment, I managed to perfect what I call the 'fake laugh'. When customers say corny shit thinking they're Jerry Seinfeld or somebody, you have to chime in on their corniness—your tip depends on it. One can narrow it down to kissing ass for a living.

"Well guys, I'll let you two eat and come back when John gets here. Hopefully, his burger will still be warm. Enjoy you guys," Tina says.

Rob snarls, "Ah, fuck him, he's a waste of fucking space anyway."

"Shut up Rob and eat your damn dinner." Jill turns to me. "Michael, it was a pleasure to meet you. Hope you'll stick around long enough to serve us someday."

"No-no Jill, the pleasure is all mine. Enjoy your dinner you guys,"

"Thanks, and good luck to you, Michael," Rob says.

"And what a wonderful smile you have," Jill adds, "watch out for this one Tina."

With Tina guiding, and to ensure I'm not hovering, I count my steps, making sure I'm always two paces behind. We head over to the end of the bar where she removes a freshly made Cosmopolitan from service. Underneath the cocktail, there's the two-ply paper that is associated with the beverage, and she stamps the ticket through a metal spike located to the left. She does a 180 degree turn and for the first time makes eye contact. "Very important to remember to stamp your drink tickets whenever you take your drink," she states.

"Usually how it goes," I reply.

"Yup, I'm glad you know where to stand. Some trainees linger like flies," she says as she speeds the beverage back to the married couple. Tina takes Jill's empty martini glass then replaces it without interrupting the couple's conversation. Tina gives a thumb up and Jill smiles back assuring that she and her husband's needs are met. Rob continues to chow down while his wife picks at her french-fries. We walk to the front entrance, past the hostess stand, on through another corridor, and enter into an unseen room of the restaurant. Unlike the barroom tables, there are more dinner tables, along with grey buckets sitting on top of every one of them. The grayish tin pails have drink and food menus sticking out. Underneath the buckets is tan-colored construction paper that covers all the tables.

Tina turns our direction back to the server station but before we enter, she snatches a smudged glass off one of the tables and carefully places it in the empty bus bin to the right of the POS. Next to that one is another one but filled with plates, silverware, and more of those tin buckets. Tina bends halfway down and swings open the door to a wooden cabinet under the POS. Inside of the cubby lies a few purses, a few stank looking shoes, and a balled-up Second House shirt. "You can throw your stuff right in here. You don't have anything important in it like money or anything like that do you?" she asks.

I loosen the straps and toss my backpack in. "Nope, just my phone, apron, and some pens."

Tina's eyes widen. "You sure you want to keep your phone in there?"

"It'll be fine. I have an old flip phone anyway; I concentrate better without it."

"Okay, if you say so… Have you seen this part of the restaurant yet?"

"No, I haven't, it looks like a sever station. There's plenty of folded napkins, extra side plates, a basket of silver I'm guessing they need polished…and bins for the dirty dishes and glassware."

Tina grazes my lower-back to gain passage to the triangle folded cloth napkins. "Yup, you got the gist of it." She pushes the guest napkins to the side of the sink, picks up the napkins wrapped in plastic, and heaves them onto the counter.

"Unlike when I worked downtown; I can tell that Second House is way more 'laxed here which is a good thing."

She rips open the plastic and removes a few napkins. "The fork and knife setups are rolled up in two, red striped white guest towels which you see over there in that corner." She throws the napkins in front of the POS, then swiftly moves in front, turning my attention to the dining room, and with her sausage link pinky finger points towards the tables. She walks out of the server station, "See the mason jars turned upside down? As you can tell those are what we use for water glasses."

"Pretty cool, but what's with the construction paper under the setups?" I ask. "What's that all about?"

"As you might know or maybe not, we specialize in barbecue and seafood here. So, instead of some fancy-ass cloth over the tables. The paper that's spread over is used for the messiness that comes with eating here. And, not to mention perfect for kids to draw on with the crayons, which we keep at the hostess station. The hostess gives them crayons or whatever and they just color on the paper since we don't have any of those coloring maps or that other funny shit that some places hand out, so the construction paper is easier."

"Oh, that's pretty cool. Very casual, so where do we get the paper from to replace it when we're bussing a table?" Tina trots out and takes a left around the station and I follow. Showing a wheel with four by four construction paper. "So, we just pull the paper out to table length and then rip across the bar?" I ask.

"Yup, but being a server, you'll hardly have to do that. That's the busser's job, let them do it. Being the fucking spics they are, they need to hustle for that fifteen percent waiters have to fork out," she says. We walk over to one of three tabletops and she continues instructing. "You see in these buckets this is where we keep our house-made barbecue and hot sauce. There's ketchup, moist wipes, and extra paper napkins. In front of the bucket, you see salt, pepper, and our house-made crab spice."

"Wow, we make a lot of condiments in-house, that's something you don't see a lot, even in fine-cuisine restaurants."

Tina snorts. "You're saying we like your work here already. Calm your fucking jets dude. Given the six years I've been here, I've heard that from a lot of new trainees, and all of them have gotten way too ahead of themselves before they made it past their third day. I'm proud to say that we do set ourselves apart from other places in the industry."

As we move into the passageway of the entrance; at the hostess stand, there poses a dark-haired, slender-bodied, young woman with a caramel complexion. She looks to be in her early twenties, or late teens. Beautifully unbothered she is, positioned behind the post nonchalantly wiping and stacking menus. Geez la weez, she is quite easy on the eyes if I say so myself. All of sudden, I feel an awkward stare coming in from somewhere. I turn to find Tina, and there she is, scolding me down as if I were a student caught daydreaming in the middle of a lecture.

I clear my throat. "Six years huh? I'm guessing you've been here from the very beginning?"

Tina's eyes roll. "You see something at the hostess stand you like, Newbie? Her name is Giselle, she's the main hostess. I'll introduce you to her in a bit. But yeah, I've been here since the owners, Martin and Scott, first opened the doors. So, what I'm going to go through with you now are table numbers."

"Sure thing, let's get to it."

She positions us at the beginning of the room, where we can overlook every seat and table. "This long table in front of us is forty and forty-one 'cause they come apart if we need to make more seating available."

"Okay, makes sense."

Tina points up and down the right of the dining room. "Now, the two tops along the wall, these tables are the banquet side of the room." Using her index finger Tina starts counting off. "Forty-two, forty-three, forty-four, forty-five, and that booth way back there is forty-six."

"Cool, that seems easy enough."

"Yup. Now, the tables in the middle of the room are the thirties. Starting with thirty-one till that round table, before server-station."

"Ah, okay."

"Yup, you'd be surprised how many trainees fuck that up on their first time on the floor when I quiz them on placing orders. They always guess the wrong table, it never fails. But, let's move on."

I shuffle behind. "I think, I got it so far."

"Good, 'cause I'm going to quiz you later on it."

As we approach the hostess' stand, I feel my back build up with moisture. Tina picks up a 2x2 glass that covers a laminated floor plan. She removes the floor layout and places it on top of the glass. "So here you see in front of us the floor plan, seating, and section chart. This is for everyone to see who's seated and what's not available. Mainly, it's the hostess' job to rotate the server's sections. Giselle usually does a great job, as for the other hostesses not so much," she laughs.

"That's because I'm the best," Giselle interrupts.

"Ah, I didn't know you were spying on us G" Tina jokes. "How sneaky of you, like always."

Giselle grins. "My typical way. Training today?"

"Yup, this is uh-uh, Michael, right?" Tina asks.

"Yes, you are correct," I reply.

"Oh wow, I remember a newbie's name for once. But yeah, he's training to be a server. Michael, this is Giselle our best hostess and my favorite."

Our brown eyes lock and we extend for a firm but gentle handshake. Off the first touch, her hand feels as if it is as smooth as a baby's bottom, doused in baby powder, and finished off with Shea Butter. "Hello, Giselle. I'm glad to make your acquaintance."

"My acquaintance? You're too cute. I'm fine, Michael, thank you for asking. And it's a pleasure to make your acquaintance as well. It's your first day of training?"

"Yes-yes, it is," I reply.

"You'll do fine, I'm sure."

"So far, I'm liking it already."

"Ah, isn't that nice. You and Michael have something in common now. You're not the only black person who works here now, G," Tina teases.

Giselle rips away her grip then reaches for the black expo marker on the side of the cash register and draws and x on the glass. "Oh yeah, I came to let you know, Tina, you now have 14b. It's just one guy I already poured water for him."

"Thanks a lot, hun. Come on, dude, time to get started," Tina says as she guides me past Giselle and head into the bar dining area. Giselle moves back into the hostess stand. I steal one more glance at her before Tina and I disappear and say, "Nice meeting you Giselle, looking forward to working with you."

She grins at me. "You too Michael, and good luck to you. Hope your training goes well."

Tina waddles over to the lone customer as I trail behind. My nose begins to tickle, and snot starts pouring down my right nostril and I try to sniff it up before it's noticeable. Then, fluid trickles down my left nostril. I drag my hand under my nose and pause to take a quick look to make sure it's just snot without Tina becoming the wiser. I wipe it off on my pants. As Tina and I get closer to the seated guest, the faint odor of cigarettes becomes apparent. I eye the customer. His bald head gleams in the dim lighting. His five-o'clock shadow is patchy, his farmer's tan covers his pale skin, and his pants are lightly caked with dirt.

"Hey Joe, just getting off? How's everything, Hun?" Tina reaches in for a cheek kiss.

"I'm good Tina. We had to do a little bit of overtime today. One of the guy's kids is sick so we were short-handed. How you doing?" Joe asks.

She sighs. "I'm alright, I guess... can't complain. I got hit with training the new guy today."

"Oh yeah, what a drag." He coughs. "Is that the rookie behind you?"

"Yeah. What can I get you? The usual?"

"You know me so well. What would I do without you?"

"Well, you're in here almost every day or every other day. So, I guess not much." She pats his back. "Are you grabbing a bite too?"

"Yeah, give me a sec. Carol might come down. But I'll grab my drink first."

"One Bud Light comin' right up."

"Thanks, Tina."

As we move through the bar to make our way back to the POS. Rob and Jill are joined by a tall, skinny, well-groomed young man who he looks to be around my age.

"Glad to see you could join us, John," Tina yells.

"You know what I always say, Tina—better late than never," John greets.

"Never late is better John. How about that?" Tina jokes.

"Yeah, whatever." He waves off her comment. "Hey, by the way, on your way back can you grab me a John Daily?"

"Sure thing. Anything else guys?"

"Other than that; I think, we're good. Thanks," Jill adds.

"Okay, one John Daily coming up." Tina scurries to the POS. I carefully watch as she starts the process of ordering. First, she presses the sleeping screen. The table section appears and hits 14. The computer prompts her on how many guests are seated, she selects one then starts scrolling a few tabs down. Her fat finger hits the bottled beer tab-quickly finding the Bud Light logo, she taps the screen again. At the bottom of the monitor, she mashes send. Within seconds; I hear the bar printer pressing out the drink order. Tina hits the exit button. The screen goes back to the bar seating. With her server number still punched in, Tina selects table 15 and finds the beverage tab, then scrolls to cocktails. She skims through the mixed drinks as if she's in uncharted waters.

"There! John Daily!" I yell.

"Oh, thanks, dude. Their son is the only person who orders that. And every time I have trouble finding it."

"No doubt, the drinks aren't in alphabetical order so I could see how you could lose track of where it is."

Tina scolds at me. "I know exactly where everything is and 'cause of A.G. nothing is where it should be. Believe me, I know where it was. I would've found it eventually, just sit back and watch. You're the one in training. The system is shit."

"Understood, *this system is shit.*"

"Good, you don't wanna get off on the wrong foot on your first day." She turns from the POS to face the bar dining. "Okay, you watched me put in the drinks. You see, Graham has the Bud Light ready for 14, now he's is finishing up on the John Daily. By the way, never wait at the bar for drinks; Graham hates that and if sees you standing there waiting, he'll take even longer to make them."

"Got it."

"Unless you're me or someone who's been here for a while. My advice is not to stand there with your thumb in your ass waiting for him to make your drinks."

"Yes, Ma'am."

"Don't call me ma'am, makes me feel old."

"Sorry, I grew up with a dad in the military. Hard habit to break."

"By the way you talk I would've thought your dad was white," She laughs. "I'm just kidding let's get these drinks."

I keep a wide enough grin walking pass 15b. Tina struggles to reach for a mini-tray on the wooden shelf to the left of us. When she finally grabs it, she slaps it on the bar and places the drinks on it, then she unlatches a jar filled with lemons, takes one out, and wedges it onto the rim. "If a drink needs any type of garnish, it's the server job to do it themselves," Tina states.

"Got it."

"What type of garnish would a dry martini need?" she questions.

"Aside from olives or a lime for a Cosmo, nothing unless the guest requests something else."

"Right… Stay here and watch me drop the drink at the Carleton's table." Gracefully carrying the tray, she moves over to John, smiles, and sets the beverage to the right of his dinner. She utters some words. Some light laughter comes from the table. Finally leaving the family she signals me with eye contact, and I follow her. Tina leads the way back over to Joe and hands him his beer.

"Can I get you anything while you wait for the Mrs?" Tina asks.

"Yeah, she's parking right now. You can put in an order of Second House wings for us."

"Alright, you got it, Hun."

Joe flips the food menu from front to back. "Oh yeah, she'll have her usual drink."

"Belvedere dry-up and one olive?" Tina asks.

"Shit, Tina, you might as well set up two cots in the back," Joe laughs.

"I'll talk to A.G. about it and see if we can't make that happen for you guys." With a more casual pace, we return back to the POS. She taps the screen, selects table 14, then appetizers and finds Second House wings.

"Michael, have you ever eaten here before?"

"Can't say that I have."

"Ok, you're not the first. But you get to taste most of the food as far as barbecue goes and the side dishes, you gotta pay for any seafood you take out. Oh, are you allergic to shellfish or anything like that?"

"Nope. I love seafood."

"Good for you. Okay now… the Second House wings are our most popular appetizer, they're flash-fried and tossed in our homemade barbecue sauce. Our barbecue is so good. You'll see when you try it, that's if you make it that far." Tina smirks at me. "I'm just kidding, tonight you get your one and only free meal unless you worked on a double."

"Awesome. Does 14 need sharing plates?" I ask.

"Yes, how'd you know?"

"With a few years of experience; I'd be afraid if I didn't know."

"Hey, don't get smart with me. You haven't been here for more than an hour and you're already getting fresh… That's your first strike, Newbie."

"I apologize, won't happen again."

Tina shuffles back to the server station and grabs two mini plates, scans them for any wet marks or food stains. "Good, I'm the last person you want to get it fucked up with," she snaps. "Matter of fact, go ahead and drop these off at 14, I gotta blow my nose, real quick. I'll be in the bathroom for two secs."

"Go ahead, do your thing boss lady. I'll be right here after I drop these plates."

"You better be."

I tread to 14. The cigarette odor is stronger than the last time I was here. Joe's wife has joined him; smiling as I set the saucers by their sides. "What's your name again kid?" Joe asks.

"Michael, Sir."

"Sir? You were in the army or something kid?"

"No, but my father was in the military."

"Oh okay. you could drop the 'sir' shit; we're not that uptight here."

"I'm sorry Si—I mean Joe. Hard habit to break, you know."

"Not many kids like you have those types of manners; it's nice to see. By the way, this is my wife, Carol. Honey, this is Michael's first day. He's training to become a server."

Carol smiles, displaying her grayish teeth and off-pink gums with her hair matching the inside of her mouth. "Welcome to Second House, Michael, where are you from?"

"I grew up right here."

"Oh, how nice, we did too. Well, I hope you enjoy working here. You'll be seeing a lot of us." She laughs. "We're the common regulars."

"Looking forward to it, Ma'am—I mean Carol. But yeah, it's nice to meet you." My face loses the cheerful smile as soon as I turn my back. Moving with vigor, Graham signals my attention then points to the bar service station.

"Hey, Michael. Whose drink is this?" he whispers.

"It's Tina's, she put it in for table 14."

"Yeah, I know that already. What I want to know is why has it been sitting here for the last four minutes?"

"No problem, I'll take care of it right now. Can you put in one olive before I run it?" I would've done it myself, but the olive jar is closer to him.

"Sure I can." Graham's hand barely fits inside the jar, so he tilts it and retrieves two olives. As soon as he drops them in, they sink right to the bottom. I pick up the glass, stamp the ticket, and place the martini on a tray. Drops of booze splash on the tray as I return to Joe and Carol.

To avoid reaching over his wife, I shuffle between him and table 13 and place the cocktail to her right. Carol's tobacco stench is unforgiving. "Thank you so much, Michael. Now the real fun starts," she says as raises her glass a few inches off the table.

Joe lifts his beer. "Thanks, Mike."

"You got it. Enjoy guys." Rushing back to the POS, Tina is there, crumbling a paper towel and then sponging her nose with it.

"Okay, I'm back. What'd I miss?" Tina asks.

"Not much. I dropped off the sharing plates to Joe and Carol. And ran her martini for you. Aside from that, not much."

"Did you remember the olive?"

"Of course."

Tina smirks and hurls the paper towel into a bus bin. "Good, there may be some hope for yet."

I grin. "Sure hope so, Tina. Nice shot by the way."

"Thanks, Blacks can't be the only people with a jump shot, you know."

FARRAKHAN

After experiencing a light dinner rush, not to mention struggling to multitask by keeping an eye on the food that left the kitchen; I was extra careful shadowing Tina. Trying my best not to poke her nerves, most of the questions I asked were about the menu and table numbers. I was repetitive but it's my mission to get all this shit down by Sunday. For the most part, I survived the first training shift. But there's always the tedious task of polishing and rolling silverware at the end of the night that every server dreads. Being the new guy or newbie, I get stuck with all the grunt work while Tina takes full advantage by having me clean and roll the cutlery while she sits and folds guest towels. Tina spent half the time scrolling on her phone. Last time I checked, unless it's an emergency, using your phone on the clock is stealing company time. Who cares? I'm not her fucking boss.

"Hey, Michael. How you making out over there?" Tina yells out.

"Few more to go. Why what's up?"

"Oh, nothing just wanted to see where you were at, 'cause it's getting close to breaking down the expo station time. And you might want to give some thought to what you want for shift meal."

I do another roll, and take the server menu from under the POS. "Okay, so the closing server has to wrap up the expo station?" I ask.

"Yeah."

Flipping the menu front to back; my stomach must realize it's time to eat because my appetite has been shot since I came in. "And what time does the kitchen close on weekdays?"

"Monday through Thursday, the kitchen shuts down at ten. Friday and Saturday the kitchen closes at eleven. On Sunday it closes at nine. But, if people wanna come in and eat at a table and come in five minutes before we close, it's your job to tell the guest that the kitchen closes in five minutes, so make sure you tell them to put in something quick or it'll be too late. After you take their order, you have to tell the cooks first, before you go to the POS. Got it?"

"Got it."

"One more thing, when you start serving—that's if you make it that far—your first few weeks, you'll have to be the closing server, so we make sure you got it all down pat."

"Sheesh, being the closing server kind of sucks," I say and shrug.

"It can, but staying late does have its advantages. If you play your cards right and don't whine about it, you'll make some decent coins."

"No doubt."

"Here, take these napkins." With a fist full of napkins, I follow her into the server station. "You're good on rollups; this should be enough for the lunch rush tomorrow. Oh yeah, and another thing, if Jackie—she is the assistant manager by the way—if me or her open the following day and you were the closing server the night before, make it your priority to fill up two bus bins of rollups and make sure the napkins under the sink and on top of the sink are all folded the right way and filled to the top. If you leave without doing any of that or you forget, it'll be ugly."

"Noted... I know what I'm having for dinner."

"Good, and made it with only four minutes to spare. I'll let you put your food in."

I tuck the extra guest towels into the bin and move in front of the POS.

Tina hovers. "Are you going to eat it here?"

"Wasn't planning on it."

She puts in her server number and a layout for the bar dining comes up. "In the right top corner, you'll find the to-go button," she explains.

I hit the tab and a keypad pops up with a blank letterhead. "Right."

"Yup. Now, type in Michael or Mike whatever's easier and then put a dash after your name and type 'training meal'. Later when Graham's not busy, he'll comp it."

"Ok, got it." I message in 'Mike'. I don't want to overwhelm my appetite, so I hit the sandwich button and select *Second House Burger*. The sandwich modifiers are displayed. "American cheese I need it; tomato, raw onion, yes. Hmm, burger on an English muffin? Sounds interesting, it's a 'go'. And the one thing that makes life better, bacon."

"Sounds pretty good. Now what?"

"What do you mean?" I ask.

"Do you want fries or another side to go with your cheeseburger?"

"I'm fine with just fries."

"Hey look, you gotta message it in. Remember there are upcharge sides, so if you ask and the customer wants fries, grits, collard greens, or sweet potato fries; the POS automatically does the upcharge. There are so many sides to choose from if they don't want fries. We're different here. So always make it a habit to ask if they want fries or something else after taking their order."

"Grits and collard greens? Whoa, that's awesome."

"Why would you say that? Don't Black people love that kinda shit?" she laughs.

"Uh, I just think it's cool to have these options. I guess I'm not your typical Black person. I never had grits or collard greens."

Tina removes her apron, rolls it up, and jams it in her purse. "Come on let you show you how to break down expo." We start to make our way into the kitchen. Soon as we set foot into the bar, the exit door is prying open. A tall man, holding a vanilla folder with reddish hair, wearing glasses, and with protruding stomach struts in with a slight grin.

"Ah, there he is!" Tina yells. "Have you met A.G. yet? He's the G.M."

"He's the man who hired me so, yes, I have," I answer.

"No need for the smart remarks dude, just a yes or no answer. That's strike two," Tina scolds.

A.G. struts over, wearing his half-cocked smile. "Hello, Michael, how was the first day of training?" He asks.

"Really good, thanks for asking," I smile. "Um, I see that you guys are really 'laxed here, and that's refreshing. And Tina has been such a great trainer... really appreciate her showing me all the ropes."

"Yeah... yeah she's good for that." He grins.

"And what's that supposed to mean?" Tina asks.

"You know exactly what that means."

"Then whatever that is, it should come with a raise."

"Yeah right, the day that comes, you'll have my job, Tina," he jokes. "You know all your table numbers, Mike?" He points to 17. "What table is that and where does position #1 start?"

"That table right there is 17, and position one is inside the booth closest to my left," I reply.

A.G. nods with a bigger smile. "Nice, you might be the first trainee ever to get that table right on the first day. Dick wasn't kidding about you."

"We'll see about that," Tina says.

"In due time, Tina... In due time," A.G. states.

I clear my throat and try to smile. "Well... Guys thanks for the positive feedback."

After watching Tina breakdown the Expeditor station, I wait for my food to come out of the kitchen while enjoying a tall gin and tonic for a shift drink. Graham is entertaining two regulars at the other end of the bar. Tina drops a check at one of the tables she has left.

I feel a light tap on my left shoulder.

"Hey."

"Whoa, there guy. Easily frightened, huh Mike?" A.G. chuckles.

"Yeah, I guess you could say I scare pretty easy," I laugh. "You snuck up on me there, I guess that's why you're the G.M., eh?"

"No kidding, that's why they pay me the big bucks," A.G. jokes, "Well, I have to say you did a bang-up job today, Michael. You exceeded all of the first-day training expectations for new employees."

I take another sip. "Ah thanks, A.G., it was really nothing new. Glad to be here..."

"You'd be surprised how many people bomb on the first day. You really did a fantastic job. Dick was pretty sound and grounded about me hiring you. Hopefully, you prove him right."

"Yeah, for sure."

"I gave you all your tax papers, employee handbook, and that other good shit like the food menu, right?"

"Yup, I'm just waiting on my free training meal while I finish up this drink."

"When are you back next?"

I polish off the rest of my cocktail. "Tomorrow night, Sir."

He smiles. "Alright, I'll see you then. Have a goodnight, Michael."

"Have goodnight A.G. and thanks again."

A.G. stops halfway towards the exit still with his back turned. "For what?"

"Hiring me."

"No sweat kid. Get home in one piece."

As A.G. heads out, here comes Tina stomping through kitchen doors with a plastic bag filled with to-go containers. She walks up to the end of the bar and slams the food in front of me. "Here you go, dude. Your cheese-burger with extra cheese and fries."

"Yeah, I mean come on now. Who doesn't love cheese?" I laugh.

"Jackie, for example."

I slide the drink glass to the side. "You mean the assistant manager?"

"Yup, she fucking hates cheese. If I were you, I wouldn't mention anything about cheese. And you might have a fighting chance tomorrow."

"Any other pointers you have that I should know for tomorrow?"

"Are you being smart with me dude? I told you about that fucking attitude and you're already on strike three!" she shouts.

"Oh no, Ma'am. I'm really inquiring.'"

Tina scratches flakes out of her hair and flicks the scum under her French-tips nails onto the floor. "Inquiring? What does that mean?"

"To have a question or be ready to ask a question. However, you want to look at it, Tina." I rise up and push the bar-seat inward.

"Oh, I knew that. But yeah, far as any more pointers; there's nothing else I can do for you. The rest is up to you, dude. Try not to fuck up too much."

I force out one more fake laugh. "I'll try." Turning my back to her, I make a slight dash for the door. "Have a great night, Tina, get home safe now."

"Have a good night, Newbie," Graham shouts.

"You too man." I turn the knob to my long-awaited escape. The summer breeze rushes to my lungs. My first few steps send stabbing pains to the back of my heels. The empty sky and warm air pairs well with this cigarette. I'm pretty sure Tracie has some booze and I could really go for another drink or two. Because the way my first day of training went, you would've sworn Tina was trying to verbally rip me in half. I mean that woman has no filter button. People from other countries swear up and down their shit doesn't stink. And her accent is the fucking worst. Fucking bitch sounds like her throat is clogged with mayonnaise. To be honest, I thought about walking out every twenty minutes. I figured out why she's been serving tables for Second House for so long, there's no way in hell any other establishment will tolerate her constant yapping. I see why trainees don't make it past the first day because Tina is training them. Man, I pray to God I make through the next five days. Defiantly going to be a test of wills if I do. And the way she was talking about this Jackie broad makes it seem like I'm going to be pushed to the maxed.

My phone vibrates with a text from Tracie: "Hey, wanna hang out? Meaning you got that money you owe me kid, lol?"

Texting back: "Sure, can you come downstairs? I'm walking through the trail right now."

"…Oh yeah! I forgot you started at Second House today. Coming down now."

Damn, forgot I owe her forty bucks. I guess I can start a new tab but what's the fucking point of doing that? This is the last bit of my unemployment money but since all my bills are paid and Second House is seven-minutes away from my house; I guess everything will work out and after the first day I had. Besides, I could use a couple of lines to take the edge off.

As I approach the entrance of the complex, I see Tracie's wide body poking out of the double doors with a cigarette lodged in between her pale fingertips. Tracie's twenty-nine but looks as if she's thirty-five and sounds as if she's forty. She another one by the way... And just like Graham, she's also taken the shape of a washed-up bartender and being that she used to bartend—I'm merely being kind about her overall appearance. Now that I think about it, she and Graham could have some relation.

We greet each other with a tender hug and a light kiss on the cheek. "Hey what's up girl?"

"I'm good, Mikey, you got that mula for me?"

"Yeah, hold on a sec." I fish in the crevices of my right pocket and retrieve a crinkled twenty. "Here you go."

"You still owe me twenty more bucks but thanks, Hun. What are you doing? Wanna hang out?"

"Sure, I'm not doing anything. Is Billie upstairs? I didn't see him at Second House tonight."

"That fat fuck had the day off. But yeah, he is, he's not doing shit but snorting all his money away." She tosses her cigarette before heading in. I follow her into the elevator. Tracie presses four.

"How was your first day, Mikey? Did you have to work with my baby, Tina? Her fine ass; I'm going to fuck her one these days, watch."

"You know her?"

"Yeah, I can tell. Not only that but her nose kept dripping snot. Oh my God, I wanted to fucking puke. Boogers were hanging out her nose the whole night," I lead the way off the elevator.

"Ah man, she's a nut on the job but she's such a sweetheart, I swear. Prepare yourself for some serious coke rage at Second House. Your safest bet is Jackie, out of all of them—she's the more levelheaded. Wait till you meet Jose, he's the dishwasher. He a cool guy. Buys off me from time to time."

"Okay, I'll be sure to keep a low-profile; I have to give myself some time to adjust to the less traditional ways of training."

"Ata-boy, and try not to look at her butt so much, ass-man. And besides, you made it past the first day and that's half the battle, and with your experience—you're a shoe in" she laughs as we make our way into her shared condo. There's Billie at the kitchen island with his fat face in a mountain of coke. What a fat-fuck he is, wasting his God-given height and decent looks on a half-ass job and seventy-dollar a day coke habit.

As he picks his face up from the coke pile, his overhanging stomach presses against the corner of the countertop. "Oh shit, that was the one right there, damn!" He shouts. "Ah, Mikey what's up man. How was the first day on the job?"

I greet Billie with a smile and a handshake. "Pretty good for the most part man, I followed behind Tina tonight so...other than that, seems like all systems are 'go'."

"Wow, Tina? A.G. had you training with that cunt?"

"Uh," I chuckle, "I guess if you want to call her that, yeah,"

Tracie moves over to the fridge and retrieves a Tito's bottle, a half-full a two-liter of Sprite, and a handful of ice out of the freezer. "You want a drink, Mikey?"

"Sure, why not," I answer

"You wanna line too Mikey?" Billie offers.

"Sure, why not," Tracie adds.

"Yeah Bill, what she said. Make my drink a little stronger than usual, Trace, today really was trying."

"You'll be okay and besides it's better than your last job." She fills the glass halfway with vodka, pours the soda to the rim, and hands it over.

"That has yet to be determined, Trace," I say and sip.

She begins to make herself a drink. "Yeah but- "

"Hey Trace, I get it... I get what you're trying to say, and I'd rather not talk about it. Let's keep the past in the past, you know."

"Yeah I get it, I'm just saying man, I'm here whenever you need to talk, Mike."

"Man, fuck all that bullshit and sniff this line before I do," Billie says and shoves a broken mirror with three bulky lines in front of me. "Fuck all that shit Mike, you're in the big leagues now, I got your back."

"I hear you guys and thanks. Hey Trace, you got any more straws or clean bills; I gave you my last bit of cash."

"Um, yeah; I got a straw around here somewhere." She scrambles around in her junk-filled purse, finally coming up with the money I just gave her. "Well, shit just use this, and don't forget to give it back."

"Come on, Trace, do I ever forget to give or pay you back anything?"

"No... But if you leave it lying on the counter or on the coffee table like you always do..." She scowls at Billie and adds, "Somehow it grows legs and walks away."

"Aye, I resent that you fat dike, I'm no fucking thief. Don't blame me when you get totally trashed and forget where you placed your shit. And besides, Black people are notorious for stealing," he sniffs.

"Hey!" I blurt out.

"I'm just kidding, Mikey, but seriously, you and Tracie get shitty every night off blow, weed, and booze. And you're going to blame me for your shit going missing when you lose everything? And to be honest, you've never lost anything that you didn't find at the bottom of that shit-filled purse the next day, so don't accuse me of taking anything. Today it's money, tomorrow it's coke. You'd lose your head if it wasn't attached to your fucking shoulders."

"Who you calling a *Fat dike*? You fat fuck. Your stomach sticks out more than your dick does. I should call you a 'dick do'!" Tracie shouts. "Stomach hangs more than my dick do!"

"Fuck off, you fat bitch. When's the last time you cleaned that dirty ass strap-on dildo you carry around in your purse?" Billie laughs.

"Yo Bill, I bet you haven't seen your dick in three years," I add.

"Oh shit!" Tracie yells, "that was a good one, Mikey."

"You're probably right, you Black son of a bitch, but so what? At least I'm not pretending to have one like some people I know," Billie says then nods at Tracie.

"While you can't see your dick, Trace is over here suffering from some serious penis envy," I joke, "Maybe that's why she hauls around a fake one."

"Shut up you, Black bastard. I hope you've packed enough cocoa butter in that backpack today," she laughs.

"Shit, I sure did. When you finally clean that fake dick of yours; I'll let you borrow some to help with the smell," I say and turn to Billie, "I may be Black, but at least I can run up a flight of stairs."

"Except athletes, the only time Black people run is when the police are chasing em'. So, you got me beat on that." Billie slaps the countertop.

"Chill out, Bill. And besides, he's gotta point —you could lose some weight," Tracie states.

"If I'm saying it and she's agreeing with it; take head Bill and listen." Finally, I roll the bill into the perfect pipeline and rail a line. The powder enters my right nostril with no hesitation. The drip hits instantly and I feel the coke run to my esophagus. The taste is so welcoming, energizing, and pure; I swear blow and alcohol are like peanut butter and jelly, they just complement each other so well. Soon enough, I'll start to yearn for a cigarette. I take a big swig from my drink. "You guys mind if I step out on the balcony for a sec?"

"Sure, it's beautiful outside, I'll come with you," Billie answers.

Tracie jumps from her chair. "Lemme go check on Cam real quick and I'll be out there... Who's got an extra smoke for your girl?"

Billie walks to the balcony entrance located in the rear of the living-room. "Mine are on the counter, right next to the mirror."

Wishing Billie would have stayed inside. I would rather enjoy this cigarette by my lonesome. I guess that's the burden of doing free drugs; nine times out of ten you're not doing them alone. And nine times out of ten, I prefer to do my drugs alone. When by myself, I'm allowed to be high and think in peace. Unfortunately for me, that can't happen just yet. The only upside when someone supplies coke on credit is that you don't have to wait idle and be miserable, the only downside is the people you have to do them with.

The screen clamps shut behind me. "Ah, such a beautiful night..."

Billie puts fire to his cigarette and passes the lighter. "Yeah, it is, and the coke is pretty good, kid, if I say so myself."

I had noticed Billie's hands were fidgeting pretty bad while we were inside. Now, lighting my cigarette, the bright blaze gave away his dilated pupils. "What? Have you been sniffing all night?" I ask.

"Actually, I have. I'm high as a giraffe's ass right now," he snorts with a laugh.

"Goddamn Bill. You have to take it easy on that shit man, you can develop a serious problem."

"Aye, I got thirteen to fourteen years on you, you Black asshole. I was sniffing this shit when you were learning how to beat your dick, so don't worry about me motherfucker, worry about securing your job at Second House."

"I got it, man, chill the fuck out Bill. I'm just looking out for you; I don't need you keeling over on my watch. All I'm saying is, be careful with that shit. And, besides I'm not worried about Second House. I got it in the bag," I inhale.

"See, there's that cockiness bullshit, right there. You don't even know the menu yet, and you're already talking cash shit. You need to humble yourself down a little bit, and shut the fuck up. I could teach you a lot about Second House. But that 'I got it' attitude ain't going to get your Black ass anywhere but tossed," he says and inhales and then thumps his ashes.

"…Yeah…" I say on an exhale.

Tracie plows through the screen door. "Hey what are you guys talking about?"

"Just telling this young buck to humble himself before he gets canned and he's not even halfway through."

"Ah shit, why the fuck are you listening to this loser? He's been suspended from Second House more times than I can count. Listening to this fat fuck will get you canned. Believe that," Tracie says lighting up her own smoke.

"What do you know? You fat bitch, you don't even have a job," Billie says letting out smoke in a huff.

"Hey, let's not even get into this. My daughter is finally sleeping and besides, you're a fatter fuck than I am. And, as long as I'm in the business to supply you coke, my money problems are non-existent," she says and smirks.

I can't help but chime in with laughing. It's funny how they both call each other "fat" given the fact they both share the same poor eating habits and lifestyle. It's like a competition on who can insult the other better. Watching these two is always entertaining. Reminds me of what "not" to do. "She's got a point Bill," I add.

"She does but just know that I'm the head cheese at Second House. I mean, aside from the owners and trust me, Mikey, I won't steer you wrong."

I think about it as I inhale, and exhale again with one word, "Noted."

"Listen, Mikey, do what you do. You rose through the ranks pretty fast when we were working downtown with Dick but that was years ago. Then your bitch-ass went all corporate. Now that all that suit and tie shit didn't work, here you come with your tail in between your legs needing a job. But I believe in you and you'll do great, I'm sure of it. But, just remember don't follow this fat asshole's ways or you'll be in a world full of shit before you know it. Next thing you know you'll be looking for another job," Tracie says.

"Thanks, Trace. I got this."

"I know you do."

I watch as Billie's cigarette falls through a fray of tree leaves, being carried by the light breeze and for a second, I start to imagine myself as that dying ember of tobacco falling so freely into my only destination. Knowing that my purpose was served. Sometimes I wish I could be a tossed cigarette—at least they have some sort of original impetus when people are through with them.

"Man, when I got back from New York today it was so nice out, I had to take Cam to the park. I tried to play a game of tag with her and after thirty seconds of running, I was outta breath. I gotta lose some weight," Tracie says as she lights another cigarette.

"Yeah, we can tell," Billie chides.

"I'll give you one hundred bucks right now if you take off your pants and without moving your fat ass stomach, tell me if you can see your own dick," Tracie challenges, and I start to crack up. "You're talking shit," she continues, "at least my mother wasn't tricking and sucking dick to put food on the table."

"Damn Bill, that's fucked up. You never told me your mother was a prostitute," I tease.

"Fuck you guys. So, what if I don't know my father. All I know is, I got a secure job which neither of you has. You wanna talk about my mother and shit, bitch, find a job first," Billie insults.

"I'm sorry that your mother had to suck a gang of dicks to put food on the table. You never know... your dad could be a black dude—you have a natural bronze to your skin, you never know." Tracie says and adds, "I mean, Italians do have a natural tan all year around. You could be something other than Sicilian."

"Fuck you and your dirty ass strapon. How many times have you cleaned that thing since you been fucking that little Puerto-Rican bitch with the fucked-up teeth, huh?" Billie shouts.

I laugh uncontrollably but manage to get out, "Oh shit."

Tracie launches her cigarette butt off the balcony and goes in deeper with, "At least my mother wasn't swallowing cum to pay the rent. Too bad she didn't swallow you."

I keep heckling from the sidelines, "Damn Trace, that's fucked up."

"I bet that dike, you brought over the other night—I bet her pussy smells like wild rice and fried pork fat," Billie says.

Tracie even laughs at that one. "Alright, alright, Bill. Calm down, you're getting a little loud over there, bud. It's all jokes, you sensitive piece of shit...geez!"

"Then stop talking about my mother sucking dick and shit. That shit ain't cool, man."

"She hit a nerve there huh, Bill? Who knew you had a soft spot and I'm sorry your mother had to swallow jizz for a living, must've been rough growing up," I say and pat him on the back.

"Shut up you Black bastard," he retorts then sparks another smoke.

I put out my cigarette. "Mind if I go inside guys?"

"I'm going to finish this fucking smoke... fucking with you... Tracie got me heated, fuck ya'll," Billie states bitterly.

"Yeah sure, a matter of fact... I'll join you and get to rolling up a blunt," Tracie says then follows as I make my way back inside. We walk over to the kitchen island. I take my drink and gulp. "I got a question," I say and reach for the mirror to cut more lines. "Why do you and Billie flick your butts over the balcony when you have a whole ashtray right there?"

"I couldn't begin to tell ya," Tracie answers as she digs in her purse and takes out a Ziplock baggie stuffed with weed. "To be honest, it's just a force of habit, I guess. I'm glad you noticed that 'cause now I'm going to say something to Billie about that shit. He actually got me into that habit when me and Cam first moved in. It's funny 'cause I bought that ashtray for that sole purpose of not having to flick a cigarette over the balcony. That shit is kinda dangerous now that I think about it. But, I blame him and I'm sticking by that."

I snort two lines and drink. "Hmm... living in a place like this, you would think there would be a stricter policy on tenants who smoke 'cause you guys do toss a lot of cigarettes out on to that walking path. And the only reason I know that is because all the cigarette butts on the walkway are directly lined up with your balcony, I'm surprised whoever manages the building hasn't said something already."

"They got maintenance on it, so I'm more than sure all those butts are getting picked up."

I snort and the drips sets in wonderfully. "That's true but you don't think you're making maintenance's job harder by the constant throwing of butts?"

"Fuck maintenance. It's their fucking job to pick up shit on the walking path. They get paid I'm sure!" she yells.

"Shit, I'm just saying."

The screen door slams as Billie makes his way through the living-room. "What's the dike hollering about now? Talking about me being loud, you should hear yourself for once. Pass that mirror though."

"Damn, Billie, you got a vacuum for a nose!" I blurt.

"Chill my nigga, I'm just living my life while being high on coke, can a nigga live? Damn," Billie jokes. "By the way, I just got a text from Tina. She's coming over."

I panic. "Tina who? Not Tina from Second House."

Billie sniffs from the pile of coke and not from the lines I prepared. "Yeah, who else would I be talking about? There's only one Tina and she works at Second House." He shrugs his way back toward the pile.

"Oh..." My heart is in the pit of the stomach, and just when I thought I was about to relax.

"You don't like Tina or something? You don't even know her," Tracie says.

"Once you see how she is outside of work," Billie snorts. "She'll grow on you eventually. She's actually a pretty cool chick even if she is a foreigner.".

"And hot too," Tracie adds.

"I'm not saying anything like that guys. How would she react if she comes up here seeing the new guy, mind you, she just painfully finished training, up here sniffing coke and smoking with you two? I mean she doesn't know me; how do I know she won't run off and tell management or some shit? She seems like the type of person to throw me under the bus if I look at her wrong," I finish my drink.

"Yo, I'm telling you she's not like that at all. Been working with her stubby ass going on six years now. She's chill, I promise." Billie reaches for his phone. "Matter of fact that's her now, she's downstairs. You know what, Mike, you should let her in," he suggests.

"That would be a fucking riot," Tracie says and licks the blunt to seal it closed. "To see your black ass coming down to let her in; that would be a fucking riot. And to think after all the times you've been up here, hanging out and shit. You've never met her. Ah man, this shit is priceless."

"You two... You two are pretty fucked up, I don't know if you guys are letting the coke talk and trying to fuck with me or not but that's fucked up. Why would you guys want to put me through hell again? That's not cool. You know she gave me two strikes today for nothing. I don't even know what that means. All I know is, I'm not on her good side."

Billie rails another line. "Chill the fuck out, Mikey, and cut the bitching—she does that to every Newbie. But I get it. She treated you like a scrub which she does to every new trainee and let me guess she said she had no clue she was training you tonight. Like I said, she does that shit to every new sucker who walks into those doors thinking they can serve at Second House. As far as that strike bullshit, it's just a scare tactic so you don't get outta line. Don't worry about that shit, she's just putting you through the wringer. You survived the first day. So, all you gotta do now is shut the fuck up and enjoy yourself. Stop being on edge all the time, shit's weird," he laughs.

"She's downstairs now?" Tracie asks.

"Yeah," Billie answers.

"Dope, I'm gonna go and let her in. And wipe the coke off your face, Billie. You fucking asshole, you're wasting it and we have guests. She slides on her house slippers and turns to me. "Ah man, this is priceless. I'll be right back." Tracie shoves my shoulder and jets out.

"Man, this can't be good," I mutter.

"What are you worried about man? She's cool. You're starting to make yourself more anxious thinking about it. Here…" Billie hands me the mirror. "Sniff some more coke and don't worry about the money, I got you."

I burry the bill up my right nostril. I'm already leaking snot from the left so it's time to try the other one. I snort hard as I can. The coke hits my nasal cavity…. "Ah shit."

"Good shit man… good shit," Billie says.

"I read somewhere doing coke causes more anxiety," I pass the mirror back.

"I don't know about that. All I know is, I love coke. Fuck all that anxiety bullshit." He sniffs a line the size of my pinky. "See, that's what the fuck I'm talking about nigga, shut the fuck up with that anxiety bullshit. What the fuck causes you to feel anxiety? You sound stupid."

The tension of having to deal with that nasty bitch Tina again and the coke is fucking with my nerves pretty bad, whoever wrote that article was exactly right. "Hey, Bill, you mind if I make myself another drink?"

"Sure, while you're at it make me another one too."

I walk over to the fridge. "What's your poison?"

"I'll take Forrest on the rocks."

"Nice, think I'll do the same." I grab the ice cubes out of the freezer and drop them in my cup before I pour about six ounces or more. I take a nice swig and suddenly, my left-hand stops shaking so I take another then set my drink on the counter. "Pass your cup, Bill."

He chugs what's left. "Here you go, bud," he says. I repeat the process and hand his glass back.

"The Rangers win tonight?" he asks.

"Yeah. Three to nothing."

"Fucking awesome! I'm ready as fuck for the playoffs," Billie shouts. "We're taking it this year!"

"The east coast is tough this year, but I think they can pull it off if everyone stays healthy."

The kitchen door opens with Tracie entering first, and Tina's pudgy body follows.

"Hey, guys look who I found!" Tracie cries. "It's your favorite server ever, my bitch, TINA!"

"Hey, Tina, how are you doing tonight?" I greet.

Billie nods, "What's going on? haven't seen you since yesterday. And believe me, I don't miss your presence."

Tracie continues to the fridge and Tina positions herself between Billie and me.

"What you want to drink, girl? Tracie asks.

"Something white on the rocks, I guess," Tina replies. "So, you guys, what's going on here? I see you got a little bit of coke, a little bit of weed, you dudes got it going on. Can I partake?"

"Girl stop asking stupid questions, you know better than that. How was work?" Tracie asks.

"It was cool. The Newbie made it easier than I expected. Oh, by the way, Michael, you did great tonight."

"I did?"

"Yeah, dude, you know your shit. You learned the table numbers and seat positions pretty fast. You ran drinks and most importantly you know how to talk to people which is really surprising because that hostess Giselle has a mouth on her but you're not like her, you actually got some sense to you."

"Thanks a lot, I try to do my job well even if I'm training."

"Well, yeah you did great just remember to stay in your place. And don't ever, try to outshine me or Billie."

"You guys are the head honchos, got it," I sip. "It's your world; I'm just living in it."

"At'a'boy," Billie says.

"Who's ready to smoke this blunt though?" Tracie questions.

"I think we all are. Fire that bad boy up!" Billie yells. Tracie ignites the blunt. I love the cracking sound it makes as the tobacco burns before catching the weed. The first couple of whiffs are amazing. Tracie makes it all the more worth-while, it's safe to say, whether it's coke or weed. She gets top-notch drugs. It's funny when you think about it, white people always have the best drugs.

Tracie blows out a smoke plume and says, "Hey, Mike, do me a solid and crack the window in the living room." I tiptoe to the end of the living room. It seems like I'm the only one who remembers a little girl is upstairs sleeping. I won't be a part of disturbing her slumber. Must be rough for Cam. She may not know it yet, but her mother's only means of providing shelter is to room with another cokehead. Poor Cam.

"Why don't we get some air guys; it's nice out. I don't see why we don't enjoy that blunt outside," I suggest.

"Well, we can't all be in shape like you Mikey, boy. Besides, these two women are just as big as that balcony so how do you expect all of us to fit out there? Not everybody chooses to walk everywhere like you, you fucking asshole. The nerve of this guy..." Billie says as he passes me the blunt. "Sorry, Mikey; I nigger-lipped it a bit, my bad."

I took a lighter from the counter and dried out his saliva. "What the fuck, Bill? Why do you always have to say that? Can't you just say 'I wet the blunt' as opposed to saying you 'nigger-lipped' it? Geez man, have some decency. I don't even say that shit, and I have every right to," I complain before I inhale, and the first drag hits strong and rough. I cough rapidly.

"What's wrong with nigger-lip?" he asks and shrugs.

"Yeah, what's up with that shit, Mike? I don't see why you get your panties in a bunch over a stupid phrase. Everyone says it, not like it means anything, you know," Tracie adds. I pass the blunt off to Tina and release my lungs of the smoke.

"What's wrong with it? What's wrong with it? You guys forget that I'm Black and I don't even use the word."

"What word?" Tina coughs.

"Nigga," Billie says.

"No, not nigga. You said nigger but nigga doesn't make it any better it's still the same disrespect," I cough it out around the smoke, but I make my point.

Tracie grabs the blunt. "I don't get it. Black people say it to each other all the time so I don't get why you guys can say it and white people can't, that's just stupid."

"Yeah, I don't get that either," Billie adds.

"During slavery, it was created to make us feel lesser than. It derives from the country of Nigeria. Somehow throughout history and the post-civil war, we stuck to it without releasing the negative content the word possesses. Blacks turned it into a word of endearment or displacement. Hence, 'my nigga' or 'who's that nigga over there?' and gradually over time, privileged whites like yourselves thought it would be cool to say it because you listened to too many rap songs and had one or two black friends who gave you a fake hood pass. So, you feel entitled to say it even though you shouldn't," I explain as the room goes dead silent, and awkward stares come from everyone. Simultaneously they all bust out in uncontrollable laughter.

"Oh shit, Mikey, you were quite the fucking history teacher in your past life!" Billie chides.

"A boring one at that," Tina passes the blunt to Billie.

"Michael, what the fuck were you talking about man? All that racist-slave shit is over now. I don't know any Black people who were slaves

46

and you should be the one to talk about privilege. You're the most privileged person in this kitchen. You actually graduated from college. And you wanna talk about our privilege, yeah, okay," Tracie heckles.

"Oh yeah, the only privilege I have is when you used to force me to drive you to Washington Heights to cop your drugs 'cause those Dominicans won't serve to anyone who's white. Yeah, privilege."

Billie chuckles hard until he starts hacking up a lung as he tries to talk. "Oh shit, he's right. Those Dominicans will sell to Mike and not you. That's fucking hilarious."

"And being able to get drugs because someone else can't isn't anything to be proud of just to let you know," Tracie continues.

"Exactly, that's nothing to be proud of at all. But what kind of privilege is that to be happy about? None… You get a better loan on a house, you get a better seat at a restaurant, servers will treat you better 'cause they think you're going to tip better. Oh yeah, and the famous one of them all; you're less likely to get fucked with by the police, can't forget about that," I say.

"You gotta be fucking delusional to think I would get better service in a restaurant because I'm white. You don't know how full of shit you are, Mike. I've been working in hospitality going twelve years now and I've never treated a person different 'cause of their skin color, man or woman, never," Tracie says as she receives the blunt from Billie.

"I'm not talking about you, Trace. I'm giving you my reality as a young, African-American, millennial male; I can't make this shit up." I reject the passing of the blunt from Tracie. "But I can't argue enough about it and I won't. You just have to understand and look at it from my perspective—me, being who I am, and not what I'm blinded by. There's something you guys might be lacking in the Awareness Department."

47

"Okay there, Mr. Farrakhan. We get it, you're a Black guy on the outside and a white man on the inside," Billie says. "But where do you get off by telling me I lack something about being aware? You're a funny guy, Mikey..." he laughs, "...a funny guy."

"Funny it is, but funny I'm not..." I polish off my drink and sneak in another line. "Well, guys it's been real but I have to get home; I'm starting to feel a little drunk." I stagger up, pace myself to the chair Tina is sitting in and grab my backpack before I head towards the hallway. "I bid you all adieu and goodnight," I say.

"Alright, Mikey, see ya later!" Tracie shouts.

"See you in a few days, Newbie. And remember to bring that same energy you brought tonight," Tina says.

"You got it, Tina, thanks," I say.

Before I'm fully out the door Billie cries out, "Aye, Mike!"

"What?"

"Your new name is Farrakhan."

"Don't call me that, that's fucked up. Minister Farrakhan is a great man. You shouldn't play with his name like that."

He laughs. "It's too late, Farrakhan, that's you now."

The door begins to close. "Fuck you, Bill."

"Aye keep your head up, brotha. And remember, 'Stay Black'..." he says as I hear their loud laughter all the way to the elevator.

WHAT WE SPECIALIZE IN

Unfortunately for me, I didn't get hit by a car on my way to work. If I were a little more hungover, maybe luck would've been in my favor. I'm pretty sure my introduction to Jackie didn't go so well. Because I can hardly catch air through my snot-filled nose, it does me no good having to either wipe or blow my nostrils every five minutes. Maybe that's why she stuck me with grunt work after fifteen minutes of meeting each other. Why wasn't the silverware done before my arrival? Who knows; I guess they figure why not have the newbie do it.

I came in thirty minutes before my shift started. I had wishful thinking that if Jackie saw that I was going over the menu before my training, I would be in her good graces. She hasn't said much but I can tell she's in a mood; whether it's to my doing or not is yet to be known. As time goes by, I find myself with a stretching anxiety on how she will receive me during training this period.

After a few hours go by, I realize working with Jackie isn't as grueling as I was led on to believe. It's not all that hard shadowing a highly attractive woman. Eh, at least my head is in the right place and I'm not talking about the one I use for cognitive thinking. Her long, golden, wave-flowing hair and milky/tan skin are really nice on the opticals. Not to mention the way her ass sits so well in the creases of her Levi's. Now with a behind like that, I would surely follow her to the depths of hell…but for today I'll settle for just shadowing.

Jackie and I are standing in front of the expo station preparing ketchup ramekins and under-liners for eight orders of burgers with fries. For the most part, I've answered the billion and ten questions she's asked correctly. At least Tina wasn't kidding about that. Jackie is definitely on top of her game. I'm just glad she's not riding my ass. I've studied the food menu throughout the afternoon. I was ready to be bombarded with a shitload of questions she might ask, which she did but I think I'm good.

I'll be damned if I don't have the table numbers down by now. And since I'm Black; I have to be prepared for everything.

"Alright Michael, you can carry more than two plates, right?" she asks.

"For sure, I can," I answer.

"Great, so we can knock out six of these burgers right now. Alright, before we run this food, can you go out onto the floor and check on Billie, and if he's not doing anything, see if he can run the last two plates for our party of eight?"

"Heard you." I rush through the kitchen doors and there Billie is, in plain sight at the bar talking it up with a guest. I feel like he does more blabbing and carrying on than he does actual work. I walk right behind the patron and wait for Billie to notice me. His attention isn't still wavered, so I slightly raise my right index finger. Finally, he's attentive. I move right behind him and tug on the back of his shirt. He jerks back.

Billie pauses with the customer, turns, and whispers, "What do you want bro? You can't see that I'm talking here? What... what the fuck is it?"

"Um... Ah, I just came to let you know that Jackie and I need your help in the kitchen running some food."

"Well... you tell that bitch I'm busy with my own shit right now and if

50

she doesn't like it, she can fuck off," Billy goes back to his conversation. I try and regain my composer before returning to the expo line; I can't believe he just went off on me like that. I mean who the fuck does he think he is? Shit, I was going to go tell that fat piece of shit to get the rest of the coke out of his nose. Forget it, he can dig his own grave... fucking asshole.

Heading towards the expo station; I grab three plates from the window while Jackie takes three more. "What was he doing?" She asks.

"Uh... he was talking to a guest."

"What do you mean he was talking to a guest?"

"He had a conversation going on at the bar and made it clear he didn't want to be bothered. I'm not throwing him under the bus here, Jackie, but he didn't seem that interested in helping when I told him... he wasn't that polite either. But I figure we can knock out these plates ourselves and besides, it'll help me get familiar with guest positions. I'll just take the extra trip.""

"It's not about that, Michael. You got the table numbers and positions down which is quite surprising, no trainee gets that right, at least whenever I quiz them. But whenever I ask an employee to do something, I expect them to do it, especially if they have nothing going on. I'm sick of Billie's shit... I really am." Following Jackie to the party of eight; I stand right behind her as she places each plate down by position number. When she's finished, she takes each dish from my hands then continues to serve. Impressive, she didn't even have to auction any of them off. When I shadowed Tina last night, she was auctioning off tables with only three plates, how can't you remember what three people are eating? It's only three fucking people. Now, my only question is what the fuck is Jackie going to do with Billie? 'Cause I'm sure as hell he won't call her a bitch to her face.

I watch as Jackie says her final enjoyment to the guest and follow her back to the expo station. We're surprised by Billie, who has the last two burgers in his hand. I can't believe you two really need help carrying out two extra fucking plates. What is this, amateur hour?" Billie scolds. You're a real piece of fucking work, Jackie."

Jackie snatches the dishes out of his hand, a few fries topple to the ground. "When I ask you to do something and you think carrying on a conversation is more important than doing your job, yes, I have a problem taking two extras plates to my table when you're fully capable of helping."

Billie removes the coke residue from his nose. "No, I was busy with my tables. And whoever said otherwise is a fucking dickhead for throwing me under the bus."

"I hope you're not referring to me, Bill," I add.

"Who else could I be referring too."

Shaking my head in disbelief. "Hey Jackie, you mind if I walk those plates over?"

"Sure, Mike, go ahead I'm going to have a word with Billie over here while you do that. You remember which one got the burger with no cheese?"

"Yes, position six gets the one with no cheese," I answer.

"You got it, kid."

As I head to the table. I force my best grin and make sure the protein is facing to their six o'clock. The head of the table rejoices and says, "Thank you, now everybody can dig in."

I smile. "You're more than welcome, Sir. Can I get you guys anything else?"

"No thank you, Michael, I'm all set unless someone else wants something." He scans the party for any request and there are none. "That'll be all for now, Michael, thanks again." I leave the table with a smile and head back to the kitchen. Before I can reach 17, Billie is waving me down to come to the service station. I'm going to regret this but here it goes… "What's up, Bill?"

"What's up? What's up with you throwing me under the bus like that, I thought you were my nigga."

"Yo, be careful with calling me *your nigga* in here. This isn't the place for that."

He sucks his teeth, "Ain't the place for what?"

"Calling me your nigga and shit," I whisper.

"The fuck do you mean, my nigga, you better stop with all that uppity shit and know it ain't like that."

"Hey man, I'm just looking out on your part. I don't want people hearing that and start thinking I'm an Uncle Tom or some shit. You feel me?"

"There you go again, bro, like I told you the other night. I'm Blacker than you."

"Just be careful man, this workplace shit is a different world. I don't want you getting into any shit, let alone myself because of your mouth."

"Worry about yourself and follow my lead. I run this shit here. Not Jackie, not A.G., and not the owners. I'm the reason these customers keep coming back. I'm telling you my nigga just watch me handle business."

"Whatever, man, just be careful with Jackie. Remember workplace harassment isn't a joke. I don't care if it's just hospitality talk or not, that shit isn't right," I say as Billie leaves to attend to his tables and I return to

Jackie. "Hey Jackie, did we get any more tickets?" I ask.

"Yeah, we got two more for the bar. One order for six West Coast Oysters and eight East Coast Oysters. The second ticket is for twelve of the Second House wings with the sauce on the side." She places both tickets in the window. "Now, do you remember the difference between the West Coast Oysters and East Coast Oysters?"

I wipe the sweat off my palms. "Yeah, the East Coast ones are brinier, saltier and smaller and the West Coast Oysters are sweeter rounder and plumper."

She smiles. "That's correct, Michael. Now, are the wings gluten-free?"

"Uhh... I think so."

She scowls. "I think so isn't an answer, Newbie."

"Yes, the wings are gluten-free, Jackie... as well as our sauce. And, the house-made crab spice is also gluten-free and if I'm not mistaken so is the chili which we make in-house as well."

"Nice job, Michael, you really prepared yourself. So far, you're the best trainee I've trained. No person who shadowed me has ever recited that before and you nailed the table numbers earlier. You'll be on the floor in no time. Keep it up, kid."

Soon more food comes out and time passes by. It's about ten minutes until the kitchen closes. The cleanup for the expo station is pretty easy; refilling all the sauces, other condiments, replenishing the coleslaw, lemons, pickles, and other side food items. It's almost too hard to wrap my head around, but in due time this shit will come together... it always does.

BOOM! Billie's fat stomach comes bursting through the double doors. "What's going on fuckers?" He dumps silverware into the dish bucket and water splashes all over Jose, the Spanish dishwasher. Remaining quiet; I continue to help Jackie. "Slow night, tonight," he states.

"Maybe for you, but me and Michael, we're back here busting our butts to drop food off to my tables and yours. You can be a fucking asshole sometimes. You gotta cut your shit and really start pulling your weight around here. I don't care how long you fucking been here. I don't care if you've been here for six years or not. I will write your ass up and push for a suspension, again, if your ass doesn't straighten up," Jackie yells.

Billie grins. "Suspension?"

"Yeah, if that's what it takes to whip your ass into shape then I'll do just that. And don't think I won't. You're on very, very thin ice, Bill." With the small hotel pan of coleslaw and tub of mayo, I scurry over to the walk-in fridge to put back the extra stock. Billie and Jackie have to be fucking. Suspension? Who the fuck is she kidding? Billie straight up violated us tonight—well he sure did, Jackie. Fuck a suspension, he's my friend and all but how can people work with that pompous asshole? Jackie has to be fucking him.

I chuckle out loud.

"What's so funny?" Jackie asks.

"Yeah, what's so funny, Farrakhan?" Bille asks with a mouth full of food from a customer's plate.

"Ah, nothing I was just thinking about how at my old restaurant job somebody shit in the urinal once."

Billie spits his food into Jose's garbage. "Oh shit, that hilarious."

Jackie frowns. "That's fucking gross Michael, ew."

"You had to be there Jackie if you were a guy you would be in tears right now," Billie adds.

She shakes her head. "Men are disgusting."

"They sure are, just look at Billie."

"What do you mean look at me? You should be worried about the trash overflowing instead of my looks. You wish your Black ass looked like me," he says and leaves the kitchen.

"He's right about the trash, you know. You mind taking that to the dumpster out back?" Jackie asks.

"No, I don't mind that at all," I reply.

"You know where it is, right?"

"Yeah, Tina showed me where it was yesterday. You head through the back exit of the bar dining room, down those stairs that lead you to the back parking lot. The garbage is all the way to the left." I laugh. "The very far left."

"Alright, you got it. Oh yeah, do you smoke?"

"Yeah, why?"

"Behind that dumpster, is where we usually take our smoke breaks. Treat yourself to one then report back."

"Thanks."

"You got it, Newbie."

The night summer air irritates my sweating skin, hauling this garbage to the back is no laughing matter. I'm praying this son of bitch doesn't rip open, there's a glass shard poking through the bottom that's going to ruin this trip if this bag touches the pavement again. With every step, my arms are starting to feel like paperweights. Just a few more steps. "AHHHH." I heave it over the city bin and into the garbage, luckily the bag tears wide open in mid-air with the debris spilling all into the waste fill. "Wrong bin bro!" someone shouts.

"What the fuck do you mean, wrong bin?" I shout back.

Jose from dish walks up. "Hey bro, that's the wrong bin." He points to another bin across the parking lot about fifty yards away.

I look at Jose as if he just punched me in the face. "You have to be fucking kidding me."

"No, Papi, I no joke, the bin over there," Jose says then slaps my back and laughs, "I joke, I joke."

I laugh with him in relief. He flicks his cigarette, goes for his right pocket, and then pulls out a clear small baggie filled with what looks like... yup, it's coke. He then takes a car-key from his other pocket and scrapes up a decent size bump and pulls it right up through a nostril.

"Yo, Jose, you sure you want to do that here? I'm mean... I'm fine with it. But someone might see you."

He laughs. "Fuck them. See poppa, I been here four years. They know me. It's okay." Jose hands the key and the bag over to me.

"You sure?"

He nods. I start to pick through the bag, edging a sizable bump out. The key bump finally makes its way into my left nostril. It hits pretty fast; the drip is a tad bit glassy but it feels alright. I hand it back. "No, poppa more, more," he offers.

I rail two more bumps and fork it over. "Thanks, man, that's some pretty good stuff." It really isn't but it's free and I don't want to insult him.

"Yes, poppa. I need for this bullshit." Jose points to the restaurant. The drip sets in and the taste is similar to Tracie's coke, but he must have stepped on this shit with baking soda or something to make it last longer. I reach for a cigarette from the pack of loosies I bought before clocking in and pass one to Jose. He takes it and pulls out his lighter but lights mine first. This is funny, the sole purpose of coming out here was to take out the garbage and have a quick smoke. Who would've thought this trip would turn into doing key bumps with the dishwasher?

"Hey Jose, where are you from?" I ask.

Jose exhales his smoke with his answer, "I from Peru, Papi."

"Cool, that reminds me of a Jay-Z song."

"Yeah, yeah, Papi, all my family there, I send money."

"That's good, you got kids?"

Jose puts up four fingers. "Cuatro."

"Damn, that's a lot of mouths to feed."

"Ye—"

"Hey!" Billie shouts from the other side of the parking lot. Jose and I head towards him. "Any of you minorities have an extra cigarette on you?" he asks. Jose declines but I give him one.

"Fine be like that, Jose, I didn't want no cowboy killer anyway. I'll smoke the Black man's cigarette. I love Newports," he laughs and lights his smoke. Jose makes his exit back upstairs. "I don't know why that dirty Mexican always has a fucking attitude, the nerve...but you see though, Mike... it's easy right?"

I take one drag before I toss it. "Jose's from Peru and what's easy?"

"Second House."

"I guess for the most part...the menu is pretty extensive but simple at the same time."

Billie pulls on his cigarette for a good three seconds and flicks it then reaches for his back pocket and pulls out his wallet. He runs through the billfold and retrieves a folded dollar-bill with coke inside. "Yup, now its closing time. You did good, Mikey, like I knew you would." He fishes up a few bumps, rails them then passes his Amex card and blow to me. I dig up a monstrous bump and snort as hard as I can. "YO!!" Billie screeches.

"Fuck you, man. After all the shit you put me through. I'm getting mine you obese fuck, you."

"Yeah, sorry about that but I run a tight ship here."

"You?" I smirk. "Get the fuck out of here. You don't sign any checks you fat asshole." I rummage for another bump, a smaller one this time. It goes right up my left nostril following the steady drip that's already there. I already feel my anxiety start to subside. This is much needed. My energy needed a boast after hauling that fucking trash to the dumpster. I give the drugs and card back to him.

"You're a funny guy, my nigga... a funny guy. You'll see real soon that I'm the head honcho around these parts," he says.

"More like the head asshole." Now, I'm feeling the drip. Air kicks in as if were my first time ever breathing through my nose. I can be suffering from a clogged nose and a couple of bumps will clear it right up. Jose giving me those first few is much appreciated but I've definitely had better shit than that. And Bill's blow—or Tracie's for that matter—is just a few notches up from Jose's. Shit, I hope that Tracie will be home after I get out of here. That shit from last night had me high as a giraffe. The first few drags of a Newport are best after the drip hits. After being exposed to what I just endured, this drip right here is well worth it. Fuck it.

"Hey," Billie spits into the lot. "You coming over tonight?"

"Yeah, sure why not? Are you all set in there? Anything need tidying up?"

"Nah, everything's good to go. You clocked out?"

"They didn't give me a server number yet, I'm just keeping track of my hours." I pluck my cigarette into the empty backlot. We walk back upstairs and say our goodbyes to the kitchen staff and Jackie. Billie hands Graham some cash in exchange for a six-pack of Miller Lite, then we make our way through the front entrance. "Trace home?" I spark another cigarette once outside.

"Nope, I think she's in the Bronx," he answers.

"To pick up or...."

"Don't worry about that fat dyke, I gotta whole eight-ball in my room."

I take one deep drag and pass him my cigarette. "Nice. You want the rest?"

Bille accepts and looks down at his phone. "Trace is coming home now." He places his phone back in his front pocket, takes two drags, and tosses it on the sidewalk.

"Word, it's a party!" I yell.

When we arrive, the front lobby of their building always gives off the lingering aroma of wet dog whenever my nose does get oxygen. And soon enough I'll be able to take in the odor of Billie's musty armpits. I usually can deal with the stench, but after a few bumps, my sense of smell decides to function and it's fucking unbearable. White people and their dogs, man. "They have to do something about the smell in this building," I follow Billie into the elevator.

"What smell?" He mashes four.

"The wet dog smell, you never noticed it?"

"Nah, I don't smell anything."

"Because, you smell like a drenched dog too," I laugh.

He takes a whiff of his armpits as if he actually cares about hygiene. "Nigga, I smell like working man."

"Nigga, you smell like a dog. You always do."

"You can only breathe through your nose when you're blowing coke. So, how can you even smell anything right now? You only did a few bumps," Billie says as he steps off and leads the way to his apartment.

"Those few bumps Jose gave me by the dumpster—helped a lot; I can breathe through my nose just fine. And you, Sir, smell as if you were a dog caught in a rainstorm. I'm not clowning you, Bill. I'm just stating the facts or that's just your natural smell; I'm used to it by now. FYI, never take off any clothing aside from a jacket whenever you're in my presence. I hate to see what your feet smell like. Working man."

Billie unlocks the door. "I have no clue what are talking about, Nigga. I never heard anyone say I smell and who is giving your broke ass coke? I know you don't have any money." He plops down on the couch and removes his shoes.

"Jose gave me some. I don't know who lied to you, and what did I just say to you about your shoes?" By the time I throw my bag on the couch and take my usual seat, a stale corn chip aroma takes over the living room. "Please, Bill, for the love of God please go and wash your feet or put back on your shoes. YOUR FUCKING FEET STINK. SHIT!"

Billie's feet shuffle back into his shoes. "My nigga you're fucking lying; I don't smell anything. And that dirty Mexican sniffs coke? I fucking knew it, that's why he gets out so fast after the kitchen closes."

"For the last time, he's Peruvian."

Keys start poking at the doorknob. "Yo!" Tracie shouts.

"What's going on, dyke?" Billie asks.

"What's go—wait..." Tracie whiffs around as she makes her way into the living room. "Damn Bill, what did I say about taking your shoes off in the living room. Goddamn, man."

"What the fuck are you talking about? My shoes are on," he cries.

"What the fuck are you talking about, Billie? Your shoes were off a few moments before Tracie came in the door, weren't they? I told you, Bill, your feet reek man. Jesus fucking Christ, get some *GoldBond* for those dogs," I laugh.

"See, I'm not the only one now. You gotta do something about your fucking feet, man," Tracie adds.

"Are they really that bad?"

"YES!" Tracie and I say simultaneously.

"Damn..." Billie shakes his head in disbelief.

Tracey runs upstairs and comes back with incense. "You got a lighter, Mike?"

"Yeah." I retrieve my lighter and put flame to the incense stick "Where do you want this thing to go?"

She gives it to me. "Crack the window right next to you and stick it in between the glass and panel, so the ash doesn't get onto the floor."

Billie dashes into his room and shuts the door. I watch the stick disintegrate then catch sight of Tracie rummaging through her oversized purse. Isn't it peculiar for a butch lesbian to have a purse? To me it seems like she's missing the point of being butch but who am I to put a label on her? Personally, I feel like she should be carrying a backpack or one of those fanny waist things.

Tracie makes it very apparent she's gay, but one can only assume she plays the dominating female in the bedroom, or should I say she does the pitching instead of catching 'cause that's what butch lesbians do. Which is why it puzzles me so much to see her sporting a 'girly-girl' purse. Maybe she's going against the grain just to go against the grain. I know people who do it from time to time just to feel different or gain some type of zest out of whatever life they're leading. It's funny to think that lesbians have sex with a strap-on. I mean, I've watched girl-on-girl porn before and one of the actors gave fellatio to the dildo. That's quite a silly thing to do or ask for in my opinion. It's understandable for a woman to be penetrated with a fake dick but to suck on it seems tedious. I actually find it to be quite hilarious even more now.

"You wanna smoke a blunt, Mike?" She flashes a quarter ounce of weed and a four-pack box of cigars.

"Yeah, I'm down but I'm not rolling it," I reply.

"That's fine…you gotta be a dick about it."

I chuckle out loud and she asks, "What's so funny?"

"Oh nothing, but your boy ill-Bill got threatened with suspension today."

"By who?"

"Jackie." I take the weed she puts in my hand and break it down on the edge of the coffee table.

"Oh shit. He's such a fucking asshole to her, I don't know why or how she puts up with his nonsense. Billie must be laying some good pipe on that poor girl." Tracie takes the broken down weed and pours it evenly through the gutted cigar.

Billie jerks his door open, displaying his pimple spotted chest. "HEY! You know I can fucking hear you, right? Stop blowing up my fucking spot."

"Fuck you, you, fat shit. It's not like it was a secret anyway, especially the way she's been spending every other night over here. Shit, I'm surprised he didn't find out sooner. I'm even more surprised how a fat fuck like you pulled a hot piece of ass like that." She twists the blunt to a cone, seals it, and places it on the coffee table.

"So what? You could have left that alone. You're just jealous that I've been getting fucked and sucked while you dwindle up your stank pussy. I bet your snatch smells like mop water." He slams his door. Tracie and I burst into laughter.

"Damn, Bill you're having quite the night," she yells and then turns to me, "Pass me a lighter, Mike, this nigga is in his feelings." She squats on the couch. "Wanna couple of lines before we gotta share with everybody else?"

"Sure, but who is everybody else?" I give Tracie my lighter.

"Oh, he ain't tell you?... HIS GIRLFRIEND JACKIE IS COMING OVER," she heckles.

"Yo, you guys are a trip. Every time I come over here it's never a dry moment. But yeah, about those lines. You want me to break something down?"

"Yeah, that would be helpful you no blunt rolling bitch." She gets up, trots to the kitchen island, retrieves her purse, and digs up another sandwich bag. She fishes around with a dollar and comes up with a sizable boulder, then shuffles back to the couch and passes the creased bill. The coke smells as if it was dipped in kerosene and has a slight glisten to the texture. This is what great coke is supposed to smell like. Comparing this to what Jose gave me, it blows that shit out of the water. "Shit, this looks and smells like some fire, Trace."

"Yeah, I know." She continues to scroll through her phone. I set the coke on the table and press against the bill with my lighter. Roughly rubbing my Bic up and down, ensuring that the rock is now all in powder form. I then grab the broken mirror at the corner of the table, place it in front of me, and spread the coke onto the glass. It's amazing how that chunk of blow refined down to smooth off-white flakey crystals.

"Hurry up and cut some fat ass lines before Billie gets out of the shower," she says. I start dividing up the coke and didn't take my time either. The lines are less than perfect but fatter than usual. They come to be the size of my index finger. "Oh yeah, I forgot to ask does Jackie fuck around?"

"Oh yeah, big time," Tracie answers. "But she's cool though, so don't worry."

"Okay, dope. You got anything bigger than this dollar bill?"

"Yeah." She digs around her front pocket and hands me a crisp hundred.

"Nice, at least we know this hasn't been up a stripper's ass." I twirl the bill up and rail one of the lines. "OH SHIT." I almost regurgitate. The coke hits instantly and the drip is spectacular.

"I know... I almost threw up my dinner on the train," she chuckles.

"You sniffed on the train?"

"Yeah, a few bumps in the bathroom. Had to see what I was working with, you know."

I sniff and rub the leftover coke from my line on my gums. "Yeah, I feel you." All of sudden there's a steady and light thump at the door entrance. It repeats.

Tracie takes the rolled bill from my lap and with no haste at all, she rails one of the lines. "Ah shit, that's probably Jackie. Man, I would kill to eat that butthole." She bolts to the door. "Who is it?" She asks

"It's Jackie."

Tracie opens the door and they embrace each other. "Hey girl!"

"What's up bitch? How are you?" Jackie says.

"Nothing much... come in, come in." Tracie follows Jackie into the living room.

Jackie's eyes immediately lock on the plate of coke. "See you guys already started the party without me. What's up, Newbie, didn't know you knew these two degenerates."

"HEY, there's only one degenerate that lives here, and he's in his room," Tracie states.

Jackie chuckles and takes a seat on the couch. "It's a small world. We had a whole shift together and you didn't say a word about knowing these guys. Well, I know you knew Billie but I didn't think you guys, like, hung out." She nudges my shoulder.

"Nah, I just like it to keep it professional, you know...you never know. Who wants their business out like that? I mean no offense; I keep quiet about a lot. It's just my nature," I say and divide up more lines.

"Alright, Mr. Mysterious over here," Jackie laughs.

"Yeah, Mikey is definitely a piece of work. For real though, Second House is lucky to have him. He knows his shit," Tracie adds.

I pass the bill and glass to Jackie. She snorts two of the biggest lines. "Whoa, that's good... Real good. Whoa. But yeah, before we hired you A.G. said you were the shit when you worked for Dick and what an all-star server you are. I'm sorry about how they just closed down like that, shit that must've been hard."

"Nah, you don't have to apologize for anything, matter of fact, don't even mention it. We got bigger fish to fry now. I'm just happy to be at Second House, you know. Let's get this money. I would toast to that but ah..." I take the plate back from Jackie.

"Oh, shit I forgot to make drinks," Tracie says and then bolts to the kitchen. "Regular screwdrivers okay, guys?" she shouts back.

"Yeah, that's fine," Jackie replies.

"I'll just have one of those *Miller Lites*, on the kitchen counter, if you don't mind." You know what... " I rise from my seat and stretch..."I'm going to head out for a smoke. Anyone want to join me?"

"Yeah, I'll come for one," Tracie says as she makes her way back to the living room with the beverages and places them on the coffee table. "What about you, Jackie? You joining us?"

"I'm good for now, I'll wait till Billie gets out here. What is he doing in there anyway?"

"Hopefully showering," Tracie jokes. "He should be out in a minute though."

Tracie and I made our way onto the back balcony with our drinks and set fire to our cancer sticks. "Yeah, man, so how you like the new gig?"

"It's cool, you know regular restaurant shit. Learn the menu, the POS system, tables and get your money, that's it," I explain.

She exhales then taps ashes over the balcony. "...That's it."

"I'm a little concerned about Bill, though. He was sniffing at work and had coke all in his nose and shit. I was about to tell him until he went off on me. Like, he really went off on me and Jackie too." I drag a little deeper and ash into the ashtray.

"He's going to get himself fired, fuck a suspension. Then he could kiss Miss Tight Ass goodbye." Tina smirks.

"Maybe so, and that'll be his own doing. The worst part is, I think some customers heard him address me as his nigga. I know what we say between us stays here, but I'm sure nobody wants to hear that at Second House—at least I don't want them to hear it. Some people aren't comfortable with a white person using that word."

Tracie reaches for her beverage. "Dude, I don't get why you're so anal about white people using *nigga*. You gotta realize times have changed. We've had a Black president now so people don't care about that type of shit anymore. It's all good in the hood."

"But—" I begin but Billie comes out with Jackie at his hip. "What are you two assholes jawing about?" he asks.

"Shit," Tracie replies.

"...Yup, what are you guys up too?" I ask.

"You smell better, Bill," Tracie states.

"I would say the same for you but you haven't washed your vagina this week..."

I chuckle. "Oh shit..."

Jackie slaps Billie in his chest with, "You're such an ass."

Tracie takes one more drag and puts out her cigarette. "Bill, Bill... you're are really a piece of work. I was giving you a compliment for once." Tracie then turns her attention to me. "Dude can't even take a compliment without getting offended."

Billie lights a cigarette. "Fuck you guys, I'm sensitive."

"We can tell." I grin.

"Anyways, I caught you flirting with Giselle tonight," Jackie interjects.

"Nah, we were just two co-workers talking. She was helping with the floor layout," I reply.

"Cut the shit, Mikey, even I saw it. She was throwing the pussy your way," Billie adds.

"Do you always have to sound like a total predator?" Tracie asks.

"Nope, but it's funny," he replies, "Giselle isn't the token anymore, so it's only right for you to take that down."

I ash my cigarette and reply, "No, you fucking idiot it's not. That's workplace harassment and I don't shit where I eat."

Jackie is right though. We were flirting and I'm very attracted to Giselle. The way her pearly, perfect white teeth shine in the dim light by

68

the hostess stand. And, the way her caramel skin glistens off the bar candles when she's seating guests is magnetic. She's a beautiful girl. It's easy for her to be flirted with and besides we work in hospitality, everybody flirts. With Tracie leading the way, everyone heads back inside. Bill grabs a chair from the kitchen island and brings it to the living room. I place myself on the couch with the coke plate right in front of me; I separate lines from what's left.

"Anybody see a hundred-dollar bill?" Tracie asks.

I shuffle around my pockets and feel it at the top of one. "Here you go."

"You wanna kill those before you give it back to me?" Tracie asks pointing to the untouched lines.

"Yeah, sure." I rearrange the roll in the bill and inhale the coke up my right nostril. "AH. There we go."

Billie pulls out more coke and then uses his teeth to release it from the bag's tight knot. "Pass me that plate, Farrakhan."

"Why do you always have to talk shit?" I hand over the mirror.

He takes a large amount out, puts it into a creased two-dollar bill, and pokes around it with his Amex. He takes a large amount and puts it into a creased two-dollar bill, and pokes around it with his Amex. "Because, you, Black bastard, are so easy to bait, you and your self-righteous Black man's 'woe is me' bullshit. You make it so easy my nigga," he and Tracie both laugh.

I take a sip of my brew. "Whatever, you fat fuck. You and your fungus feet need to see a foot specialist with that unholy smell you got going over there. You should be the last motherfucker talking."

"Damn, my brotha. WHY SO SENSITIVE?" He shouts.

I finish the rest of my beer. "You don't have to belittle my Blackness every time I come over here. Just break down some lines and chill the fuck out."

"Anybody want another drink?" Jackie asks.

Tracie rises from the couch. "Yeah, I'll help you. You want another beer, Mikey?"

"For sure, thank you," I reply.

"See, that's what I'm talking about, bro," Bille says and divides the coke into eight, pinky-sized lines then rails two. "You think you carry the Black race on your shoulders and you don't. Shit, I'm blacker than you. I bet you can't even moonwalk." Billie hands me the plate. "Shit, I bet Jackie can even moonwalk," he laughs.

"HA. I can moonwalk!" Jackie shouts.

"See..." Billie heckles.

"Nah, I don't see. You're a real piece of work, Bill." I snort my lines and slide the mirror back.

He smirks. "Why, because I can moonwalk?"

"No, because the fact that you can imitate Michael Jackson doesn't mean you're blacker than me nor does it solidify my own Blackness, you prick."

"So, you admit to not having rhythm as a Black person?" he questions.

"Does that define me being black? FYI, I can dance. Hey, Trace while you're up, can you grab me a tissue, I'm leaking over here."

"There's tissue under the coffee table!" she yells.

I reach under the table and snatch three Kleenex. "Thanks."

"We got you covered, snotty," Billie jokes. The girls find their way back into the living room. Tracie hands me a Coors Light with a side of water. One thing about working in restaurants, you carry over being hospitable outside of work. People can only appreciate the mannerisms that working in hospitality can bring.

Jackie places herself on Billie's lap. "So why were you saying Mike can't dance Bill? Is it 'cause you can't dance?" she laughs.

"You never seen me dance, Jack. And, besides my mother was a dance instructor before I was born. Of course, I can dance. Especially better than Farrakhan over there." He holds the mirror to Jackie's nose. She sniffs one line and passes the plate to Tracie.

"Oh really," Jackie scoffs, "you never mentioned that before.

"It never came up and we've never been dancing," Billie replies.

"That reminds me, when are we going to go on an actual date?"

"Don't hold your breath, Jack," Tracie says, rails three lines, and then gags. "You gotta better chance of seeing Mikey moonwalk."

Billie chuckles and says, "You know what Trace, you're probably right."

Jackie smacks his chest. "Asshole."

"I would pay to see Farrakhan moonwalk," Billie laughs.

"I would pay to see you lose weight. And you're going to stop calling me that, you fat fuck."

"Why don't you like being called Farrakhan? Isn't he like an ah-civil rights leader or whatever?" Jackie asks.

"Not whatsoever. And he's that and much more. Plus when Bill calls me that, he doesn't mean it out of respect, he's trying to be funny."

"Good one, Farrakhan." He retrieves more blow, puts it in the bill, and hands it to Jackie. "Here, break this up."

The drip comes back with full force when I breathe through my nose. "Tread light, Bill, you're lucky you're my friend. Because, one day you may run into a person of color who isn't going to take that *nigga* shit likely and that nigga might fuck you up," I say.

Tracie reaches over the table and gives Jackie more coke to refine as she addresses me. "You gotta take a chill pill, Black man, it's not that serious. You can't take a little joke? How many times I gotta tell you? It's not 1954 and niggas ain't marching through D.C. and shit."

I clinch my beer tighter. "Yeah, whatever. Coming from a white lesbian that's easy for you to say. Only thing you're fighting for is same-sex marriage. Black people have been fighting for equality for years—up til this day shit isn't right. Having a Black president is cool and all but that doesn't change four-hundred years of systematic oppression."

Billie points at me. "See, there it is that Farrakhan shit I was talking about. My nigga, what the fuck you know about four-hundred years of systematic bullshit? Nigga, you never had an oppressed day in your life. I told you that before. You're as privileged as I am fat."

"And what does me being a lesbian have to do with anything?" Tracie asks.

"We're all fighting for something in this life. I'm fighting for equality, you're fighting for gay rights, and Billie's fighting to lose weight."

Billie snorts a humungous line. "Whatever you say, Farrakhan." They all laugh.

"You're a real piece of work, Bill," I forced a chuckle. 'You mind if I get a couple lines before I get out of here?"

"You're leaving so soon?" Jackie asks.

"Yup, I have to get some sleep to study the menu some more. You know how it goes." I take the plate from Billie's hands.

"Are you kidding me?" Jackie wipes snot from her nose. "You're the most knowledgeable person I've trained since I started at Second House. You got that shit down and it's just your second day, you should relax and stay awhile."

"Nah, it's getting late anyway. And I'm working with what's-her-face tomorrow—Tina. I don't want her riding my back all night." I rail my last lines.

"I feel ya," Jackie replies.

"Nah, tell her the real reason why you wanna leave. It's 'cause Billie is getting under your skin like he always does," Tracie states.

"Nah, fuck you guys, it isn't that serious. Wouldn't give him or you the satisfaction. I enjoyed your hospitality, but I must bid you guys adieu." I stood up, gave Bille a handshake, Jackie a light hug, and Tracie a fist pound before making my way out.

"Aye, Farrakhan. Stay Black!" Tracie shouts.

Before making a full exit, I poke my head back into the kitchen. Aye, Trace stop asking your girlfriend to suck your strap on. Don't you know you can't feel anything? Newsflash, you don't have a PENIS. And Billie you smell you take naps in the backlot dumpster. Goodnight, Jackie; I'll see you tomorrow."

FRONT OF THE HOUSE

Tonight, it's more than hectic at Second House—a shit show to be exact. After Tina tripped over the expo mat with three entrees, the kitchen has been playing catch up ever since. I'm just finished with cleaning up her spill now. Given the fact that one of the bussers called out; I can't imagine how the tables look. This mess has taken a solid ten minutes to clear. Jackie for whatever reason cut Billie early and doesn't do us any justice. I swear this place is worse than high school. I haven't seen Tina since her catastrophe, either she's too embarrassed to help or too lazy. It's probably all the coke she railed before service started. The coke residue coated all under her fingernails is a dead giveaway, real professional. This place is something else.

Jose comes over with a mop to put the finishing touches on the spill. "Thank you, Papa." I smile.

"No, Papa, thank you," Jose pats my back. "Papa? You have cigarette?" he continues to wipe the floor.

"Yeah, I do, just let me know when you go out. They're in my bag. Once I hit the floor, they're going to need me. But when you're ready to go, come find me, Pa."

"Okay, Pa," he trots back to the dish station.

Tina's stale face pokes through the kitchen windows. By accident, I make eye contact. "Damn, Newbie. I know Black people are always late, but I never heard of you dudes being slow. It took you that long to clean up? We need help out there. You're taking too long back here. Get your ass out here NOW!" She shouts.

"Calm down, Tina. If I had some help maybe this would've been faster but that wasn't so... I'll be there in two secs."

"Who are you talking to, Newbie?" she scolds. "You should know fucking better than to talk back while you're training. I'm sure A.G. would love to hear about your mouth."

"I'm sorry, Tina... I'll be right there." Wish I had enough balls to tell her to eat a dick and who cares if she tells A.G. I'll call immigration on her ass, see who gets the last laugh then. But that's not the case. I'm the bitch in this scenario and, Tina made that very clear. "Oh, shit," I laugh.

"What's so funny, Papi?" Jose questions.

"Oh, nothing man. I was just laughing, you know." I hand him the drying towels.

"Se' Se'. Don't let that pig make bad you feel. She get no fuck from man so she's always mad." He does a jerk-off motion to the air to demonstrate what he means. I reassure him I'm content by forcing out another chuckle and nodding in assurance.

I make my way towards the dining room floor. "Ay, Pa, remember to come find me when you want to go smoke. OK?" Jose nods and waves me out. When I exit, the temperature suddenly drops ten to fifteen degrees. Feels as if I was in there for a lifetime. First things first, start clearing every table in my visual. With a handful of plates and my fingertips cusping the inside of four beer glasses, I find relief in coming back into the kitchen.

"Ay, Pa, you fast, really fast!" Jose cries.

"Just doing my job, brother. Ain't nothing to it but the right attitude and right sneakers." I dump the plates in a bin under the dish station and

Jose without pause takes the rest from my arms.

"Thank you."

"No, thank you, Pa," he says.

One of the cooks rapidly hits the service bell and I jolt to the expo line. Waiting in the window are five entrees on one expo ticket for Tina. Three Snow Crabs, one Rib Eye Steak—med-rare, and one filet mignon, rare. I grab the steaks and one crab leg dish. Soon as I do a one-eighty turn, Tina's pudgy figure enters through the double doors. "Where you going with that?" she scolds.

"Your table, Ma'am."

"What table?"

"Uhh... 13b. The rest of the entrees are in the window."

"Ok, Newbie, I'll follow you."

Instead of waiting for her stubby legs to catch up, I march out, passing by the bar, and avoiding Billie as he does the tip out for his tips. Still, he waves me down. But little does Billie know, I could care less about whatever nonsense he's got going. Before arriving at the table, I watch Jackie seat a Black couple. They have to be the only persons of color I've seen thus far other than Giselle. It's kind of a relief. It shouldn't be, but it is.

I set the plates down at a table by positions. The guests switch dishes and I realize Tina put them down not knowing which entree belongs to which person. This is the only time where the auctioning of plates would work. Only if she would do her job right for once. I catch one of the three women staring a little too hard.

"Ladies, Tina is right behind me with the rest of your dinner. I assume we're sharing everything?"

The women nod simultaneously. "Thank you," position two says and adds, "Before you rush off, what's your name, handsome?"

I blush and then answer, "My name is Michael, Miss."

"Ok, Michael, you have great teeth to match that great smile. You're a breath of fresh air, you are. When did you start working here, Michael with the great teeth?" She teases.

I blush again. "Two nights ago, I'm a server in training."

The guest reaches for my hand. "Well, I'm Sage, and these are my sisters, Patricia and Shirley. It's nice to meet you, Michael. I'll make sure to tell A.G. to stop hiding you in the back."

As I release Sage's firm grasp, her wedding ring scratches my palm.

All of sudden, someone nudges my back. "Hey ladies, is Michael bothering you?" Tina asks.

"Oh, heavens no," Patricia answers, "we've been blessed to have our food delivered by this beautiful Black man."

"He's the sweetest," Shirley adds.

Sage touches my left bicep. "Think you'll be seeing more of us. Now, that you guys finally hired some eye-candy," she says and giggles.

"Thank you ladies, you are too kind. I'll be sure to say goodbye before you leave." I smile and speed back to the expo line. To my luck, there are orders for the bar ready. I prep ketchup, blue cheese, and liners for wings and fries. "Where you going with that?" Tina shouts.

"Ah-the bar?"

She snatches the food out of my hands. "My tables need water and clearing. NOW!"

"Ok. I got it."

"Yeah, but you don't talk to my tables; I don't want you fucking up my tips. Who knows what the fuck you been saying to those ladies." She waddles forward.

"But I didn—"

"I DON'T CARE! Know and stay in your place and do what you're told, Newbie, and everything will be fine." She vanishes through the doors.

I head over to the server station to retrieve the ice pitcher and to my surprise, Jackie is there putting something into the POS. I straighten up my face. "Hey, Jackie, how's it going?"

"I'm alright, glad we're finally caught up with all the tables and the bar has everything they need." She continues to punch at the POS. "What are you up to?" she asks.

"I'm just making sure everyone has water." I scoop ice and pour water into the pitcher.

"Awesome, did Billie leave?" she asks.

I poke my head into the dining room, then scan the bar. "I don't see him. Yeah, I think he left."

"Okay, did he tip you out?" Jackie makes eye contact.

"No, I wasn't under the impression he was going to, after all, I'm still in training."

"Yeah, I know but Pepe called out and you bussed all the tables and ran food. So, you're entitled to some cash."

"That's dope, maybe he didn't know." I shrug.

"Oh no, he did. I told him mid-shift. What a dick..."

"Don't sweat it, I'll get it from him later." I grin. "Do you need anything before I head back onto the floor?"

"Nope, thanks though. I saw Sage and her sisters getting talkative and handsy with you. Which is funny, they don't care too much for the guys who work here. They love me and Tina but hate everyone else. So, it was funny to see them flirting with you."

I grin. "You're right, that is funny, but I guess that's a good thing."

"It is, now go water some tables," she directs.

As I bounce around from guest to guest refilling glasses until there is nothing to pour, you'd be surprised on how many people don't even touch their water, especially considering the water crisis in California. I mean, sure, this isn't California but the number of guests who rapidly order alcohol by the glass is nuts. Their heads must be throbbing in the morning, poor souls. I head back to the back station and I start stabbing the block of ice with the scooper.

Que esta pasando?" I ask.

"*Cigarrilo?*" He does a smoking signal with his hands.

"*Se, un momento.*" I place the pitcher on the side of the sink and rummage through the bottom cabinet to find my bag. "Ah, here we go…Man, it fucking stinks in that shit." I fish through my pack and hand Jose two cigarettes.

"You're right Papa," he says, and we laugh. Jose drags his feet back to the kitchen and I go assist Tina with clearing and wiping tables. As time winds down, the patrons vanish from table to table and the restaurant becomes calm. After I wrap up the expo station and stock all the to-go supplies as well as start to wipe down the silverware. When I'm finished, I pass off to Tina to roll. Feels good to see her actually doing server work, it's about time.

"Hey, Mike!" Jackie yells.

"What's up, Boss Lady?"

"You're outta here, have a great night." She continues to do the numbers for dinner service.

"You sure? Do you guys need anything else?"

"Nope, great job tonight, order yourself something and get outta here, kid."

"Nah, I'm actually good."

"Curbed your appetite?" she asks.

"Nah, not at work," I chuckle. "I've actually got some food at home, something my mother made. She's trying to make sure I'm not surviving just off Second House."

"Right, good... Must be nice. My mother lives all the way in Mass and she rather drink than cook."

"It is. So you're from Mass?"

She shuffles more receipts around. "Yeah, Dorchester to be exact"

"Damn, that's a pretty rough area."

"You ain't lying."

"Glad you made out."

"Shit, me too."

"Well... I guess that's it; have a goodnight. I'll see you tomorrow," I say and grab my backpack. I take my phone out then stuff it into my back pocket as I head towards the bar.

"Oh, before you forget," Jackie shouts, "make sure, Tina tips you out, ok?"

"Got it, thanks." I turn towards the kitchen where Tina is wiping silverware and stuffing her face with fries which I'm pretty sure are lukewarm by now. "Hey, Tina."

Tina continues to chew, "What?"

"Jackie said you had some tips for me?"

"Oh, yeah." She reaches into her back pocket and hands over three crumply twenties.

"Thanks."

"Yeah, we did pretty decent tonight," she says and swallows.

"I can tell, thanks again." I head towards the doors.

"Oh, yeah Sage and her sisters left an extra twenty in there for you," she says.

"Wow, that was really nice of them."

"Yeah, it was. Don't know why they like you so much, they don't like anyone. So, what makes you special?"

"Apparently I'm Michael with the *nice teeth.*"

"Well... *Michael with nice teeth.* Get your Black ass out my face, you're annoying me," she says and frowns.

I smirk but manage a reply. "Alright, have a goodnight." On my way out of the kitchen, I give Jose a fist bump and another cigarette. I wave at Jackie as I pass the dining room and see Graham signaling to approach the bar.

"What's going on?"

"Where you are going? You bussed tonight right?" he asks.

"Uh...yeah, I did."

"Okay then, let me pay you," he says and opens the bar register and pulls out a twenty. He lifts the cash holder then retrieves a white envelope. "Here, this twenty is from me and the money Billie left for you is in the envelope."

"Thanks a lot. Guess I'll see you tomorrow."

"Yup." He waves me off. Before hitting the exit, I stop at the end of the bar to count what Billie left. "Whoa, sixty bucks. Not bad, Bill... not bad," I mutter and mix the cash with what Billie left before I slip it all in back my pocket.

"Hey, Weathers!" Giselle shouts.

"Oh, what's up, didn't know they kept you here this late."

She sighs, "Yeah, Jackie likes to keep me on the clock whenever A.G.

is not here. And, she'll have me do all this unnecessary shit, like sanitizing all the menus and buckets. This shit is way too fucking much."

I chuckle, "What else does she have you?"

"Cleaning and organizing the reservation book which is way overbooked. Honestly, it's whatever…I guess someone has to do it."

"Wait… If you're organizing the reservation book then why doesn't she make Tina clean the menu and buckets?"

"I know…right? Oh, yeah before I forget some white lady dropped this on my podium before she left, it's got your name on it. She seemed rich." Giselle hands over a white torn piece of paper with a number on it, and Sage's name written in cursive.

"Sage?" she asks and grins.

"Yeah, she came in with her sisters earlier; I think she's married," I tear it in half and chuck it in the hostess bin. "Yeah, fuck that."

"You're funny."

"Nah, man, I'm just a Black man trying to stay employed. These white people are crazy," I chuckle.

Giselle smiles. "Yeah, they're definitely something."

"Alright then, Giselle, I bid you adieu and goodnight."

"Wait…where are you going?"

"I'm headed home, why?"

"Well, if you're too tired… but if you're not; you wanna grab a drink?"

"Ah, sure why not. Where do you want to go?"

"Hold on a sec, I'm going to check with Jackie if I'm all set to go. I'll be right back." She marches to the back of the dining where I last saw Jackie. Damn, this is intense. Why the fuck does she want to grab a drink with me? With me, of all people…Goddamn, Michael you better not blow this.

Gisele rushes back. "Come on, let's go." She moves behind the hostess stand and grabs her oversized Louis Vuitton purse (a bag this size is overkill if you ask me). I hold the door open as we make our escape. We take a left after reaching the sidewalk. "Do you have a car?" she asks.

"My car broke down a few days ago, but lucky for me I live within seven minutes of walking distance."

"Oh, nice."

"What about you, do you drive?" I match her walking pace.

"Yeah, my car is parked over there." She points directly across the street into the transit driver lot to a tannish early 2000 model Mercedes Benz.

"Hmm, nice."

"Thanks, it was my dad's. He got a newer one and gave me that."

"Must be nice."

"Not, really. I still live at home, unfortunately. Do you live with your parents?"

"Fortunately, I don't," I laugh, "I proudly live alone."

"That must be fucking nice."

"It is... wait where the hell are you taking me?" We stop at the corner of Canal and Main street.

"Oh shit. You've never been to First House, right?"

"What's First House?"

"Oh my God. Nobody told you what First House is?"

"Nope."

"Damn, whoever's responsible for your training sucks. Anyway, First House is Second House's sister restaurant, by the same owners. Nobody told you that?"

I laugh. "Nope. The servers here are a class-act," I say as we turn on Canal.

"Class-act," she scoffs. "You gotta be kidding me, they're all a bunch of cokeheads."

I gulp. "You don't say?"

"You can't tell? Just look at Billie, shit look at Tina—their attitudes are always on ten. And they always have some white shit on the corner of their noses. They're always running back and forth to the bathroom and shit." She stops at the crosswalk and starts digging through her purse then comes up with a pack of Newport shorts, then puts a flame to one.

"I didn't know you smoked."

"You want one?"

"I got my own but I'll have one with you." I retrieve my cigarettes and light one. She leads the way crossing the street. The overhead sign reads *First House Tavern*. It has the style of an old tavern from the late 1800s. Big brown wood doors, 4x4 windows, and gold brass door handles. Looks comfy. We stand off the side of the building about ten feet away from the entrance while we smoke.

"So how old are you Weathers?" she asks.

"Twenty-six. You?"

"Wow, you don't look a day pass nineteen or twenty-one. I'm twenty-three."

"Thanks. You don't look past eighteen. I thought you were much younger."

Giselle laughs and ashes. "You know what they say, right?"

I exhale my smoke. "What?"

"Black don't crack."

I laugh. "You're right, I've heard that too many times... must be the cocoa butter."

"Must be..."

I flick my butt into the street. "Being Black comes with blessings and curses, I guess..."

"It sure does, especially working at Second House," Giselle says and tosses her cigarette. "You ready to go inside?"

"Ready as I'll ever be." I let her guide the way in, but not a second before I grab and hold the door open for her.

"Such a gentleman, you are," she says.

I smirk. "My father is to blame, I apologize."

She directs our movement towards two open seats at the crowded bar, "Good, Keith's working. First rounds on me."

"No doubt." I pull her chair out and can't help but notice the way her full thighs and voluptuous ass hit the stool. How the fuck can her stomach and waist can be so tight with an ass like that? Jesus Christ.

"What are you having?" She questions.

I adjust in my chair and reply, "I'll have a Hennessy on the rocks."

It isn't long until the bartender notices us. He waltzes over wearing a pressed, long-sleeved white shirt with C.J Brian's printed in black cursive letters on the shirt pocket. He wears the sleeves halfway rolled up. A tannish brown belt holds up his faded Levi jeans and a black apron that almost touches the floor, just like the ones at Second House. Keith's gelled up hair glistens of the dim bar lights. He looks good for his age; I'm assuming he's anywhere in his mid-thirties-early forties. He greets us with a big smile. "Second House in the house!" He shouts then reaches over the bar to plank a kiss on Giselle's cheek. "Who's your friend G?"

"This is Michael, he is a server in training at Second House. We both just got out and decided to come for drinks."

"Ah, welcome to the company, Mike. As you probably know now we're the sister restaurant to Second House, and I've been here since the beginning of course—and that was back in '99." He extends his hand.

I shake his hand and smile. "Glad to be a part of it." I notice Giselle raises her eyebrows and grins.

"Glad to have you, buddy. Pick your poison, Mike," he says.

"I'll have a Hennessy on the rocks, please."

"You got it, and for you G, the usual?"

"Yeah, Remy Martin and Coke. You know me so well," Giselle giggles.

Keith slaps the counter. "One Hennessy on the rocks and Remy and Coke coming right up." He grabs two glasses, fills them ice and water, and places them in front of us.

I reach for my water. "So, I'm guessing, you don't do coke since the waiters are all cokeheads?"

"Hell NO. My father was in and out of jail for drugs. Me and my brothers learned our lessons with an absent father. I smoke a little bit of weed but that's about it. I hope you don't fuck around with that shit," Giselle says and reaches for two coasters and places one on the side of my water.

I clench my glass. "Nah, can't say that I do... How many siblings do you have?"

"Three... I'm the youngest. You?" She takes a sip of water, her lipstick leaves its mark on the glass.

"It's just me..."

"Lucky."

"Eh, I guess."

Keith, wearing another smile, comes back with our drinks and places them next to our waters. "Enjoy guys." He walks away to the end of the bar joining the patrons who are watching the Rangers game on the big screen.

Giselle and I look each other in the eye and lift and graze our glasses. "Cheers," she says.

"Cheers."

Giselle reaches for two more coasters and sets our drinks on top of them. "So, tell me about your life?"

"What do you want to know?"

"Well... what was your last job like?"

"Uh... where do I begin... Well, let's just say I was a copywriter at LBS. Litigation Bank of Switzerland, I was there for the latter half of three years. I was basically just someone stuffed in a backroom with other creative people and our sole purpose was to come up with marketing content, basically making ads to sell to the other companies."

Giselle sucks her drink halfway down. "Sounds like a great job, why would you leave that just to wait on tables?"

I sip and consider my answer. "You want the fake version or the real version first?"

"Hmm. Let's hear the fake version first."

"I got overlooked and denied the promotion I sought after since I'd been there; it was devastating so I quit," I say, polish off the rest of my drink, and signal Keith for another round.

"Now the real version..."

I begin to play a game of chess with a salt and pepper shaker. "One night, I was working late, right? So I went to the copy room. When I got there, I noticed there was coffee spilled all over the copying machine and...."

Keith pushes our second round in front of us.

Giselle finishes her first drink, pushes it aside and replaces it with the fresh one. "...And..." she asks.

"And... you sure can put em' away," I laugh.

She slaps my shoulder. "Come on, finish the story."

"Alright, alright, no need to get violent." I push my empty glass away, grab my second, and take a big sip from the straw. "So, where was I?"

"You were working late, and something about the copying machine."

"Oh yeah, so. Tammy Bell..."

"Who's Tammy Bell?"

I smirk. "If you let me finish, I'll tell you who she is."

"Okay, I'm sorry, go ahead and finish."

"So, Tammy Bell... a name, I will never ever forget. She was the secretary of my department head. But that night I was in the copy room, Tammy came rushing in with a bunch of paper towels. I figured she was the one to spill all that coffee, every morning she used to have that extra-large mug filled with it, and all damn day her breath would be lingering of stale coffee."

Giselle giggles.

I laugh. "Nah man, I'm serious her breath was like that teacher you had in high-school who always had that oversized cup of coffee in the morning. Well, that was Tammy, serious homeroom breath. Anyway, I guess Tammy was just as shocked to see me as I was to see her, 'cause I never stay late, but on that particular night I did. She probably thought everybody in the department was gone for the night."

Giselle squeezes the lime into her drink, "So...she spilled the coffee?"

"Yeah, that goes without saying." I toss the straw from my new drink into Giselle's old glass. "So Tammy starts looking at me crazy as hell—like I was a ghost or some shit. She literally turned white-- not knowing I could care less that she would spill coffee everywhere. Anyway, so Tammy starts panicking then she's swearing up a storm. But, earlier that day I'd seen my boss scold her pretty bad. I think she was on her way to being fired or something, she was always getting reprimanded for something. But that morning, I knew she was on her last leg. So, after she starts to panic and all of that, she calms down for a bit. Tammy then looks at me with this… soulless stare, almost like she was having a brain aneurysm, you know… Then says *you did this.* I'm like 'what' *no,* you know damn well this is your mess. This crazy bitch starts shouting in my face saying this, saying that, and how she's going to tell Human Resources I groped her off-camera."

Giselle gasps, "Wow."

"Wait, I'm not done. So, Tammy continued to threaten me with all kinds of false accusations and what really put the icing on the cake is, her saying these exact words: *who the fuck is going to believe your Black ass anyway? You're just another uppity nigger who's only here because of Affirmative Action.* So, when my boss and the tech guys came around asking questions about the xerox machine; I kept quiet—I didn't know how to deal with Tammy and what she said. Just having to look at her every day was nauseating so I gave HR my two weeks, and two weeks after that, I ended up getting an interview for Second House." I tilt my glass. "Now, here I am talking to you."

"What the fuck? That's some shit, Weathers. Did you ever tell anybody?"

My parents wanted me to sue—well my mom did, but I didn't want that in and out court shit. I'm not a fan of being paraded around like some charity case, I just wanted to be seen as another 'out of the way' employee. But because of pigment, Tammy baited the fuck outta me and won. Whatever, I just wanted it all behind me, so I left."

Giselle slips her hand onto my lap. "I'm so sorry you had to experience that. It's a day-to-day struggle to be Black in this white man's country. The battles that are being fought just to get ahead in life will make anyone go insane. I'm glad you kept your composer but at the same time, you had every right to work in that office building. And it's crazy crackers like that Tammy bitch who should've never been born."

"Unfortunately, the condom her father was using popped."

She laughs. "It's good that you can still make fun of it, especially after what happened. If I were you, I would've decked that bitch...well... Maybe not deck her but something would've happened. I guess it's easier to give an opinion when you're looking on the outside in."

"I guess it is... Do me a favor G?"

"Sure, what is it?"

"Please keep what I just told you between you and I. To be honest, I don't care that you know but I really don't need those guys in my shit, you know…"

"No problem, I totally understand."

"Well... enough about me and my bullshit. Let's hear about your life," I say and take another sip.

Giselle grins. "What do you want to know?"

"Anything..." We pause for a second and gaze openly at one another. I think she can tell that I'm sincere with my inquire and not how people usually fake introductory questions. You can't put a price on honesty, or maybe you can but I'll like to think at this moment, I'm not paying for it.

"Well uh, you know I've been a hostess at Second House for a while. I actually like being a host, it's a simple enough job where I don't have to put in a lot of effort. As you can tell, I don't wanna be bothered by anyone else in the front of the house, they're all on coke and feel entitled. Other than that, when I'm not at school or work; I'm usually smoking," she laughs and catches Keith's attention for another round.

"What are you in school for?"

"I wanna be either an LPN or maybe a therapist, I really don't know. Something in the medical field I guess."

I scratch my head, "Isn't that the same thing?"

"No, LPN is a therapist who can prescribe medication. And a therapist is just someone you talk to and figure out what's wrong and what can help fix what's wrong. To become an APRN I would have to go to med school which would take longer or whatever..." she says as Keith comes back with our new drinks and walks away with our old glasses.

"It's not whatever, Giselle, that's fucking awesome, you wanna help people. You have goals and not a lot people have that."

"I'm glad you think so, cause my father thinks I'm wasting time not studying law..."

"At least you got parents who want the best for you." I chug the rest of my second drink.

"Yeah, but what about what I want? I have my own best interest at heart, things that I wanna do, you know. And what about your parents... Do they support every career decision you make or made?"

"Surprisingly, yes," I chuckle. "They're nuts, even after I quit LBS, they've supported my every decision. I could say I'm truly blessed and thankful to have them as my parents; I don't know where I would be without them.

Do you have siblings or no?" I ask and watch her swirl her drink

91

around.

"Just me... What about you?"

"I'm the youngest of three and the only girl."

I chomp the ice around in my glass. "That's crazy."

"Yeah, so I know how to fight," she says and smiles.

"With older brothers, you definitely should."

"Yeah... I guess. So, Weathers, you dating anyone?"

My eyes widen. "What do you mean?"

"Are you single?" Giselle blushes.

As a distraction, I start to swirl around the ice cubes in my drink. "Yeah, I have been for some time now. What about you? Are you single?"

"I'm not seeing anyone. Shit, I don't even have time for it. My ex was something else. I thought I was into him but after a while, I couldn't help but be sick by the sight of him," she sips and laughs.

"Wow, how long were you guys together?"

"Eight months or so. I would've left sooner but hey, he had a big dick." She laughs a little louder and I can't help but laugh with her.

"Sex can complicate things, I can relate to that." I raise my glass and we cheer. "Was he Black?"

She squeezes the lime into her drink then buries it to the bottom, "No, he wasn't, he was a white guy... I never dated anyone Black."

"Why not?"

"I didn't really grow up around too many Blacks, I had a few in my class but they were like you..."

Turning my attention away from my glass to make eye contact. "What do you mean, *like you*?"

"You know... like they weren't Black, Black. They were smart, white talking Black kids."

I laugh. "Wait.... what do you mean, *white talking?*"

Giselle sucks down the rest of her drink. "Like... How you're all polite and shit. I mean it's a good thing. But when we first met, you said it was nice to make my *acquaintance.* Most Black people I know don't talk like that or have the type of manners you do. The only person I know like that is my mother. That's funny, you kinda remind me of her by the way you talk and carry yourself," she laughs, "It's cute."

"So, you mean to tell me... I'm not Black-Black. That's like saying I'm not Black enough. Did I miss the memo about my skin color or something? 'Cause last time I checked, I was born Black and I'm going die to Black."

"Whoa there, Weathers, calm down. I didn't mean it like that." She signals for another round.

"Then how did you mean it? Sure sounds like you made your case about my Blackness crystal clear." I push my empty glass out the way.

"What are you talking about? You should consider yourself lucky you're not another cased-up, uneducated nigga walking around with a ton of felonies or gang of baby-mamas, shit—sometimes both."

"So, let me get this straight, being uneducated, and having court cases defines Blackness?" I scoff, "I can't... I know... You don't even believe that."

"It's what I know, Michael, and I know you feel the same way too. You know that's how the world works for us. There are two different types of African-Americans. Blacks, who are like us—respectable, honest, educated, and goal-oriented. Then there's niggas, who are unfiltered and disgraceful ...need I say more?"

I laugh. "Please, don't."

"Don't be rude, Michael, I'm just stating facts."

Keith returns back with our drinks. "How you guys feeling?"

Giselle wraps her purse handle around the back of her bar-stool and answers, "Good, glad to be outta work."

Keith lifts our glasses and starts wiping away all of the condensations that were left behind from beverages, "Was it busy tonight?"

"There was a steady push. Hey, are the Rangers winning? I ask. "I can't tell from here."

Keith glances at the screen. "Yeah, they're up by two. You into hockey, Mike?"

"Yeah, I played as a kid."

"You don't say..." Someone shouts Keith's name. "Hey, Mike hold that thought. Let me go see what these crazy fucks want. I'll be right back," he says and jolts to the other end of the bar.

Giselle squeezes and buries her lime. "See, you even played hockey. What nigga you know grows up playing hockey?" she heckles.

I shake my head and laugh with her. "I can't lie, Giselle, you got a point. But given the fact you do make some kind of sense still doesn't solidify you questioning my Blackness. My parents just saw to my interest, and that pertained to what I was around. My dad introduced me to hockey which I happened to excel at 'cause that's what he did as a kid. I went All-American on those white kids I played with and against. So, fuck you," I chuckle.

"That doesn't surprise me one bit," she sips, "but, see that makes you different from the rest."

I draw my attention to the big screen. "See, that's where you're wrong. 'Cause I'm still an African-American and yes, my upbringing was a bit privileged but no matter what I do, I will always see me as a Black man... that'll never change."

"Yeah but you're the Black man who can blend in with white people. You're the pleasant, educated Black person that whites want to have around."

I force the rest of my drink down. "Giselle, I hope you not calling me a house nigga."

She smirks. "You said, it first."

Keith returns with a bottle of Fireball and three shot-glasses, "Shots on me guys?"

Giselle claps and smiles. "Yay!"

He lays out the shot glasses and pours until each rim is full. Giselle and I pick up our shots and happily cheer with our graceful bartender. After Keith shoots down his, he slams the glass on the bar. "So, Mike, you said you played hockey growing up?"

The liquor torches my chest as it goes down. "Ah, that sure does burns. But yeah, I played center, my whole life."

"Wow, you must be pretty fast."

I chuckle. "I'm alright; I guess."

"What the hell is a center?" Giselle asks.

"Basically, he's the front runner of the offense and defense. Pretty much the team's go-to guy," Keith explains.

"Oh...Okay, Michael, I see you... you were running shit huh," Giselle says.

She can't tell but I'm blushing like a motherfucker right now but I answer. "I mean... I just held the team down and helped secure wins. You know, team effort."

Keith slaps the bar with his bus rag, "OH SHIT, DUDE. I remember reading about you in the paper a few years back. How old are you,

Mike?"

"Twenty-six."

"You graduated in 2002 right?" He questions.

"Yup."

"Holy shit man, yeah I remember you. You were All-State, and your senior year you got the national rank. You were the only Freshman in the state's history to start for varsity. You guys made it to state's every year, holy fuck."

"Yeah, but never won."

"Yeah, I know, but you're one of—if not the best center in the state— maybe this side of the east coast. Holy shit, you didn't play in college?"

"Nah man, after high-school I just wasn't feeling it anymore. And besides the thrill of making it to state every year just killed my entire drive to even play the sport."

"Shit, Weathers, sounds like you could've gone far with it," Giselle says.

"He could've. Mike here was great, man. I remember you averaging 30 to 40 goals after your freshman year. Damn man."

Giselle checks her phone and asks, "Is that good."

"Hell yeah, fucking great," Keith replies.

My phone vibrates with a text from Tracie: *what up Farrokhan? What you doing?*.

I reply back: *"chilling just got off work, what's good?"* I put my phone back in my pocket and say, "Hey, Keith mind if I get the check?"

"Lightweight huh?" Giselle jokes.

Keith laughs. "The man knows his limits, you don't gotta bust his balls, G. Yeah, I'll get that for you." He heads to the POS.

Giselle glances at her phone. "Wow... I didn't realize it was so late."

She puts her phone in her purse and pulls out her wallet.

Following her lead, I retrieve my wallet. "Why? What time is it?"

"11:30."

"Damn, it is late."

Keith comes back with a check creased in half. He places it in the middle and grabs the empty glasses. "Here you go guys."

I grab the check before Giselle can. Keith comped two drinks, the whole bill came to $20.35. "Don't worry Giselle, this one's on me."

"No stop," she pleads.

"No, no. Don't worry I got it." I pull out a ten and twenty and put it under the check. "Hey, Keith!" I shout.

He scurries over. "What's up?"

I hand him the cash. "That's all you, bro, thanks."

"No, thank you, man. Welcome to the team. Hey, if you ever wanna strap on those good ol' skates. Me and some of my friends play in a league from January to April and we'd love to have you, Mike."

"Thanks man, I'm glad to be here. Keith extends his hand, his grip is stronger than before. "For sure man, let me know." He then reaches over the bar and plants a kiss on Giselle's cheek. "Alright guys, have a goodnight and get home in one piece."

Giselle smiles. "You're the fucking best Keith, goodnight."

"Be safe bro, thanks again and goodnight."

"No problem guys, I'll see you soon." He bends under the bar and comes up with a bus bucket filled with glasses, and plates then haul it off to the kitchen.

Giselle gets up from her seat first; I stagger behind. She holds the door open for me and walks over to the unofficially designated smoking section, reaches in her purse for smokes, pulls out two and lights them both. "Here, you go."

The filter has a print from her lipstick, which I don't mind at all. I use to think girls who smoked were unattractive but she pulls it off. She makes it look so sophisticated and elegant. "Thanks." My phone goes off again, another message from Tracie. "*Tryna party?*" Knowing that I shouldn't. Ay, who cares, I'm drunk. I reply back, "S*ure, be over in 10*"

Giselle blows thick smoke and taps her cigarette. "What are you doing after this?"

"Me?"

"No, the brick wall behind you. Yeah, you dummy."

"I was going to go home and get some sleep. I got this thing with my mom tomorrow and she'll kill me if I'm dragging my ass," I explain.

Giselle exhales and ashes. "What do you have to do?"

"Uh, I gotta go to my parent's house; I promised to cut the grass."

She nods. "That's cool you don't live with your parents... I'm so jealous."

"Yeah, it is... My mom still does my laundry though and sneaks her cooking into my apartment—she definitely going through some separation anxiety," I smirk.

"Aww, you're so lucky. Sounds like you have a great mom and you're such a great son."

I chuckle, "Thanks... she's not so bad." I toss my cigarette and watch it fly into a drain pipe.

She throws her butt into the street.

I try not to stumble into Giselle, as we make our way up Canal. For whatever reason, she wraps her arm around mine. Her perfume overpowers the tobacco smell. I can almost taste the alcohol on her breath and I'm pretty she can smell it on me as well. You know, I would play this out and take her back to my apartment. It would be pretty grand to enjoy some sex on this beautiful summer night. Drunk sex under the air conditioner is fucking amazing. The way that ass might look bent over and the panties slid to the side for clear entry. I bet her moan is sexy too, and the way her big lips sit on her wide mouth, she can probably give one hell of a blowjob. I wouldn't mind if her lipstick left stains on my dick; I wouldn't mind at all. Jesus Christ, how drunk am I?

Giselle finds her keys and mashes the unlock button, and out of nowhere, her car starts. "Nice! You have a car starter," I remark.

She leads as we cross the street. "Yup, comes in handy during the winter." Giselle continues to the driver's side, "Do you need a ride home?"

"Nah, I live a few blocks from the complex and it's beautiful out. Why not enjoy a nice walk?"

"You sure? You've been on your feet all night."

"I'm good, thanks though."

She smiles. "I don't know how you do it."

"I don't know either, must be the liquor."

All of sudden, Giselle forces her lips on mine, then her tongue slips in my mouth. Out of nowhere, our tongues start playing a game of tag. It's spectacular. The moisture and wetness are arousing with every kiss. Giselle presses even harder for about five seconds, then softly pushes off.

I struggle to force down my boner. "Uh, what was that?"

Giselle presses her lips together as if she were fixing her lipstick, "Mmm, I don't know, must be the liquor." She gazes aimlessly into my eyes. "I like you, *Michael with the nice teeth.*"

I snicker, "Ah you got jokes."

"I gotta get going."

"Ok..." I steal another tongue kiss and it's more arousing than the last.

"Mm, you're a great kisser," she says and begins to rummage through her purse.

"I can say the same for you. What are you're looking for?"

She pulls out her phone and hands it to me with the new contact displaying on the screen. "I need your number, Mr. Nice Teeth."

"Cool." I type my number in her phone, save it, and call myself. "Hold on, I'm calling my phone."

"Ok..." She kisses me again while my phone is vibrating. Her tasty lips are dreamlike. I grab a handful of Giselle's fat backside and squeeze tight as I can, capturing this moment as hard as possible so I have something to beat off to later. With swiftness, I open the door to her running car.

"Tonight, was awesome," I say.

She places herself in the driver's seat, straps on her seatbelt, and concurs, "Yeah, it was."

I push her door shut, and she rolls down the window. "You working tomorrow?" she asks.

"Yeah, I'm training with Billie for the next two days sooo… Yeah."

"You'll do fine, you're better than all the other servers we tried to hire."

"Thanks, I appreciate that."

"Don't let it go to head, Weathers, I haven't seen you in action yet."

I laugh, "How the fuck, do you know my last name?"

"When I was in A.G.'s office, I looked at your I-9 papers," she giggles.

"Wow, aren't you something." I stick my head in the car for another kiss.

Giselle ends our lip-lock by biting on my lower lip and whispering, "I guess I am."

"That you are, Ma'am, get home safe. Text me when you get there just so I know you made it home safe."

"Will do, you be safe getting home yourself, Sir," she says and puts the car in drive.

"Will do, don't forget to text me when you get home."

She smiles. "I won't, see ya tomorrow."

Watching Giselle speed off is bittersweet. I guess Billie and Jackie were right. Most things I think are happening usually turn out to be the opposite. After a few drinks, I guess anything can happen, especially what you think won't happen. With what just did occur, A.G. could demote me to a fucking busser and I'll still be wearing a fucking smile. As I cross the street someone shouts, "AY, MIKE. I SEE YOU FINALLY GOT GISELLE!"

To my left, there's Tina and Jackie closing up the restaurant. "WHO'S THAT?" I yell, trying to fake it as if I were someone else.

They both light smokes as they walk towards me. "Fuck, do you mean who's that?" Tina cries.

I should keep walking but, it's way too late for that. Cover blown. "Oh, I didn't know who you were for a second."

Jackie slaps my back and Tina nudges my shoulder. "Look, at you, Newbie," Tina says and smirks. "I bet it's wonderful to experience Black on Black love instead of Black on Black crime."

"You guys are too cute," Jackie adds.

"I don't know what you're talking about."

"Stop lying Michael, me and Jackie just seen you two all in each other's face. You don't have to lie and what's there to be ashamed about?

Giselle is a pretty girl," Tina says.

Jackie lets her hair down and plays with it until it's somewhat even. "I thought you were going home? You've been clocked out for over an hour now," she laughs. "We saw you coming up the street just now, then peeped you guys smooching at her car."

"*Smooching.* What are you, 60? Who the fuck says *smooching.* I don't know what you saw but you didn't see that."

Tina ashes. "Newbie, Newbie, Newbie...... It's okay you can hook up with her and not have to worry about management, as you can tell by now, Jackie doesn't give a shit."

"I don't," Jackie adds.

Tina throws her cigarette into a sewer drain. "It's cool, Newbie, don't worry. Where you headed anyway?"

I fire up a cigarette. "Tracie's."

Jackie flicks her butt into the street. "Cool, we are too."

Tina and Jackie march past me, leaving me to trail behind. "Aw, Newbie you're just full of surprises, aren't you... Let's go, I can't wait to tell Tracie and Billie what we saw," Tina says.

"You and G would make a cute couple. You're going to fit in just great, Newbie," Jackie states. My spine cringes as I count the cracks in the sidewalk. "Ah, I'm glad you feel that way. Glad to be here."

IDENTIFICATION

The worst part about being a Black waiter in a predominantly white restaurant is you can't help but make the correlation to the slave period in America. The "house nigga" was the worst thing to be, against the image of all the slaves laboring under the scorching sun while dealing with breathtaking humidity. Praying they picked more than their weight in cotton just to avoid the overseer's whip for a day. All while the lighter skin slaves are catering 'inside' to the master's needs, eating their fill in scrapped meats and drinking the corners of their owner's wine glasses. At night, they slept in basements quarters, in their own bed.

All the cooks here look at me as if I was the 'house nigga' even though I'm not light-skinned. Yet the fact I'm not on the line sweating over burgers and fries makes me out to be somewhat of an Uncle Tom. They look at me as if I'm not to be trusted; as if I'm not just another minority trying to earn his way. Anybody who's held an occupation in food service knows that all the revenue is in the front of the house.

But to be Black and work as a waiter in a well-to-due establishment is the same as it was to servant in the Big House. You gotta be one polished 'nigga' to do so. You have to be extra with everything you do…"yes, ma'am" - "no, ma'am." When serving the fairer-skinned, their needs and wants become stretched to the extremes. Back when I waited tables downtown, the service had to be impeccable, not one mistake. After working there for about a month, I felt like I was one table or guest away from saying, "Would you like me to wipe your ass for you, Sir? We have the Charmin Brand or our house toilet paper which is two-ply, and just like Charmin, it's soft to the touch with an elegant finish. Leaving your butt-cheeks with a "fresh" clean feel, and please, feel free to help yourself to the complimentary baby wipes ."

Even though Second House is way more "laxed" in service, it's no different from when I was downtown; at least I'm not the only person of color here.

"What's up Farrakhan?" Billie shouts as he bursts through the kitchen doors.

I shake my head. "You know you're late, right?"

Billie takes a stack of fresh plates from the dish station. "So what, nigga, you don't sign my paychecks."

I laugh. "You're right..."

"Damn straight, I'm right... Looks like you're training with me today, Black man. You ready?"

"Ready as I'll ever be."

"I'll take that as a 'yes'."

I fill the hotel pan with the last condiments; a tub of mayo and a hotel pan filled with coleslaw. I struggle to find space for it in the kitchen fridge. "Ahh, finally; it fits. Oh, by the way, you got anything you need me to do before get bombarded?" I ask.

He sets the dishes on the expo station, then takes half of the stack and places it in the expo window. "Just make sure you stay three steps behind me at all times. If any of my tables need anything and I'm not there, you come find me right away. I don't care if you got a million dirty plates in your hands or whatever the fuck you're doing, you come find me first. I don't want your Black ass fucking up my shit, got it?"

"Anything else?"

"I know I just said it, but just to make sure you're not one of those motherfuckers who have selective hearing, so I want to make myself clear again: don't, and I mean do not talk to any of my tables," he scolds. "I don't care what happens, don't talk to any of my guests... Just keep your Black ass moving. We're going to be busy tonight, we have a lot of reservations to cover and I need you to be on the go and not making friends."

"Ok. Got it."

A.G. enters the kitchen by cracking his knuckles and flexing his shoulders, "You guys ready for tonight?"

"You know better than that, you should be asking this scrub," Billie jokes.

"Well," A.G grins, "Michael are you ready?"

"Ready as I need to be."

"Good, keep that energy where it's at. As you know already, you'll be following Bill here, but try and buss as many tables as you can. Pepe is our busser tonight; he'll be helping you as much as he can."

"Cool, I'm ready for whatever."

"Awesome. I'll be running the point at the hostess stand," he instructs, "I'll switch over to the expediting food when it starts to get busy, but if you guys need me to run food or bus tables; don't be afraid to ask."

I dust my hands off. "For sure."

"See you guys in the trenches... Oh before I go, Michael do you smoke?"

"Yes, is that a problem?"

"No, not at all, just go and have a smoke now, it'll be your last one for some time."

I wonder if my slave ancestors got a smoke break before they attended to their masters. "Okay, thanks."

"And what about me?" Billie chuckles. "What am I chop liver?"

A.G. grins, "You been here six years and still asking dumbass questions." He shakes his and shoves through the kitchen doors.

Billie hawks up mucus into the trash "You got smokes, Farrakhan?"

"Yeah."

"Cool, let me get one."

"I have to get them out of my bag, I'll meet you downstairs, fat boy."

Billie stops restocking the ticket printer and turns. "Why you gotta call me fat, Black man?"

"Why do you gotta call me *Farrakhan*? When you stop calling me that, I'll stop making fun of your weight." Instead waiting for his rebuttal, I start for the dining room with haste; I spot John and his parents at the same table they were seated the night before last. They wave and smile, and I return their kind gestures. When I arrive in the back station, the bus bin is overrun with dirty dishes and glassware. I retrieve my cigarettes first then proceed back to the kitchen with the bus bucket in hand.

A six-foot, tannish looking Dominican or Cubano maybe- in his late teens cuts off my path, in a deep Spanish accent he says, "Excuse, but I take."

"Pepe?" I ask.

"Yes," he replies.

"*Como estas hacienda mi hombre es* Michael," I greet then extend my hand.

"*Tu hablas español?*"

"*Un poco...,*" I shrug, "Very little."

106

"*Se' se'* How long you work-- here?" he inquires.

"Uh, uh—*cuatro dias*, ah, *ahora*. You?"

"Ahh se'. Me, January."

"Good, well you and I will be working together tonight. And I will help you much as I can, *Señor*," I smirk, "*mas* helped—please."

Pepe nods with a smile then starts for the kitchen as I head to the back exit, and straight downstairs. And just like clockwork, there's Billie, standing outside, peering through the glass and signaling to me hurry up.

He holds the door open, "What took you so long?"

"I ran into the busser-- Pepe, nice kid," I hand Billie two cigarettes.

"Fuck man, you're wasting our smoke break talking to that *mida-mida*. He's just a fucking worthless busser," he states, "There's nothing to talk about," Billie then sets fire to one of his cigarettes.

I spark one as well then quickly inhale and exhale, "What do you mean? He's our co-worker. I should know or be aware of who he is."

Billie sighs out his smoke, "I wouldn't even consider him that, he's just another Mexican or whatever shithole country he comes from," he says before he ashes and adds bitterly, "Just another spic for America to take pity on, that's it. That's all he'll ever be just another spic. If I were you, I wouldn't waste time getting to know him or any other beaner while you're in training. The only thing you need to worried about is making sure Pepe is keeping your tables clean, and you'll be fine. This isn't like that downtown spot you and Trace were working at, where everybody is all professional and corporate. These spics here are lazy as shit. Always asking for breaks in the middle of rushes, always talking to each other in Spanish and shit, and most of the time they're probably talking shit about us."

I pause. "Like you're doing now..." I reply.

"Walk with me over to the dumpster, we're going to do some bumps before the shit show starts."

"You sure? I don't know if that's a good idea man. We're about to be crazy busy, right?"

He scoffs. "I do it all the time."

"I don't know man, A.G.'s here and shit. Seems like a bad idea."

"Come on, Farrakhan stop acting like a little bitch... Nah, you know what? Fuck it. More for me." He shuffles pass, and plods towards the dumpster. I still feel like shit from all those drinks last night not to mention all that coke Trace kept putting out. You know what? Ah fuck it, I could use a little pick me up so I say, "Hey, fat ass. Wait up." I jog lightly catching up to him. Billie maneuvers his weight between the dumpster and cardboard boxes. He struggles to catch his breath as soon as he does, he pulls out the coke and what seems as if it business card— from Second House. He dips into the sandwich bag and snorts three bumps in a row. "AHHH, SHIT."

I take the contraband. The card reads, Anthony Gloss, General Manager of Second House with the restaurant number, and his email printed below. I didn't know that's what his 'G' stands for—Anthony Gloss. That name has a ring to it, I don't know why he prefers to be called A.G. "So this coke is good, right?" I question.

"Nigga, you already know it is. Tracie hasn't missed with this new batch, this is crazy good if you ask me."

I scoop up sizable bumps for each nostril and repeat and wait for the drip to set in. The powder kicks at my esophagus. "Goddamn, this shit is good."

"Told you... You know what?"

I sniff. "What?"

He takes the card and coke back. "Still can't believe you passed up on getting some ass, especially from Giselle. See, and I told you she wanted your dick," Billie rails four large bumps in the same nostril. "That's a tight little piece of brown sugar, if I ever seen it... If I were you, I would've had my face in her ass soon as you two left First House," he hands back the contraband.

I rip two bumps, "You see, Bill," I snort, "It's that kind of talk that makes you sound like a fucking creep. *Your face in her ass?* Damn bro, who the fuck says shit like that? And you need to stop worrying about what I'm doing with my dick, aren't you fucking the assistant manager? Handle yours and I'll handle mine," I rail another two bumps before the drip disappears... and BOOM! It's returns as if it's never left. This is great coke. Now I feel alive--I feel fresh--I feel ready... My phone screen makes for the perfect mirror to check for any coke boogers or left-over residue. "So, we're going to be busy tonight?"

Billie wipes his nose. "Yo, I'm good?"

"Yeah, you're good."

"Thanks, but yeah we should be busy, especially going into the weekend and it's nice out. Since you're bussing tonight, a majority of your tips are going to come from me and Jackie. I don't know what's Tina's deal with you but don't expect much from her."

I remove two more cigarettes, light one, and give Billie my last loosie and ask, "Why, isn't tip out fifteen percent? Since there are two bussers, I would assume that fifteen percent is split between me and Pepe, right?"

"He'll get something but not that all of it."

"What do you mean, not all of it. That's fucked up, that kid works hard."

"Nah, son you my nigga so I gotta look out for the American citizens first," he laughs.

The drip is overpowering but phenomenal. I snort as hard as I can to catch the phlegm running from the cocaine that's building throughout my sinuses then expel it into the parking lot. "But, that's not fair. Only difference is, I'm following you the whole night."

"I don't care," he cries, "That fucking *mida-mida*, Pepe is probably fucking illegal anyway, shit, if I had to guess probably ninety percent of the beaners that come through here, are."

The high from the coke is taking its course. I want to tell this Fat Fuck off and let him know that his racist remarks make him shallower than what I just spat on to that cardboard box. Instead, the smoke from this Newport keeps my frustrations at ease and besides, why would I waste this perfectly good drip on berating this idiot. "That's real fucked up, Bill. You shouldn't do that to him, like I said before he's a nice kid."

Billie flicks his ash, "Fuck all that shit. Let you get some money for all this bullshit grunt work you gotta do. But, I'm not going to lie, it feels great bossing you around. Who knew I would be telling what do you," he heckles, "You're a long way from LBS, Mikey."

"Yeah," I sulk "Don't remind me."

Billie turns to spit out whatever he just hawked up. "If I were you, I would've stayed. You had it pretty good there. Your little collared shirts and khaki pants, looking like a fucking dickhead."

"Fuck you man, only thing I miss about that bullshit is that I didn't have to work weekends. It sucks coming back to the shit."

"You'll make good money here though; you already know how to talk to people."

"What does *me* knowing how to talk have anything to do with making great money?"

"Come on bro," he pauses, "You know how to talk to people, you're educated—at least you got more schooling than me. And, people like shit like that, you know. Especially seeing it come from a Black person."

"Bill, Bill, Bill..." I smirk, "Come on man. If you're looking for a way to hype me up about working here, you're doing a horrible job. I could sell salt to a snail, shit man I can sell water to a fucking fish. How hard can it be selling a few steaks and keeping the drinks filled?"

Billie stomps out the cigarettes' embers then fingers his nose. "Pretty damn hard. I haven't sold a steak in a few months, shit, maybe even longer. So believe me when I tell you, just focus on learning the menu and the POS and you'll do fine here. Just don't step on my toes, comprende?

I take one last drag, flick the cherry off, then toss the butt into the garbage with, "Got it."

"Come on," he says, "Let's get going, A.G.'s probably looking for us." Billie struggles to squeeze his stomach between the boxes and the dumpster-- I can't help but crack up.

"What's so funny?" he cries.

"You are... You really are out of shape. I just don't understand how you're cut out to be on your feet all night serving tables. I mean, your legs are kind of muscular, but your gut sticks out so bad, you almost look pregnant. It really amazes me, like how the fuck does your body keeps its balance? Like, how the fuck do you manage?... You have to lose weight man."

Billie continues to march through the lot, then leading the way upstairs he turns and says, "You know, I may be fat but at least I'm not bussing tables tonight. Unlike some people I know."

"What the fuck are you talking about, bro? It's your job to help with bussing tables, that's literally your job. You bring the food and drinks and then take it away when the customer is finished. Oh, I forgot the tips on your checks are still in ten to fifteen percentiles. So, while you wait for the busser to grab all empty plates or refill someone's water, you've not only lost money for yourself but Pepe has to suffer too because you're too lazy to do your job. In the grand scheme of things, everybody losses except the owners; they're making money regardless of how bad your service is. But who am I to talk? I'm training under you so what does that say about me? Not much, I guess."

"Fuck you, Farrakhan. You don't know shit, about this restaurant," he scolds.

I follow him into the server station. "That's true; I don't know shit about this place. But what I do know is, you're really out of shape to be in this profession and how you manage to keep it up is beyond the laws of physics."

Billie starts folding a bundle of guest towels and sets them in the bin. "Whatever nigga, you still gotta follow me around the entire night like a lost puppy, picking up after my tables, and you're right since you're here, I'm not touching one fucking plate or refilling any water. I guess you were right about me not doing my job 'cause tonight it's yours."

I laugh. "I guess that's fair."

"What's fair?" A.G. suddenly interjects.

"Nothing... just schooling the young buck here, that's it."

A.G. chuckles, "I don't think there's a need for that, Bill. This kid has only worked in one restaurant and has food critics on his resume. To be honest, I think he can school you on the steps of service. Now, what did I come over here for?... Oh, I just made the floor plan for tonight, in other words, Michael, the sections for each server. I'm giving Jackie the dining

112

room and you and Bill here are covering the bar dining. Oh, I almost forgot, I just sat three at 13, they just sat so you could give them a minute," A.G. pats my back, adding, "Alright, see you two out there, and make sure to wash your hands, Mike."

"Got it."

Billie digs into his apron and comes up with a server pad. "Way to kiss ass, Farrakhan. See, what did I tell you about stepping on my toes?"

"Stepping on your toes? Kiss ass? I didn't do any of that just now so watch your mouth. I was just standing here while you were folding napkins, if anything I look like I should be doing something. You know what, I take back what I said about doing bumps before service started. Look at you all paranoid and shit. I'm not fucking here to step on your toes or whatever. I got rent to pay just like everyone else. So, please spare me all with all that hate coming from your fat lips."

Jackie shuffles pass and stops. "You ready, Mike?" Even though she's unaware that I'm high as a giraffe's ass right now, I scurry to the sink, mash the soap dispenser a few times, and scrub away the tobacco stench.

"Ready as I'll ever be, Boss Lady, why what's up?"

Jackie smiles. "Good, don't let this asshole get the best of you tonight." She then slaps his chest with a checkbook.

"Oh, I'm going to get the best of him and my money's worth. I'm going to work him like it's 1860, except I can't whip him when he gets smart," Billie laughs.

She hits him again.

"Hey. I was just kidding. Come on, Mike, let's get to it," Billie says as I trail behind and we make our way to 13. As we approach the table. I can't help but think that the gentleman seated at position #1 looks as if he's a cheap rip-off from the *Sopranos*. Needless to say, something about him screams, "I'll fucking kill you if you don't have my money the next time I come back here." Aside from being younger looking faces, positions #2 and #3 seem no different. They're all dressed in nice pressed shirts and pants which go along with their slicked-back hair. Add a few gold rings, and tucked necklaces that sit on their chest hairs as they shine through the top part of their shirts. I can tell by the overuse of their hands when talking and their thick New York accents, they're obvious Italian. Whenever we return to the POS; I wouldn't be surprised if one of them calls me 'moolie' under their breath or at least not in earshot distance. And, it may not come from the youthful two, most likely it'll come from their elder. Older Italians don't take too kindly to people of color, especially the men.

Billie greets the table with a smile then leans on a vacant chair chatting. "How we doing guys? My name is Billie and tonight I'll be shadowed by this handsome fellow here, he's a server-in-training and his name is Michael."

"AY, MIKEY!" Position one shouts.

We both laugh.

"Nice to meet you guys. I'm Pauly and these two are my sons, Tony, and Pauly Junior. We eat here for lunch all the time and Tina usually takes care of us. But Junior thought we should skip on lunch and see what all the fuss is about on your dinner menu. We always see a gang of folks, young and old, piling in here around this time, so I figure why not? We'll see what their dinner has to offer," he slaps the table, "so, we're here."

"Your dinner menu is good, right?" Junior asks.

I lean in and whisper, "Yes, Sir, it is.."

"I'm just messing with you kid. What's with the 'sir' crap, kid? Save that for my father."

Pauly Senior strikes Junior over the head with a menu, "AY! You could learn a fucking thing or two from this kid. He's a well-mannered young man, what's wrong with you?" He focuses his attention on me. "I appreciate your manners son, your parents did a good job."

"Thank you, Sir."

"Can I start you guys off with something to drink?" Billie asks.

"Dewars Scotch with the big cube, please," Pauly Senior replies.

"Bud-Lights for me and my brother," Tony adds.

"Coming right up guys." Billie scratches their drinks onto his pad before he directs the way to the POS. He punches in his server number. "Alright Farrakhan, let's see what Tina and Jackie been teaching you. Go ahead and put their drinks in."

I scan for the alcohol tab. "Boom." So, far Bud-Light is the easiest to find; I hit two for quantity and find Dewar's two tabs down, message in one ice cube, and send.

Billie grills the screen. "Way to go, Farrakhan, good job. And, I'll give it some time before we go back over there. You down for another bump nigga?"

I laugh, "Nah man, I'm good."

"Alright, more for me then. If anybody asks—"

"You went to take a piss... yeah I got you covered. Remember to check your nose."

"Whatever, nigga," Billie says and walks out the server station and turns towards the bathroom. I wonder, if he were Black and acted in the same manner he does, would he still have a job? Nine times out of ten probably not. I don't blame him for railing more coke. Shit, I could use another bump myself. That's the fucked-up part about cocaine if you're not wanting constantly, it's kind of pointless. Maybe that's what Billie feels. Maybe he's stuck in the idea of wanting more. Yet, knowing that leads to the thought of what will happen when that bag of blow eventually runs out. It's funny when reality sets in and the high is gone, you realize how much of a piece of shit you are. And when it comes to Tracie; she can't sell coke for the rest of her life, she has fucking kid God's sake. She and Billie can't be roommates forever because he's falling into an abyss. Hmm, maybe we all are.

"Hey, Mike," Jackie calls, "Where's Billie?"

"He had to use the bathroom really quick."

"Of course, he did. I just walked past the bar and there are two beers and a drink just taking up space. Get to it, kid."

"Right away, Boss Lady." I head to the bar and place the beers onto a drink tray first; and before I forget, I snatch a cocktail napkin to set under Pauly Senior's scotch. Before running their beverages, I wipe both palms on my apron. "Ok, everybody here are your drinks," I announce. Pauly Senior recives his first, Tony next, then Junior.

Tony flashes his Rolex. "Thanks, Mike."

Before I can turn around, Pauly senior shouts, "Ay, Mikey wait one second... what's under my drink? I've never seen this before," he snickers, "I mean I've seen it before just not here."

"Seen what, Sir?" I ask.

Pauly smiles then points to the napkin under his glass.

"Uh, it's a coaster, Sir, or should I say cocktail napkin. They're right next to where your drink was made, I figure it's the proper way to enjoy your drink so you don't get all that condensation from the ice under your glass. As you know, it keeps it from sliding."

Pauly Senior scoffs. "Ay, look at this, boys, you would've thought we were downtown Manhattan or something," he says and they all laugh.

116

Beads of moisture begin to trickle down my back. "Is something wrong with the napkin, Sir? I can rem-?"

"No son, not at all. I come here three days out of the week for lunch, sometimes four with my sons or my other associates, and every time I come here, I order the same drink, every time. Tina never brought me a fucking cocktail napkin," he chides. But, you do, you did good, Mikey, you did *real* good."

"Why, thank you, Sir. Billie will be right out to take your food order."

I try to make an exit and Pauly Senior tugs my arms and stops my movement. "Ay, Mikey, not so fast."

"Yes, Sir."

"You look real familiar where'd you go to high-school?" He questions.

"Here in town."

He sips his scotch and stares. "Your last name wouldn't be Weathers would it?"

"Yes, that's my last name."

"See Pop!" Junior yells, "I fucking knew it was him!"

Tony nudges his brother. "Calm down numb-nut, we're right here."

"Holy smokes, kid. What a fucking small world," Pauly Senior says and extends his hand. His grip is almost crushing. "I can't freaking believe it's really you, you're one of the greatest scorers I've ever seen, you could've gone pro. Not to mention, you made us a lot of money, kid, I mean...during the regular season of course. It's a shame you guys could never take states. That bum of a coach sure knew how to tank."

I force a nervous but calm grin. "Glad I could be of some service to you."

"Back when you played," Tony smacks the table, "you were something else on that ice, kid."

Junior swigs his beer then belches. "No kidding man, I couldn't believe how fast you were. Whoever said hockey was a white man's sport never saw you play. For real, Mike, no kidding. Remember Pop, I would jump out my seat whenever I saw him controlling the puck? I couldn't believe your backhand shot and passes, I would be like look at that mool—"

"What my son, was is trying to say," Pauly Senior says as he gives Junior the death stare, "...you could've went collegiate, hell kid, you were NHL 'good'. You had serious talent, son. Why'd you stop?"

"Don't know... Guess I just lost interest. I mean... after all those regular season wins and then having a national playoff schedule... it just puts a toll on your body and mental. Overall, my morale was just shot, so I just wanted to relax for once."

"You were something special kid," Pauly Senior slouches back. "Now, I know *that* you know that I *know*, you're smart young man and that goes without saying. But never let someone else's mistakes dictate how you move or be an alternative to what you deserve. Because they're going to be people in your life that will just be fucking miserable, excuse my language. But, those those miserable sacks of shit are going to try and put their misery on you. You're young so you have to deal with a lot of people who think they have the answers, but in actuality, they don't. Ultimately, you have to decide the best outcome for you, and no one else. Never forget your purpose son, never forget where you're going. Got it?"

"Yes—sir, Understood."

He pats my shoulder, "Alright, where's that Billie guy? Think we're ready to order an appetizer or something."

I place the drink tray on table 14 and retrieve my server pad, with pen in hand ready, "I'll be more than happy to put in some appetizers for you and your sons."

"Well... let's start with an order of your house wings and some onion rings," Tony states.

"Okay, anything else?" I ask.

They all silently decline.

"Alright then gentlemen, I'll go and put those in for you right now, sit tight." As I speed to POS; I scribble down their order, there's still no sign of Billie. I flag down Jackie and wait for her to finish attending to a party of six.

She moves with haste as she paces over. "What do you need?"

"Billie's still in the bathroom and I need his server number to put in appetizers for 13."

"Got it." Jackie jumps in front of the POS. I turn my back as she puts in her number. "Alright, put in the food."

She hovers as I scan for the buttons. "Boom," I yell, "All set!"

"Nice, you pick up fast, Mike, I like that. I guess A.G. was right about you, you're a quick learner."

I grin. "Thank boss lady, you know, this isn't my first rodeo."

"I'm sure that's what you told Giselle last night," she snickers.

"I can't confirm or deny that statement. Since you're closer, can you do me a solid and pass me three side plates, Boss Lady?"

Jackie slaps my shoulder and reaches for the dishes and says, "Hey, you better treat her good, or else." She hands over the plates and vanishes into the bar dining. Now that I think about it, Billie's been gone for some time. Hope he didn't die in that stall. I should go and check on him. On second thought, this is my time to show them what I can do, fuck Bill; he could stay in there all night... wait, who the fuck am I kidding? I need that fat piece of shit. I have no clue where half the buttons are on this damn computer. Ten to twelve minutes pass and still no sign of Billie, I read over the menu to pass the time. Figure it's about time to get 13's starters. As I head towards the kitchen, surprisingly, Jackie passes by with their appetizers. She flaunts her smile as she greets the table. After she sets down the food and turns, all three men become hypnotized by the hard switch of her hips. Junior taps his brother on the shoulder and whispers something to Tony, causing him to smirk.

"That's a great looking piece of ass if I should say so myself. What about you, Mikey, would you tap that?" Junior says as he's the first to reach for a wing. Tony hanks the back of his brother's hand before he touches the chicken.

"Uh, yeah- Jackie's nice," I reply.

"Good, answer kid. Where's that Billie kid," Tony asks, "Think we're ready for another round of drinks."

I glance at the back of the bar. "Um, good question but once again I'll more than happy get you guys another round."

"Looks like we'll be tipping Mike tonight," Pauly Senior jokes.

"Oh no, Sir, I'm still in training. I'm not allowed to accept anything just yet."

Pauly Senior fills his side plate. "Ah, that's a load of bull, you're too modest, son."

I smirk and return to the POS. To my surprise, Billie's standing in front of the server sink with his phone in hand and high out of his fucking mind. Good God, he's really a piece of work. "What'd I miss?" he snorts.

"Aside from your decency," I joke, "Not much."

"Stop fucking around."

"Ah, Okay, you're serious...so, yeah, 13 just got their appetizers and they want another round of drinks."

Billie clinches his jaw. "What do you mean just got their appetizers? I was only in there for ten minutes."

"You got be kidding me right now. It's been at least fifteen minutes since I dropped their drinks; they wanted to order starters. What the fuck do you want me to do? I can't keep them waiting, I should have pulled you out the bathroom?" I say.

"What did I fucking tell you man, not to talk to my tables. You should've come and got me." He turns to the POS. "What the fuck do they want now?"

"Another round of drinks, that's it," I answer.

Billie's going through some serious coke rage right now. He can barely punch in his server number. "How the fuck did you get into my login anyway?" he scolds.

"I got Jackie to do it and she was fine with it."

"But I'm not. You're really stepping on my toes here, Mike. You need to chill the fuck out. And stay in your fucking place."

"I get that your upset, but you need to watch your tone. Nobody told you to spend twenty fucking minutes in the fucking bathroom. You have to calm down."

"Listen, Mike, you could either shut the fuck up and listen or there's no place for you here; I'll make sure of that. If you wanna play this fucking game, I can't play it better, try me. I fucking dare you."

A few seconds of silence linger... I clear my throat. "I should let you get to that. 13 is ready to order their entrees whenever you are."

"Thanks, come on let's go take down their order." Billie leads to their table. He manages to somewhat smile. "Sorry about that gentlemen, my mother called and I needed a moment. I see Mike has been holding the fort down... I heard that you guys are ready to order dinner, so what can

I get you?... Oh before I forget, the filet mignon is available right now, very tender, very juicy, and cooked to the temperature of your liking." He then fidgets in his apron for his pad coming up empty.

Pauly Senior downs the rest of his scotch. "Yeah, you heard correct, Bill, and for the record, Michael here has been doing a great job. He'll be an excellent add on to you guy's restaurant."

"We only hire the best. And he is sure one of em. So, we got your second round of drinks coming. Now, let's get started on your dinner. What are we having?" Billie digs in his apron again and realizes he doesn't have his notepad. While the family runs through the menu, I slip him mine.

"What are you having, Junior?" Tony asks.

"Uhh... I think... I'll have the New York Strip, med-rare with fries and carrots," Junior answers.

"That sounds good, think I'll have the same except I want mashed potatoes with mine," Tony states.

Billie's hand is moving so fast across the pad, he probably won't be able to make out what he's even writing down, "Got it. And for you, Pauly Senior, how about that filet?"

"Eh, I don't really like how you describe it so I think I'll pass if you don't mind. But what I will have is a Second House Burger with sauce on the side, rare, with a side of asparagus. Oh, can you bring a side of fries just to pick on?"

"Good God pop, you get that shit all the time, be a little spontaneous for once, will ya?" Junior cries.

"Watch your mouth, you idiot. Me and your mother didn't raise you to curse at the dinner table. She would be rolling in her grave right now." His sons share a moment of silence and simultaneously cross their hearts.

"So, two New York Strips, med-rare, both with carrots and one with fries, one with mash. And for dad our Second House Burger with the sauce on the side and a side of asparagus," Billie repeats.

"Don't forget about our drinks," Tony adds.

I tug on Billie's shirt and lean in. "What temp does he want his burger?"

"Oh, before I forget, Sir, what temperature would you like your burger to be?" Billie asks.

Pauly Senior rubs his chin and peeks at his Rolex. "We'll do medium, how that's for being spontaneous." He and his sons smile.

Billie snorts. "You got it guys. I'll be right back with your drinks."

We march back to the POS and Billie is so out of his mind, he fumbles my notepad and manages to drop it again as he tries to pick up. He aimlessly stares at the page. "Holy shit, what the fuck did I write?"

"I don't know, Bill, their order maybe?"

"The father wanted a New York Strip too right?" he asks.

"Nope, he wants the Burger, medium, sauce on the side with asparagus and a side fries."

"You're right and what did his sons get?"

"Damn Bill, how fucking high are you?" I whisper.

"Not now, Farrakhan, tell me what the fuck they ordered?"

"Uh-uh, wait... Ah, two New York Strips. One with fries and the other with mash but both with carrots."

"You sure?" He sweats.

"Positive, both steaks are medium-rare."

"Alright, follow me while I run their drinks." He hands back my pad, covered in his palm sweat. I throw it in the back server garbage. I trail behind as we pick up 13's drinks, Billie calms his pace as we return to the table. I hope that's a sign of his coke rage coming to an end. He serves the brothers first. Luckily enough for Pauly Senior, I stuffed a cocktail napkin in my apron before we left the bar. Soon as Billie turns his back on the table, I lift the scotch and gracefully slide the napkin under it. Pauly Senior doesn't utter a word, and with his sons buried in their phones, they didn't even notice. He winks and I gladly wink back. I sidestep behind Billie before he notices what I've done. To be honest, if he would've caught me in the act, fuck it. What's the worst that could happen?... Billie's so worried about not fucking up their entrees, he couldn't care less.

Thank God, 13's dinner comes out as they order. Amid the first push, I got called into the kitchen to expo. And dare to say, I expedited those tickets flawlessly. Shit, I even surprised myself. The fact A.G. had enough balls to ask is beyond me; I really didn't mind standing line for that hour or so. Jackie helped as much as she could while managing her own tables. As for Billie; I'm pretty sure that poor bastard looks and smells like shit, especially since he sweats so profusely, his entire shirt looked damp. Billie didn't show much of his face in the kitchen when I got pulled from the floor, so Jackie had to run most of his food. I helped as much as I could. Thankfully, I was on top of things. All the starters and entrées were sent to all the correct tables and that's what I was most concerned about. Everything came out promptly. The overall wait time on food is about twenty minutes which isn't bad on a busy night. As the tickets keep flying in, my composure stays the same. I was real careful about making sure what plates needed garnishing and the most annoying part of making sure everything dish with a side of fries has a ramekin of ketchup.

A.G. enters the kitchen. "AHH. Great job tonight, Michael. You did one hell of a job, man. Give yourself a pat on the back."

"Thanks, A.G. I appreciate that." I continue to wipe and separate the silverware.

"No doubt man, like I said, Dick wasn't kidding about you."

"I'm glad to hear that. Four years seems like a decade ago, but I guess the food industry is kind of like riding a bike"

He begins to make an exit saying over his shoulder, "For sure. Once again, great job, kid, keep it up."

I make sure all the cutlery is packed tight. "Well, Jose that's the last of it."

"Se' papi, you do good tonight, I see," Jose says.

"Nah man, you did good."

He smiles and waves me off. As I enter the dining-room, Jackie's at her usual seat, and Billie is nowhere in sight. I heave the silverware onto the back-server counter and search for a clean guest towel to remove the sweat from my face. "You did great tonight, Mike," Jackie yells over the dining-room.

"Thanks, Jackie, much appreciated."

"Really kid, don't know what we would've done without you. I had tables and so did Billie. A.G. had to host and manage. You came in clutch kid. 'Cause if Tina was back there, she would've had a total fucking meltdown. It's happened before, I've seen it," she laughs.

"Nah man, it's cool. I'm just glad to be here. I mean, restaurant work is not for lighthearted, but if you like what you're doing along with some thick skin, you can come out okay... I guess."

Jackie smiles. "Yeah..."

"Who knows...but ah, I'm going to help out Pepe and bus some of these tables, is there anything you need from me?"

"Did you clean the silverware already?"

"Nah, I didn't."

"Well I nee—"

"—I'm just kidding, it's back here on the counter,"

She chuckles. "Get outta here."

"Ah, there he is," Pauly Senior shouts.

Surprised that they're still here; I walk over with haste. "Hey, guys is there anything I can get outta your way or can I get you gentlemen some more water?"

"Nope, we're good, we're just waiting for that Billie fuck to come back with our check. We gave him the cash already, just waiting for my change. But here, I want you to have this." Pauly Senior snatches my hand and shoves a hundred-dollar bill in my palm. "I know you're in training, but even for a rookie you did one hell of a job tonight kid, you're the best waiter I've seen in here, and you're not even a waiter yet."

"Sir, I don't know what to say. I'm thankful but I can't..."

"...Ay, just shut up and slide it in your pocket son, you deserve it, don't let anyone tell you different. And do yourself a favor... stay away from that fat fuck server you had to train with tonight. He's no good, no good at all."

"Tell me about it," Junior scoffs, "Fucking idiot kept going to the bathroom every ten minutes, we even timed him. He didn't even try to get rid of the coke off his nose. What a fucking loser."

"Do you ever shut the fuck up? Huh? Please, shut the fuck up for once," Tony scolds.

"Your brother is right, Junior, shut the fuck up for goodness sake, will ya?" Pauly Senior slides his glass to the edge. "Michael, you'll do great things here. You'll rise up the ranks fast if you stay who you are and just keep your nose clean alright, son?"

"Will do, thank you, Sir."

"No, Mikey, thank you," Tony says.

As they exit through the back entrance, wish Pauly and sons a "goodnight." I try not to sulk returning to the server station, but Billie is in a near panic, running after Pauly Senior and his sons. How long does it take for someone to get change? The father and his sons aimlessly stare. I would have to say I'm a little embarrassed for Billie; I truly am. It's sad 'cause he's kind of the reason why I'm even here. He said to use him as a reference and I did. Now, I'm starting to regret it, maybe, because he's been here since the beginning, and after all that time he probably has it down to a science when and when not to rail bumps on the clock.

Somewhere down the line, Billie lost all ability to control his habit. He can't function without it. I'm afraid he's so far gone, there's no going back to who he was when we first met. Bill would have to enter some type of inpatient treatment. And even then, he wouldn't be the same—he can't be. I've been here three days now and he's become more and more of a fucking degenerate. It's not so much about how he treats me, but he needs this job. This restaurant is his life. Jackie is a wonderful girl and from the looks of it, she's not all that into coke which is cool. The fact is, she does it merely because Billie does it. But as long as she works here, she'll just fall deeper and deeper into the abyss.

As mundane of a task as this is, for whatever reason, I'm relaxed by rolling the silverware. All of a sudden, Jackie yells, "Newbie!"

I poke my head around the server station to see where Jackie's coming from and she's in the front of the dining room, seated at the eight top that hasn't been taken apart yet. I speed over. "What's up, Boss Lady?"

"Here you go," she says and places three twenties and one ten-dollar bill in my hand. "Good job, I threw in an extra thirty, 'cause you handled expo tonight. Don't go putting all that up your nose now," she laughs.

I smirk. "You got jokes."

"I'm busting your balls, Newbie, but hey, where'd you learn to expo? It wasn't in your resume."

"Shit, man, working downtown. No telling what you were going to have to do when you showed up. Serving was what I got hired for. But somedays I had to expo, bus tables, be a host and sometimes help wash dishes while waiting tables," I explain. "To be honest, I did a little bit of everything but manage."

"Even bartend?"

"Nah, Tracie would scream and possibly hit you if you stepped behind her bar."

"Whoa, kid, before you know it you'll have my job." The service bell rings twice and Jackie is quick to get up.

"Relax, Boss Lady, finish what you're doing." I lift my body up by the heels and add, "Still got some life in these bad boys."

She takes back her seat. "You got it, Newbie, you don't gotta tell me twice."

When I arrive at the expo window, there's a ticket for the bar: chicken tenders with buffalo sauce on the side and an order of twelve house wings—extra hot. I stamp the ticket and head out. When I approach the bar counter, I patiently wait for Graham to finish a cocktail to put a face on the food. I spot a boisterous, seemingly belligerent patron having a few words with Billie when he should be restocking or doing rollups.

Their conversation doesn't look as if there's much to gain. Graham slides the drink in front of the woman who's sitting next to where Billie is standing. When he sees me with an order, Graham gives a thankful nod and directs me to the man who's conversing with Billie.

As I move towards the man's seat, he aggressively rises from his chair and looks as if he's trying to showcase some type of two-step. He begins to flail both arms around then thrusts his waist back and forth, at the same shuffling from side to side. I don't know what type of dance move he's demonstrating, whatever he's doing he needs to stop, it's fucking horrible. I smile and try to maneuver between his dancing and table 15.

As I try to move in between the barstools and the man dancing, all of sudden, he throws his body into a spin only to bump into me, which knocks the plates out of my grasp causing the food and sauce to splatter all over his silk shirt and denim jeans. "What the fuck asshole!" He yells. "Look at what the fuck you just did, this is Versace, you idiot."

In complete shock, I just stare. "Uh—uh, oh my God-- I'm so sorry Sir, I was trying to get around you and the table. Ah man, I'm terribly sorry, let me get you some club soda and a few guest towels to clean up."

"What the fuck is that going to do?" He tenses up. "This shirt is ruined, fucking ruined. Five-hundred bucks just pissed away."

"Sir, if I move fast I'm pretty sure we can still salvage the fabric, Sir."

"Yo, Mike," Graham interjects. "Here." He sets a glass of seltzer water, and two cloth napkins on the bar. I sigh in relief as I dip one of the napkins in the seltzer, and begin to dap the man's shirt.

Suddenly, my body is thrown into table 15. A chair breaks my fall. "First you spill food on me, then have the nerve to touch. Someone teach this nigger some manners," the man shouts.

"—Hey!" Graham yells as he rushes from behind the bar. By the time I can come to, Graham already has him by the collar. The guy's arms flail around and his legs kick as if he were a misbehaving toddler being picked up. Graham carries him outside then tosses him on to the sidewalk as if he were last night's trash. "If I see your face in here again, I'll call the cops," Graham states.

I pick up the man's cell phone and wallet then jog outside to give it Graham. "That son of bitch, drop these."

The man dusts himself off as he staggers down Main Street. "Don't forget your phone and wallet. Fucking piece of shit," Graham throws his belongings across the street as the man crosses to the other sidewalk. His phone nearly shatters as it smacks the payment. The man holds his scraped face with one hand as he gathers what's left of his phone, and stumbles till he finds his wallet. "Fuck you guys," he cries. I've been kicked out better places than this. What happened to free speech? I thought this was fucking America. Go back to Africa, Nigger."

I try to lunge after him yet Graham's massive hands keep me from breaking free. "Yeah, you're a fucking tough guy," I yell.

"Calm down, Mike, he's trash, lower than trash. A real piece of shit and he's not worth it. Look at that frail piece of dog shit. You'll kill him."

The man still stumbles around across the street searching for his phone and steps on it. "FUCK YOU NIGGER, THIS IS YOUR FAULT. I THOUGHT THEY KEPT THE MONKEYS CHAINED IN BACK! YOU CAN'T EVEN CARRY FOOD WITHOUT RUNNING INTO SOMEONE!" I finally break from Graham's grasps and being to go after him. The man tucks his wallet and begins to jolt soon as he sees me sprinting across the street. Out of nowhere, a patrol car comes down main with the sirens blaring, blocking my path as the man escapes around the corner.

A slender policewoman jumps out with her gun drawn, "Stop right there," she shouts. I freeze dead in my tracks and throw my hands up as she draws her firearm. The bar crowd begins to pile on the patio as they stare, A.G. comes rushing to my aid.

"Officer, what seems to be the problem?" He asks.

"As I was pulling on to the street to meet my supervisor for the shift change, I spotted this guy running after someone who looked pretty beaten up," she says and holsters her pistol, unclips handcuffs, and begins to detain me adding, "The person he was chasing down Canal, I'm sure he's long gone by now."

"Excuse me, officer, there is no need to place him under arrest, he didn't do anything. Please remove those cuffs," A.G. pleads.

"It appears he is a suspect in an assault. If he didn't do anything then why did I stop him from catching that man, and only God knows what the damage could've been done if I didn't show up when I did. I'm placing him under arrest. Please stand back."

"No, officer, you're making a mistake. This young man works here, he's the victim here, that man he was running after shoved him to the floor inside the restaurant. The reason why that man you saw him chasing looks beaten up because my bartender," he points over to Graham, "tossed him out. He must've hit his face on the pavement, and that would explain the scrapes on his face. I can show you the footage inside if you would like, but I assure you that placing this young man under arrest would be a big mistake. He just lost his cool for a second, he didn't lay a hand on that man, please."

She stares, and tugs on the cuff. "Is this true? Did that man put his hands on you?"

"Yes, Ma'am, he did," I reply.

"Would you like to press charges?" she questions.

"N-no, please, it's fine, can you just uncuff me, please?"

"Sure. First, got ID on you, Sir?"

"My wallet is inside, Ma'am. I've never been arrested in my life, I swear. To be honest, this is my first ever being handcuffed. But my name is Michael Weathers, W-E-A-T-H-E-R-S. I'm twenty-six, and I live at 350 Baldwin Ave, it's just a few blocks from here."

"Still need to run your, I.D., kid, that's just how it goes, I don't make the rules."

"Officer, can you just let this time slide once? I mean we've got customers outside making a spectacle of this whole ordeal," A.G. states. "Please, Mike's a law-abiding citizen and we run a background check on all applicants before we hire them. I'm promising you he's a good kid. Please, spare him the extra embarrassment."

She turns to the other patrol pulling up next hers, thinks, and then answers. "Uh, I really just want to get home. But, if you're vouching for him, then he's your responsibility." The policewoman finally uncuffs my wrist. "Alright kid, no more chasing people cause they pushed you, next time just call us, got it?"

"Yes, Ma'am."

"Thank you for understanding, we didn't mean to cause you any trouble. Please, get home safe," A.G. says.

"You're welcome, you have a good night yourself," the policewoman says.

A.G. takes me by the shoulder as I step forward, and before the Officer makes it to the driver's seat, she turns and asks, "Hey?"

"Yes," A.G. answers.

"The food any good here?"

"The best barbecue in town, you should try it sometime."

"The kitchen still open?"

A.G. checks his watch. "Sorry officer, you just missed it. They shut off

132

the grill off five minutes ago, sorry."

"Ah, alright then, maybe some other time."

"Maybe... take care, Officer."

"You too, ay kid, no more dropping plates on customers," she laughs.

I grin, "Thanks for the advice, will do." The officer slams her door then speeds towards the bus terminal. The onlookers pile back into the restaurant with Graham, while Jackie and Billie approach. "You got a smoke on you, Jackie?" I ask.

She hands over two Marlboro lights and a clear lighter. "Here, you go."

I tuck one behind my ear and light the other. "Thanks, Boss Lady."

A.G. turns to Jackie. "You finish checking the server receipts?"

"Yup," she answers.

"Make sure Billie tips out Michael and tell Graham he can have whatever he wants as a shift drink; I'll be downstairs. Mike before you clock out, come downstairs so we can talk for a moment. Cool?"

I breathe out slowly, "Sure." He pats my shoulder and returns back inside.

"Holy shit, Farrakhan what happened back there?" Billie asks.

"What the fuck do you mean what happened back there?" I snap. "Your fucking buddy fucking freaked, puts his hands on me, and called me a nigger, that what happened, Bill, that's what fucking happened."

"Whoa, calm down I was just asking a question. Nobody told you to spill shit all over him."

"Fuck you, you were fucking chitchatting him up when all that shit started. Why did Graham have to come all the around the bar to get that guy the fuck out of there? All you did is watch. Fuck you."

"Chill out, Mike, you're real hot right now, and I get it. You have a reason to be, but it's not Billie's fault what happened to you. Take a minute to let that sink in, and cool your jets, kid," Jackie says,

The moment is broken when Billie asks for some of my cigarette, I give him the rest and head inside. To avoid the embarrassment of being seen, I stroll right through the dining room and straight into the server station. Before clocking out, I yank my bag out of the cabinet. Before I can make an exit, Billie stops me to hand over my tips. "You going to be good, right?" he asks.

"Yo, you're really asking me that right now? You're a piece of fucking work."

His eyes widen. "Nigga, you acting like it's my fault, what's wrong with you?"

"I really just need to get the fuck out of here."

"Why? A.G. said to talk to him before you clock, I'm assuming you didn't talk that fast."

"I'm go—"

"Hey, Mike," A.G. interjects.

"Yeah, what's up?"

"You gotta minute?" He smiles. "It looked like you were getting ready to leave before speaking with me."

"Nah, I was actually just heading down there. But Bill here was so gracious to tip me before heading to you."

"Oh, how nice of him. He usually forgets," A.G. says and smirks.

"Come on, I'm not that bad," Billie adds.

"Nobody said anything about you being bad, you're just forgetful. But do you mind giving me and Mike a minute?"

Billie answers with a nod then disappears into the bar dining. A.G. paces to table 47 and pulls out a chair but positions himself in the booth.

I take the seat he's prepared. "So, what do you want to talk about?" I ask.

"Well from the looks of it, something you obviously don't want to talk about so I'll say only a few words. Look, Mike, what happened tonight shouldn't have happened at all. And I'm terribly sorry you had to experience what you did. I can't apologize enough. As your G.M. I'm supposed to make sure assholes like that keep their hands of my employees. I heard that fuck called you a racial slur, is that true?"

"…yup."

"Once again, I'm sorry, I know me apologizing can't fix what happened but I owe it to you anyway. Without stating what's in plain sight, I can't relate how it feels to hear something like that. I can't but I understand that it makes you look at working here differ—"

"With all due respect, I don't mean to cut you off but look… A.G., if you think I'm about to quit off what that son of a stupid son of bitch did, think again. I've heard—been through worse. I'm more mad at the fact I couldn't catch that motherfucker after he pushed me. Other than that it's water under the bridge. But if I ever see him outside of here; I owe him one, for sure."

A.G. smirks. "Honestly, I have no control over what you do outside of the restaurant, and if I were you, I'd probably say the same thing so I'm not shocked by that at all. Just know that you do add value here, and it requires someone to have tremendous strength to go through what you just went through and not just say 'fuck it'. You're an intelligent young man. You'll find another job soon as you walk out of here. But, if you can allow yourself to move past what you experienced tonight and work with due diligence, you're going to make great money here."

"That's the plan. I can't let what happened to stop me from making a living. That's just plain stupid. You gave me a job when you hired me, and I intend to do just that."

"What's that?"

I stare. "Serve tables."

"I like that. Um, if you need the day off tomorrow to—"

"No," I say, and force a smile. "We're not doing that, I plan to show up as scheduled and finish another day of my training. I don't see a reason for a day off. Let me finish what I have to do to start making the *big bucks* as you would say."

"Good, glad to hear that."

"No doubt... well, if there's nothing else you want to discuss. Is it alright if I take off?"

"Yeah, for sure. One more thing. Is everybody treating you okay? As far as the staff here goes?"

I pause. "So far so good."

"Great, great... you'd tell me if someone was mistreating you, right?"

"Sure, I would."

"Alright then, have a good night, Mike, I'll see you tomorrow."

"As you will."

A.G. smiles then extends his hand. He gets up first and I throw my bag over my shoulder and head towards the front. "Mike!" he shouts.

I turn. "Yeah?"

"Was that really your first time being handcuffed?"

"Yeah, why?"

"I'm sorry."

"It's not your fault, man, she was just doing her job, right? Shit happens, what can you do..."

"...Yeah, *what can you do*. I'm kind of jealous that was your first time being cuffed."

"Why?"

"Well, my first time being cuffed-- arrested, it was for streaking bare ass through the campus green when I was in college. It was in the middle of January, so it was so flattering," he laughs. "Especially when I got to the bookings. All they had were clear garbage bags to cover me up, I looked like a used condom."

I laugh, "Holy shit, that's hilarious."

"Yeah, tell me about it. Get home safe, kid, see you tomorrow."

"Yeah, you too."

Finally, I'm able to heave my ass home. I remove the cigarette from behind my ear and retrieve a light from my bag, then start for the street.

"Yo!" Billie shouts.

I turn, "What now?"

"This is from Graham, you forgot the bar has to tip you out 'cause you bussed. So here." He hands over a mini yellow envelope with words that read, "For Newbie."

"Thanks."

"You got it, Farrakhan... Where you about to go?"

"Home..."

"Nigga, let's party a bit, you ain't got shit else to do right?"

"Is Trace home?"

"Yeah..."

"...fuck it, I'm down."

YOU'RE USED TO IT RIGHT?

Last night, I left Tracie's a little after 4 am, drunk, and higher than a satellite when I arrived home. My drunkenness was so overpowering, I passed out as soon as my head touched the pillow. I'm surprised there's still half left of the liter of *Jameson* I bought before going over there. A majority of the tips I got went to coke, *to say the least*. Tracie looked out on her part but I could care less if she contributed to the pile or not; I just wanted to get fucked up, plain and simple. There's really no other way to cope with what happened but to just let it go. If I catch that son of a bitch from last night; I'll be sure to give him a dose of his own medicine. As for now, I just want to make it to work before this downpour hits.

Usually, I'm getting there earlier especially to go over the menu a bit and grab whatever staff meal they got going, but luckily enough, there's was a plastic container stuffed with my mom's famous rigatoni on my kitchen counter. That's what happens when your mom demands an extra key to your apartment. Random homemade plates that magically appear or my laundry just happens to do it itself. Half of the time, I don't even hear her come in when does her little surprises. If she didn't spend thirty-odd years working at Town Hall, she would've been one hell of a burglar.

As I enter the path, I spot Cam on the balcony waving and smiling but before she starts screaming at the top of her lungs I yell, "What's going on baby girl, how are you doing today?"

"Good," she giggles.

"That's good, where's mom?"

"She's in New York, I think..."

"So, who's watching you, baby girl?"

"Nana's here."

"Oh, okay."

"Hey Michael," Cam's grandmother shouts.

"Hey Miss Lorna, how you doing?"

"I'm doing ok honey, how are you?" she asks.

"I'm good, on my way to work."

"That's nothing new, get that money, baby. Sure wish Tracie would get off her ass and get a job."

"She will in due time. You know she has her hands full."

"How when I'm always watching my granddaughter all the damn time, she's got time to run the streets but don't have time for her own kid," she scoffs. "Why can't she be more like you huh? You went to school, got yourself out your mama's house to go to work every day like a real person should. I'm mighty sure your mom and dad are proud of the son they raised. You know, it's a shame those motherfuckers at that office wouldn't give you that damn promotion. Lord knows you deserved it, and you know why they ain't give to you? You know why..." She points to her skin. "Those racist motherfuckers ain't want a nice-looking Black man with his shit together in a position of power. Fuck em', you ain't need them sons of bitches no way."

"You know that's right. Well, Miss Lorna, it's always a pleasure seeing you. But I gotta get going."

"Okay baby, it's always good seeing you, have a blessed day. Oh yeah, next time you see my good for nothing daughter, try and talk some sense into her please."

"Will do."

"Alright baby, I'll see you later," she says and vanishes back inside.

"Are you still going to take me ice skating Sunday?" Cam shouts.

"Yeah, baby girl; I wouldn't break my promise but let me get going, I don't want to be late to work. I see you later okay?"

"Okay, have a good day, Michael."

"You too baby girl! When your mom gets back, tell her I might be by later."

"Okay, bye-bye." Cam waves me off and returns inside. When I reach the sidewalk that leads to the restaurant entrance, my phone begins to vibrate.

I answer, "Hey, mom. What's going on?"

"Hey hon, what's going you with you?"

"Nothing much, just getting ready to walk into work. Where's Dad?"

"He's in the back, firing up the grill, we got some porterhouse steaks going. We're just going to hang out by the fire-pit as the night comes, wish you were here baby."

"That's nice, Mom; I wish I was there too. But unfortunately, your baby has to work..."

"You're right, honey. How's the adjustment going? The people you work with are treating you as you should be treated, I hope."

"Oh, it's really good and yeah, for the most part, everybody is very nice. Yeah... ah- all my coworkers are great and the food they serve is delicious, you and Dad are going to like it when you guys come."

"That's great hon, how are the customers? Are you getting familiar with the regulars?"

"Um, haven't met many of them yet but the ones I have are really nice. I got tipped a hundred bucks last night. So yeah, that was cool."

"Oh wow, I was a little worried at first, Michael, but I guess your father was right…don't tell him I said that, you know how he gets whenever someone tells him he's right. He'll never let it go. But yeah for last night's supper I made that rigatoni you like so much and since I was in the area running some errands, I figured I'd drop you off a plate. I didn't wake you, did I?"

I laugh, "I knew you were going to ask that. I got it on me now, thanks mom and no you didn't disrupt my sleep, you never do. Seriously thanks, I'm going to eat it before the dinner service starts."

"Okay, good... Hey, Michael, I saw a bottle of alcohol on the living room floor when I first came in. Now, you're an adult so you don't have to go into why it was on the floor like that but I hope you're drinking responsibly. Before I put your dad on the phone, I have one more question for you sweetie… Are going to your therapy sessions? You know, your father and I pay good money for those sessions and Michelle hasn't billed us this month. It's for your own good, hon, and she's a good person to talk things over with," she advises.

"I'll make it a point to see her. I've just been so busy with training and learning the menu, you know. But, I'm fine Mom, really I am. And if I start to feel, I don't know, depressed or something. I'll set up a meeting with Michelle; I promise."

"Ok, Michael, I just want you to take care of yourself. You're my only baby. I want you to be independent but just know it's okay to talk about things."

"I know and I am. Being an adult requires your *only baby* to work mom," I joke.

"I know... I know you have to work and I want you to do what makes you happy but at the same time son, you have to make sure your head is on straight. I still think you're getting another job too fast. You know if you need time away, we'll always look out for you like we always have son, but I'm through talking. Hold on, your father wants to say hello..."

"Hey, Mikey, what's going on?" he says.

"What's going on, Pop? Heard you got some steaks going on the grill. And without me? You're a jerk, you know that," I joke.

"I'm the jerk," he chuckles. "You haven't been by in a month or so and you're calling me names." He laughs again. "You got some nerve son. You know your mother had to do a covert mission today to see if you were replaced by a robot. But yeah, son, we got the grill going and some of those double IPA's you were talking about the last time we spoke. Oh yeah, and your favorite—a pint of Hennessy. You're working tonight?"

"Yeah, Pop, you know it."

"Well, kiddo, you gotta work; but remember, you gotta show your face from time-to-time. Your mother and I miss your face, and you know how she worries."

I wipe away the tears forming and clear my throat. "Yeah, I miss you guys too. I'm off the day after next. Why don't I treat you guys to lunch or dinner here at the new job and we can catch up then?"

"That's great, kiddo, your mom would really like that. But ah, let me see... me and your mom got this retirement party we're going to for someone she works with the night before you want to meet but how does eleven work? I shouldn't be too hungover," he jokes.

"Perfect."

"Alright, it's set. Anyway, you see any girls you work with that catch your fancy?"

"You know Dad, there's one. But I'll play it by ear, I'll let you know for sure though."

"If you end up on a date with her just remember my advice."

"Dad...."

"I'm just saying no woman can resist that Weathers' charm. Your mother couldn't..."

"Too bad you'll never say that while mom is right next to you."

"He won't," Mom shouts.

Dad whispers, "You didn't hear that."

"Well, I did. But ah, Pop, I'm actually walking into work now, text me later. I'll message you the address when I get off, its actually down the street from my apartment. But hey, I gotta go. I love you guys and tell Mom I said thank you for the rigatoni."

"You're welcome honey, and we love you too!" she yells. "But remember what we talked about, Michael."

"I know you heard that," Dad laughs.

"Yeah, of course, I did."

"Alright, text me later. Give em' hell, kiddo."

"Will do."

"Alright, son, love you."

"Love you too, Pop." I end the call.

Giselle isn't at the hostess stand when I first come in. I walk through the dining room to avoid anyone who could've been a witness from last night. Before I head into the kitchen; I remove the rigatoni and toss my bag in the cabinet. The only people in the kitchen are the prep cooks and Jose. For a brief moment, I become envious that I'm not one of them. Their job is simple and out of the way. More than half of the cooks can't even speak English, so even if the servers are talking shit, they can't even comprehend what they're saying, so it makes doing their job easier. I guess that's the old saying, "ignorance is bliss." They pay me no mind as I microwave this container I set for three minutes. When the timer goes off; I mix the pasta around and put it back for another minute and a half.

Jose lets me take one of the clean entrée plates from the dish-rack. I scoop four forkfuls onto the dish and let it cool off. "What's up newbie?" Tina says as she enters. "What you got there?"

"Some of my mom's rigatoni," I reply.

"No fried chicken and collard greens? Wow, must be nice."

"Nope, not today, Tina. Sorry if I don't fit the description. But I got more than enough if you would like some."

"You know what, Newbie, I'll take you up on that. Never knew Blacks to cook Italian food," she grabs an entrée plate from expo and a fork from the silverware tray. Tina scoops three forkfuls worth of pasta and digs right in. "Hmm, hmm, damn, Newbie, who knew? This is pretty good if I say so myself. Your mom put her foot in this."

"Thanks, it's my favorite thing she makes."

"So… how did last night go?" Tina continues to chew.

"Um, uh, there were steady pushes throughout the night. A.G. needed me to expedite, that was cool."

"You what? Expo? Yeah right."

"Nah, I'm serious."

"Wow, A.G. got you driving the bus already. I'm pretty sure you fucked up on a few tables, right?" she laughs.

"No actually. Every table and person who ordered was on time. But believe me, I was just as surprised as you are. To be honest, I didn't think I had it in me still, I use to expo from time to time with when worked downtown."

"No way; I can't believe that."

"Why?"

"'Because I know the only person who never fucks up expo is A.G. What makes you so special? You gotta be lying..."

"You're right, everybody makes mistakes and I'm not saying I'm immune to making them but I don't know what to tell you; I know I'm not lying, why would I do that?... All I can say is what I know. And, as far as last night went, I didn't have one problem doing expo. I mean once you've expedited at one restaurant, you've kind of expedited at them all. I mean, some expeditors may use pencils or pens, some use highlighters or permanent markers... all-in-all, it's the same, as long you don't send the wrong food to the table or whatever. It's not rocket science, Tina."

"Still don't believe you."

"Why do you think I'm lying? No offense but who are you for me to lie to..."

"You gotta be lying," she scoffs, "I've never seen anyone who was training not mess up at expo. Hold up, now that I think about it... I've never seen someone in training do expo, what the fuck makes you so special?"

Jackie waltzes in. "Howdy everybody."

I wave. "Hey, what's going on, Boss-Lady?"

"Nothing much, what's good in the hood?" She hugs Tina and squints at my plate. "What you got there Mikey? Looks and smells amazing."

"Uh, some of my mom's homemade rigatoni. There's plenty more to go around, you want some?"

"Nah, I hate cheese but thanks. Hey, whenever you're done with that can you clock in early, so we can prepare for a party of sixteen at five-thirty in the dining-room?"

"Yeah, for sure." I chuckle. "Are you lactose intolerant or something? Because who doesn't like cheese?"

"Nah," Jackie shrugs. "I just don't like the taste of it, the texture alone grosses me out. I'm half Irish and half Italian, believe me, Newbie, that doesn't sit well with a lot of people—especially my family," she smirks.

Tina pokes at the food as if it were poisoned. "Hope, you didn't spit in this. Newbie..."

I frown at her. "Don't flatter yourself. I wouldn't dare disrespect my mother's cooking and you shouldn't either."

To be honest, I should've spat in it.

Tina teases, "Ok, mama's boy, don't get touchy. I was just fucking around with you, relax. But to be honest, this is really good pasta. Who knew Blacks could cook anything other than collard greens and pig-feet? This might be the best rigatoni I've ever had."

"Thanks, I'm glad you like it. To be honest I thought you would've—uh never mind. I'm glad you like it."

"What, Newbie? Cat got your tongue? Giselle couldn't kiss your boo-boo from your fall last night," Tina heckles.

"Alright, Tina, leave Newbie alone and finish up in here so we can set up for tonight," Jackie interjects.

"Yeah, yeah. Oh, Jackie, I wanted to ask you something?" Tina swallows.

"Sure, shoot for it."

"Who ran expo last night?" Tina asks.

"Newbie did, why?"

"He said he did, and I didn't believe him. Did he fuck up?"

"Nope, A.G. put him on mid-rush and he did a pretty good job if I say so myself. I didn't notice he was expediting till about eight-thirty or nine. Everything ran as smooth as a baby's bottom."

I grin. "Told you."

"Whatever, Newbie, you think you're such hot shit, huh? Time will show... you'll fold under pressure. And I'll be there to watch you crumble like a stale cookie."

Jackie frowns. "Tin—"

"—No Jackie, I got this..." I set my plate down and turned to Tina. "You know, one of your regulars tipped me a hundred dollars last night?"

Tina's eye's jolt. "Oh yeah, who the fuck would do that, huh?"

"Pauly Senior," I reply. "You know, Tina, for the first time since he and his boys have been coming here; last night was the first time ever that he got served a scotch with a coaster. And if we're keeping score then yeah, I'm pretty good at my job. I'm sick of you always playing me like I'm some simpleton. Last time I checked, I was a college graduate and documented. Excuse me, I stand corrected, a natural-born citizen."

Tina dumps her entire plate in the trash then storms out.

Jackie gasps. "Oh, shit, Mike, where did that come from?

I shrug. "Man, she's been giving me shit since day one, honestly, fuck her. It's about time she got a dose of her own Tylenol."

"Geez, Newbie, I had no clue you felt that way, I'll talk to her later about taking it easier on you, she can get a little territorial. She's like that with anyone new, maybe that's why they never last," she says. "You think you got it bad, you should've seen how she treated Pepe when he first started and he's just a busser. To be honest with you, I think you're the first server-in-training to ever stand up to her. And you don't have to take shit from anyone, I get it. Nobody likes to be a tattletale. I just don't get involved in shit that's none of my business, but I'll talk to her."

"Boss-lady, I get it, or maybe I don't but she's really a piece of fucking work, and she threw my mother's food away. I mean, what a bitch. Who acts like that? And even for her age, it's not only immature but utterly disgusting."

Billie charges in and shouts, "Sup' Bitches?" He pecks Jackie on the lips and pats my head. "What's wrong with Tina? Seen her outside before I came in. I think she smoked a cigarette in one drag. What's up her snatch?"

"Newbie just cursed her out," Jackie says.

Billie begins to tie on his apron. "Holy shit! Not Farrakhan?"

"Yup, it was pretty intense if ask me," she replies.

Billie notices the container of rigatoni and starts to poke around it with dirty fingers. "Who brought this in?" he asks. "Looks and smells bomb as fuck, umm."

The sight of him touching it makes my stomach turn. I actually planned on having some more. "My mom made it, but you can have the rest; I'm good."

His eyes widen. "Oh word? Good lookin' out, Farrakhan."

"Yeah man, that's all you," I say as I pull Tina's plate from the garbage and take mine and hers to the dishwasher. "You like the food, Bill?" I ask.

With his mouth full he answers, "Hell yeah, I gotta meet your mom one day. All the shit she makes is amazing. Remember those peanut butter crunch cookies and those banana-nut brownies? Man, your mom sure knows her way around the kitchen. What Black person could finesse rigatoni like this? I gotta thank her one day."

"Yeah, one day... You ready to set up that party, Jackie?"

"Yup, all we're going to do is just put two long tables together and round up sixteen chairs from the back hallway. Simple." Jackie leads the way to where the extra chairs are kept. We each carry two oak chairs to the front of the dining-room and return to the hallway until we reach the amount she needs. And of course, no help from Billie, but Tina and A.G. both help by putting the tables together. Before we can finish setting up, A.G. is rushed off by a beer vendor. I watch as Jackie pushes in the last seat. "Alright, I think that's it," she says and counts out sixteen positions. "Okay, Newbie, thanks for all your help but around 9:30 or so I'm probably going to need your arms again to help break this down after they leave, but I'll try to get to Billie to do it if he's not speeding to get outta here."

"No doubt but what about water glasses?" I ask.

Jackie fixes her hair into a ponytail, "Eh, we'll worry about it when the times comes. What time were you scheduled to come in?"

"Four o'clock but I still have about twenty minutes to kill, why what's up?"

"No, I'm just saying go have a smoke or two before your shift gets started, we're going to get slammed tonight. A.G. is expecting it to be busier than it was last night so..."

"So, I hear. Well, I'll be back, Boss-lady," I say.

As Jackie instructed, I make my way through the back exit to a smoke break. Before I reach the bottom of the stairs, to no surprise there's Billie, lighting up a cigarette and scrolling through his phone.

When Billie spots me coming down, he holds the door open. "Join the party, Farrakhan."

"You really have to stop calling me that," I say and light a smoke as I follow him into the parking lot.

"Why? I like it. And it fits 'cause you're such the *enlightened* Black man," he laughs.

"Enlightened my ass, you just sound stupid, and may I add racist," I say. "Anyway, how'd you like my mom's food?"

"That shit was great, it's kinda funny, I've never seen you try any of the black dishes- we have but a nigga comes in with some authentic ass pasta..."

"What the fuck do you mean by that?"

"You know like-- the grits and shit," he says.

"Just because you been selling grits for the last six years doesn't mean all people of color eat that shit too...You know, sometimes, you can sound as dumb as you look. You might be the dullest tool in the drawer, but that hasn't stopped you from succeeding; the way you got Jackie hooked," I scoff. "Guess you're not doing so bad for yourself after all."

"I'm going to pretend you just didn't say that last part, and assume that just you're letting out some of the steam you have left over from last night... Come on, let's a take a trip behind the dumpster real quick, I still got a little pick me up." We head over to the garbage pickup. I get in between the cardboard and trash dumpsters with ease but watching Billie's struggles to get through almost takes the air out of my lungs. "Damn," Billie struggles to catch his breath. "I gotta lose some fucking weight," he huffs.

"Who are you telling?... You don't want to get diabetes, that's if you don't have it already. And, you since you want to be Black so much, I'm going to give you a rapper name. I'm going to call you, Blood Sugar." I pretend as if there were microphone in my hand and I'm hyping up a crowd as I introduce Billie to overly anxious raps fans, "Ay, I want ya'll to put your hands to together for Big Blood Sugar, got the most insulin shots in the game right now," I heckle.

Billie laughs along as he digs in his dusty pants pocket, and his hand shifts around until he pinches from what looks like a mini rubber ball. He then comes up with appears to about less than half a gram. "That's pretty funny," he says.

"There's nothing funny about diabetes, Bill. Wait a minute... didn't you wear those khakis yesterday? And now that I think about it, you wore those pants the day before yesterday..."

He undoes the knot, scales through the bag with his Amex, and then quickly sniffs two bumps off the corner of the card and answers, "Yeah... so, they're clean. What are you trying to say?" Billie passes the contraband. "What the fuck you worried about my pants for? What's gotten into you today?"

"Well... First, I think you still might be drunk from last night... Second, stop calling me Farrakhan while you got the nerve to be shaped like a limp penis. And third, if Tina gives me any more shit, I might throw a plate of piping hot mac and cheese in her fat face," I say as I try to manage getting the coke to stay on the corner of his Amex. Finally, I get it up my left nostril, giving my clogged airway just enough air to get another bump through. "I mean other than what happened last night; I'm okay. Why? Does something seem off with me?" I snort.

"Yeah, a little. You've tapped into your inner asshole. I love it."

I rail two more. As soon the powder hits the back of my throat, a tingly sensation runs from shoulders to toes; and the drip sets in. "Well, I'm not an asshole. I'm just questioning why you have on dirty pants, and most importantly she didn't have to bring up what happened last night, she fucks with my head 'cause she can and I'm sick of it." I snort and add, "So, I'm sorry to inform you, there's nothing for you to love."

"I sure love this coke, and I know you do too, so there's plenty to love right about now."

I shrug. "So we're going to be busy tonight?"

He sizes up the bag, sets it down on a cardboard box, and pulls out two cigarettes.

"Yeah, looks like it. I checked the guest book before coming out here and there is supposed to be 250 covers including that party of sixteen. So minus sixteen, what's that, ahh..."

"234. You got another bogie?" I ask

"Yeah I got you," he replies, "it's going to be a shit show, though." I light the cigarette, quickly inhaling and exhaling. "It won't be if you don't spend every twenty-minutes in the bathroom getting high. You're bugged out."

"It isn't that long." He exhales. "Who are you shadowing?"

I ash. "You."

Billie chuckles. "Damn, not again, just remember not to talk to my tables, you didn't listen to me last night and overstepped your boundaries."

"Excuse me, if you didn't spend every twenty minutes in the bathroom I wouldn't have to. Not only do you put yourself in jeopardy, but you also put me at risk. What the fuck was I going to say if A.G. noticed you were gone? Or even worse, what if a customer complained to A.G. then you would really have been in for some shit, I tell ya."

"Whatever, Farrakhan, you think you know how this shit goes but you have no idea, I know exactly what I'm doing."

"I beg to differ, my friend, you just haven't gotten caught it yet... there's a difference."

Out of nowhere, a faint female's voice yells, "Hey, what you are doing back here?"

I immediately jump out of my skin as my butt falls to the ground. To nobody's surprise but my own, it's Jackie; who laughs as her slim figure eases its way through the dumpsters. "What the fuck man? You play too fucking much." I pick up my cigarette. "How the fuck did you even know we were back here?"

"Don't worry about it, Newbie," she laughs. "Nah, Billie told me, that shouldn't be so hard to figure out. Your heart skipped a few beats when I shouted, huh, Newbie? Damn, kid, hate to see what would happen if you dropped a plate or something," They both chuckle.

"Shit, Farrakhan, how can you lead your people to freedom but you're scared of your own shadow? "No one likes a scary-cat, Newbie," Jackie snickers. "Oh yeah, Giselle asked about you soon as she clocked in."

"Really?" I ask.

"Yeah, you better get up there before she comes looking for you," she says.

"You said I could have a smoke break before dinner starts."

"You might want to stay... well, least until these lines are gone," Jackie says and reaches around to her back pocket. She pulls out a mini square mirror along with what looks like about two grams or so of cocaine. I'm not certain, all I know is, it's noticeably bigger than what Billie had. Billie passes her his Amex as soon as she pours half of the bag onto the glass. Jackie proceeds to fish and dice around the powder, making sure it's as refined as possible. She hands me the mirror, goes in her front pocket, and removes some-what of a clean twenty dollar bill and rolls it. I hand back the mirror and watch as she sniffs two out of the six lines she divided. "Ahh, that's what I call a wake me up, your turn,

Newbie," she says with a snort.

"You mind holding it for me? My right nostril is clogged," I ask.

"Sure," Jackie replies. My cigarette is near the filter, and so I toss it behind Jackie as she holds the mirror steady while I press on the right side of my nose and try to get the lines up my left nostril. I manage to get half of the first one up and it causes some airway to push through. I snort as hard as I can and hawk up phlegm. Behind Billie is the safest place to spit it out; it lands on a piece of cardboard. All I care about is that it's out of anyone's sight, and most importantly, both of my nostrils are finally clear. Jackie patiently holds the mirrors as I readjust the bill. Without any hesitation, the line and a half that was leftover, quickly finds its way through my nose and straight to the back of my esophagus. I gag, "Holy shit, that one hit. Yup, umm hmm. Pick me up for sure."

Jackie smiles. "Glad I could help you out there, Newbie. I didn't want to say anything while we were upstairs, but I could tell you were struggling, that's why I told you to go take a smoke break."

"No, no, I appreciate it. Thanks, Boss-lady. Uh, you wouldn't happen to have an extra smoke on you would you?"

"Yeah, I do." She retrieves two cigarettes from her back pocket. Jackie lights one and passes it off to me.

I grab it with, "Thanks."

"You got it, Newbie," Jackie says.

Billie takes his bag of coke off the cardboard and dumps what's left onto the mirror. Jackie's small pile now merges into a miniature mountain. He rubs the plastic together to make sure he's gotten every last particle onto the glass. When I think he just about through the hit, he then licks the inside of the bag, and without a care to where it ends up, he tosses it into the summer breeze. "Is that the pack I bought you last night?" He questions.

"Yup," she answers. "I'm surprised we didn't run through this whole pack; we were partying hard last night." Jackie hands back Billie's Amex. He then uses it to separate more lines. As he prepares the cocaine, my right nostril starts clogging up again, so I snort as hard as I can.

The snot from my nasal cavity rushes to my throat, immediately and I expel it to where the last spit lies. With the saliva comes a new and revived drip. With every drag from this Marlboro Light, the high intensifies, my focus sharpens, and my confidence heightens. Yet, just as I know with most things, this feeling won't last forever.

"What do you mean?" Jackie laughs. "I'm going to pretend you didn't just say that. It's your third day and Billie's already got you following in his footsteps. FYI, Newbie, this spot is no secret. The only person who doesn't know about it is A.G. As far as anybody knows he doesn't party. To be honest, I'm glad he doesn't 'cause somebody has to be in their right mind to run this shit show. But like I said, I only come back here when I know it's going be a shit show on the floor, or in most of the cases, if I partied too hard the night before like we did last night."

"Ah, I get it. These dumpsters serve more purposes than trash, I guess," I reply.

Jackie clears her nose. "Oh yeah, for sure. Only me, Tina, Billie, and Jose come back here, and I guess you now, Newbie."

"Figured that much."

Shortly after, another round of lines followed by sucking down our last cigarettes before returning upstairs; I find myself cleaning more silverware. Billie is somewhat preoccupied with folding napkins, Tina looks to be replenishing to-go containers and refilling the ketchup and barbecue bottles. I want to say Jackie is downstairs doing inventory, and

A.G. is assisting her. As for Giselle; she's at her usual post, doing whatever she's paid to do. While looking more breathtaking than ever in her tight, ripped jeans with a halter top that leaves room for the naked eye to wonder some ungodly things, but she keeps it elegant with a pink blazer which matches her flat-footed shoes. Instead of being graced by her presence; I'm just going to wither away in the server station, hoping my high goes down before we get bombarded.

As I'm wiping down the last of the forks, cheap perfume begins to creep through my nose. I turn to see where it's coming from, and Tina is right behind me. "Hey, Newbie, can I have a minute?" she asks.

I pause. "Sure."

Tina waddles to table 47 as I trail behind. She takes a seat in the booth and I pull out a chair to face her.

"I just want to say sorry about throwing your mom's food in the trash and that was really disrespectful," she says.

"Thanks..."

"And, I just want to let you know, Jackie told me what happen to you last night."

"Oh, really?" I sneeze twice.

"Bless you."

"Thanks." I sneeze once more.

"Damn, Newbie, bless you. Must be those pre-shift bumps."

"Nah, more like some off-brand fragrance. Low-cost perfumes tend to bother my allergies. But as you were..."

I trail off as I watch Tina frown. "Um well, Jackie also said you got called a *nigger* too, but that shouldn't matter much right, Black people hear that all the time—you must be used to it by now. I don't know why she made it seem like it was the worst thing to ever happen. I told her

156

you're probably over it already by now."

I rise and push the chair in. "I really appreciate you apologizing about my mother's food, it was heartfelt, I guess. Thanks again, Tina."

"Wait... you're not going to say sorry for calling me an illegal alien?"

"I didn't call you anything. All I said was, I'm a citizen, take it how you want to but I'm not apologizing for nothing I said earlier. Why should I? You've been giving me shit since I first walked through those doors. To be honest, I could've been a lot more an asshole but no one deserves that, not even you."

Tina abruptly rises from the cushions then forcefully brushes past, making sure her shoulder is felt. As I stumble back, I catch myself by the edge of the table. At this moment, it's taking every ounce of self-control not to punch her in the face. "So, I guess that makes us even huh?" Tina says as she turns into the server station.

I take a deep breath before marching towards her. I force a smile as I hover right over her and whisper in her ears, "You know, you've been pulling my chain ever since we met, ever since we fucking met. I get it, you've been here from the start and see me as a threat to your job, shit, maybe even to your entire existence. You probably think, 'how can this Black motherfucker be so good at this job?' When it took you six years to finally make some decent money, but you know nothing about me, nothing at all. And not to add insult to injury I don't want your fucking job. I'm here for my own money. Far as I'm concerned, you don't sign my checks. From now on, if you have nothing informative to say to me while we're on the clock, don't say anything to me at all. And you throwing my mother's food in the trash was real mature. Aren't you like thirty-something?"

For a moment Tina stares then flashes a devilish smirk. "Wow, you got some pair of balls on you, Newbie. You think you're hot shit, huh?" She smirks. "You're just another uppity nigger that thinks he can fit in with the whites. You know something, Newbie? I might be from another country and so what if my papers aren't legit. I'm the right skin color, at least I have that going for me. That's more than I can say about you, and since we're being honest, being white gives me all the advantages that you'll never have." Tina nudges my shoulder as she storms out.

Man, I should've taken A.G.'s advice, and taken the fucking day off. Maybe mom was right; I'm in way over my head. Tina's apology turned into an ugly truth of belittlement with a fresh reminder of where my place is. I feel as if history's starting to repeat itself.

Before I can do away with the silverware tray, someone sneaks to my blindside and covers my eyes.

"Guess who?"

"Beyoncé?" I ask.

Giselle throws a fist into my lower back. "You're funny, Weathers."

"So, I hear."

"What's wrong with you? Tina fucking with you again?" she asks.

"Nah, she was just giving me a few pointers with POS. What's going on with you?"

She slaps my chest with a bus rag. "Nothing much, I just finished printing the new specials list. I missed you last night..."

"And this whole time I'm thinking you were home, sick; I should tell A.G.," I grin and say.

Giselle snickers. "Shh, shut up. Was it busy?"

"Yeah, nothing I couldn't handle. Got most of the food coming out, so that was good."

"Hmm. Maybe after tonight, you could handle something else..."

"Oh yeah, and what would that be?"

Giselle presses my body against the counter then brushes my top lip with her index finger. "Maybe you'll see later." Her hips switch harder than usual as she moves back to the hostess stand. I turn to face the sink, run my hands under cold water, and I count to fifteen. Wrong time to have a hard-on especially with the dinner crowd beginning to pile in. After my excitement subsides; I return to the silverware tray to dish. Within ten minutes, Giselle starts seating more customers and before I know it, every table is occupied by groups of friends and family or candid couples. Billie's section is 13 to 16. Mostly two tops but if it weren't for me shadowing him, Billie would be in the weeds. So far, I haven't seen him pick up so much as a salad fork.

Yet the ambiance is vibrant and fast-paced and I'm engulfed by it. Some patrons set aside their appetites as I pass by to smile and side-track with their engaging but inquisitive comments. One customer stops me and says, "By the way you're moving and how you know what's going on, you could've fooled me, I'd have thought you been here for years." Right after that a lady seated at the bar compliments my mannerisms stating, "It's so nice to see a handsome young man like yourself knowing how to talk to a woman, I bet you're radiant to all the girls your age."

All I can do, is what I always do; smile and chuckle an utter, *is there anything else I can get you?*. Even if it's not my section, I figure since I'm employed, I'm obligated to make the guests have everything they need. They don't care if you're pressed for time, they want what they want, and want it now.

My high wore off about an hour ago; I could feel the pressure from the snot in my nose starting to build up. I tread quickly to the server station and make it seem as if I'm refilling the water pitcher but in all actuality, I really need to blow my fucking nose. As I'm hitting the soap dispenser Jackie approaches. "Newbie, I need help bussing this party," she demands.

"Yes, Ma'am, just let me wash my hands and tell Billie I'm helping you."

"There's no time for that, just wash your hands, he'll be alright. He should be thanking you; for once he's not in the fucking weeds. Let's make this quick, yeah?" she snaps.

"Yes, Ma'am..."

Jackie pats my back. "Attaboy." With her leading the way; I take whatever plates I see to the side first. If I'm not too sure if a guest is finished, I politely ask, "excuse me, are you done with that?" and they either nod or state, "I'm still working." Doesn't matter to me if they use manners or not; I'm just trying to get this done as fast as possible. Politeness does go a long way. From what I experienced, they don't want to be interrupted and when they're cut off by a Black man asking to remove something, it's always a shock, always. Some customers look as if I'm about to mug them in the middle of dinner.

It's funny... let's say if the noise from the chatter is overwhelming and I couldn't get their attention and they're obviously through with their course; once they see my copper fingers on the edge of whatever I'm attempting to remove, it is almost too hard not laugh at their reaction. Some are so surprised, they quickly pick up their phone as if I'm planning to take that too, or their eyes widen as if I'm some dancing dog.

See, I have a way I go about giving dining guests great service or at least using what I learned working downtown. For example, if a customer's napkin falls to the ground and they've been a dick to me all night, I won't even pick it up, shit, I won't even acknowledge it if they don't. That dirty cloth will stay there till the check is paid. If they've been nothing but kind; I spot whatever mistake there is, like a napkin on the floor and I will make it my duty to retrieve a clean one. And it doesn't stop there; I'll refill water with fresh lemons; even if they didn't ask for it I'll bring the wedges anyway. Good tippers and people who work in the industry people notice shit like that.

With our hands full, Jackie and I speed to dish and pile them neatly on the track. She jumps to the expo which A.G. is handling. He passes the entrees off to her and yells, "Position one, Burger med-rare, position two Burger-med well and position sixteen!..."

She returns to the floor. "Hands!" A.G. shouts.

"I'm right behind you," I answer.

"OK, New York Strip position ten, shrimp and pasta position nine, and Snow crab legs position seven," he stares at a ticket then the side dish," Mike, come back for position ten's side of broccoli," he says.

"Got it." I turn to Tina standing directly in my path. Carefully, I catch my balance and steady the scorching plates. "You're supposed to stay behind, Tina," I scold.

She shrugs. "Oh, I did—I thought you heard me, sorry."

There's no time to bicker; I dart towards Jackie's party, as I'm walking past the server station, she speeds past and back into the kitchen. Counting the seat numbers in my head as I match the seats they go to; I set position nine's dinner down, all of sudden she's asks, "Wait, did I order this?"

I being to perspire. "Uh, I believe so Ma'am."

"Honey, that is exactly what you ordered. You'll have to excuse my wife young man; she likes to confuse the busboys," position eight-person interjects.

"Luckily for me, Sir, I'm not a busser. I'm currently a server-in-training. Please enjoy your dinner." As I walk away from the table, I wipe the perspiration from my neck soon as I enter the kitchen. And there's Jackie again, with three more plates hurrying out; I quickly sidestep as she dashes out.

"Hands!" A.G. yells.

"Right here," I answer.

"Okay, position one's burger is rare, position two's burger is rare, if you forget, just remember the rare burgers are stuck with toothpicks. No, I'm sorry position two is medium-rare," he says and removes one of the toothpicks. "And position three's burger is medium-well. You got that Michael?"

I count the positions and temperatures in my head, "Yeah, I got it." As I'm rushing back to the party, Tina passes by but doesn't forget to flash her bitch of a smile along with her sausage link middle finger. Before reaching the table; I pace my heartbeat, and once again I take a minute to count out the position and the burgers that match. party and one by one I place the correct burger in front of each guest.

"Excuse me, busboy?" Position nine shouts.

"What can I do for you, Ma'am?" I ask.

"I need a refill, Ketol One vodka, dirty with two olives," she says.

"I'll inform your waitress," I smile.

Before I can turn, she tugs on my shirt. "Why can't you do it?"

"I'm just a server-in-training; I don't have the proper access to put in another beverage for you. I apologize, but I will notify Jackie as soon as I'm done here."

Her eyes roll. "That's stupid. Well, tell whoever can do it and make it fast, will you?"

"Right away, Ma'am."

Soon as I finish setting down the entrees, I spot Jackie in the server station fixing her hair. "Hey, Boss Lady, you got a minute?"

"Sure, kid, what's up?" she asks.

"Position nine needs a refill. Ketol One martini with two olives."

Jackie grunts, "That's like her third one, this is going to be her last one."

"Yeah, for sure. You need anything from me?"

"You can run this fried shrimp to 15," A.G. cuts in then asks, "Where's Billie? I gotta get back in the kitchen."

"Don't know, but I'll take it." As I'm dashing towards the table, Billie races past, speeding towards the POS but Tina beats him to the punch. When I arrive at 15, to my surprise, it's Sage and her sisters. I force the best smile I can. "Hello, it's so nice to see you all again."

Sage places her hand on my forearm. "*Michael with the nice teeth.* How are you doing sweetie?"

"I'm well Sage, thanks for asking. How are you ladies doing on this rainy evening?"

Patricia and Shirley nod and smile simultaneously. "We're going to have a few drinks and drown our fat-asses in some of this fried shrimp," Sage snickers. "I'm so happy to be graced by your beautiful Black presence. But, Michael, ah how can I put this… our server, ah-ah— Billie? I don't want to offend anyone when I say this… But my dear, Micheal, that Billie is something else. It's like he's never heard of a shower. What's the deal with his body odor? It's repulsive and almost insulting the way he smells," she says and sips her wine, frowning.

I chuckle. "That's peculiar, I never smelled any stench of his." Of course, that's a lie but what the fuck can I do? "I'll make sure to tell him in the most subtle way possible ladies; I apologize for any further inconvenience," I say.

Sage grazes my chest. "Well, Michael, do what you can. But you shouldn't be responsible for anyone else's body odor."

"Understood, if I don't see you ladies for the rest night. Please, enjoy yourselves and get home safe," I grin and state. Before walking away, Sage shoves something down my back pocket but not before she grabbed a handful of my right buttock. I look back and smile. What else can I do? I guess this is what a complete violation feels like. And to think it mostly happens to women. Goddamn, white women are the scariest ones walking around this country and they don't even know. If I were to do such a thing, I could kiss my whole life goodbye. What in the world gives a white woman the right to feel me up as if I'm some cabana boy waiting on her every beck and call?

Once again, I'm at the server station and Billie is nowhere to be found. I walk towards the counter sink to check what Sage stuffed in my pocket; two twenty-dollar bills. Holy shit, what the fuck is wrong with that crazy bitch? I can't return the money 'cause that will be a sign of disrespect and I can't tell A.G. he'll look at me as if I'm some kind of homosexual. This shit is killing me. "Hey, Newbie!" Tina shouts.

I bury the money in my apron. "Yeah, what's up? What do you need?"

"Where's Billie?" she questions.

"That's a good question... Is there something I can help you with?"

"Yeah, I need you to go get Billie so he can serve his tables, so hurry your Black ass up and go find him."

"Yup, I'm on it." I bolt to the bathroom. "Billie, you in here?" I whisper.

A man in the stall yells, "Nope, just Phil!"

I chuckle. "Sorry to bother you, Sir."

The only place to look now is out back. Soon as I step into the parking lot, I become drenched. I don't even know why I came back here to look for this fat fuck. I poke my head between the dumpsters and just my luck; he's nowhere in sight. Why would he be? It's pouring out. I sprint back to the entrance. Before heading upstairs; I begin to breathe through my nose to catch my breath. Haven't run that hard since my hockey days. Damn, I need to get back in shape. I jog up the stairs only to see Billie is chatting it up at the table next to Sage and her sisters. At the back server station; I try to dry off my clothes using bus rags and realize this is going to take a lot more than a bunch of guest napkins cause I'm fucking drenched.

Jackie approaches. "Newbie, where were you? One minute, I saw you talking to Tina, and the next minute, Billie's looking for you... and why are soaking wet?"

"I went outside to look for Billie and got caught in the downpour, just my luck huh," I toss the rags into the dirty bin.

"Tina didn't tell you?"

"Tell me what?... she told me she was looking for Billie."

She starts putting in another round of drinks for her party. "I sent him home; he forgot his wine key, 'cause Graham couldn't spare his and neither of us has one so I let him run home really quick."

"I have a wine key in my bag, somebody should've asked."

"You should've said something, Newbie. You know why I sent Billie to get wine. You're smart, Newbie, you can put two-and-two together. He's probably high as a giraffe. Good luck, shadowing." Jackie walks off.

As I try to finish drying off, Billie pinches the side of my hip. For once, there's no coke residue on his nose.

"What's up, Farrakhan? What did I miss?" he asks.

"Shit numb-nut, let me see... Uh, how about leaving me to attend to your tables when I should be following you?"

"Chill the fuck out. You're a pro right..."

"That's not the point."

His voice rises. "You're a pro right?"

"Yeah, I am."

"Then stop whining. You know, you sound like a little bitch right now," he chuckles. "Keep acting like a little faggot and I won't share none of the goodies I got."

"Oh yeah, what did you get, more coke?"

Billie takes out a wine key with a wooden handle, you could tell he spent at least fifteen dollars or more on it. He then flashes a rocked filled baggie. "You bet your Black ass I do, you know I had to get some more rocket fuel."

"Cool, let me get a couple of bumps."

"Oh shit, what happened to *I don't fuck around on the clock*," he snickers.

"What? Do you not see me right now, dumbass? I got caught in the fucking pouring rain looking for you. Shadowing you will be the death of me. Now, do me a favor and slide me that bag of coke before I go ape shit."

Billie slips it into my apron. "There you go, Farrakhan, be gentle."

I smirk. "Be gentle my ass."

"Nigga, don't kill my shit... Let me get to the floor," he says and stares into the bar dining area. "Yo, A.G. is coming this way. Make sure that shit don't slip out your apron." The coke is stuck at the top of my

166

apron and lodged between my server pad; within a split second, I manage to jam to the bottom.

"Quick question, why are you wet, Michael?" A.G. enters and interjects.

"Uh-uh, um; I-I a-had to take out the trash for Jose, he didn't ask, of course, I just saw that he was busy, and the garbage just happened to be overflowing so I figured why not take it out. Just my luck to get caught in the downpour, right?" I snicker.

A.G. chuckles, "That's what I like to see, but next time get Pepe to do it, he's your busser. And your presence is needed on the floor, regardless of training."

"Understood."

He taps my shoulder with his vanilla folder. "I'm not coming down on you Mike, so don't take it as such. I'm glad you noticed it, lord know how many times I to rush that garbage out back. But, just understand your job here is bigger than to worry about the trash overrunning. I'm sure you know that already and I also understand you're new, and the last time you were working in a restaurant, your job extended from server to taking out the trash," he says and smiles. "We're much different here, and with time, you'll see for yourself but save the grunt for the people we hire to do the grunt work, cool?"

I nod. "Cool."

"Okay then, I wanted to ask you, well, since you're training and you did such a phenomenal job with expo last night, you mind giving it another go tonight?"

"Sure, when do you want me to start?"

A.G. turns to Billie. "You all caught up with your tables?"

Billie gazes into the POS. "One sec, let me... ah, yeah we're caught up, and ready for the next wave right now."

A.G. strokes his beard. "Alright, well you should start printing whatever checks you can, so we can get those tables prepped. Uh, Michael since you're still in training, how about you take fifteen minutes to drive off and go smoke; since you're going to be in the back for the rest of the night, sound good?"

"Sound good to me," I reply.

A.G. smacks his folder. "Billie, get your ass to it. Michael, I'll see you in fifteen. Alright, gentlemen let's have a good night."

They both march out to the floor and I feel around the outside of my apron for the coke; it's still intact. For a moment, I thought Billie forgot to tie the bag in the midst of him trying to be slick. Can't even fathom the thought of all this blow found its way out the plastic and crumbled within the crevices of my apron. A man is occupying the urinal before I can enter, and we make eye contact. "How's it going?" he greets.

"I'm good, thanks for asking," I say and lock the stall door.

"My name's Kyle; I'm in all the time, you new here?"

"Nice to meet you, Kyle, I'm Michael; I just started training to be a server for when the patio opens up."

Kyle flushes and turns on the sink faucet. "That's awesome, man, you're going to make good money for sure. It gets crazy busy out there. Sure, you can tell by now. Hey, don't mind me asking but aren't you the kid that almost got arrested last night? I don't mind me prying but I was outside smoking a butt when it happened, was that you?"

I use one of the bills from Sage to pour some of the already broken up coke into. "Unfortunately, some drunken piece of shit called me a nigger then pushed me. I would've caught that fuck if it weren't for that cop. But, yeah, I'm sorry you had to see that."

"Yeah, man, the police in this town are a fucking joke, but as far that *drunken piece of shit*. His wife left him for a Black guy," he chuckles. "It's actuality kind of ironic, but don't mind him if you ever see him in here. He is always taking out his frustrations on the least suspecting, it's been that way since we were kids. And, last night you just happened to be that person."

"Wait… you know that son of a bitch? Do you know where I can find him?"

He cuts off the faucet then hits the paper dispenser twice. "Sorry, pal, can't do."

"Why? I'm not going to hurt him; I just want to find out why he would do such a thing."

Kyle approaches the stall. "He's my older brother, that's why I can't tell where to find him, and if you see him, which would be no time soon I'm assuming, I'd advise you to just let it go. I'm sorry for what Jack did to you; we don't come from a family that sees color. Like I said, he's been a headcase since we were kids. But you'll be alright, that type of shit happens to Black people all the time, right? ? I have a few Black friends, you should hear the shit we say to them. Anyway, I gotta close my tab but it was nice meeting you, Matt."

"Michael!" I shout.

"Matt, Mike same difference, right?" He jokes. "Well, gotta go but good luck, brother. You're going to make a lot of money here."

Once the door latch clicks; I start the process. The powder blends into the off-white color of the toilet tank, which makes it hard to see how far the flakes are spread out. So, I scrape up the angles of the base and settle for two fat lines. This will give me a second wind for sure. Need all the energy I can muster, only God knows what's only waiting for me when this break is over. Before rolling the bill; I crease it to fish out more cocaine. I manage to get what's already broken down, and there are a few tiny pebbles that seem small enough to pass through my nasal cavity.

Andrew Jackson turns into the perfect cylinder. Getting the first line up my right nostril is nearly impossible; switching to the left is my best bet. I breathe in so deep my chest starts to congest. There's only one thing that will work for sure, inhaling through my mouth, which I hate. It's harsh on the throat but the drip hits instantly. I suck through the twenty. Without any hesitation, the coke smacks my esophagus. I begin to dry-heave and then all of sudden, I regurgitate my mother's pasta directly into the toilet. I use toilet paper to wipe the corners of my mouth and to remove the specs of vomit from the seat.

"Pull it together, Mikey. This isn't amateur hour," I coach myself. The drip takes place and feels phenomenal. It's so electrifying what great blow will do. I've never thrown it up before but I've seen Tracie puke after a few lines more times than I count. Unfortunately, having a nose like mine is not useful at all, a dead giveaway to those who are suspecting. I get why people smoke it instead of sniffing it.

Whenever I start to come down, the airway in my nostrils becomes plugged with fluid and no matter how hard or how much I try to clear it, the snot comes back making it impossible. Then, if I'm lucky after the snot dries, I can breathe through my nose when I blow it. A nasally whistling sound happens when I can finally catch air and it discloses to anybody who is wise to drug abuse that I sniff way too much—better I shouldn't be sniffing it at all. But smoking coke only leads to smoking crack, at least that's what I assume. And from the looks of some of the addicts at the bus terminal and even worse downtown, they can't back from smoking crack; I don't think anyone does... Shit, I'm lucky not to be addicted to anything else; it could be worse. Hypothetically speaking, I could be in some back alley mainlining heroin, next thing you know my forearm veins collapse then I'm injecting a needle into my toes and hands. "Ah, shit," the sight alone sends chills through my spine.

Finally, an airwave through my right nostril gives way, I take the bill and rail the remaining line. I cough and almost spew again. My heart starts to kick so I put the seat down and sit. It's funny how things are playing out. It seems like the worst things get, the better the coke gets. Shit, maybe I'm just forming a habit. Who knows? On the contrary; I'm high and this drip is amazing. A cigarette would serve a great justice right about now. Before exiting; I run my middle finger across the tank, picking up any visible leftover residue then I rub it against my gums.

"Wait, wait, what the fuck am I doing?" I rush out the stall and hurry to the sink and I try my best to rinse out my mouth, but my body is telling me no matter what I do, there's no undoing the germs that I just put in my mouth. I gargle hot water for a few seconds, spit into the sink, repeat, and then hit the towel dispenser, removing any all evidence from the rim of my nostrils to the corners of my lips. Don't know if there's more shame in finding myself in here during work hours or sinking low enough to scrape up remnants of blow off that filthy toilet tank—and God only knows what kind germs I just put in my mouth. Oh man, after last night I thought it could get any worse—boy was I wrong. I shouldn't say that because after saying, 'things can get worse', they usually do... that's Murphy's Law for you.

After fetching a loose cigarette from my bag, I place myself downstairs, a few paces away from the entrance. This drip is paring great with each drag from the slow-burning tobacco and the menthol flavor just gives it such a nice finish every time I exhale. Man, I wish this feeling could stay, but it never does because it can't. It's not supposed to. That would defeat the purpose of doing it. The haste that cocaine gives, is always and forever fleeting. You would think one would come to the conclusion to hate drugs in its entirety after coming down from it. But, that's the gimmick. The high eludes the user then leaves them with a weary mind and body. Whatever poor bastard that choose to sniff blow, including myself, is left to crave and chase for more. What horrible evils drugs are to be brought upon the lost souls of this bitter word. God must've never forgiven Adam and Eve for that bullshit they pulled. As if The Good Lord himself were punishing us with his leftover vindictiveness he had for those two. *"Forgive me Father, for I know not what I do,"* I mutter into the rain.

"You talking to yourself, Newbie?" Jackie interjects.

I jump back, "WHAT THE FUCK?.... Where the hell did you come from?"

Jackie flips her hair then smirks. "From upstairs Sherlock." She laughs again then lights a smoke. "You didn't hear me walking out? I mean it is raining pretty hard so I guess it would nearly impossible to hear someone walking up."

I flick my butt into the downpour. "Fuck no, either the rain is too loud or you're just really light on your feet. Man, you scared the living shit out of me, again."

She hands me a cigarette. "Yeah, I can see that. Were you just praying out here?"

"Yeah, I do that sometimes, it's a great way to meditate in peace. Shit, to meditate in general. I used to do it when I worked downtown, it helped then maybe it'll help now. You got a light? I just used my last match."

"That's good, at least you're not ruining to the bathroom every twenty minutes, like some people we know here," she hints.

I set fire to my cigarette. "Can I ask you question. Jackie, if you don't mind?"

"Shoot."

"I'm not even remotely jealous of Bill, he's my friend after all. But in confidence, between you and me...what do you see in him? I mean, you're a pretty girl and all. And I watch the way some of the high-rollers you serve, and the way they look at you. You could have any one of those guys and be taken care of, not that I'm calling you a gold digger or anything like that, but you would be set. Given all that, I guess what I'm trying to say or ask is, why do you choose to fuck around with Billie? And it's none of my business or anyone else's for that matter; I'm not trying to offend you whatsoever. But WHAT THE FUCK do you see in that fat asshole?"

Jackie chuckles. "You're cute, kid. And no, I'm not offended in the slightest bit, you're asking an honest question and I respect it because you're the first to ever ask about what I see in him..." She inhales and exhales thinking. "You know, Newbie, when I moved here, I completely started my life and after my dad died—well after I buried the son of a bitch—I had a little bit of money left over from his insurance. I searched for places where a waitress could make good money, well at least better than what I was making back then, and mind you, I was severing at two restaurants at that time. But this place was the closest and most affordable.

At the same time, I was running away from my ex-boyfriend, who would get all liquored up and forget I wasn't a punching bag," she explains. "But yeah, as for Billie...we were just something that happened when it happened and I just rolled with it like I always do. Billie's sweet when he wants to be and smells good when he wants too."

We both laugh. "In all seriousness, he doesn't put his hands on me. His shit-talking, I can put up with; I'm used to it anyway, by now, it's kind of normal, if that makes sense.

After a long shift, when I don't feel like going home; whenever I just finished working a double and his flappy arms are holding me tight and I'm all snug and shit…and right before I pass out on his fat stomach, there's this moment that I can't really put into words but all I know is, I just-I just feel safe, you know."

I stare. "Damn Jackie, that's intense. I'm sor—"

"It's cool newbie. I'm kinda glad you asked. Shit, I've been here for a little over two years now and not even my roommate has heard as much as I just told you, let alone Billie or the rest of those clowns upstairs," she says and ashes.

"It stays between us; I just want you to know that."

"I know, Newbie, I trust you. Remember when we first met, and I had to find out later that night after our shift that you're friends with the guy I'm fucking. I know you'll keep your lips shut, you don't like to boast, I don't know if that's a good thing or a bad thing, all I can say is, I like that about you."

"You're too much sometimes, Boss Lady. But thanks, I guess." I inhale and exhale giving that some space then add, "Oh yeah, I wanted to ask you how that conversation with Tina went. Did she realize she was out of order?"

She exhales then taps her cigarette. "Oh shit, I totally forgot about that. Don't mind her at all. Half the time she's just blowing hot air, and the other half she's blowing her nose. Between you and me, Newbie, she actually wants your dick."

I gasp. "Shut up! That cunt? Yeah, the fuck right, good one Boss Lady, good one."

"No, kid, I'm serious. You gotta understand, she's from a country where they have little to no people of color. And the day after you trained with her, she couldn't stop talking about you. I guess foreigners have a weird way of showing interest."

"You don't say."

"Listen, Newbie, just keep doing your thing as far as your job goes. That chubby Dane is mad that she can't have you. So, to make herself feel better, she's going to treat you like you're less than shit in a toilet. Till she gets her way or you quit, you're going to have to develop some tough skin, and pretty quick."

I exhale my disgust. "Are you serious? Tell me you're not serious..."

Jackie laughs. "I'm just fucking with, Newbie, don't quit your job because of some thirsty bitch. Remember, Tina doesn't sign your checks." She puts her smoke on the arm railing and tosses it into the lot.

I nod and hawk up a loogie then expel it into the downpour. The drip hits again but this time, at full force. As I lick my chapped lips, it's almost as they're not even there. The only sense of taste I have is from that grade-a cocaine, I just railed. I could go for another cigarette better yet, a stiff drink to wash down the tobacco.

"Hey, you got that on you right?" Jackie asks.

"Uh. Yeah, I do," I reach inside of my apron and retrieve the coke. "Here, you go. Hey, I know I sound like a fucking mooch right now—I promise I'm not—but you wouldn't happen to have another cigarette, one you could spare?"

"Yup, you're pretty banged up huh, Newbie?" She laughs the passes me a Marlboro Light.

"Hell yeah, this shit is really good. You're about to rail a few?" I light the cigarette.

She starts toward the entrance. "You know it. After that smoke, you're back on the floor—I mean expo, right?"

I blow smoke and answer, "You bet."

Jackie smiles. "Nice, it's going to be another shit show so enjoy that smoke as much as you can 'cause there are no breaks when you get to that window." She forces the door to close, then pops back out. "Oh, A.G. told me to tell you, he had to run to C.J's for something. You're cool with being up there by yourself?"

I nod.

"Alright, Newbie, when you finish that we'll be knee-deep in the trenches. Make sure you wash your hands good."

"For sure." I watch Jackie run back up the stairs; I try to savor the last drags before the drip subsides. At least I'm alert and present. The hangover I had coming in has passed, maybe that's why I threw up. If I wasn't drunk; I sure as hell felt like it. I wish I could upchuck anxiety. The cigarette incinerates pass the filter and burns the tip of my index finger then falls into a puddle. The rain finally gives way to the sun as the drops disappear, and the onyx clouds vanish into the horizon. For a brief moment, I feel invincible. Strong enough to push through, strong enough to see this through.

GISELLE'S AMBITION

The last rush was fucking terrible; I sent two appetizers to the wrong table. And, as luck would have it while running a baked chicken entree for Tina; I crashed right into her exiting the kitchen. It's quite ironic because the order was for her. As Murphy's Law puts it: anything that could go wrong did go wrong. As if there was this looming air of anxiety that seeped in and robbed everyone's ability to focus (either that or the coke was wearing off, maybe a combination of both). Pepe managed to split his thumb open on broken glass, I ended up puking in the trash after he ran into the kitchen with blood squirting all over the place. Forgot to mention I'm squeamish on my application. Jackie got so overwhelmed, I'm almost certain she found time to break down and cry in the ladies' room because when she came back to expo, her eyes were all bloodshot. I even noticed she removed her eyeshadow, I'm assuming it was the tears that ruined it. Yup, safe to say tonight has been a total shit-show. I'm more than elated it's finally winding down.

After breaking down the expo station and helping Pepe buss and clean tables, I somehow managed to get Jose to wash three trays of silverware before he started to scrub the pots and pans. I remember Billie saying, "Getting Jose to wash all the cutlery before dishes and pots is a total waste of time" luckily for me, I'm not Billie. There's no waiting around tonight. Billie's folding napkins, I'm wiping the cutlery, and Tina is stocking all server stations. Everyone appears to be broken but we all do what's needed and we do it in silence. One by one, I hear guests cheering Giselle, "goodnight" as they exit. Her heels clomp around the hostess stand and into the dining room. I poke my head around the server station and don't see her. All of sudden, someone's hands cover my eyes. "Get your fake sick hands off me," I command. "You don't want to sneak up on someone while they're wielding a knife."

Giselle swings me around. "Boy, please, you're cleaning forks and some dull ass steak knives. Who the fuck do you think you're going to hurt with that, huh?"

"Shit, if I'm lucky, I'll hurt you," I say with a grin.

She throws her weight into my chest. "Don't threaten me with a good time."

"That was good."

"I know," she says. "What are you doing after they cut you loose?"

"Shit, I don't know. What are you doing? Did you get cut?"

"Yup, A.G, said I could leave after the menus are cleaned and guess what... they're clean."

I point to the left of the sink. "Oh yeah, what about those?"

Giselle gasps. "Shut up, I'm done. I had enough of this fucking place," she chuckles and pushes my shoulder. "Anyway, you wanna grab a couple of drinks at C.J's, after you wrap up?"

"Hell yeah, might be more than a couple, tonight was brutal." I grab more forks.

"What... tell me about it. I got asked to help with bussing. Ugh."

"So, what's wrongs with that?"

Giselle drops her jaw. "Excuse me, what's wrong with that? Weathers, you're not stupid—well I hope you're not that stupid, but do you see the nails?" She flashes her hands.

"Yeah, so..."

"So? You are stupid, and just when I thought you had some wits about you. Well, Weathers, you're a hockey jock, but let me add that they look great and Ling Ling did a wonderful job. I can't fuck the gel up by bussing tables, that's just out."

I heckle her. "Is that your nail designer's name? *Ling Ling?*"

"No... well, I don't think so but that's what I call her."

"You call her that to her face?"

"Hell no. I call her Ling Ling in my head stupid, that would be racist."

I shake my head. "Wait... By you calling...or saying it in your head...you're too funny G."

"Shut up, let me get to these menus so I can get drunk already. Find me in the front when you're ready."

"Will do, Ma'am."

She frowns, "Now you got jokes, I'm not a ma'am.

"You're a woman, right?"

"You wanna see my dick?"

"Well, that would be unfortunate."

She slaps my bicep. "Shut up."

"Nah, but for real. My dad was a marine so everything growing up was, yes ma'am, no ma'am, you get what I'm saying? It's a sign of respect, you know." I shrug.

"Um, I get it, and it's really respectable coming from a young Black man, but that 'ma'am' shit just makes me feel like I should be drinking unsweetened ice tea and playing bridge. I just feel like my grandmother."

"That's far from my intent, Ma'am."

She pinches my face. "You need to quit while you're ahead,

Weathers. Anyway, meet me in the front whenever they let you go."
Giselle's hips switch as she stomps her way back to the front. Every time
her heels smack the floor tiles, her buttocks jiggle with every step; her
perfect figure along with her full thighs are too much for the average man
to bare witness to. Everything about her frame seems so inviting yet, so
untamed; as if she were a lioness grazing under the shade—I would have
to image, I would be helpless pray if we were in confines of the Serengeti.
It should be a sin against God to be so beautiful; I would spend an entire
eternity in hell to be considered an afterthought. I'm not too proud of my
lust, but I'll ask for forgiveness later.

"Yo, Newbie!" Jackie shouts.

"Ye-yeah, what's going on Boss lady, what do you need?"

She slaps my back. "Geez, dude stop staring so hard, she's ain't going
anywhere."

"What's with everyone and the jokes today."

"What are you talking about?"

"Nothing, just some silly shit."

"Whatever... anyway, here you go." Jackie hands over a tip envelope.

"Thanks, Boss Lady."

"You got it, Newbie, you did good tonight. A.G. put an extra twenty
in there."

"For what?"

"I have no idea, Newbie, he just told me to tell you that that's an
extra twenty there He gave it to you, and you got it which means you
deserve it. If you don't want it, shit, I'll take it."

"Again, with the jokes," I smile.

"I could've done stand up but unfortunately I'm here with you,'" she
chuckles. "When you're finished with all that shit you can get out of here;

I'll be downstairs doing inventory if anyone needs me."

"No doubt, in case I don't see you, have a good night Boss Lady."

Before walking off she turns. "What was good about it?"

"You know, comedy could've been your calling, but here you're here with me."

Jackie yells, "Say's you. Later, kid!"

I shout back, "Later!"

Billie struts over as he drops a settled check on table 17. He begins to collect forks and knives as he says, "Good job on the silverware, Farrakhan. Usually, I got to run them back through the washer again, but you did a good job if I say so myself..."

"Thanks, Bill, I guess that means a lot."

He starts rolling silverware. "No doubt, but yo, I'm crashing hard my nigga, I killed the rest of what I had about an hour and a half ago, you know that was supposed to be my second wind. Don't know how I'm gonna push through, I know you feel like shit."

"You know for a second; I did, but after some espresso; I perked up really quick, why don't you have one, it'll help."

"Get the fuck outta here...espresso," he grunts. "You probably took some coke out and saved it for later. You holding out nigga? You can't pull that spook shit with me, my nigga. I know the game."

"Yeah right...you should be the one to talk." I grab a few napkins and helped roll.

"Fuck do you mean by that? I get it, Farrakhan, I get it, you're still making love to your hand when you go home at night. So, you need coke to get over your urges. You don't gotta steal man, just ask. You living up to the stereotype," he heckles.

"Shit, you might be right. I guess it takes a cokehead, to know a cokehead."

"Oh yeah?"

"Shut the fuck up and finish rolling this bullshit silverware." I take two handfuls of rollups and jam them into the bin. "See Bill, it's just that easy."

Billie shoots a snot rocket into the trash. "Whoa, needed to get that out. Anyway, what you doing after this Farrakhan?"

"I don't know, probably going home, I need to catch up on some sleep, BAD."

"Welcome to the club Farrakhan."

"Nope, I'm good on that membership," I stuff down more rollups.

"Too late nigga, you've already been initiated, congrats."

"You're a real piece of work, Bill, just don't quit your day job man."

Out of nowhere, Tina squeezes her wide body in between Billie and I, and throws to-go containers under the sink and forces Billie out of her way to get to the staff cabinet, then hanks out her bag. "Later Bill, I'll see you at your house," she says.

Billie stops and turns. "I know you see us doing rollups, and I know you're not fixed to walk out that door without doing any."

"Hell no, I restocked everything and cleaned both coffee pots, fuck you. I'm outta here." She throws her bag around her shoulder and storms into the bar.

Billie mutters, "Fucking cunt."

Tina redirects and marches back. "What'd you say, Newbie?"

"I didn't say shit," I reply.

"You fucking lie, you did say something, you called me a cunt."

"Whoa, you're outta fucking line bitch!" Billie shouts. "It was me who said it, now get your wobbly ass out of here before I call immigration."

"Fuck you, Bill, you piece of shit—I wish you would shut your fat mouth for once."

"You should be the one to talk. You're a sandwich away from being just as big as me. Go P.M.S. somewhere else, you fucking hobbit."

Tina storms out of the restaurant. "I'm sick of her shit, what a fucking cunt. I hope she gets fucking deported, she just wanted to pick a fight to give her a reason not to do rollups. She knows good and well I called her a cunt and still, she found a way to attack you. Ay, Mike my bad man."

"Well, that's a first."

"What is?"

"You apologizing."

"My nigga, that was all my fault but fuck her." He throws the entire tray of cutlery.

"Whoa-whoa-whoa, chill the fuck out man! Tina isn't worth losing your shit over, not to mention throwing silverware all over the place. Believe me, I've seen worse."

"What do you mean? You're not talking about last night, 'cause that was a whole nigga that pushed you and—"

"You know what, just forget it, just know there are people far worse out there. Come on, I'll help you pick this shit up." I pat him on the back and use my feet to shuffle the silverware to one pile.

Billie tugs my shirt. "You know, don't even bother, I got this. You got some pussy waiting for you, and besides I'm shocked you even showed your face after what happened to you last night, you got balls, Farrakhan, you got balls."

"I don't know about that," I chuckle. "Are you sure you don't want me to stay? You don't have to feel sorry for me."

"Nah, my nigga, get the fuck outta here, I got this."

"Alright man if you don't hear from me tonight, I'll see you tomorrow." We shake and embrace each other.

"Alright, Farrakhan make sure to get a few pumps in for me when you get in that later."

"If that were to happen, which it won't, what makes you think I'll be thinking about you?"

"It's only right, you gotta think about your homies," he chuckles. "Ay, get the fuck outta here."

We wave each other off as I make my way to the entrance. Giselle is seated to the side of the platform with her face buried in her phone. I lightly smack her device upwards.

"Hey, you break it, you buy it," she scolds.

"You ready to go?"

"Yeah, let's blow this popsicle joint."

Giselle trails as I lead out the door. Soon as we touch the sidewalk, she fires up two cigarettes and hands one over. "What was all that commotion in the back?" she asks.

"What commotion?" I exhale.

"Tina and Billie. They were arguing, weren't they?"

"Oh, that commotion. It was just Billie coming at her for leaving and not doing any silverware, nothing crazy, just some bullshit between the two, that's it."

She exhales. "There's more to it than that, I know there is. I've only known you for a couple of days, so get it...the business of telling fibs. Now, what really happened, Weathers?"

"Basically, Tina was asked to help with rollups and she didn't feel inclined to, Billie called her a cunt and she flipped out."

As we turn on Canal, Giselle bursts into laughter. "No the fuck he didn't. That's fucking crazy, I swear that motherfucker Billie does the most and gets away with it. He's so fucking disrespectful it's not even funny. Doesn't he know that's the worst thing you can call a woman."

I smirk, "apparently not, that's the second time I seen him do it."

"Goddamn, you know; I'm not surprised in the slightest bit. Since I've been working there, I've learned that cokeheads have a horrible temperament. She wasn't talking to you when she yelled out Monkey."

I clear my throat. "She was talking to Billie. Uh, I'll be damned if that bitch were to call me a monkey." We stop at the crosswalk; a few cars pass and we make our way across. I take her hand as she hikes up the curb; she leads the way to the side of the building. I take one more drag and discard it into the sewer drain.

She exhales and ashes. "I know that's right, these crackers have no fucking sense, especially that fucking Billie. He swears he's Blacker than anyone who is actually Black, can you believe that?…and he's always saying nigga, my nigga this, my nigga that. I cringe every time I hear it."

"You never confronted him about it?"

She breathes in the last of the smoke then flicks it into the street and explains. "When I started getting comfortable being the hostess, so did he—a little too comfortable. I nipped that shit right the in the bud, but when I hear how he talks with Tina or any of the other staff, I just brush it off, as long as he doesn't bring that shit this way; I'm good or least pretend to be." Giselle presses her body against mine as I lean on the brick wall.

"You never went to upper management about it?"

"Did you go to your higher-ups when someone said some racist shit to you that made you feel uncomfortable?"

I look away.

Giselle snatches my face. "Exactly, and besides who the fuck is going to care? Billie's fucking the assistant manager and A.G. looks like he's never heard of racism. And who am I to get in the way of the money? They're giving it away for nothing. I'm pretty sure I'm the highest-paid hostess in this town. So yeah, once you get settled you don't have put up with Billie's bullshit, just learn what's useful and forget the rest... Oh yeah, and play the house nigga role for this check, these crackers love a well-behaved nigga, and you know how to play it, Weathers."

"As I should..."

She pecks my lips. "You have no choice but too."

"Can I ask you something?"

Giselle nods.

"Take a look at people smoking in front of the entrance. How come we smoke over here when people are smoking right outside the door?"

"Shit, Weathers, you still don't get it, huh?"

I smirk. "Apparently not."

"You're not stupid but you play dumb too much. Isn't it obvious?"

"What is?"

Giselle frowns. "They're white."

"So what, just cause they're smoking in front that means we can't? Who the fuck wrote that law? This isn't 1950; I don't see any 'Whites Only' sign? That's not right."

"Listen, Weathers, I just enjoy the discount and stay out the way. That's how things work here. And besides, you know white people get fucking weird during hockey season and shit. They wanna be all in your face 'cause their team won a game. They get a little liquor in em' and start to feel brave enough to drop Black jokes and shit. Fuck em' let's get drunk." With her arm wrapped around mine, we enter C.J's. It's more

186

crowded than the last time. Keith is running a full bar. We pick a two-top table just a little passed the bar. She takes her seat first.

"What are you drinking? Remy and Coke?" I ask.

"Wow, Weathers, good memory and yeah, I am."

"I know, be right back." The fray of Ranger jerseys it makes it extremely hard to maneuver. When I finally reach the bar, Keith is juddering a cocktail in an upwards motion. I watch as he scoops ice into the glass. With confidence, he turns from the drink while the alcohol is pouring over the cubes to look at the TV above the front entrance. Without anyone else paying attention; I glance up and become a little tense after realizing the Bruins now have control over the puck, then turn back to Keith. I'm not sure what he's making but it looks tasteful. He finishes the beverage off with a lemon peel then hands it over to a gentleman who then passes it off to a lady. He then marches past and signals that he sees me. He bends down to the beer fridge and grabs three IPA's, cracks them with a flat bottle opener, and gives them to the same gentleman, who then passes the cans to two other men as one of them shouts, "Go Rangers!!" It causes a chain reaction, most of the customers even Keith yell, and cheer. I crack a smile.

Keith trots over and grins. "Mikey, what's going on, kid? How they are treating you down the street?"

I extend my hand and smirk. "Good man, good. Everything is going as it should, I only got two days of training left, then it's official."

"Attaboy, what can I get you?"

"Ah, Giselle wants her usual and I'm going to go with gin and tonic. House liquor, please."

"You guys just getting out?" he asks.

I turn to the big screen. "Yeah, we just got out."

187

"You know, Mikey boy, I think she likes you."

"What's not to like?"

"Nice... When your drinks are ready, I'll walk em' over, you wanna start a tab?"

"Sure, you need a card?"

"If you were Billie or Tina, sure, but you're good here man. Your drinks will be right up, Mike."

"Thanks, Keith. We're right over there."

Giselle's dusting her cheeks as I return and adjust my wobbly chair. It's funny, even when she's self-absorbed this girl is absolutely breathtaking. The structure of her cheekbones shines perfectly off the candlelight and her lip-gloss burnishes magnificently as she smacks her lips together. "Keith said he'll bring over our drinks."

Giselle shoves her makeup back into her purse. "Great... Ugh, I fucking hate hockey. Is this shit almost over."

"Five minutes left in the third. And the game is tied. Might go to sudden death."

"What the fuck is a sudden death, are they about to kill each other or something?"

"Two things can happen in the next fifteen minutes. First, you'll see some very happy, loud drunk white people. Second, some very angry drunk white people but less loud."

"So we still have to deal with drunk white people."

I heckle her, "You wanted to come here."

"Eh, Keith takes good care of me and unlike Second House the food isn't so greasy and fattening and after the night we just had I need something to take the edge off and fast. So, this is where I come to maximize my unwind time," she grins. "Are you hungry?" She then reaches over to the next table and grabs the menu standing between the salt and pepper shakers.

"I could eat." For a quick second, I take my attention off Giselle and glance back at the flat-screen above the entrance and it's a little under four minutes left and the Rangers are controlling the puck. They're now in the powerplay as I spot Keith rushing over with our drinks.

"Here you guys, go," he says and sets them down with coasters underneath, and then plants a kiss on the side of Giselle's face. "I would stay and catch up guys, but we got a packed house tonight."

"Yeah-yeah, we know you got better things to do, we're not as cool as them," Giselle smiles. "Keith baby, but can you slow down for a second and put in a small cheese pizza and an order of well-done fries for us, pretty please," she begs and bats her eyes.

"Perfect timing. The kitchen closes in five. Anything else guys? And even if they were closing, how could I so no to such a beautiful face?"

"Thank you, Keith baby."

"Cool, one small cheese pie and well-done fries coming up." Keith speeds back to the bar. Giselle and I take our drinks and cheer. She takes the first sip.

"Did you see your girlfriend tonight? She came in with those unruly ass bitches again."

"What the hell are you talking about and who the hell are you talking about?"

Giselle presses the lime garnish. "You know what and who I'm talking about," she laughs.

I slap the edge of the table and grin. "Oh, you're funny."

She laughs harder. "I am, I am... She left her number again and gave me ten dollars to make sure you got it this time. For some reason, she doesn't think I gave it to you the last time. Fuck it, I'm ten dollars richer."

I mix the ice around and dump my straw onto the table. "So, where's the number now?"

"You don't need it."

"Why would you assume that."

She stares.

"I like that."

"I know." She brushes her foot against my leg and keeps it there. "That woman is thirsty for some Black dick. So thirsty, I have no doubt in my mind she would pay for it, I wouldn't be surprised if she has already."

"You think she's thirsty?" I turn to the game.

"Hell yeah, you know how privileged white women give it up. They fuck Black men just to piss off their cracker ass daddy. Then again, Black men look at white girls like trophy prizes and get excited when they pump out a baby just so they can have a confused ass kid with good hair and start a whole new gene pool of good hair having ass babies. I don't know who's worse, White Women or Black Men."

"That's interesting, I never heard of that before—I mean, I have but not how you just put it into perspective like that. It resonates."

Giselle sips as her eye widen. "Wow, Weathers, I'm surprised..."

"By what?"

"You?" She finishes the rest of her drink.

"With..."

"When you came out with me the other night when; I was surprised. To be honest, you're cute and all but I thought you were into the Becky's."

"What's a *Becky*?"

"A White girl, stupid."

I turn back to the Big Screen. "That's a wild assumption to make and you don't even know me or what I'm into. I've never really been bias on who I'm into. I was brought up to think, if we like each other than we like each other, right?" I chug the rest of my drink.

"Right, but understand the culture we come from. Black men are taught from infants to despise their counterparts. Anywhere you go in this world, Weathers, anti-blackness is universal. My first thought of you, when we met and the moment I heard you speak, I thought you were mimicking a white person. But, the fact you're here with me now, proves me wrong. You weren't acting that day and I hope you aren't acting now; but going back to when Tina introduced you to me, you were just being yourself and that's what I like about you the most. You're different."

"Wow Giselle, thank you, I guess. You know, I was attracted to you from the first time I laid eyes on you. I was so relieved to see another Black person. The only other people of color at my last job were the janitors, but still, I talked to them every chance I got. I felt so alone back then but here, right now with you, it washes away any loneliness that I felt at LBS." We stare for a moment then embrace each other's lips. We've kissed before but for some reason, this feels like the first time. I press back in my seat. "You want another drink?" I ask.

"Sure."

"Okay, I'll be right back." Before I can get up, she pulls on my arm and drags me in for another lip lock. "What was that for?" I smile.

Giselle begins to blush. "'Like what your girlfriend said, you got nice teeth."

"You're a piece of work you know that?"

She giggles, "Get our drinks, Teeth Man."

As I try to get to Keith, it's a constant motion of dodging and sidestepping the anxious crowd; I somehow manage to glide my way to the middle of the bar and spot Keith cracking the tops to a few Bud Lights. When he finally becomes aware of my presence; I signal for another round. He replies with a thump's up. Before leaving; I check the big screen. The game is down to fifty seconds with a timeout called by the Bruins before it goes to a commercial break; I don't know why but it seems harder getting back to our table than it was getting to the bar. Soon as I departed from Keith, some woman, who looked as if she was on the wrong side of thirty-five, spilled her entire martini on my shoes. My feet were dry for about an hour and soon as I start to feel comfortable, BOOM. My toes go back to being uncomfortably damp; not to mention my shoes squeaking with every step. Good God, I hope Giselle doesn't notice, well she didn't notice it on our way over here and it's quite loud so hopefully, she won't think anything of it.

I return to my seat. "Awesome, the foods here."

"Yup." Giselle wastes no time separating a slice but not before drenching it in grated parmesan. She places two pieces on her side plate, picks one up, and delivers heavy blows to cool it. Once she's satisfied with the temperature, she shoves nearly half it in her mouth. Her mouth becomes a greasy, cheesy mess. Strangely enough, watching her stuff her face, she's still beautiful.

I start pulling apart a slice. "How is it?"

With a mouth-full, she nods.

"Good." The cheese doesn't seem so hot as Giselle made it out to look; I lightly blow on the cheesy surface and to my surprise, my first attempt to bite into it torches the shit out of my tongue. As a painful reaction; the slice falls from my grip and onto the table, missing the plate completely.

Giselle laughs uncontrollably. "See, that's what you fucking get. You know that shit was piping hot and didn't blow on it enough, you could've let that shit cool off first but nooooo," she continues to howl. I reach for a napkin and wipe the corners of my mouth then pat my tongue thinking it will help subside the pain. "You know what, fuck you and this damn pizza," I chuckle. "That shit burned the fuck out of me."

We both bust out in hilarity. I chuck a fry at her face, and she returns the gesture. Our amusement gets louder than the speakers projecting the game and constant bar chatter, and our behavior causes for some of the fans and waitstaff to stare. Amid our hysteria, Keith arrives with our next round.

He serves up a smile with our drinks. "What's so funny guys, I did miss something?"

Giselle is laughing still. "The hockey star just burned the shit outta his tonged," she continues to heckle.

Keith stares and smirks. "Come on, Mikey what the hell you doing? You're supposed to fold the slice, blow on it for about ten seconds, then bite into it, come on." I remove the slice off the table in order from him to wipe away the grease and he pats my back before scurrying off to the bar.

Giselle snickers. "You're a mess.".

"Tell me something I don't know." There's barely any heat coming from the slice as I bite into it, the taste alone washes away my previous embarrassment.

"There you go, good job," Giselle cries.

Still chewing I say, "Fuck you."

"Aww, you're mad, 'cause I laughed at you," she says and pinches my cheeks.

"That wasn't funny, that shit really burned the fuck out of my mouth."

"Your ass should've known better." She presses tight on the lime, pokes it to the bottom of the glass then sips.

"I can't even be mad, you're exactly right." I remove the straw from my drink. As I take in a mouthful of liquor; I let a few ice-cubes fall into my mouth, and bite down on them to take my mind off the lingering pain. We enjoy your food for a moment then out of nowhere, loud cheers and yells ring throughout the bar. Everyone is full of joy and complete strangers embrace each other with hugs and the type of high-fives that look as if they would cause some minor pain after contact.

CJ's is in a frenzy. I glance at the big screen. The score is 3-4 Rangers over the Bruins. Memories of me being on the ice reappear; the feeling of winning division games and rejoicing with my teammates over our hard-fought victory, and with me leading us into battle and drawing first blood, or putting the icing on the cake to secure a win. Ah, man what a feeling, what times they were.

It's funny, except for the opposing team, no one ever judged or ridiculed me when I was on that ice, no matter who we played, my teammates always reminded me I was worthy of skating on the same patch of ice. Most of my teammates saw me as one of them. As a brother, friend, a teammate, and the best of all, their leader.

And, the ones that didn't, hardly got any playing time. It's funny how sports can bring people from all different walks of life together.

"What's going on? Why are they all hugging each other? Did

somebody win?" Giselle questions.

"Yup, big win in a big situation, The Rangers got the win." I polish off my drink.

"White people are too much when it comes to this hockey shit. I can't tell you how many fights I've seen over this. Shit, sports in general. Why are men so stupid?"

"I'm not surprised. Hockey is one sport, they let the players fight so the fans feel encouraged to follow suit. And, for that comment you just made about men being stupid... you might be right." The fries have lost their warmth; I eat one anyway.

Giselle smirks. "See, I knew you were smart. But no really, no wonder white people go ape shit for it, especially if all they do is throw the players in a box after a scrap... Did you ever get into fights when you played?" She sucks the straw, depleting the rest of her drink.

"Sure, I did. But I was also targeted a lot because of my rank and the color of my skin. So, it was kind of expected in every game to fight, no I couldn't back down. Some games were so brutal and some games I left without a scratch. It's the territory that comes with the sport especially if you're ranked high in the state, at least that what my parents would say..."

"How'd you get into playing hockey, anyway, isn't that for white people?"

"My dad played. He wasn't as good at it as I was but he wanted me to do something he liked doing as a kid, so he introduced me to it and I liked it. It was kind of fun when I look back on it."

Giselle stabs the ice in her drink. "That's pretty dope, you know I don't even know how to ice skate. Can't even rollerblade properly without falling on my butt."

"How come?"

"Nobody in my family knows how to fucking skate, let alone skate on ice," she laughs, "and now that I think about it, I don't think my mom or dad knows how to rollerblade so learning to skate was definitely out of the question growing up. I could hear my mom right now, fuck you wanna skate for,? That's white people shit. You know, I still have my first pair of rollerblades I got for Christmas a few years back.

I'm assuming they still fit because my foot size hasn't grown at all. But it's funny, I asked for rollerblades knowing I couldn't skate for shit, and I remember my dad saying, 'What the hell you want rollerblades for? You can't skate,'" she laughs, "but he still got them for me anyway."

"You know, if you want or whatever, I could teach you sometime."

"Really... I would like that."

"No doubt. Then I could finally get a laugh out of you busting your ass after you let me burn the shit out of my mouth."

"See, you're already going in with foul intentions on the offer to teach, how does someone do that? That's fucked up, Weathers. No one told you to burn your fucking mouth."

"It would be my pleasure to teach you how to skate and it would also be my pleasure to watch you bust your ass."

She heaves a fry at my face. "See and that's why Black people can never stick together. Always hating on the next person's progress. You're foul."

"You know, you're so aware of who are, and I dig that. I don't want to sound dumb by asking you this, but how did you get like that?"

"Well, my grandparents are former Black Panthers, on my father's side. Basically, the trickle-down effect. What they taught him, he taught me."

I clench my glass. "That's deep."

"I guess, unlike any other five-year-old, I was well aware of racism. I remember my father took my family out to this five-star restaurant, well I don't know about five-star but the shit was really nice. I was crazy excited to be there, being five years old and all. There were nice white tablecloths over every table and the crystal glasses. It made me feel like a Disney princess. I thought we were royalty or some shit. And, I remember after we got sat, our waiter came back and asked if we could pay for food ahead of time."

I gasp. "You're kidding."

"Nope, my dad flipped his shit and dragged us the fuck outta there not before knocking the entire table setting over."

"And that was my first experience with racism, in a fucking restaurant. And the irony about it is, some odd nineteen later, I end up working in one. If you can't beat em' join em right," Giselle says and grabs another slice.

"Still, that's fucked up, it's disgusting how people treat us. And for what? We should be afraid of them."

"No, we shouldn't, Michael, don't you ever say that. We come from kings and queens. Here, we were slaves but on the other side of the ocean, we come from greatness."

I run my finger through a paper napkin. "Greatness, huh?"

Giselle stares. "Yeah, greatness." The bar crowd begins to die down.

"You want another drink?" I ask.

She shrugs. "Why not."

From my seat, I'm able to signal Keith our final round and the check and turn back to Giselle, "What do you mean by greatness?"

"The reason why Blacks excel at anything we put our minds too is in our DNA. Look at Michael Jordan, Tiger Woods. Shit, even yourself, Weathers. You think, 'cause of hard work and practice you just happened to be good at hockey?"

"Well, yeah."

"Yeah, that may be a part of it, but your DNA structure allows you to be faster and stronger than all those white kids you played against. That's why you had to fight so much. Whether they wanted to admit it or not, they knew the minute you put on those skates and stepped on that ice... you could be better than them, and news flash, Weathers... you were."

"Interesting."

"Interesting," she echoes. "I'm sure your parents have told you about your history and where your ancestors come from, haven't they?"

"For the most part they never really touched on the topic, aside from my own research; I did a lot of reading about Black leaders, like Garvey and Farrakhan, just to name a few, outside of MLK."

Giselle tilts her head back, "Garvey and Farrakhan huh? Intense, there maybe be some substance to you yet, Weathers."

"Well, a lot of stems from my parents bei—"

Keith abruptly interjects while setting our drinks down, "How bout' those Rangers kid? Clinching the playoffs by a hair. That game was tight, but we got the win."

"What do you mean Keith, I'm a Bruins fan, Beantown baby, you know what it is," I grin.

His jaw drops. "You're kidding right, please tell me you're kidding."

"Of course, I'm kidding. You should've seen your face just now, you looked like a gift-less kid on Christmas. Holy shit, you were about to cry, weren't you?"

"Ah dude, I was ready to kick you the fuck out."

"I bet, I know Giselle can't stand hockey, but you want to do a victory shot?

"Hell yeah, with a hockey legend as yourself and with a huge Ranger win tonight, it would be my honor. What we drinking?"

"Jameo?"

He claps. "Coming right up. You're going to have one too right, G?"

Giselle sighs, "Sure, why not."

"Nice." Keith speeds behind the bar, yanks the Jameson from the second shelf, and grabs three shot glasses then bolts back. He places the glasses down and pours till the rims overflow. We raise our shot. "To the Bruins, let's hope they have the longest bus ride of their lives back to Beantown," he shouts.

"To a long bus ride home," I repeat. Our glasses chime before we throw the shots back.

Keith slithers a bit. "Ahh, good choice, Mikey. I always forget how straight Jameson burns on the way down, it's the perfect thing to enjoy after a big win or drown in after a bitter loss." He begins to clear the side plates, and pizza tray, only to leave the table with glassware, "Ay, Mikey boy, you ever think about joining the league I was talking about the other night? I was telling some of the boys about you the other day and they—I mean we would love to have you on the ice with us, give us a real chance when January swings around, what you do you think?"

"I still have to give it some more thought, you know. To be honest with you Keith, I been so busy at Second House. I haven't even had time to even think anything. But you know what, maybe when the season comes around; I can check out a practice or two and see what you guys got going on. How does that sound?"

"Hey, that's better than no."

"Cool, you know what, I'll follow you back to the bar with the rest of these empties, that way you don't have to haul yourself all the way back over here to clean up."

"Thanks, man, I really appreciate it." As I follow Keith to the bar; the lingering Ranger fans are still in high cheers. Making my way to Giselle is much easier this time around and every time I come back to the table, her beauty shines brighter than before and her body becomes more and more enticing. Yup, the booze is definitely kicking in, better cool my jets. But it's nearly impossible not to be engulfed by her full thighs and the plumpness of her hips as her butt overlaps the seat. Her whole being is nothing short of magnificent.

"Oh my God, what the fuck was that shot you got us drinking? That shit is disgusting and it burns way too much." Giselle coughs.

"Jameson. Why? You don't like it?

"It would go great with ginger-ale or sprite even, but straight, hell no. That shit has crazy white boy written all over it."

"You think?"

"Hell yeah, maybe that's what that cracker who called you a nigger last night was drinking before he put his hand on you. Man, I wish that motherfucker did that while I was there, I would've had my dad to teach him a valuable lesson in minding his manners, fucking bitch ass cracker."

I rub my face and pause for a moment. "How'd you find out about that?"

Giselle's clicks her nails against her glass. "Come on Weathers, you've worked in restaurants before, you know everybody gossips like it's in high-school all over again. I'm pretty sure that's what any job is like, more-so hospitality work."

My fingers lock the under table. "Who told you?"

"Does it matter?"

"Well for me, it kind of does, I won't say anything."

She shrugs. "You will, but I don't care, she's a bitch anyway. Tina told me and made it seem like it was the funniest thing that ever happened, and she wasn't even there."

My foot starts to tap against the base of the table, "You're right, she didn't work yesterday, so that means either Jackie or Billie said something. Shit, even A.G. could've told her."

"Told you, like fucking freshman year all over again."

We sit in silence. This moment of awkwardness is more than unsettling. I resort to the salt and pepper shaker and pretend to play a game of chess and to no surprise; I'm losing. "Well, now that I'm aware that you know what happened last night, did anyone tell you how I chased the son of bitch and how scared he was?"

"No, but she did say how A.G. pleaded with some pig bitch not to arrest you. And, for what? You did nothing wrong. I bet she didn't even radio for the racist fuck that pushed you. Did she?"

"That motherfucker was fast, shit." We both chuckle and the moment of amusement kills the embarrassment that washed over me. "You ready to get out of here?"

Giselle reaches for the check. "Sure, I got this one."

"No, no. I got the bill." I try and tug the checkbook out of her grasp. She then snatches it back.

"Like I said, I got this," she scolds.

"Shit, you got it."

"You damn right, come on, Weathers, let's get out of here." Giselle leads the way to the bar. She interrupts Keith as he is wiping down the countertop. She slips him her debit card and he swiftly runs it through the POS. Two receipts print. Giselle crumples one and draws an "x" through the other and then hands Keith the ten dollars Sage bribe her with. They wish each other a goodnight followed by cheek kiss. Keith waves me off followed by a thumbs up and a smile. I give him one back and hit the exit with my arm around Giselle. The early summer air is as cool and calm as I feel right now. Giselle forces our way over to our unofficial designated smoking section and I lean on the bricks and watch as she rummages through her bag. She lights two; I take one, inhale then gaze into the starry abyss. Giselle joins in for a brief moment of silent bliss and transparency.

"Hey, you wanna smoke?" Giselle asks as she presses against my body.

I exhale, "We're smoking right now."

She slaps my chest. "No dumbass, I meant weed. I have a blunt rolled in my car."

"Uh-yeah, sure we could head over to my apartment if you want."

"Eh, not really. I should've been home by now, but I can drop you off after."

"Whatever works for you, but if you just want to get high in your car, sounds like a plan to me."

"Let's head over there now, I'm parked in the lot right across the street from Second House."

"Cool."

We toss our cigarettes as we make our way down Canal. Before reaching the halfway point to Main, I can hear Keith inside the bar yelling, "GO RANGERS, GO RANGERS!" The outside crowd accompanies him in his cheers which causes more commotion.

"You know what's so funny?" Giselle asks.

"What?"

"You see all that yelling and carrying on they're doing?"

I glance back. "Yeah, they're having one hell of a time."

"Yeah, they are. You know why?"

"Uhh, cause the Rangers clinched a home-field advantage. I don't know, why?"

"Ah, come on, Weathers for a person who reads Garvey and Farrakhan. You should know why," she cries.

"Yeah, I know; I know it all too well, they can be drunk and loud as they want because they're fucking white. White privilege is why we can't smoke in front of the entrance. I guess we didn't come so far in 2009 'cause if that were a Black bar, the police would've been parked across the street all night and the moment they saw too many of us outside, cheering about a game, boxing match, or whatever; here they fucking come with their sirens blaring and their nightsticks out. Yelling over the loudspeaker, telling everyone to clear out. Yeah, I know."

Giselle smirks. "See, Weathers, that's what I was talking about right there."

I stop and rip my arm away. "Now, I don't know what you're talking about. Are you trying to insult me or something, are you trying to call me an Uncle Tom or something—I don't get you, Giselle, I really fucking don't."

She takes back my hand, "Look, I'm not calling you an Uncle Tom. I'm not insulting your intelligence at all only questioning it," she smirks, "like I did tonight, and the other night, that's it."

"Questioning what? What's that?"

"You play dumb for the sake of playing dumb. What are you Waiting Face for?"

"Waiting Face? I heard of saving face. What the fuck is that?"

Giselle wraps her arm around my waist as we approach her car and continues, "My dad says it all the time. It means, like, in a situation are you were trying to justify, or pin-point some kind of identity, more like present a false calm to someone or something. Like, you were trying to wait face between you and those crackers back there. You're funny, Weathers, but not stupid. If you look at Obama and his campaign for president, he didn't say too much about the struggles our people still go through, like being able to smoke in front of a bar or being subjected to racism or for us to be okay with someone's racist undertone. Obama knows he was going to be the first Black President whether he chose to accept or not. What I'm getting at is he didn't speak on the Black struggle, he just spoke on shit that appeals to everyone. Which pertained to what's current like the shitty economy, health care, at the same time, straying away from what's happening to us and focusing on what could be. What's happening to his people and what's good for the country are two different things. Get me?"

"Let me get this straight, I know that I'm Black, that's clear. But what you're saying is, I play dumb while waiting to find an identity or something like middle ground or medium to where I fit in between white people and my own kind?"

She smiles. "Yes. Don't assume that's a bad thing, you're better off than some people I know, like Billie for example." We laugh as we approach her Mercedes. Giselle mashes the key fob and I wait for her to get in. As soon as she slams her door, she reaches over to the passenger side and unlocks it. My mom's car reminds me of hers, the passenger seat cluttered in most of her unessential nonsense. It's actually kind of funny, women are parallel to each other when it comes to their cars.

Giselle slaps the passenger seat. "Your throne awaits, Sir."

"You're really playing out that king shit, huh?" As I climb in, Giselle opens the center console. She fishes around for a bit then pulls out a blunt. It's a little misshapen and the leaf around the mouthpiece is slightly coming undone. Giselle's applies moisture from her lips to seal it back.

"There's nothing to play with, Weathers, that's exactly what it is, what you are—a king... You need to stop playing and realize who the fuck you are," she states. Giselle then puts the blunt to her mouth and fires it up, "Yeah, for a girl. I can roll a blunt with the best of them."

As she inhales, Giselle lets smoke out then catches it through her nose and proceeds to turn the ignition halfway. The indicators lights light up as Bobby Caldwell's, "Do For Love" creeps out the speakers.

"Did you just French inhale? Wait, that's not important... what the hell do you know about this shit?" I ask.

"What's a French inhale? And fuck you, what do you know about Bobby Caldwell?"

"It's what you just did. Letting out a little bit of smoke then inhaling through your nose. And second, Bobby is an honorary Black person, this song is a fucking classic."

Giselle inhales, "So, that's what that is. I never knew there was a name for it. One of my brothers taught me how to do it when I first started smoking. And what do you mean about Bobby? He's not Black?"

"Hell no, he sounds like it though."

She coughs, "You got that right. Oh shit, I guess it's true, every day you learn something new, I would've never guessed it. I been getting high to his soulful sounding ass for years."

"When did you start smoking?"

She inhales then passes the blunt. "When I was fifteen or fourteen I think. Somewhere around then. You?"

I take three decent hits and hand it back, "Same. This taste really great by the way."

Giselle takes in a huge hit and covers the windshield with smoke. "Thanks, I usually cop off one of my brothers. If not them, I get it from Billie's roommate Tracie, you know her?"

"Kind of. She's sort of heavyset, right?"

She passes it back. "If you wanna call her that, but yeah."

"That's funny, she has some great weed, though; I'll give her that." I take three more drags and exhale then give it back. We become consumed by the smolder as it fills up the car. After those first few hits; my eyes start to feel heavy and a tad bit of anxiety seeps in; I don't know why, but I'm a little anxious.

Giselle exhales. "Yeah she does, but she sells everyone coke too."

I take the blunt. "Really?"

"Yeah, you'll see her from time to time coming in Second House with her kid to get food and in most cases she making a drop, to Billie, Jackie, or Tina," she smirks. "Shit, maybe all three of them."

"How do you know she dropping off coke?"

"Either, Billie or Jackie will be posted in the server station waiting for her pop up, that's a blind spot for the cameras. And, she'll walk straight back there, she always hands them something; anybody with half a brain can put two and two together. One time, Billie dropped some right after she gave it to him. He's so stupid cause he had a two-top right in the dining room, and you know how the hostess stand is literally in eyeshot distance soon as you poke your head around that corner. I can see everything. I'm just waiting for A.G. to catch them out and when that day comes," she grins. "I hope I'm there to see it."

I exhale, "What do you think he'll do to the first person he catches, you think he'll call the cops?"

"I don't know," she coughs, "probably fire whoever he catches in the act first, I really can't tell you. I doubt if he'll call the cops or anything, but I know his only daughter overdosed on heroin a few years back, don't tell anyone I told you that. I'm the only one who knows that 'cause she was in my graduating class; we both were cheerleaders and she was the captain. When she died, I didn't know that A.G. was her dad until the day I first came in with my resume. I didn't say anything about her, I don't even think he knows I knew her, but I wouldn't be surprised if he did. I mean, the whole cheerleading squad attended her wake and funeral, I do know he keeps a picture of her in his desk drawer," she takes the blunt.

"Damn, that's sad as hell. Poor A.G.," I state.

Giselle breathes in the smoke, "Yup. He really doesn't care about weed much, I had to give him a ride this past winter 'cause his car wouldn't start and my car always reeks of weed and all he did was laugh when he got in."

"I really can't believe they have Tracie making drop-offs in the restaurant, while they're on the clock, they better chill the fuck out. Losing your job over some shit like that isn't a joke."

"Who cares? They'll deserve it. They take this place for granted and everyone knows it, even you."

"You got a point there, but Jackie is pretty legit. Don't you think?" I squint through the windshield to see Second House, but every one of her windows is smudged with fog. Giselle and I are fully submerged in marijuana smoke, and to think, we're not half-way through with this blunt.

"Jackie's cool as fuck, she's from the school of hard knocks—I can't tell she's been through some shit but she never talks about it—at least with me anyways," Giselle says as she almost burns my fingers handing over the blunt, "My bad."

"No harm no foul but yeah, she told me," I take a pull.

"Yeah, she's not like Tina or that fat fuck Billie," she coughs.

The weed is in full effect. My eyes start to sink more as I recline my seat back, "Not to change the subject... but I got to give you props on having a Benz. These power reclining seats are everything.

"Hell yeah, I love this car. Shout out to my parents."

I ash before passing it back, "For real, how many miles does this have?" Styles P's, "I Get High" starts playing.

"A little over 185,000. I got it at 100,000 miles, so..." she inhales.

"That's dope, you basically got this car brand new."

"Basically." She turns the volume knob to the right. "I fucking love this song."

"Hell yeah, this song is a certified classic. When this first came out, I had no clue what the fuck he was talking about, but one thing for sure; I knew he was my shit."

"Same here." We both drift into the melody...

What You Wont Do, Do For Love, You Tried Everything...

"Same here."

I turn down the blunt as she tries to pass it. "I'm good. I'm high as shit from this baked ass car," I laugh.

"I didn't even realize how smoked out it was," she laughs, "you think I should crack a window?"

"Hell no, and fuck up this perfect bake. That would be a fucking sin against Styles."

"You're exactly right." She clips the blunt and slides it in the ashtray.

"I haven't been this faded in a while, I'm feeling nice," I say.

"Yeah, me too, I haven't baked in since the weather started to break. You want a bottle of water?"

"You know I do; this cottonmouth is killing me."

Giselle starts laughing hysterically. "I can't with you," she continues to crack up.

I tease, "For real though, you know how it is. Can't even form spit, my fucking mouth is so dry."

"You're something else, Weathers, something else." She rises up and reaches in the backseat with her ass directly in my face. The pink bra she's wearing is slid up as her shirt moves forward. She flops down back into her seat and hands me a bottle of Poland Spring. "Hope it's not too warm for you," she says.

Sweat starts to form on the back of my neck. "Um-no, ah-this is more than fine. Thank you." I twist the cap and drink.

"You're welcome." Sade's, "Smooth Operator" slips through the thick smoke into my eardrums.

I place my water in the center consoler cupholder. "I have to say, you got pretty good taste in music."

"I try, I try… but thanks. Whatever you hear in this car is just what I picked up from my parents and my brothers. You wouldn't know but being the youngest and all, you really don't have a choice in what to play every Saturday morning, when my mom would force us to clean the house."

"Still, that's pretty dope. Not going to lie, my mom did all the cleaning, occasionally I cleaned my room, but she did most of the sprucing up," I say and wipe my palms on my jeans. Wow, this weed has my anxiety at an all-time high, no pun intended; either I'm paranoid or just overthinking but I have no fucking clue how this is going to play out. Shit, maybe I should just head home. Thank God for the music, it's blocking out the rapid beat of my heart.

"Hey, Weathers can I ask you something?

I shut my eyes. "Shoot."

"Remember when I told you—you sound like a white boy?"

I laugh, "you're a trip, yeah why?"

Giselle bites on her thumbnail. "What that dick look like, though?"

I clear my throat. "Wh-what, excuse me?"

Giselle pounces out of the front seat and hops on top of me. She then forces her tongue into my mouth. The fullness of her lips and the lingering alcohol on her breath snatch my sense of taste. She begins to suck and bite on my bottom lip, the combo sends my dick upwards, and just like that, my penis is harder than Quantum Physics. I don't want to make this awkward at all and but at the same time; this could be considered as rape; I didn't consent but I'm not halting whatever is going on so I assume that this her consenting; I grin, and steal a glance of myself in the passenger-side mirror. With my right hand, I grip her entire neck, my left-hand finds it way under her shirt.

I try and get a handful of her right butt cheek but there's so much ass meat; I would imagine if we were in my bedroom, I'd have to use two hands just for one cheek. Oh my god, the softness of her butt is more than I fantasized. I mangle the crouch of her underwear to the side and become taunted by a slight bit of moisture from her vagina lips. As I try to penetrate her with my fingers, her jeans make it impossible. I try again, no luck. Removing my hand, I drive it right up under her shirt

210

and through her bra. Giselle's tender breasts are fuller than I thought, it's easier to caress these C cups than her ass. She begins to kiss harder as I fondle and pinch each one her nipples.

"I wanna suck it," she demands.

"Yes, Ma'am," I say and unfasten my belt while Giselle unbuttons my pants. We jump into the backseat and I lay down on the cushions. She readjusts to snatch my boxers off. There's no turning back now; she's in full attack mode and I'm so erect, it kind of hurts. Giselle hikes her head over my shaft and gazes into my eyes as her mouth gets closure to the head. I watch as the saliva drips down to the head and trickles down to my testicles. She strokes it from the bottom up, making it slick just enough to tease then stuffs it in her wet mouth. Giselle wastes no time shoving it to the back of her throat.

Her tonsils tickle the top then she takes my hand and forces me to press down. She gags twice and comes up for air, soon after she catches her breath, she ejects all the accumulated spit all over my cock and balls; I never in my life had my dick sucked in this manner. Jesus Christ, this is amazing. Containing the semen that I feel coming up is going to take a miracle; I start to picture images of the early mornings had at the icehouse. Man, I fucking despised every single practice. And just like that, it softens up a bit; but Giselle's aggressive mouth doesn't.

She stares directly at my pupils. "Again, I want that dick in the back of throat again, you taste so good." I form her hair into a ponytail and use it as leverage. Before I know it; I'm stiff as a board again. Giselle's head bops up and down in a repeated motion. She takes it out then beats it on her beautiful face. Every time my dick makes contact with either jaw or cheek, I can feel it becoming heavier. She spits on it once more then tugs it, her grip is rough but with all the salvia, it feels superb. With every stroke, she gets it harder and stiffer than I ever thought possible. Yup, this is the best blowjob I ever received.

"Finger my asshole, Weathers," she whispers.

There was never a time a girl invited me anywhere near her rectum, there's really nothing to say; I just do as I'm told. I shove my left hand up and under jeans. The heat coming from it turns me on. To test the waters, I push down on it, and her suck is even harder. She slaps her face with it again. Giselle then cuffs my balls with her jerking hand while she's sucking; the tip of her tongue teases my balls. Apparently, she thinks my nuts aren't moist enough so she starts sucking each one, making a soft but hard popping noise, but it feels great. Now, my finger is submerged her ass. I gyrate it in and out. Giselle moans, "You want this pussy?"

"Yes please," I beg.

"You want this pussy, daddy?" She puts my dick back in her throat.

"Ahh, hell yeah."

She gags, "Take it then."

I push her off, she kicks off her heels, and then I help remove her pants. Giselle slides her thong to the side, licks four fingers, and rubs herself up and down as she gets ready to hop on top. Once she's ready for entry, she guides my dick in her tight gateway and whines so beautifully from the temporary pain; and to be quite frank, this is enough to make any man prematurely cum. Once she feels it reach the bottom of her cervix, she loosens up as she becomes more lubricated with every inch penetrating. Giselle's moans become constant and louder. With one hand on her ass and the other around her neck. I lean forward and whisper in her ear, "It's so good."

She mutters, "It's all yours, daddy." Giselle rides harder and faster. The car begins to rock. Between the smoke and hot air; I can't even see across the street. As she grinds, her juices start to run down to my testicles.

"Weathers," she pauses, "I'm about to nut all over your dick."

"What's a nut?"

She grips my ears and bites on my forehead, "That means, I'M ABOUT TO CCCCUM. OH MY FUCKING GOODNESS, I'M CUMING ALL OVER YOUUUU." My only reaction is to squeeze her breasts. She yanks the back of my head and moans. The pace slows as her love rains down. I can feel every crevice of her walls. She carefully gets off and to my surprise, she starts sucking on it again. The funny thing is, with any other sexual encounter I ever had; I usually have to ask for fellatio and Giselle seems more than willing to give it. "Ah, I love the taste of my pussy juice," she whispers, "I want you fuck me from the back."

"Ok," I reply.

We maneuver around and put ourselves in position, before I can penetrate; she moves the front seat up and taunts by shaking her backside. I smack it and pull her back, then I slide in with a gentle but forceful drive. I start off slow then begin to pick up the rhythm. Each thrust is longer and harder. She's going to cause a climax; I feel it. I keep the same pace but steadier. The rhythm is what I'm focused on and suddenly, I feel a stream of water smack on my thighs and all over the back seat. She doesn't care and neither do, I just keeping thrusting and stabbing. She squirts again, a little more this time. I keep a tight grip on her hair and smack that ass again and again until her caramel skin turns copper. She moans louder and louder. At this point; I don't think either of us cares if the cops come. Unfortunately, they'll be no one to file a report because her vagina is about to fall victim to homicide.

Giselle arches her back, buries her face in the seat cushions, then hikes her butt up commanding, "Stick a finger in my ass."

The amazement of her asshole as I spread her cheeks, keeps my penis rock hard. I spit around her rectum and gently rub against it with my thumb, then finally forcing it in. Giselle's sex cries are the biggest turn on; I hit her with a few more thrusts then I start to feel the semen pulsate through the shaft. I groan, "I'm about to cum baby." Giselle spins around and with a few tugs of her mouth, my sperm splatters directly on to her tongue and face. It makes quite the mess, she even swallows some. You would've thought she was a porn-star in her past life. I mean goddamn, I think she drained my entire nut-sack if such a thing were possible.

"Goddamn, Giselle. Holy shit, good God, I've never seen that before." I fall back on the seat while she tugs and licks my penis spotless.

She smirks. "Don't use God's name in vain, Weathers." After a moment of tender embrace, we search and find our clothes and shoes; I help her wipe down the back seat with the spare napkins she had in the glove compartment. Giselle retrieves two cigarettes, signals with a nudge to get out the car. I spot my wallet on the floor as we make way into the soft breeze of the night. Giselle hands over the first smoke she lights then sets fire to another one. The first drag is everything, now that I think about it, smoking after sex might be my favorite thing about intercourse, and to be honest, this might be the first time I really enjoyed one after sex. I'm mean, I get it; it's so relaxing and buoyant. No wonder all the Hollywood writers implement smoking after the intimate scenes. It's just the right thing to do after fucking, if there was a "right" thing to do after. It would be smoking, for sure.

"When does the open patio up?" I ask.

Giselle exhales. "Uhh, I think next week, whenever your training is over; I know that's the day, cause that'll be your first section. Monday I think, Tuesday maybe, you gotta ask A.G. I never keep track, I just prepare for it to be a madhouse."

"When is it never?"

She smirks. "You gotta point."

My phone vibrates, it's a text from Billie. "Yo nigga, when ur done fuckin, come thru and chill."

I reply back. "Got u."

Giselle stares. "Who are you texting?"

"My 3 am," I smile.

"Well, I would beat the hell out of you and make your life a living hell at work, but first I would beat the hell outta you so, yeah." She wraps herself around my waist.

I embrace her supple body. "That's nice to know. So, what are we?"

She plucks her cigarette. "Well, I like you and I don't play games." Giselle grabs my crotch and continues, "And you got good dick, Weathers but..." Giselle yanks my scrotum, "But I have no problem Lorena Bobbitting you if you play me like a fool or even think about it. I'd like to see where this goes. What about you? What do you want?"

"Whatever you want." I steal a kiss.

"Good... need a ride home? I'm going to get outta here."

"Uhh, I'm good. After what we just did; I need to stretch out my legs."

"What about that third leg." She grabs it again. "I'm going to be so fucking sore tomorrow." She slaps my arm.

"HEY!" I laugh and open the door for her. Giselle climbs in the driver seat, places the key into the ignition, turns the engine, and switches on the headlights then rolls down her window.

Giselle pokes her head out for a quick lip-lock. "You got some real good dick, Weathers. And if Tina ever calls you a monkey again, I'll beat the shit outta her. You're a horrible liar by the way, but that's a good thing. Remember, you're a KING."

"Wait... you heard that?" I question.

Giselle stares as if I just asked the stupidest question to ever come out of someone's mouth. She puts the car in drive, pulls off the curb onto the street, and hits the horn twice before she drives off into the night.

RANGERS WIN!

The night breeze finally arrives as I make my way towards Billie and Tracie's apartment. As the cool settles in, the streets quiet down except for the police car that just circled twice. Oh well, that's what they do. I'm not bothering anyone, so, I continue to walk. Passing the Off-Betting Track, I could hear the river push against the current. The air becomes cooler with the blowing leaves. The entrance to the complex is no more than twenty yards ahead. But, wait... I see a familiar hairstyle and body shape walking out of the building. It's that bitch, Tina. Yup, I better wait a sec before heading in. You know what? Fuck that, there's nothing to be afraid of; I got a better chance of being shot by that cop than her doing something to me.

I jog to the door before it closes shouting, "HEY, TINA, TINA!"

Tina squints and yells, "Who that's?" The lobby entrance clamps shut as I catch my breath.

"It was me calling you, you couldn't hold the door? I know you heard me."

Tina switches her purse from her left shoulder to the right then flips her hair, "Well, you could've been anyone. All I seen was some Black shadow running towards me. Shit, I was about to take off my damn self."

"Come on, Tina, that's fucked up. I repeatedly called out your fucking name. It's almost been a week, and you still don't recognize my voice...un-fucking-believable."

She lights a cigarette. "What is?"

"You are!" Realizing that out of frustration, the pitch in my voice is raising, I calm it; I don't want someone calling the police about a loud Black man outside of their complex yelling at a white woman. Let me check myself before I'm sleeping in a jail cell. I whisper, "You are, Tina. I don't know what your problem is...but you got some serious issues under your belt that you need to adjust."

Tina glares at me. "Are you trying to call me fat again, Newbie?"

"Oh my God, is that all you care about is your weight? I don't give a fuck about your size. Maybe that's why you're so insecure, and why you treat me like some shit you stepped in. Whatever man, if you don't get it then that's your problem, not mine. I'm sorr-—nah, why even am I trying to apologize for how you treat me? If you don't fix whatever issue you have with me, I'm just going to treat you as a waste of space." I whip out my phone and go to recent calls, search for Billie's contact, and then hit send.

"You know what, Newbie?" She blows smoke my way and continues, "The thing with you people, is that you feel so entitled to everything. I get it, I really do. Slavery was fucked up but that was years ago. You need to get over that shit and realize your place in this world, especially at Second House. Maybe in the world you live in outside of Second House-"

Billie picks up. "Yo, you downstairs?"

"Hold on, really quick." I mash mute. "Finish what you were saying, Tina."

"All I'm saying is, know your place at Second House, and remember you're a third-class citizen when you walk through those doors. You're only there to keep the Blacks that come in to eat happy. You're just

218

another... uh-uh what's the term I'm looking for... Oh I got it, you're just an uppity nigger who we need in the front of the house. But don't be sad, Newbie," Tina says then ashes on my foot and blows a cloud of smoke in my face adding, "You're not alone at Second House that's why you got your little fuck buddy at the hostess stand." She turns and starts toward the street then yells, "I don't know what you see in her anyway, don't Black men prefer thick white women anyway? That big dick you got should be inside something pure and wholesome like me."

I unmute Billie. "Yo, I'm down here."

"Tina should be down there, have her let you in," he says.

"Uh, I think I just missed her. Actually, I just saw someone walking towards Main, when I got to the door. And, from the looks of it, I don't see any lights shining on the elevator indicators, so yeah unless you come down; I'm going home."

"Ah fuck, alright. I'm coming. Don't be scaring any of my neighbors coming into the building, they know no Black people live here," He laughs then hangs up.

Can't really make out what Tina was just talking about but I'm pretty she just referred to me as a slave but not quite a slave but not free either; basically what she was trying to say is I have no rights or value at Second House. Fuck her. The elevator indicators to the floor levels start to flash. Billie exits the elevator wearing blue pajama bottoms and a stained white tee shirt. He looks banged up as usual. Billie presses up against the door and lets me in. "What's good nigga?" he asks.

"Shit, C.J's was packed," I reply.

He leads the way into the elevator. "Yeah, Rangers game. I watched it. It was a tight win but they got it done."

"That's for sure," I say as I mash the button to his floor.

"You went with Giselle?"

"Yeah..."

"You hit that, didn't you?" he smiles.

"Nah, just chilled and smoked, besides its none of your business what I did with her."

"Nigga, you hit that."

"Don't worry about what I'm doing. Worry about doing your laundry and washing your ass." The elevator comes to an abrupt stop then squeals as it creeps open.

"Giselle has always been a little prude anyway so you probably didn't fuck. But one thing for sure is ya'll like each other."

"She's cool, for sure. Trace home?" I ask

Billie pushes open the door to the apartment. "Yeah, but she's putting Cam to bed. But, I got some shit left out if you wanna quick bump."

"Most definitely, I'm kind of drunk right, now some lines would help. And I got some cash for some more lines."

Billie stands over the kitchen island while I pull out a chair. He slides over a straw and a broken mirror with lines ready to go. This coke has a yellow shine and orange flakes in it, from the looks of it; it's over cut. Most cocaine is cut, but this shit is so bad, you can just tell someone fucked their money up. I hold the straw to my nose and inhale. The powder immediately irritates my nostrils causing me to sneeze twice.

"Bless you," Billie says.

"Thanks." I sneeze once more.

"Bless you."

"Tha—" I sneeze twice more.

"Damn nigga, shut the fuck up already!" Billie cries.

I laugh, "I think that was it." No drip hits, I rail another asking him,

"Where'd you get this shit from?"

"I got it off Jose before leaving work. You know I needed a little pick me up. It ain't that bad, got it for a good price."

"Well, you need to ask for your money back. This shit basuda." He reaches for the mirror and empties the coke he got from Jose on it; he cuts up six lines and sniffs three before he slides back the mirror.

Billie snorts. "I think this shit is okay, I mean sure it's not the best but it gets the job done. Maybe I should invite Jose over sometime for a drink."

I do the rest and push it to the side. "Whatever happened to him being nothing but a lazy Mexican?"

"He's from Peru, and what do you mean? I never said that."

Finally, some type of drip sets in. The taste is disgusting as if it were mixed with Vitamin B or Adderall. "You're so fucking fake. Jose sells you a little bit of coke and now you want to be his friend. You're a real piece of work Bill."

"Hey, people change my nigga. You just have a negative outlook on things." He passes me a cigarette.

"Nah, bro I don't. You on the other hand have a very poor view on things. Especially hygiene," I laugh and head towards the balcony.

Billie fingers the mirror clean and rubs it between his gums. "I smell fine today."

I hold the screen door open and light my smoke. "Yeah... today. But you have to start showering before work, man. You know, one of your tables complained about your odor."

Billie puts fire to his Newport then quickly inhales and exhales. "No, they would've said something to A.G. about it. You gotta be lying. See, there you go telling lies again, just because I ride your ass all night at work, doesn't mean you have to come with elaborate stories to get back at me."

I frown and turn. "You know, I'm trying to help you be better at your job, and for whatever reason, you think I'm lying—or trying to step on your toes, whatever the fuck that mean. Bro, you can lose out on money if you want to. I can't afford to move back in with my parents, maybe you can but that's a risk I'm not trying to take… Whatever dude, if you get fired from Second House, it's your own doing."

He taps his cigarette and stares. "You know, you can't believe what Black people say, anyway," he smirks. "I'm kidding... But yeah, I'll start showering before work instead of after."

"My nigga, do both! You smell like the dumpster in the back lot."

"But I still get pussy, so what do you have to say about that?"

"Good for you, Bill, good for you. But let me remind you, anybody can pay for sex."

"What's that supposed to mean?"

"You figure it out for yourself."

Tracie pushes through the screen door, "Man, it took forever for her to go to sleep." She shoves my shoulder, "What's up, Mikey? You make it to work on time?" she laughs.

"Always do, how's baby girl doing?"

Tracie sparks a cigarette. "Good and happy. She keeps asking when are you going to take her ice-skating again."

"Maybe on my next day off."

She nods. "I need some time with my girl so I'll hold you to that.."

"Mike thinks the shit I got off Jose is trash. What do you think, Trace?" Billie asks.

"It is, I would ask for my money back but you probably did it all," she responds. Billie drags the cigarette halfway down to the filter and in frustration, flicks it over the balcony.

"Watch out, Mike, I'm about to shower up before Jackie gets here." The screen door slams behind him.

Tracie exhales. "What's his problem?"

"You never know these days. He doesn't shower or wash his clothes and he buys shitty coke. Every day it's something with him."

"You got a point."

I scrape the cherry of my cigarette in the ashtray. "You got anything?"

"You know it," she tempts.

"Cool, let me get a ball. It's on me tonight."

"Oh shit, look at you, big balling tonight huh?" she laughs, "Finally contributing to some big shit. How'd you come up on cash? A.G. gave you an advance or something?"

"Nah, I've been pulling more than my weight at work so I've been getting tipped out for the last three days. And there were a few customers that really looked out especially this one chick." The thought of Sage groping my ass sends nervous chills through my spine but I manage to continue… "But, you been looking out since this transition started so it's my turn to provide, you know."

She tosses her butt into the trees. "Cool, let me run upstairs really quick. If you want to make a drink or something, Billie picked up some beers and Henny."

I lead the way inside. "Think I'll do just that. I have to wash the taste of that crap ass coke out of my mouth." Before doing anything, I count out $150 and hand it over.

Tracie laughs and pats my back. "You ain't lying! Be right back." She tiptoes the entire way to her loft. Billie's door is closed, and I could hear the shower running from his bathroom. Guess, I'll help myself to some good old Cognac. I strut over to the fridge, grab the liquor, drop a few ice cubes in a clean solo cup, and count to four as I pour and then stop. The first sip is cooling and refreshing but doesn't flush out the after taste of Jose's coke. I add a little more Henny to my cup. The second sip of liquor comes to my relief, it finally washes away the horrible drip. Tracie meets me in the living room with my purchase. It's mostly in rock form and looks as if it were compressed by a machine. The sandwich bag it is knotted in is a dead giveaway, but hey, I'll take it. and telling from the tiny crystals glimmering through the plastic, this shit doesn't come close to what Billie gave me.

"Where's Bill?" Tracie asks.

"From the sounds of it; I think he's taking a shower...for once." The bag is almost impossible to open and I don't want to put my mouth on it because God only knows where Tracie's hands have been.

Tracie chuckles, "You have trouble over there?"

I wedge the knot free and showcase my independence. "All good over here and I didn't poke a hole."

"Good job, you want an award," she laughs.

"Fuck you, you got a surface under the table or should I grab the mirror from the kitchen?"

She bends down under the coffee table and comes up with a gloss-plated slab of some sorts, it looks as if it some sort of tile sample, you would get at a hardware store. "You're in luck, I thought Billie had that shit in his room. After I tried that bullshit coke he had, I told him to take it in his room while I watch TV with Cam; I guess he forgot to take it up with him, there's still some of that bullshit coke on here, hold on a sec."

Tracie takes the slab into the kitchen and runs it through the sink faucet for a few seconds, and dries it clean with a paper towel then returns to her seat. I take from the bag what could be over a gram and set it on the glass.

"Oh, that's cool and much safer, he was using that broken mirror on the counter when I first came in. You got an extra bill on you?" I question.

"Yeah," she says and passes one of the twenties I gave her and asks, "Broken mirror?"

"Yup, right there on the kitchen island." I lay the money on top of the coke and press down with my lighter and lightly rub across it until the boulder breaks down. Once it crumbles, I apply more pressure to the twenty. When the bill is completely flat, I retrieve my debit card and turn the bill over, shave off any coke stuck right on to the slab, and then mold a miniature mountain, making sure no spec of coke goes un-sniffed. Unfortunately, you never can get all of it.

"Broken mirror, you don't say?" Tracie asks.

"Say what?" I dig into the pile and begin to separate lines.

"That Billie was using a broken mirror."

"Yeah, on the kitchen island like I said." I place the rolled-up bill to my left nostril and rail the two biggest lines. Every hair follicle on my lip stands up. The powder hits instantly causing a vengeful drip to course it's way directly to my esophagus.

"That's funny 'cause that mirror was in my room. Now it's down here."

I sneeze.

"Bless you," she offers.

"Thanks, you sure you didn't leave it down here from earlier?" I take a sip and the Hennessy calms the drip.

"Yeah, I'm sure, 'cause I was with Cam all day and I remember doing key bumps last night 'cause I didn't want to wake up Cam."

"That's funny..."

"It is. And now that I think about it, I'm missing a few grams of coke."

My eyes widen. "oh shit. Are you serious?"

Tracie leans forward with her fingers locked, lowers her head for a bit then stares, "Yeah man, dead serious."

I divide two nice lines and slide the slab. "You sure you didn't separate some for personal use and misplace it? You're always losing shit. You probably hid it so well; you can't find it."

"Nope, I put my entire stash where I always put it. And I threw it on the scale for safe measure and when I did, it was way off. Can I see that bill?" She takes it and doesn't come up for air until the lines are gone. "Ahh, damn that's some good shit."

"You think—I mean... would Billie even think about something like that, let alone do it?" I reach for the slab.

Tracie starts to massage her temple. "Shits always coming up missing, you know that."

"Yeah, but you guys live together, you shouldn't have to put up with that." I cut out more lines.

"When I first moved in, my shit was always where I left it. Remember when you first told me about leaving LBS?"

"Yeah," I snort.

"Since then, a lot of shit goes "misplaced" or I "lost". 'I' lost mind you—at least that's what he says. I mean, how can somebody lose money and coke every other day? Shit, Mike, I think he's been taking my soap."

"Soap?" I chuckle. "Sorry, I don't mean to laugh but that's the last thing he should be stealing or maybe the first thing in his case."

But then again when's the last he used soap or even bought some."

Tracie smirks. "I know, right? And it's always too late to question him about it. He'll get all defensive and start an argument or some shit and wakes up Cam."

I rail another one and slide the slab. "If you really know he's taking shit from you, what are you going to do about it?"

Tracie prepares her own lines. "Probably tomorrow…I gotta see if my mom can watch Cam tomorrow. I got a few moves to make and there will be no reason for Billie to get loud—and if he does it won't matter 'cause she won't be here. But if I can catch him before he goes to work, I'm going to confront his thieving ass."

"What time is that?" I snort and cough up a heavy amount of nasal drip, I grab a napkin from under the table and spit the phlegm into it; I ball it up and tuck it away in my bag.

"He told me he got called in for brunch, supposedly you guys are going to be really busy. I think A.G. is setting up the patio or something."

"Oh okay, well I hope you guys can come to a mutual agreement and he will finally own up to his shit."

"Honestly, Mikey, it's whatever, really; I'm over living here. He looked out on letting me and Cam stay here. In the beginning, everything was chill; then he just starting taking advantage. I'm just going to start looking for more apartments in the morning. I'm sick of this shit. I really am." She takes the glass and divides her lines.

"Damn girl, what do you mean looking for apartments? It's that serious?"

Tracie does every line she made then gags. "Ah shit, I almost threw up my lunch there, kid. Goddamn, I forget how good this shit is…damn." She clears her throat, "But fuck yeah, it's that serious. Even though I'm just now telling you about it, this has been an issue for a while now."

"You know, now that I think about it, he did leave work tonight to get a wine-key. Well, Jackie told him to."

"That makes sense 'cause I was gone then." She suddenly claps. "That makes perfect sense, now. Has he been disappearing from Second House since you've started?" She moves the slab across the table.

"Uh, he goes to the bathroom in between tables a lot but today he vanished without telling me until Jackie said something." I glance at the slab and realize the mountain the coke that once was, has now turned into a small hill. Shit, if Billie really did steal her stuff then that means I was sniffing her shit too. "Well, I guess that puts a face to what's missing," I say and take a sip of my drink.

"Yeah man, I can't live here anymore, especially if I'm getting this shit fronted to me; and at the same time be expected to pay my connect back while Billie's putting his fat fingers in my shit. Not to mention, I got a daughter who has a birthday coming up and she wants to do shit, as she deserves to. I don't know anymore, Mikey, I really don't."

"So… wait a minute, you're getting the coke you sell on credit?" I begin to realize that I can't feel my lips move as I talk so I rub my cheek to see if…yup, my entire face is numb. Wow, she wasn't just talking, this blow is spectacular.

"Yeah man, for a while now. I do buy a good amount upfront but that's not nearly enough to help with all the shit I got going and having a habit doesn't do me any good. But, yeah he usually tosses me half on top of what I buy, but even then I have to find a connect with the same prices and the same quality of coke."

I start to crush more blow. "Why? If this guy is reliable and has constant product."

She looks away. "You promise you won't say anything?"

"Promise."

"There have been a bunch of times where I sniffed too much or I gave out a bunch; and who know how much that fat fuck in there has gotten me for, but ah. Sometimes Primo-"

"Who's Primo?"

"My connect, stupid."

"Oh, my bad."

Tracie lowers her head. "So yeah, sometimes I um, um, suck his dick or let him fuck me sometimes, whenever I come up short. He considers the debt paid. He's never forced himself on me or anything like that. I'd just rather find a new connect."

"Do you make him use protection?"

She reaches for a loose cigarette on the coffee table and lights it. "Nope. And, I'm late..."

"What do you mean late?" Tracie waves her cigarette and signifies she's hinting at something beyond tardiness. Then it hits me, she's referring to her monthly visit from Mother Nature. My jaw drops. "Oh. Shit..."

She signs with her smoke, "...Yup."

"Shit man, I don't know what to say...

"Yeah, I know." Tracie blows a cloud of smoke then passes the cigarette. I down the rest of my drink and ash in it. We sit speechless for a minute, I guess we're just trying to figure out the next thing to say but come up with nothing but silence. Watching the tobacco disintegrate is the most peaceful thing about this entire night. Sure, I got drench by rain, degraded twice by an undocumented citizen, sniffed coke on the job. I'm pretty sure Giselle is a clean girl, but who really feels safe after unprotected sex with a woman you just met? But, like my dad always says, 'It could be worse Mikey'. But for Tracie, it is worst. All I can think about is that poor little girl upstairs. I can relate to Cam more than she'll ever know, only thing is, I had a fighting chance. She may not get one.

I dead the butt in the melting ice and ask, "Does he have other kids?"

"Of course, he does, he's fucking Dominican." We both laugh. She takes the coke I've broke down and carefully pours it onto the slab then divides four fat lines.

"Could her dad keep her for you while you get your shit together?"

Tracie rails her two and shoves the slab. "Shit, Mike, I haven't seen that fuck since she was born, even if he could, Cam doesn't even know who he is."

"Now that I think about it, back in January, when I took her to the ice rink, she did ask if I knew who her dad was. She was real down after I couldn't give her an answer, so I brought her a Slushie."

"She told me about the Slushie part but not about asking you about her dad. She never even asked me about him." Tracie's face turns from worry to disgust as Billie comes out, and into the living room

"What's good niggas? I see we got some lines going on here. Who's it on tonight?" he laughs.

Tracie rises saying, "I gotta get to bed, you guys have fun."

"So soon?" Billies asks.

"Yeah. See ya."

"Goodnight, Trace, keep your head up," I say.

She chucks a peace sign then tiptoes back up the stairs. Billie heads to the kitchen and pours a drink. When he returns to the living-room, he takes Tracie's seat. "What's up, nigga?" he burps.

I can't help but feel anxious sitting across from him. "You're what's up. You want some lines?" I pass the surface with prepared rows ready.

"I'm down with that. Is this my bill?" He snorts the biggest line.

"Nah, it's mine."

"You sure?"

"Positive, Bro." I watch as he chugs his drink. Now that I think about it, I'm pretty sure he went into his room to beat off. "What were you doing in your room? Talking to Jackie?"

"Yeah, she's about to come over." He slides the slab.

I smirk, "It took you twenty minutes for her to tell you that?"

"Yeah, why?"

"Nah, just asking. You were in there for a while after you cut the water off." My nose starts to drip so with the inside of my shirt, I catch the snot before it grazes my lip. For whatever reason, I decide to divide the rest of the blow into six big lines. Soon as I rail three; I shove the slab in front of Billie, then I force myself up and into the kitchen to refill my cup. "Ay, Bill you want to go out for a smoke?"

"Yup, this shit got me jonesing, perfect timing, Farrakhan."

Today's downpour returns as before I reach the screen door, Billie's sticks in a cigarette while smoking one. "This rain gotta go; I'm sick of this." Billie states.

I light my smoke. "Why? I love it."

"Why? Are you depressed or some shit? Only people who are fucking sad all the time like the rain. The rain ain't nothing to like, Farrakhan. Ain't nothing to like at all."

Hypnotized by the precipitation, I stare for a bit. You know, rain is one of the most meticulous things about this planet. How it just knows the purpose it serves is amazing. It never has to question its job or place in the world. When it's time for it to rain, it just drops from the sky. "I guess you got a point there, Bill. Hey, can we talk about something for a minute?"

"If it's about Tina, man—"

"—No, Bill. Not at all," I interrupt.

"What then?"

"Have you been taking shit from Tracie's stash?"

"What? No, why?" he shouts.

"Look, just calm down and listen real quick. She's missing coke and money I guess; I'm not accusing you. Hell, it's not even my problem. But I'm coming to you because I don't want to see you without a roommate and most importantly a friend."

"What do you mean by that? She told you she's moving?"

I exhale, "I can't say all that but she's pissed and thinks you have something to do with her coke being gone. Cam didn't take it that's for damn sure. It's only you two who live here so you have to talk to her before it's too late. 'Cause you know damn well you can't afford to live here without her especially with all the money that goes to your nose."

Billie remains silent and leans on the balcony. I finish my cigarette and nudge him for another one. "You ever thought about giving yourself a little break from the blow?" I inhale smoke and ask.

He rubs his face. "I don't know man, ever since she moved in, it's been non-stop. And, I know I've been fucking up at work but this shit got me by the balls." He lights another cigarette.

"Well, all I can say is that I'm here for you if you need help. Shit, I'll go sober with you. But you need to get your shit together before you hit rock bottom. Who wants to lose it all before they realize they fucked up?" I pat his back and notice a few tears welling up. "You'll be alright, man, you helped me get the job at Second House, and I'm going to help you keep yours. But, you gotta want it for yourself first man, I can't make it happen for you.

He wipes his eyes, "Thanks, my nigga. No matter what people say about you, you're a good dude."

I bristle. "What are you talking about? What do people say about me?

Billie teases, "Look at your face, I'm just fucking with you man, calm down."

"Whatever...you're always playing around. You need to grow the fuck up. That's why you're in the shit you're in now. You never take shit serious."

"Well, tomorrow is a new day; I'll start to be serious then."

I exhale towards him, "If you say so. It's your bed either way you make it, you got to lay in it at the end of the day, not me."

"Yeah, yeah. You got anymore shit?"

"Umm, hmm." I dead my smoke in the ashtray and Billie flicks his over the balcony. I lead the way into the living room. I throw myself in the same spot and bust out more coke before I hand him Tracie's twenty to break it down. While he's doing that, I enjoy my high along with my drink. Billie grinds the TV remote against the twenty; I guess he's too lazy to ask for a lighter. When the coke is all refined, I let him do the honors and getting the first few lines. Boy, if there's one thing he can do right, is sniff blow. "Isn't Jackie coming over?"

Billie does his lines. "Ahhh," he cries, "Man that shit is fire. What'd you say Farrakhan? My bad."

I shake my head. "Isn't Jackie coming over?"

"Yeah." He rails another line then pushes the slab. When I pick up the bill, Billie's snot and blood are on the rim. For a second, I thought I was going to puke for the second time today. I unravel it and lightly put flame to it. "Yo, blow your nose."

"Why?"

I flash the twenty. "You got shit all over it and your nose is bleeding. But go in the bathroom to do it, so you don't wake up Cam."

He wipes his nose with his right index finger. "Shit, you're right." Billie quietly speeds to his room and shuts the door. Still, I hear him clear his nose, but it's discreet enough not to travel. I finish my drink and cut more lines. Billie makes his way back to the couch. "Damn, there was some blood coming out there, boy I tell ya."

"All the more reason to give yourself a break," I suggest.

"Yeah, I guess you're right about that one. I mean, there was a lot of blood coming out my nose, that can't be good." He grabs the slab.

"No kidding, you could rupture your nose cavity after a while."

Billie sniffs. "Really?"

"Yeah, you fucking idiot. How are you thirty-six years old and don't know that? Weren't you the one that said you dropped more coke than I've done?" I chuckle, "You're a piece of work."

"Yeah but I didn't know all that." He snorts again.

"Well, now you know. Anyway, how is Jackie getting in the building? When she comes I could let her in. I'm leaving soon anyway."

Billie passes back the slab. "You're good. She'll let herself in I gave her the code but told her she can only use it when Tracie's not here or sleep."

I make more lines. "Ah shit, someone's getting serious."

"I don't—"

Jackie comes through the kitchen door with, "—SECOND HOUSE IN TH—"

"Shhh. Cam's sleeping, why are you so loud? Why you didn't text me?" Billie whispers.

Jackie adjusts her tone and quietly steps into the living room then she pecks Billie's lips before taking a seat. "My phone died, I'm sorry," she murmurs.

"What the fuck does that have to do with not waking up the entire building," Billie scolds.

"Sheesh." Jackie wraps her arms around his waist, "I'm sorry but you know how you guys are always up, partying, and whatnot. Sometimes we get so fucked up; I forget Cam even lives here," she chuckles.

"I get it, but you did come in a little hot just now," I add.

"My bad, my bad. I said I was sorry. Now, can I get a line please; I have cash." Jackie stares at Billie.

"Don't look at me, talk to Farrakhan."

"Hey, Newbie, I have som—"

"It's all good Boss Lady, help yourself. Hold on a sec, let me get mine first." After railing three lines; I cut out six more and then slide the slab.

Jackie removes her clutch from her handbag, retrieves a fifty-dollar bill, and then rolls it. "Thanks, Newbie. You know tonight was brutal and don't even ask me about doing inventory. That shit took forever, then A.G. had the nerve to say we're missing a few liquor bottles from yesterday's delivery." She snorts two lines then tilts her head back. "Oh wow, this is good shit. Seems like Trace keeps getting better and better coke." She turns her attention to Billie. "I thought the shit you brought to work was fucking horrible and it had my nose sore as hell but this tastes pure as shit."

Billie becomes disgruntled. "Hey Jack, can you remember to keep your voice down, you want Tracie coming down here? Keep your voice down for fucksake, there's a sleeping child upstairs"

"I'm sorry," Jackie mutters, "I thought I was talking in earshot distance."

"Apparently you weren't," he states.

There's about a little less than a gram left on the glass. I retrieve my coke from my tube sock and break off what looks like a half a gram and place it on the surface. "Well guys it's getting late and I haven't slept much since my first day of training. But you guys can enjoy that, I know Trace is coming back down tonight." Before getting up, I sneak Tracie's bill under the cushion and bury it deep.

"Are you sure you don't want cash?" Jackie asks.

"It's cool, they'll be other times you got it. That's why they pay you big bucks," I laugh.

"You're so sweet." She hugs my shoulders and pecks my cheek.

"Don't sweat it. I'll see you guys tomorrow for dinner."

Billie extends his hand to me for a shake. "Tomorrow is your last day of training, right?"

"To be honest, Boss Lady, I'm so high right now," I smirk, "Can't even tell you, but nonetheless, can't wait till it's over."

"I bet," Jackie states.

"Yup, so I'll see you two tomorrow; same time, same place."

"Remember A.G. called me in early tomorrow, so I'll be there before you for once."

I chuckle. "Yeah for once. Alright, guys, I'm out of here, goodnight."

"Goodnight, Newbie, sleep tight."

"Yeah, Farrakhan get home safe and avoid any police brutality on the way."

I smile, "Fuck you, man." Before leaving, I fill my cup halfway with more Hennessy. I wave one more time before closing the door. On my way down to the lobby; I text Tracie to let her know her twenty bucks is in the couch cushion, where I was sitting. The elevator doors open and a woman walking her dog gets in as I walk out. I hit the entrance door and once I'm outside, I toss my empty cup and it lands on top of the bush right outside the lobby. Soon as light my last smoke the rain stops. All of sudden my phone vibrates. It's Giselle calling. Before picking up; I snort and hawk up a heavy but soothing amount of drip; I spit onto the payment and accept her call. "Hello?"

"Hey, did you make it home safe?" she asks.

"Uh, yeah; I did. Thanks, I have had to take out some garbage so I'm actually outside right now." I start for the trail.

"Oh okay, you sound like you're outside."

"Yeah, what are you up to?"

"Nothing much. When I got home; I had to wrap my hair and jump in the shower. Now, I'm just laying here. You said you were going to call, but you didn't so I figured to call you to make sure you didn't get kidnapped or some crazy shit."

The stream catches my attention so I decide to lean on the guard-rail. "Tonight was great, totally unexpected, but great nonetheless," I say with a smile.

She pauses, and I can sense a strong grin coming from the other side of the phone. "Yeah, you're not so bad yourself, Weathers. I could not talk with all those white people yelling at the top of their lungs. It's only a fucking game, Jesus."

"Well, it's that you see two rivalries take it all the way to overtime, and for the Rangers to come through in the clutch. To be honest, if I wasn't with you I would've gone home and tuned in and watched. It's just, I watch it 'cause I played it. But, no...." I laugh, "I never yelled like that unless I was on the ice."

"It's just funny to me 'cause I see it as the whitest sport ever, I mean there's golf but then again Tiger Woods is the best golfer in the world and he's Black. Whenever he's playing I'll watch with my dad and he doesn't know shit about golf. He's just cheering for the Black man," Giselle yawns.

"I get it. You sound tired, you want to get going?"

"Yeah, I suppose I should. See you, tomorrow right?"

I smile, "You will."

"Alright, Weathers make sure you get some rest yourself. I think you're training with Tina again tomorrow."

"Ah, man. Don't tell me that. Well, at least I know what to expect, right?"

"Right."

"Okay, Giselle, have a goodnight."

She yawns again, "You too... Wait..."

"...Yea."

"I wish I could share my bed you...wait is that too much."

I pause. "No, not at all. I wish I could too. Goodnight."

"Goodnight" I stare at my phone and wait for her to end the call. Jesus Christ; I'm fucking high. It took every ounce of self-control not to keep yapping it about hockey and Blackness.

Holy shit, that conversation could've got deep. Probably would've talked her to sleep if she wasn't already tired. The thought alone of her ass in doggy-style while I was in and out is giving me a half chub. To be honest, Giselle's right about Billie and Tracie. Mostly, Billie… that guy is going nowhere fast and I don't want to be in the passenger seat when he gets there. Once, I'm done with training, I'll be able to distance myself from him entirely. I mean, I appreciate the fact I was able to use his leverage to get in the door. But, at what cost? What price do I have to pay to be accepted? As long as I'm a respected worker, they could have their pound of flesh.

Out of nowhere, a flashlight shines to the left of me. "What the fuck, who is that?" I yell.

"Don't you fucking, move!" the man shouts. As he approaches, the police badge on his chest glimmers off the street light. "Put your hands in the air and turn around slowly."

I do as he directs. With the blinding light and his gun drawn; I try to steady the pace of my heartbeat and make no sudden movements. "What seems to be the problem officer?"

He takes a step closer and tucks his flashlight, "I've seen you walking around for the last few hours, you look too fucking suspicious if you ask me."

"Well, I am asking you, Sir."

The cop rips my collar and lifts my body about six inches off the ground. He presses me halfway over the guard rail then shoves the barrel of pistol into my temple, "You want to get smart, asshole?" He shouts. His breath smells as if he just ate a bowl of shit. From the looks of his yellow incisors, he doesn't have very good oral hygiene.

"I'm sorry, Officer if I offended you in any way. I was just sitting on the bench while I was having a conversation with a girl I work with," I plead.

He lowers his gun. "Where do you work?"

"Right there, Second House; I'm a server in training."

He loosens his grip on my neck and puts his weapon in his holster. "Let me see some I.D."

I rummage through my bag. I totally forgot to put the coke in my sock. Like a fucking idiot, I placed it in here when I was getting my debit card and wallet together. Without panicking, I tuck it into the inside pocket then hand over my license. My left foot starts rapidly tapping; I force it to stop. "Once again, I'm sorry if offended you, Officer."

He slides my license into his back pocket then unclips black metal handcuffs from his belt saying, "Put your hands behind your back." I turn around and he latches each cuff as tight as possible; I can feel the blood circulation slowing down in my wrist. He forcefully positions my body onto a trail bench. "You move so much as an inch; I'll beat the Black off you."

I nod. "Yes, Sir." He takes three steps towards my bag and removes my I.D from his back pocket. "Dispatch, this is Officer LePore, come in."

"This is dispatch, Office LePore, what's your 10-4?" The voice from his radio asks.

"Uh, I'm on the walking path of the Lux Apartments off Main. I have a Black male, height about 5'10, weight 175 pounds, brown eyes. Name: Michael H. Weathers, W-E-A-T-H-E-R-S."

"Copy, sit tight, Officer."

"Copy." LePore scoops my bag up and peeks inside then places it at my feet. "Weathers, Weathers. Why does that sound so familiar? You've ever been arrested before?

I sweat. "Uh, no sir. To be honest with you sir, this is my first time in handcuffs."

LePore lunges forward and smushes my head into the bench. "What

the fuck did I tell you?" he shouts. "Move again, and see what happens."
I fight back tears of fear and start to shake. I look down and feel wetness;
I pissed myself. I'm overwhelmed with shame and regret. I don't care
about him finding the coke, I just want to make it out of here in one
piece. He paces, flicking my license with his middle finger then comes to
an abrupt halt. "Weathers, why does your name sound so familiar? You
sure you've never been to jail or arrested?"

I shake my head.

"Okay, kid, I find out your lying to me; you're in a world of trouble,"
LePore says and picks my bag off the ground and begins to search
through it.

The Dispatcher cracks in over his radio, "Officer Lepore, come in."

"This is Lepore, over."

"Nothing came back on your perp," she says.

"Nothing?"

"Nothing, Officer."

"Thank you, Dispatch." He continues to go through my bag, "Where
were you coming from kid?"

"C.J's, Sir."

"What were you doing there?"

"Having a few drinks with a co-worker, the Rangers were playing so I
figured it would be a great way to unwind."

He stops then stares. "You watch hockey?"

I clear my throat, "Yes sir, I use to play."

LePore gasps then lets my bag hit the brick pavement, "That's it!" he
cries, "You're Michael Weathers! You're one of the best center-forwards
this state has ever seen, shit that I've ever seen. Holy shit!"

I lift my head. "Yeah, that's me."

"You still hold the record for most hat tricks in a season."

"Yeah, that was junior year."

"Wow, man you don't remember me? I was your assistant coach your freshman year. I left to go the police academy. "

To get the fuck out of these cuffs; I pretend as if I know who he is. "Oh yeah, Coach LePore, you had us working on our backhand passes. Now that I think about it, if weren't for you, I wouldn't have led the state in assists that year."

"I mean you were a freshman starting varsity, I kinda think you had no choice but to pass the puck but thanks anyway; that means a lot. Remember that game against Lincoln, when you scored on the top-ranked Left-Wing that year? Man, you whooped his ass. That was the tightest bare naked choke I've ever seen."

I smirk. "Not as tight as these cuffs."

"Oh shit, let me get those off you man," LePore says as he helps me to my feet and then uncuffs my wrists adding, "Hey Mike, I'm sorry about being such a dick to you. If I knew who you were, I wouldn't have been so rough. It's just protocol, you know. No hard feelings, right?"

I dust myself off and throw my bag around my shoulder, "Yeah man, I get it. I really do. And, I apologize if I caused you any discomfort; but I'm glad we can leave here without incident."

He smiles. "Yeah, me too. You need a ride home or something?"

"Thanks, man, but I'm good, I live two blocks away from here."

"You live around here? Come on, let me get you home. That's the least I could do." LePore slaps my shoulder.

"Sure, why not. Where'd you park?"

"Right along the bus terminal, come on." LePore marches through the path as I trail behind. The tightness of the cuffs has broken the skin on both of my wrists and caused some heavy swelling. I don't know if I should just decline this ride or not. Something tells me if I do, he'll take it as a sign of disrespect and really ruin my night. If I didn't have this shit on me, I would file a complaint. But, what good will that do? He knows where I work and live. I'm better off just taking that beating on the chin and moving on. "First time in a cop car?" He opens the back passenger door.

"Uh, yeah. Can I sit in the front with you?"

"Oh no, I'm sorry, Mike, it's just protocol even if I was to give my own mother a ride, she would have to sit in the back. I don't make the rules; I just follow em'."

I duck under his arm and sit down as I throw my bag against the dividing glass. Needless to say, the plastic seats are less than comfortable. I couldn't imagine being in here with my arms restrained behind my back. I wonder how many Black people had to endure this dickhead's wrath then had to be pushed into the hot ass backseat with the circulation in their wrist cut off? I can't imagine that pain, I can't imagine it at all.

LePore slams his door and turns the engine. "Dispatch this is LePore, going back to my beat. Over."

"Officer LePore, this is Dispatch, that's a copy. Finally a night without an arrest. I'm lost for words."

"I still get an hour and a half before shift change, I'll find something," LePore jokes

The Dispatcher laughs, "Good luck, Officer, see you at shift change."

"Copy." He clears his throat. "You're on Baldwin, right?"

"Yeah, 350 to be exact."

"Alright, you got it." He turns on the siren, speeds to the end of the terminal, and straight through a red light. Taking a hard right then another one; my body slides towards the divider. I catch a glimpse of a bruise above my left eye. Shit, how the fuck am I supposed to explain this tomorrow? To the touch, it stings. And I'm pretty it looks worse than it feels, but I may be singing a different tune when I wake up in the morning. LePore shines the patrol light on the houses looking for my place. "350 Baldwin, right?"

"Yeah."

LePore gets outs and walks around to let me out. "Hey, man, once again I want to apologize for how I acted back there. Like I said if I knew who you were, I wouldn't ever have stopped you."

I grab my bag and stand up. "Nah, I get it. It's just protocol."

He pats my shoulder. "That's it... just protocol."

YOU'RE UP KID

For the first time in days, I'm not hungover. Today, I'm feeling somewhat good. Disregarding my bruised wrists and black eye; I'm alright. Not to mention the few bumps I took before heading out. It's funny how coke can subside physical pain. I don't know if it can do the same for mental ailments but I'm not that far gone. That blow definitely put a little extra pep in my step. The sun is shining and there's not a cloud in the horizon. For once, I didn't have to race across the street to beat oncoming traffic. When I got to the trail, Cam caught my attention from the balcony, and wouldn't let me leave until I promised for the thousandth time to take her ice-skating tomorrow night. How could I say no to that little girl? When I enter Second House, Giselle greets me with a kiss and hug. "What's going on hon?" I ask.

Giselle smirks. "I'm having a tough time walking today, we had too much fun last night." She smiles and adds, "What's going on wit—wait." Giselle grips my jaw and examines it from side to side, "What the fuck happen to your face?"

"Ah, nothing..."

"I know you didn't lose a fight with a door."

I chuckle and take her hands. "Nah, nothing like that. After you left, I got stopped by a cop. He ran my name and he roughed me up a bit, no biggie. I play hockey with kids who hit way harder than that asshole. I'm fine."

Giselle looks down. "Oh my God, look at your wrist, they're completely swollen, did that pig cuff you?"

"Yeah but, that was just protocol."

She rips away from my grasp. "Don't feed me that bullshit, Weathers, you know that fucking pig was just flexing his authority, and for what? Just so he feels safe? And if you weren't cuffed, just imagine him putting three warning shots into you while you reach for your license." Her voice raises as she continues, "Come on, Michael, look at you. Did you get his badge number? Or his name?"

"Giselle, calm down, take a deep breath. It's okay, he actually apologized for the incident, and to be honest with you, the guy who did it used to be my coach. After he ran my name and everything checked out, he offered me a ride home and not to make the matters worse, I took it. Because if you look at my face, he could've taken it to a whole other level. I had to play his card so I wouldn't get three warning shots in my back."

"Giving you a ride home isn't justifying the ass whooping he handed you."

"And you're right, but the truth of the matter is…" I take her hands again, "I'm alive."

A tear trickles down her cheek and splashes onto a special's menu; I wipe her face dry and kiss her forehead, "Hey, G. It'll be okay like I said, it looks worse than it feels. I'll be alright."

"I hate to see this happen to you, Weathers. Poor eating habits, racists cops, and drugs are the main threat to us. And it gets me so frustrated to see this happen to someone I care about. I don't care how you know him or what he used to be to you. He had no proper cause to fuck you up like this." She walks around the hostess stand and gives me her tender embrace adding," And, you're right. The fact is, you're in front of me breathing and walking. I guess you made the right decision. If that pig would've killed you, and made me deal with these crackers by myself, I would be in jail." We both laugh. She says, "Well, I'm glad I could bring you some joy even though that fucking asshole bruised your handsome mug." She kisses my blackened eye and marches behind the hostess stand. "Oh, before I forget A.G. wants to talk to you."

I clench my bag. "About what?"

"Fuck if I know, he just told me to make sure you talk to him before you clock in."

"And he didn't say about what?"

"For the last time, no. I'm sure it's about nothing. You don't do anything wrong, shit he may even want to give you more hours. Now, stop being so scary and go see what he wants. I gotta make sections and call the reservations. Now scoot."

"You're right it's probably nothing." I reach in for a kiss and head to the back-server station and to my surprise, nobody is here. All of the rolls up are done but there are napkins to be folded. Guess they left that for the newbie to handle, oh well. I throw my bag into the cabinet and tie on my apron. The bar is empty as Graham cleans and prepares for the happy hour rush. "Hey Graham, what's going on?" I greet.

He jumps back knocking over a few rock glasses, and barely catches the bucket of sanitizer. "Oh shit!" Graham shouts, "Holy fucking shit, kid." He laughs. "You scared the living shit out of me."

"My bad, I was just saying hello. I hope you didn't shit yourself."

"No kid, my undies are stained free... I hope." He chuckles. "I guess your mother was right about you, kid."

"Right about what?"

"About you having the element of surprise."

"Mom knows best."

"As they all do. Hey kid, what happened to your face?"

"Uh," I chuckle. "Lost a fight with a door."

"You'll always lose that one kid, hey but look on the bright side, at least you know the odds every time you pick a fight with an inanimate object."

"For sure."

"I know the past couple of days have been rough on you, kid, but once you get your feet planted, you'll be alright."

"You think so?"

"I know so, you're a good kid, Mike. A little wet behind the ears when it comes to dealing with Tina but you'll get there. Don't let anyone stop you from being who you are, you deserve a shot like anyone else."

"Thanks, Graham, that means a lot to me."

"Don't mention it. This is your last day of training, right?"

"Yeah, about that… Giselle told me A.G. wanted to speak to me before I clocked in, and I actually have no idea where his office is. Can you point me in the right direction?"

"Sure kid, when you get to the end of the stairs before you reach the door leading outside, you'll see a gray door to your right and in that room is the beer room. It should be unlocked but if it isn't come just yell and I'll toss the keys down. But yeah, when you go through that door you're going to walk past the walk-in fridge which I'm sure you know where it is by now. You walk past it and you'll see where we store all the beer and spirits, keep straight till you get to another gray door, and you'll be at the office."

"Thanks."

"You got it." He goes back to work and I continue through the back door, downstairs, and just as Graham instructed: I enter the beer room and walk past the walk-in fridge. I can't help but notice the various amounts of bottles and cans of beer. All different colors and names. There is even a non-alcoholic brand. The only thing I don't see is forty ounces of malt liquor but I don't think any bar or restaurant would serve forties. Be funny if they did. The office door is adjacent and before I walking in; I knock three times.

"Who's there?" A.G. shouts.

"It's Michael Sir, said you wanted to see me before I clocked in."

"Oh yeah, just the man I've been waiting for. Come in, come in." His office is rather bland. Just a desk with a full computer set. But the picture of his daughter that Giselle mentioned sits right next the monitoring screen with every camera view of the restaurant. I catch an image of Tina and Jackie in the kitchen but no sight of Billie. I wipe my palms before shaking his hand. "What happened to your eye?" he asked.

"Uh, after leaving C.J's last night, turns out I had a few too many. And I somehow managed to get knocked out by my entrance door which happens to be pretty heavy, and when I woke up there was this," I laugh. "So, yeah..."

"Ah man, I've been there before. Back when I was in college; I got so blackout drunk, I fell face-first on the corridor pavement. When I came too, my entire face was black and blue. But that's another story for another time, take a seat, please."

"Sure thing."

"You know why I called you down here, Michael?"

"No, sir I don't."

"Well, I wanted to thank you for all the extra effort you've been putting forth. You've been put in some tough spots and I know how hectic expo training can get, it's a lot to remember. Overwhelming even. And you've shined on every occasion even when that racist fuck started shit with you. It took immense strength and will to show up the next day and not let it affect your work performance. Plain and short, that was the most impressive thing I've seen in twenty some odd years of being in this industry. I can't imagine how hard it was to deal with that. And if you need to talk about what happened that night or anything else; my door is always open."

"Thank you; I really appreciate your kind words, but I know you didn't call me all the way down here to talk about my strong will. I know you're a busy man and all, and I took a peek at the guest list and tonight and we have a shit-ton on of covers so what is this all about..."

A.G. smirks. "I like that, Mike, straight to the point. So I guess I'll cut straight to the point then: as of 12 pm, William Tills, or Billie, is no longer with Second House."

My jaw drops. "Wait, what did you just say?"

"We let Billie go, meaning he's no longer employed here."

"Why? I don't get it, he's been here forever."

"Yes, he was and due to his neglectful tendencies, while holding an occupation here, it was time to part ways. There were a lot of things that configured his departure."

"Like what?"

"For one, he was stealing alcoholic beverages by the six-pack and liter. I know you two are friends and he referred you to me but were you aware of his substance abuse problem?"

I lower my head. "I had no idea, I guess he did a great job of keeping it under wraps."

"Well, it was no secret to me or the owners. We even offered some type of treatment facility which at that time, the owners even offered to finance it, but due to the theft and erratic behavior, we had to let him go. I didn't call you down here just to inform you of Billie's termination; I have to ask you to sign a covenant to not sue." A.G. slides a contract in front me.

"Why, what is this?"

"Well, another reason why I had to fire Billie…a few customers on numerous occasions heard him address you by a derogatory name. And it is in your right to quit right now and file a lawsuit but if you do stay employed here, you have to sign this letter stating you won't later file against Second House or C.J.'s."

"What? I ju—I mean, Billie uses the N-word all the time. He drops the hard "r" and uses it like people…like myself who can say it, and I never felt discriminated against or anything like that, ever."

"I get what you're saying, Michael, and maybe that's fine and dandy outside of work even, but I still disagree with that type of language whether you take offense to it or not. He shouldn't be allowed to say that in your presence, at all. It's disgusting and disrespectful, he should be ashamed of himself. My girlfriend is African-American and I feel for you, Michael, even if I can't fully understand or console you. But the truth of the matter is, Billie had to go, he just had to. He was becoming too much of a liability."

I shake my head then rub my face. "It's just, I don't know, like why couldn't he get let off with a warning of something, I know stealing is one thing but couldn't he just pay back what he took or something? Shit, wash dishes for a month… I don't know anything but fire him."

"We did, time after time and again, even after six years of employment; he just kept fucking up. No matter how many times I reprimanded him, he would always overstep his boundaries. Next thing you know, he would've been stealing from you or anyone else who works here to support his habit. I have a duty to manage and protect the staff here. Billie was treated as if he were family, and that hurts the most."

"Yeah, it's just he got me the job here, and... now, he doesn't have one."

"Well, Michael, you shouldn't. This was his own doing. You did nothing but show up and do the job you were asked to do." "Well, Michael, you shouldn't. This was his own doing. You did nothing but show up." He pauses for a second. "I know this is a lot to take in, Michael, but I have a job to do and that includes looking out for the restaurant's best interests. Turns out Billie didn't fit those criteria but you do. So, I'm going to ask you again will you sign this letter because I have a full-time spot to fill with your name on it, and if not you, then I have to find someone else."

I stare at the off blue fountain tip pen sitting on top of the contract, something possesses me to pick up it and scratch my Hancock across the dotted line and so I do. "Well, I guess that's that."

A.G. pushes off his desk and the wheels of his chair glide to the wall. "Wow you know, Michael., there hasn't been one moment you have ceased to amaze me. Most people would have sued and settled out of court, obviously, that isn't what you want. Can I ask why?"

"What's the point? What's me suing going to prove? It won't heal help fix anything."

"Fix what? Did somebody else say something derogatory towards you?"

"No, not at all, and I meant nothing by what I just said. It's just... I just... I just want to be accepted by my peers for reliable and consistent work performance, not because of affirmative-action. That's why I chose to sign it. It's hard to explain. I don't expect you to understand."

"No, no, Michael, I think I do but you are accepted here and if you should ever feel that you aren't, you come to me and we'll address it together. You're not alone here, Michael, and I want to make sure you are well aware of that, and that you deserve your job here. You bust your ass for it. So why not?" He removes the contract off his desk and places it in a desk drawer.

"Yeah, but for whatever reason, it doesn't feel like I belong here. I don't know. Guess, we'll just have to wait and see."

"As long as I'm here, I'll make it my business to make sure you're treated fairly and respected."

I nod, rise, and push my chair in.

"Before you leave, Michael, one more thing?"

I turn to face him. "Yeah, what's up?"

"Since I had to let Billie go, we're shorthanded a server tonight. And you progressed through your training pretty fast. Would you mind if I put you on the floor tonight instead of shadowing? To be honest with you, there's nothing else for you to do and it's your chance to make some serious cash as well."

I pause. "Uh, yeah it's a little sudden but sure anything to get the job done."

"You're going to do great, I just know it. Anything you want to ask me before the night begins?"

"No, oh wait... do the others know about Billie getting the can?"

"Yes, everyone who needs to know has been informed. I'm working on the schedule now; it'll be posted in the back-server station later on tonight. Check-in with Giselle for your section."

"Does she know?"

He smacks his folder against the desk. "Oh shit. Thanks for reminding me; I actually forgot. I thought I said something when I told her to tell you to speak to me. Come on, I'll follow you back upstairs to let her know about him and giving you a section." A.G. trails behind as we make our way upstairs and through the bar. When we arrive at the hostess stand, Giselle has just finished confirming another reservation for tonight. She pencils the name into the guest book.

"I hate it when you hover A.G.," Giselle laughs. "But that party of twelve that's supposed to be coming at 7:30 pm is now fourteen and they need a high-chair."

"Okay, noted just make sure you inform Jackie about that. Did you make the sections already?" A.G. asks.

"Yup, Tina has the back of the bar dining starting from 15. Jackie has the dining room as usual, and Billie has the front of the bar from 14 and down. Why?"

A.G. removes his glasses and takes a cloth from his back pocket then wipes the lenses. "Don't kill me G, but I forgot to tell you when you came in that Billie was let go and to—"

She gasps and smiles. "Really, why?"

"I won't get into all of that right now." A.G. pats my back. "But, Michael here is all set with his training and is willing to step up to the plate and fill in. So, would you be so kind to etch out his name and replace it with Michael's?"

"I'll be more than happy to do that," she says as she erases Billie's name faster than I could blink and dots the I in my name with a heart.

"Well, with that being said. If anyone needs me, I'll be downstairs doing paperwork and getting prepared for tonight." He turns towards me. "Okay, Michael you got this, let's rock n' roll. Any questions you know who to ask. Knock em' dead, kid." He marches through the bar dining and vanishes downstairs.

Giselle, filled with excitement, scurries from behind the hostess stand and wraps her arms around my neck. "Oh my goodness, I'm so happy for you. They gave you that fat perv's job and all his hours I bet." She grins. "You're going to make great money. I'm so happy for you." I can't bring myself to embrace her. She lets go and stares, "What's wrong aren't you happy you don't have to deal with that fat fuck anymore?"

"Uh, yeah I guess but he got me the job and..."

"...and what?" she shouts. "He's always coming late, coked out of his mind, and always harassing me. Plus, he smelled like shit. I don't see why you feel sorry for him. He brought that shit on himself, all you did was show up and do your job. If I were you, I'd be jumping for joy right now. There's no need to feel bad for that degenerate, not one bit. Fuck him, good riddance."

I force a smile. "I guess you're right."

She pecks my lips. "I always am. You'll find out soon but get to work. Service starts in thirty."

"No doubt, I guess this is it. Wish me luck."

"Luck!" Giselle shouts. "Wait a sec, did A.G. tell you why he was fired? It was the coke wasn't?"

"Uh, that was a part of it but it turns out he was stealing booze and customers kept complaining. And a bunch of other stuff he didn't want to mention."

Giselle begins to clean the dinner menus, "Well, I'm not surprised one bit. Like I just said, good riddance. He had it made here. Like to see him pull the crap he was doing here at whatever place hires him next."

I grin. "That would be a sight to see, but, yeah, let me know when I get seated, will you?" I leave her a smile and proceed through the dining-room and straight into the kitchen. Soon as I enter, Tina gives me a dirty look and bumps into me as she marches out. I pay her no mind. Jackie usually says hello, but she continues to set up expo. "Hey, Boss Lady, you make it home okay last night?"

"Yeah." She brushes right by to grab entree plates.

"That's good, we're going to be busy tonight, looks like you and Tina took care of everything already."

Jackie starts to dry each plate. "Yup."

"You know, I heard about Billie and I just think it's fuck up. And we just talked about him taking a break from partying and getting better here at work."

"Uh-huh." She moves past again.

"And I had no clue A.G. was going to let him go."

"Nobody did."

"I haven't texted him yet, how's he tak—"

"Look, just keep Billie's name out your mouth, 'cause it looks like you took his job," she scolds.

"Bu—"

"But nothing, Newbie, just shut up and get to work." She storms out of the kitchen. After taking a few bumps in the bathroom, I'm in the backlot trying to find solace in this cigarette. There's about ten minutes until service starts and it'd be a shame for this drip to go to waste but pending on Jackie and Tina's mood, it will. I texted Billie but no reply. Who knows what's going through his head right now. He probably thinks I was hired to replace him but I told that stupid fuck to watch his mouth at work. I fucking told him. Now, everybody thinks it was my intention to get him canned. Should have just walked out and not sign that fucking contract, but I can't go through that shit again. What would my dad think? My mom would go ballistic, pressing for a lawsuit for sure. I guess it's time to go see Michelle after all."

"Hey, Weathers!" Giselle shouts from the backdoor entrance.

"Yeah."

"You got sat, 15b four top. They're regulars so..."

"Got it." I flick my smoke into the lot and rush back upstairs into the bathroom to wash my hands but not before railing a few more lines. The drip comes back and my attitude shifts for the time. The facet always takes fucking forever to get warm. I check my nose for specs and catch a glimpse of the piece of shit I've become. How could you do this to Billie? He's the reason why you're even here. You don't deserve this job. Who are you trying to fool? You're better off washing dishes with Jose or better yet, hanging from a tree like the disobedient house nigger you are.

I shake my hands, pull twice on the paper dispenser, and then wipe my nostril clean. Maybe I should do another... I hurry back in the stall and sniff three bumps off the corner of my notepad. I check the mirror, then dash to 15b. It's Joe and Carol from a few days ago. They have happy hour menus which I'm not too familiar with but we'll see how this goes. "Hey, Joe, how are you and Carol? It's nice to see you guys again." I smile.

They both look surprised and not too happy about my approach. "Hey man, Mike right?" Joe asks.

"Yes, sir, Mike it is and I'll be waiting on you tonight. Can I get you two anything to drink?"

Joe scans the bar dinning. "Where's Billie?"

"Uh, unfortunately, Billie is no longer here," I answer.

Carol drops her menu. "What do you mean, no longer here?

What happened? He was great here."

My palms become moist. "Uh, all I know is, upper management decided that they should part ways..."

"...So, you took his job?" Joe scowls.

"No, not at all, Sir."

His wife's face washes over with discontentment. "But you replaced him so you took his job."

"No, Ma'am, that wa—I mean that was not my intention at all. Can I start you off with some Bud Lights? Or..."

Joe belches. "You might as well, you sure as hell took you long enough to get here."

I grin. "Okay then, two bud lights coming right up." I jolt to the POS only to find it occupied by Jackie. She's slower than usual so I just face the dining room and try to make it like I'm not in such a hurry.

"Newbie, can you not fucking hover over me. It's creepy. I'll be done in a minute," she says.

"Got it." I take two more steps into the dining room. Without saying a word, Jackie speeds into the kitchen. The POS seems brand new all of sudden as if I never used it before. I punch in my number in and the screen takes forever to load. When it finally does, I can't find the bar dinning button. I'm such a dumbass. Turns out I was on the correct screen this whole time. I find 15 and ring in their two Bud Lights and move to the bar. By the time I get to Graham, he's already twisting the cap off the second beer. Before I can grab the bottles, Giselle informs me she sat two people

at 13. When I return to 15, Joe and Carol look even more agitated.
I set their beers in front of them. "You guys ready to order?"

"We've been ready," Carol barks.

"What can I get you?"

"Well, start off with wings with the sauce on the side, a Lobster
with the greens and mac and cheese, and my wife will have a large
Cobb salad," Joe orders.

"Would you like the lobster and salad after the wings?"

Joe looks as if I just asked the stupidest question ever, "What do
you think genius?"

I force a chuckle. "Okay, so as a second course."

"Bingo, hey hon and this is the guy they got to replace Billie,"
he heckles.

"Oh be nice, he's still new."

I smile. "Will that be all?"

He picks at his incisor with a matchbook. "For now, run along."
I get to the POS and Tina's here, deliberately taking her time.
When she finishes sending in her orders; she pulls out her phone
and starts texting.

"Excuse me, Tina, can I put some food in for my table or are
you just going to stand there?"

"Who the fuck you talking too? Oh, wait, I'm sorry, Newbie are
your feelings hurt now?" Tina laughs. "Are you going to run and
tell A.G. how I was mean to you?" Tina nudges pass as she leaves
the back-server station. Jesus Christ, this shit is getting out of hand.
I put 15's order in and bolt to 13. It's a Black couple and they look

relatively young; I would say they're younger or somewhere around my age.

I approach the table wearing a smile. "Good evening, welcome to Second House. My name is Michael and I'll be your server tonight. I see you two have been eyeing the drink menu, can I start you off with something, or do we need more time?"

The gentleman smiles. "Hello Michael, I'm Greg and this is my sister Georgia. I'm going to have a Gin and Tonic. Sis?"

Georgia grins. "Hi, Michael, how are you?"

"I'm good Georgia, thanks for asking. What would you like?"

"I'll have a Makers on the rocks with a side coke but if you only have Pepsi that's fine."

"Okay Georgia, one Makers on the rocks with a side of Pepsi, I'll check and see if I got Coke in the can, I think we do. And, Gin and Tonic for you Greg. Do you prefer a certain type of gin?"

"What do you suggest?" he asks.

"Well, when I'm trying to save money, I just stick with the house brand but when I can afford it, I drink Blue Coat."

"I'll try the Blue Coat, thanks."

"Okay guys, your drinks will be right up and if you notice the paper menu between the salt and pepper shakers....those are the specials for tonight. I'll be right back with your drinks." As I head towards the POS system, the service bell goes off. Tina is standing at expo. I glide right pass and see wings with the sauce on the side. I check the ticket, stamp it, and take the wings from the window. When I turn around Tina is standing right behind me. "What happened to staying behind?" I ask.

"What happen to not throwing people under the bus?" Tina replies.

"What's that supposed to mean?"

"You know what it means, monkey, you think you're hot shit now. Well, as long as I work here, I'm going to make you always know your place."

"For what? I never did shit to you, Billie, or anyone for that matter." I try to move past and she blocks my path.

"See here, Newbie, you're exactly what's wrong with this country. Blacks think they're so entitled to everything that the whites lay out for them. You're just another excuse for taking a perfectly fine white man's job. You're just a piece of shit who took another white man's job just to meet the quota."

"Fuck you, Tina. And if you'll be so kind as to get the fuck out of my way; I'm working."

She leans in and whispers, "I should spit in your face, nigger."

You spit in my face and you'll have a face full of hot wings. You're lower than dirt. Now, please if you would be so kind as to let me pass." I stare her down as she moves out the way. I return to 15 even though I'm holding their appetizers; I'm still greeted by their same looks of disappointment. I carefully set the dish in between them. Both of their beers are three quarters down from being empty. "Would you guys like another round?"

Joe digs into the food first. "Yeah, like yesterday."

I grin. "Okay, coming right up."

Jackie is at the POS. I wait a minute or so and make sure not to hover. She grunts as she leaves. I put in 13's drinks first and reorder Bud Lights for Joe and Carol. Before moving to the bar, I take a second to process what Tina said. Maybe she's right. Maybe I'm only here to meet the minority mark as if I was to be the token server or some shit. You know, I can't imagine how Billie is taking this whole ordeal. I fucking told him and I get blamed for the shit he pulled while all I did was try to help. "Ay, Newbie, your drinks are ready!" Graham yells from the bar.

I grab a tray and place cocktails napkins under Greg and Georgia's drinks. When I get to 15; I replace their empties and leave with a grin as I return to 13b. "So guys here are your drinks. And Greg, I have to tell you, I'm excited to see how you like the Blue Coat so please tell me what you think."

"I'll tell you right now." He sips from the straw and pauses. "Hmm, you know what, Michael? This might be the best gin mix I ever had. Great choice, man."

"Why thank you, Greg, I'm glad you like it. Now, are you guys ready to put in some starters or do you need a few more minutes?"

Georgia glances at her brother. "Uh, we're going to do tonight's special, the diablo mussels, are they—"

"—Yes, they're quite spicy," I add.

She smiles. "Perfect. I haven't decided on my entrée, what about you, bro?"

"Um, I'm between the House Burger and the filet. Which one would you prefer, Mike?"

"This is going sound a little crazy, but I'm actually on a bread diet right now, so I haven't tried the burger yet. This is my first day as server."

Georgia gives a mean side-eye then grins, "Really? Your first day, well Michael you're doing a wonderful job."

"But the burger seems to be a fan favorite, and the filet might be the best steak I've ever had. Nonetheless; I would assume the burger would be served well over a garden, but that's the bread diet talking," I say.

"Hmm, a burger over a salad that sounds so healthy and yummy, might have to give that some thought. Especially for this weight," Georgia giggles. She is a little on the heavy side, so maybe that wouldn't be a bad idea. "What weight?" I say anyway.

She smiles. "You're the sweetest, Michael, thank you."

"So, I'll put the Diablo Mussel special in for you both and check on you in a few. Now, Greg, give that burger some thought ."

"You know, I'm leaning towards the filet, but we'll see when you come back, Mike." He sips.

"Okay, great your appetizer will be ready shortly."

I fetch two smalls plates and a water pitcher. When I return 13, I don't interrupt their conversation; I quickly refill their water and march back to the POS. Finally, there's nobody here. The special's button took all of three seconds to find and luckily for me, my table gets the last order. So, that means I have to go out of my way to tell the others we ran out of mussels so they don't look stupid if someone were to order the special app. I find Tina first and she just shrugs me off. When I told Jackie, she forced a 'thank you'.

But what she really wanted to say was, 'Why are you bothering me?'

I guess someone at the bar tried to order the mussels special and Graham yelled out "eighty-six." That's code for "no more" or "we ran out" of a certain food item or a keg has kicked and there's no backup.

When I check on 15, the table is a fucking mess. You would imagine these people had more table etiquette than what they're displaying. Before interacting, I see wing sauce all over the place, both of their guest towels on the ground, and a ton of paper napkins covering a toppling of plates and the table. So when I get back to the server station to get a tray. I wet my bus rag. I do my best on trying not to touch any of the bones or napkins, and pile trash all on to the tray. "Can I get you guys another round?" I ask.

"Sure, while you're at it check on our food, I'm fucking starving," Joe whines. "Or did you forget to put it in?"

I smile. "No sir, it should be right out."

On my way to the server station, A.G. comes out of the kitchen and signals it's Joe and Carol's entrées he's carrying. I expected him to just stand there and wait until I dispose of their trash but he does me a great service by serving them. As I'm scraping the plates into the garbage, A.G. approaches. "You know 15 got their last course, right?" he questions.

"Yes, I do. Thank you."

"You're welcome, we're starting to pick up now so I'll be on expo. You already know to try and run your own food. But if I can, I'll help run food while you're in between tables, that'll be a big help. You're finding everything in the computer, okay?"

"Yup, some things were confusing at first 'cause there's nobody hovering over," I chuckle. "But other than that, I figured it all out pretty quickly. I'll check on 15 in a sec after I put in another round of Bud Lights for them. It's like every five minutes they need another beer. They can sure put em' away."

"They sure can," He chuckles. "Joe and Carol have been coming here since the start, at some point, I have to break the news to them about letting go of Billie."

I send the drinks to the bar and turn to face him. "I already did, when they asked for him earlier. And, they did not take it so well."

"Oh geez, well yeah, he was a favorite of theirs. I'll go over and talk to them, try and ease their minds about his departure. Billie did fill a lot of seats here. That's one thing you didn't have to worry about when it came to him." A.G. pats my back. "Well, you're doing great kid, you know where to find me when the shit starts to hit the fan." He strolls over to 15 and starts talking. I'm glad he wants to ease the tension, but there's no undoing their ugliness. The service bell goes off, I rush to the kitchen. Before grabbing the mussels out the window, I fill the breadbasket with three more dinner rolls just in case Greg and Georgia think of asking for more bread and place cocktail forks into the dish. This should be more than enough. I take the appetizer and move to their table. "Okay, here is your Diablo Mussel along with bread for dipping."

Georgia grins. "Oh my goodness, it smells and looks so delicious. I thought we had to request for bread. I like how you think ahead. And, I'm starting to think you were lying about this being your first day,"

"You're welcome very much. Now, have we decided on our dinner?" I ask and tap my notepad.

Greg places his napkin in his lap. "Sis, you go first."

"Well, Michael the fact that you're crushing the bread diet..." she chuckles.

I laugh, "I don't know about crushing but it's worth a try."

"So, I'm going try your idea with the house burger over a large house salad, may I have that chopped with the dressing on the side?"

"Yes, you may. How would like your burger cooked?" I ask.

"Medium-well, please."

"Would you like cheese on your burger as well?"

She pauses. "Uh, do you have cheddar?"

"We got cheddar," I nod.

"Great, Greg you ready?" She hands over her menu.

"Yup, I'm going with the filet, medium-rare, please."

I point to the bottom of his menu. "It comes with two sides."

"Oh okay. Hmmm, I'll do asparagus and fries."

I take his menu. "Great, you guys good on drinks?"

Georgia picks up Greg's glass and eyes it for a bit. "Yeah, we'll do another for sure thank you, Michael."

"Great, I'll put those in along with your food. Enjoy the

mussels." I speed to the hostess stand and give the menus to Giselle. She blows a quick kiss then I stop and smile before I continue to the bar to pick up Joe and Carol's beers. A.G. is still at their table. They haven't touched their food yet nor have they finished their second round. I keep a grin as I set the bottles next to the unfinished ones. Back at the POS Tina is here, buried in her phone just taking up space. "Excuse me, Tina. Some people are actually working here."

She moves over to the sink. "You got 13 right?"

I reorder the sibling's drinks. "Yeah, why..."

"...Everyone knows that Black people don't tip, or tip good enough." She peeks into the bar dinning, "And from the looks of it, they might not even leave one, that's gotta suck."

"Are you done?"

"I told Giselle to give you 17b."

"Why?"

Tina smirks. "Because I know your kind doesn't tip," she says. "Now I'm done. See you later, Newbie, you're going to need it." As she waddles into the bar dinning, I give her the finger then complete 13b's order. I return to Joe and Carol. The lobster tail is hollowed as it sits on his plate and she hasn't touched her salad. Yet, they finished their second round of beers. "How's everything going so far?" I ask.

He laughs. "We're not dead yet. Hey, kid, let me ask you something... Billie was really stealing booze huh?"

"I wouldn't know, Sir, luckily for me that's not my department."

"Seems to me like he was set up, none of that stuff was a problem until you started working here, and all of sudden he's stealing? Something doesn't add up," Carol says.

"Like I said, Ma'am, I wouldn't know if he were committing theft or not. I'm just doing the job I was hired for which is to make sure you're fully accommodated, that's it. It's unfortunate if that was the case and still, I wish Billie the best. But I'll reassure you once more, I had nothing to do with upper management's decision. With that being said, can I get you another round?" I grin.

Joe wipes his mouth. "Sure kid. Hey, you know what? You're pretty fast," he states. "I've seen you whizzing around this place faster than my eyes can blink. You're no Billie but at least you got that going for you."

"And what's that, Sir?"

"Being fast. I guess that's something your people are born with even though most of them use it only when they're from running police," he laughs.

"Good one, Sir. I'll be right back with your drinks." I should piss in his fucking beer. The nerve of these fucking two. Jesus, I just can't get a break today. As I grab a tray for 13's drinks, Giselle is approaching 17 with menus and crayons.

"Hey, Tina asked if you could take 17. I told her you would cause you're next in the rotation anyway but they wanted a booth, obviously, that's her section but she insisted on you taking it," she says.

"She told me already, and I'm on it, thanks."

"That Tina hates to pull her own weight, it's like she doesn't want to make any money."

"Believe me, you don't want to know."

"I don't care to know." She smiles. "I'll keep you updated."

"Alright, pretty lady, you do that."

Before I can jet off, Giselle plucks a few white specs off my shirt. "You're too cute. I'll see you later," she says.

As I make my way to Georgia and Greg; I wonder if that was spilled coke on my shirt. Fuck it, who cares. I replace their empty drinks and remove the devoured appetizer and one piece of bread they left untouched. "Glad, to see you two enjoyed the mussels," I say.

"Oh my God, they were so good, compliments to the chef," Georgia smiles.

"Yeah, Mike, we did everything but lick the bowl clean," Greg laughs.

Georgia grills Greg. "I wish you would."

"You know I was just joking." He smirks. "Do you have siblings, Mike?"

I shrug. "Unfortunately, it's just me."

"Consider yourself lucky, Mike, you don't have someone always ratting you out," Greg says, followed by his sister sticking out her tongue to taunt him.

"You know, I kind of wish my parents had another kid so all the attention wouldn't be on me," I chuckle. "Who's older?"

"I am, by two minutes." She flashes her tongue again.

"Oh, wow. So, you guys are twins, that's so cool."

"Yup, he's stuck with me till the casket drops."

"Very true."

I collect small plates first and tuck them in the bowl with the shells and then sit the breadbasket on top. "That's awesome guys, well let me go check on your dinner and I'll be right back." I dart to the back-server station to dump the dishes. 17 looks adjusted; I'll ask for drinks soon. But before I greet the table, I put in Joe and Carol's Bud Lights. I wait for a second for Graham to read the ticket and grab the bottles. Soon as he uncaps them, I swoop in and drop them off.

"You guys okay, here?" I ask. Joe doesn't say anything and Carol just nods. I turn to 17; the family looks restless and hungry. The dad seems content by scrolling through his phone while mom has her hands full calming down their rambunctious children. The kids are between the ages of three and nine. Two girls, and a boy being the smallest. "Hey everyone," I smile. "How's everyone doing this evening? Welcome to Second House, my name is Michael and I will be your server. Would you like to start off with some drinks?"

The mom grins and her husband says, "Hi Michael, I'm Stephen, this is my wife Joanna and these are our girls. He points the oldest first. "Gina-"

"—Gina with a 'G'" The oldest interrupts.

I smile, "Hello Gina with a G. I'm Michael."

Stephen grins and continues, "And that little lady next to her mom is Samantha." With his arms around the boy, he gives him a playful shake. "And this little guy right here is, Stephen Jr."

I smile and wave to the children. "It's my pleasure to make all your acquaintances. Now, mom and dad is there anything I can start the table with?"

"My husband and I will have a bottle of chardonnay, The William Hill," Joanna says.

"Yes, ma'am. And for the kids?"

"Milk for everyone, please."

"But I want a root-beer." Gina cries.

Joanna leans into Gina's ear and mutters something I can't make out but poor Gina is silent after. "Everyone will have milk, Michael, thank you."

I smile. "Okay, the coldest milk in town."

The husband and wife both chuckle. "Is it too late to put in an order of chicken tenders and fries for the kids now? They're really hungry as you can tell," Joanna states.

"Sure, it'll be my pleasure. Would you like their milk in kid's cups?"

"That'll be great, Michael thank you."

"No problem Joanna, I'll be right back with your wine glasses."

I move through the kitchen doors and Tina is standing with 13's entrees, she's clinching the filet mignon with a paper napkin. "I'll take those, thank you very much," I say.

Tina smiles, "Careful, those are really hot. You don't want to burn yourself."

"Fuck you," I mutter.

"What was that, Newbie?"

With A.G. being present she knows I won't repeat myself. "Oh, nothing." I scurry to Greg and Georgia, I set the food down trying to hide the agonizing pain. "Well, guys the moment you've been waiting for." Though I never had the filet, it doesn't half look bad. Georgia's salad looks great, overwhelming, but great.

Georgia grins, "Oh my God Michael, this looks so wonderful. I can't wait to see how it tastes."

"Yeah, this looks great. Man, I can feel the heat still coming off this thing," he laughs. "Hope you didn't burn yourself on the way over here."

"Nah, it wasn't that bad. You guys enjoy now, I'll be back in a bit to see how everything is going."

Back at the POS, I punch 17's order and grab two of the cleanest wine glasses from the side shelf and grab three plastic cups with lids, then prepare the kid's milk. When I return to the family; mom disperses the beverages to the children. I look to Stephen, he shows no signs of wanting to order appetizers. So, I check the bar for their William Hill. Graham hasn't gotten to it yet, the perfect time to get belittled by Joe and Carrol. "Hey, you two how are things over here, ready for the check?" I grin.

Joe belches and rubs his stomach. "The check? What about dessert?"

"Okay, terrific. What will you two be having or do you need some more time to figure it out?" I take his empty plate and with my rag, I clear all the mess on his side of the table into the dish.

"What do you think honey bun? Dessert?" He asks.

Carol's eyes light up. "Ooo, do you guys still have the fudge brownie sundae?"

"Yes, I believe so."

"Well, is that a yes or no? It's too hard to believe anything these days," Joe says.

"Yes, we have it."

"Have what?" Carol asks.

"The brownie fudge sundae, you want for dessert," I respond.

"Good, don't forget to bring two spoons and another round? And make it quick, you been a little slower since that Black family came in. Don't forget about who was here first."

"Believe me, Sir, I can never forget about you, no matter how hard I try. Now if you'll excuse me, I have to go put in your dessert and Bud lights." Joe's jaw drops and his wife stares aimlessly. "Oh, before I forget, can I wrap that up for you Carol? You barely touched it. I'm sure it'll make a good lunch for you tomorrow."

She nods and Joe is still speechless. I take her salad and leave it in the back station while I grab Stephen and Joann's wine. When I get to their table, the kids are more unruly than they were before. I can tell the parents have had a tiring day. They're not even trying to settle the behavior of the children. Mom utters a few "stops." But they just carry on.

"Would you like to taste the wine before I pour?" I ask.

Stephen grins, "Thank you, no, thank you. We've had this

William Hill before and ordered a bottle of wine from that waitress right over there." He points over to 15 where Tina is taking a table of three's order. "She never asked—and to be honest we hated the bottle she preferred. Usually most servers at the restaurants we've been to ask that before pouring. Thank you, Michael."

"I'm going to check on the kid's food and hopefully when I come back, we can get you two started on an appetizer."

Joanna smiles, "Thank you, Michael, but take your time we got our wine now."

I leave with a grin. Before heading to the kitchen, I stop at the POS, unfortunately, it's preoccupied by Jackie. She's finally putting in the order for her party of sixteen so I decide to check on 13. "Hey, guys how are we liking everything so far?"

Georgia with her mouth full just nods and gives a thumbs up.

Greg continues to chew. "Hmm Michael, you might be right about this filet man, it's slammin'."

I chuckle. "I'm happy you guys are enjoying everything. When I was coming out of the kitchen with your burger Georgia, the only thing I could think is how good this burger will mesh well with the salad...so jealous." I smile. "Anyway, would you guys like another round of drinks?" They both nod then I trot across the bar through kitchen doors and like clockwork, A.G. hands over the chicken strips and fries. I head back to the family and watch the two girls hawk over their food while Stephen Jr. stays under his father, waiting for his portion to appear in front of him. Joanna and Stephen seem as if they want the chardonnay to settle before they order.

I return to the back-server station to wrap up Carol's salad, and put in their dessert, then 13's third round. While Graham makes their drinks, and Joanna and Stephen are still idle, this is the perfect time to go kill the rest of this coke. I head straight into the bathroom stall and dump the rest of the powder on my notepad. There's one tiny pebble that happens to be in the pile. There's no sense of breaking it down; I twist up a dollar, scrap up one fat line, and then snort as hard as I can. Tilting my head back to catch every last bit of substance I think, this last bit has to last. "Ah man, damn this shit is good." The drip hits faster than I thought it would.

Now that I got a second wind. I can push through the next wave.

In the kitchen, A.G. puts whip cream as the finishing touch on the vanilla bean ice-cream as it drips over the warm brownie. "Hey Michael, I didn't look at the ticket, this is for 15, right?" A.G. asks.

"Yeah, why?" I reply.

"No particular reason. I had a feeling it was for them, 'cause they order the same shit every time they come in here, and to be quite frank with you, I don't really care for them or their business. They just happen to be good friends of the owners. Do me a favor..." He passes the dessert.

"Yeah, sure what is it?"

"When they settle of their bill, let me know if they leave a tip?"

"Okay..."

"They can be pricks, just let me know what they left you, got it?"

"Got it." A taste of the coke comes back as I move to 15. The smell of the hot chocolate makes me want to puke. I try my best to hide my nausea as set the sundae onto the table.

"Thanks... uh what was your name again?" Joe asks.

"Michael, Sir."

"There you go, Mike. Moving a little faster now and working for that tip like a good waiter should."

For a second, I imagine what would it be like if I shoved that pastry in his fucking throat. Boy, it would be worth all the shit I've been through these last few days. "Well, Sir, I take constructive criticism very well and thank you for noticing. I have Carol's food packed; I'll make sure to bring that right away."

"There may be some hope for you after all." He pokes into the brownie.

"Why thank you, Sir." I wish I could say there's some hope for Carol's face, instead I'll just leave with a smirk. Soon as I turn my attention to the bar I can tell right away, Graham seems agitated. I already know he's going to complain about the drinks sitting for too long. But from what I can see, they're perfectly intact. Luckily for me, a customer grabs his attention before I can reach the bar. I carry them over to Greg and Georgia. They've taken a small break from eating. "Here are your drinks guys, glad to see that we're pacing ourselves, making room for dessert, I hope."

Georgia finishes chewing. "Everything has been great tonight,

Michael thank you so much. How long have you been working here?"

"Not even a week."

Georgia places her napkin on the table. "We would've never known that. You've been excellent and it's so nice to see a Black man getting his money, and not to mention at the same time excelling at it. You know, there are so many Black men who would achieve great things in this field. I don't want to hold you up, but can I ask you something?"

"Shoot."

"What were you doing before this?" She asks.

"Uh, I was in finance well, sort of; I was a copy-writer at LBS."

"No kidding, I've been at LBS for three years or so. You were on the fifth floor with Mark Cannon and those other guys."

I clear my throat. "Yes, yes I was ."

"If you don't mind me asking why did you leave?"

"There was no room for promotion. As you know, the department heads aren't going to retire anytime soon, so I left."

"And you've worked as a waiter before, somewhere else I'm assuming?" Greg questions.

"Yes, throughout college, I worked in a fine dining restaurant, downtown in the city. Soon as I graduated, I got the position at LBS and stopped working in hospitality."

"Wow, okay. Where did you attend college?" Greg asks.

"I went to Upper State University, graduated in 06'."

"That's cool we went to Howard and we both graduated in

05'," Georgia states.

"Dope, it's pretty awesome you guys went to college together. I hate to cut the convo short but I got to check in with another table. You guys are still working on your dinner or can I clear your plates?"

"I'm still working, I'm trying savorer every bit of this steak," Greg laughs.

Georgia glances at her half-eaten burger. "Yeah, I'm still picking too, but yeah come back when you got the time, Michael. Everything has been so great, thanks again."

Before approaching 17, Stephen signals he and his wife are ready to order. Even though their kids are messy, they're cleaner than Joe and Carol. "So, we're ready to order?" I inquire.

Stephen grins. "Yes, we are, Michael."

"Okay then, I'll start with Mom first, what would you like your first course to be?"

"Um, how are your crab cakes?"

"They're superb, as you may or may not know that blue crabs are in season which the crab cakes are made from. With the freshest crab meat tossed in our house-made batter, pan-fried, then finished off in our gluten-free fryer."

She smiles. "Ooh, gluten-free. Well, I'll start with the crab cakes and for my entree well... Let me ask you this, Michael, how is the Alaskan Cod?"

"The cod is pan-fried as well with minced garlic and olive oil, garnished with scallion and cilantro, and comes with two sides of your choosing." I show her the list of sides.

"Hmm, well I'll have that with a side of sweet potato fries and the chard broccoli." She hands over the menu.

"Awesome, and dad what will you be having?"

"Can I choose a side to start with instead of an appetizer?" he asks.

"Yes, Sir, you can."

"Well, I'll start off with a mac and cheese."

"I'm definitely picking at some of your mac and cheese," Joanna chuckles.

"Take notes...when you get married, Michael, know that everything you own isn't yours anymore, even your food." Stephen's comment is followed by a chest slap from his wife.

I smile. "Will do, Sir, so mac and cheese as an appetizer. What will you like for your main course?"

"How's the filet mignon?"

"Great, you know I suggested one to the gentleman sitting closes to the front entrance and he couldn't be more satisfied."

"Great, I'll have that with chard broccoli and sautéed spinach."

"And how would like your steak cooked?"

"Medium-ish.."

"Sure thing, so I'll go put that in for you guys right now." Before leaving, I top off their wine then proceed to the POS.

As I'm typing in the order, some of the drip comes back; the taste has me yearning for more. I should call Trace but I'll just wait... I print the check for 15 and grab Carol's leftovers. Dropping the check for Joe and wife is the best part of my night, and this is the first time while being at their table I didn't have to fake a smile. I return to 13b. Greg's plate is scraped clean while Georgia still has half her burger and salad left. "Hey guys, how are the dynamic twins doing on their dinner?" I grin.

Greg glances at the floor then laughs, "Oh my God, Mike, you sound just like our mother and it's scary."

Georgia chuckles, "Yeah, I got to agree that's something our mother would say."

"Damn, guys and I just thought we made a connection tonight, now I'm sounding like your mom."

"Nah, you're good, bro. We're just messing around with you but that dynamic part did sound like our mother," Greg says.

"Well, I'm glad to sound like a familiar voice. Is this your first time here?"

"By ourselves. Our mom took us here once during the grand opening. And we haven't been back since. So, we decided to come and experience it on our own," Georgia adds.

"Oh, okay, cool. I haven't been here long enough to tell you what changed but I'm glad to have been you guy's waiter, we had a lot of fun. Before I print your check, would you like to take a look at our dessert menu?"

"You know Mike, I think I'm good." Greg pats his full stomach. "What about you, Sis, some dessert?"

She flips the dessert menu then glances at the special's list. "Um, you know that key lime pie you guys have looks delicious. Is it made with key lime or do you guys just serve it as cheesecake with the flavoring?"

"That's a good question, Georgia. I will run to the back and check that out."

"Nope, it's okay, Michael, just put in one key lime pie and bring two spoons please."

"I'm not having dessert, I'm too full," Greg states.

Georgia's eyes roll. "Bring two spoons, please."

I chuckle, "You got it. Can I wrap the rest of your salad?"

"Please and thank you, it'll make for a great lunch tomorrow. And after you put in the pie can you bring us the check?"

"Sure, I can." I clear the plates and glide to the back-server station and there is Tina with her sausage finger poking away at the POS. I dump Greg's plate, and scrape Georgia's food in a to-go and seal it closed.

"Hey, Newbie. How does it feel to be the first Black server for Second House?" Tina laughs.

I answer with silence and reach for a take-home bag for Georgia. "...You know you're the mascot of this place now. You should talk to A.G. about getting you a monkey suit and you could stand out in front with a huge sign that says *Second House Home of the First Monkey Waiter*," she giggles. "I'm sure they would pay you more, and now that I think about it...it's an unusual amount of Blacks in here tonight. Hmm, first day on the floor and you're already bringing in new customers." Tina mashes send then finally moves from the POS.

"You know Tina, that's not a bad idea at all."

"It isn't?...Well, I'm glad you think so."

"Pardon my back, but I'm working." I fire 17's first course, then Georgia's pie. "You know what, Tina, maybe we could alternate wearing the suit... Oh but wait, you would have to get one two or three sizes bigger. Ask A.G. if they make a one size fits all monkey suit," I say and smirk.

"You think you're funny?" She laughs, "You're ju—"

"Yeah, yeah; I know. I'm Black and you're still fat, yeah I get it, Tina. Instead of worrying about my skin color, you should focus on getting more tables or better yet, losing a few pounds. You sure look and sound like you should."

With Georgia's doggy bag, their check, and two dessert spoons; I brush pass Tina and return to 13. I set down the utensils, place the bill in the middle and hand Georgia her leftovers. Back to **POS** and I print out Joe and Carol's check so they can finally get the fuck out of my sight.

"I'm glad you're enjoying your dessert guys. Can I get you guys anything else?"

Carol takes her brittle face away from her phone to say, "We'll do another round of Bud Lights, and then you could bring the check."

My left eye begins to twitch. "Oh okay, two more Bud Lights and the check." The way Joe is devouring the brownie while his wife pokes around it, looking for scrapes is almost sad.

Well, that's marriage for you. I'm not for domestic violence but if you ask me, nine out of ten I put my money on Carol definitely walking on eggshells whenever the two are home alone, assuming that's a decent portion of time to be walking on eggshells—shit that's like the rest of her life. She just looks miserable. I'd like to think she wasn't like this before she married him. Who knows, maybe she had some decency before Joe came along. Maybe Carol had dreams and goals. Maybe she wanted to be something other than a passive-aggressive wife.

Section 17 seems to be more settled. The kids are eating while their parents are cuddled up talking about whatever it is they converse about. I picture their conversation consists of what work needs to be done around their house, or if the sitter will be available for their date night next weekend. They seem as if their marriage is a good one and their children want for nothing. Stephen seems as if he's a great provider and I imagine there's enough room for Joanna to be a homemaker or if she wanted, she could be a realtor or something business-oriented. Joanna and Stephen look happy and most importantly so do their kids. One big beautiful family.

At the POS, I fold whatever loose napkins are around and wait for 13 and 15 to finish their dessert. 17b is nursing the wine while they wait for the apps. Giselle approaches the back-server station looking flawless as usual. "Hey, love how are you feeling?" she asks.

I continue to stack the guest towels. "Aside from Jackie giving me the cold shoulder and Tina, being Tina...other than that, I'm alright... How are you feeling?"

Giselle throws her face into my chest moaning, "Is it over yet?"

I chuckle. "Nah, I don't think so but this first push is about to be done. And from the looks of it, no one is getting cut early so I would suggest you drink an espresso or something."

"Thanks, Weathers, I might just have to do that. But back to Jackie giving you the cold shoulder, why would she do that? 'Cause her piece of shit boyfriend got fired for shit he did?...Fuck her and anyone who thinks differently. How many times do I have to drill it into your thick skull? You deserve to be here, you worked for it." She pokes my chest. "Now, it's your job to prove Tina, Jackie, and whoever else wrong. This shit is yours." Giselle grabs my face and plants a wet kiss on my cheek.

"Thank you, no bullshit, thank you..."

"Don't let those trash ass crackers get to you, Weathers."

I move the folded napkins to the side of the sink and say, "Working for the man is never easy." I force a chuckle.

"Never is. What are you doing after work?"

"I'm probably going to head home. I'm taking my parents out to brunch and I want to be somewhat functional when they get here," I joke.

She glances over to the entrance and turns back. "Oh, that's really sweet of you. Where are guys eating?"

"Uh, here."

"Why here? Don't you wanna take them somewhere nicer than this place?"

"You know, my parents just want to know what's going on in

286

my life so I figure why not bring them here. The food is pretty good, so that's half the battle and I get a discount so, there's that."

"I guess you got a point, Weathers. That discount is nice and the food is not that bad. I just can't stand the people we work with."

"Oh yeah, what about me? You can't stand me either?" I tease.

Giselle snatches my dick. "Especially you..."

"Hey!" A.G. shouts, "G, two guests are waiting at the door and 17 got their appetizers, Mike. You should fire their entrees in a few, and Joe and Carol want to settle up."

"Got it," I say.

Giselle scurries back to the front.

"Sorry about that, got caught up there for a second."

He grins. "I could tell. It happens sometimes but don't make it a habit. When you make certain shit a habit, things can go wrong, really fast. It's okay to converse during pushes but watch the floor."

"Yup, thanks for dropping 17's apps by the way."

"You got it, Mike. Remember to fire their entrées soon."

"Heard you." As I approach the table, the checkbook is sitting on the edge with a credit card on top, I grab it without saying a word and head back to the POS. The Bank of America card is a little mangled and the magnetic strip has seen better days. I type in my server number, press their table, and swipe the card in the processing slot. Lucky for them their card didn't decline. The merchant and customer receipts begin to print and I place them both on top of the original bill before I proceed to Joe and Carol. I slide the book in front of Carol since it was her card.

"Well guys, it's been my pleasure to wait on you two, and thanks for making work fly by. You guys have been wonderful, safe travels home now. Looking forward to seeing you soon." Once again, I manage an artificial grin.

"Well, Michael you're no Billie but I guess you can manage," Joe laughs

"Joe," Carol interjects.

"What?" He belches. "I'm just being honest. It's not like I'm saying he isn't good even though he took another man's job."

"With Billie's untimely departure, he left here with some pretty big shoes to fill and there's no replacing his knowledge and work ethic. Speaking for myself, I'm happy you thought I did a decent enough job serving you two tonight. And, again, I look forward to building a rapport with you two."

Carol coughs. "That's sweet Michael. And you'll see us here every week, at least three times or more."

I grin. "Couldn't be more excited, you two get home safe and enjoy the rest of your evening."

Joe burps again. "Thanks, kid, will do."

I turn from the table with a frown and make my way to table 17. Jesus Christ, I wish I had more coke for this next push. Greg passes the checkbook. "That's all you by the way, you've been wonderful to us tonight. When's the next time you work?" he asks.

I laugh, "Unfortunately, the schedule hasn't been posted yet. But, I'll be here on the weekends for sure."

"You know what Greg, I think we should bring Pop-Pop here, he loves dry rub ribs."

He nods.

"Well, if you guys do bring your Pop-Pop; I sure as hell can't wait to meet him. And you'll have a chance to explore the food menu since the specials change every weekend."

"You know, Michael, you are so knowledgeable and diligent at what you do. It's a shame you quit LBS, we could've sure used your talents on the trading floor while you were there. It's such a shame they let you slip through the cracks. There's gotta be some way we can get you back in there with a better position," Georgia states.

"Thank you for the offer, that's really kind of you but I think I'll try my chances here first.

You know, waiting tables is less responsibility and I make the same amount of money as I did when I was copy writing, give or take, mostly take," I smirk

"If it's the money you're worried about we could definitely make something work in your favor. All jokes aside Michael, you're a smart guy and you're Black, which carries more weight to why I would personally, advocate for your return. And the reason why I say that is when we were eating our dinner; I pulled your resume from your department head from *monster.com*, and I have to say it speaks for itself."

I laugh, "That's hilarious."

"Not to intrude into your personal life. I know you left for some reason other than wanting a promotion or money which is none of my business. But whatever it is that led to your departure, don't let that be the reason you rob yourself from achieving bigger and better. Georgia reaches in her clutch and removes an off-white business card. "Here. You could bring in a lot of clients being the head of our creative department. With a smile like yours, you could do wonders... Mr. Weathers."

"Wow, you really did some digging there, Georgia. I'm honored you think so highly of me and you sure know how to make a grown man blush," I say with a grin, "But yeah let's see how this goes. I did leave LBS for a reason, and maybe things would be different if I went back, but my morality wants to give this place a few months before I leave. I have your contact and will tuck this in the depths of my wallet like a lucky charm 'cause you never know."

"See, Mike, that's why we like you so much, you stick to your commitment. I dig the fuck outta that!" Greg says loudly.

"Thanks, I appreciate you both; you guys made my first night of serving one to remember. Hence, why it might make going back to LBS a tough decision. So, with that being said I bid you two twins farewell and a great night. And I'm looking forward to meeting your Pop-Pop next weekend."

They both smile and stand up. Greg shakes my hand and Georgia reaches in for a hug and a cheek kiss. The twins adjust back into their seats. I wave them off and return to 17. Stephen and Joanna pick at their appetizers while their two youngest children are fast asleep on the cushions, and Gina is steady coloring. "How we doing family?" I ask.

Joanna smiles. "As you can see Michael we're finally at ease."

"It's amazing how sound asleep they are, especially with the music and bar crowd, I'm really at a lost for word right now. But looks like everyone is enjoying themselves so I'm going to go ahead and fire your main courses now, can I get you anything else in the meantime?"

"Yeah, you know, Michael, you can. Do you guys sell this wine by the glass?" Joann asks.

"Yes, we do."

"Oh, wonderful. Well then, when our dinner comes we'll just do two more glasses of the William Hill if it's not too much trouble."

"Now, Joanna, you know that it would be my pleasure to do just that. Does Gina need a refill on the milk or?"

"She fine, Michael, thank you," Joann whispers, "But can you bring a root-beer in a kid's cup?"

I smile. "Someone has been on their best behavior, I see."

"Finally," Stephen grins.

"Okay family, I'll be right back with the root-beer and your entrees should be arriving shortly." My pace begins to slow as I head back to the POS. Holy shit, I'm crashing. I have no idea how I'm going to make it through this second push. I need a fucking miracle. My vision starts to blur as I stare at the screen. I manage to fire their last course but it took more time than I thought to find the root-beer tab. Once I hit send, I go inside the server cabinet to fetch my phone. I text Tracie; "You home????"

A few minutes go by and she finally replies back. "Yeah, what's going on?"

"Need a ball, you good?" I reply.

"Yeah, where you at?"

"Work, waiting for the next wave. How fast can you get here?"

"Leaving now, see you in two minutes."

"Cool." I throw my phone back in my bag then kick the door shut. The service bell goes off so I jolt through the kitchen doors and like clockwork, there's A.G., standing with my entrées.

"You've been kicking ass tonight, Mike. I only had to run for you once. I don't think any server has ever been as punctual as you. I'm impressed, man, I really am. I know your resume speaks for itself but you certainly back it up."

I force a smile and take Joann's and Stephen's dinner. "Thanks, A.G. that means a lot to me. Really, thank you."

"No problem, kid, no bullshit. You're a rock-star..." He dings the service bell. "When you drop that off find Tina and tell her the apps for 16 are ready."

"Heard."

Oh yeah, a few reservations canceled so I'm going to cut you after 17 leaves. Cool?"

I smile. "Cool." Joanna and Stephen's eyes light up when I return with their main courses. "Okay guys, what we've all been waiting for. Here you go." I serve her first then her husband. "Are you guys still working on your apps? Or..."

Joanna considers them. "You know what, Michael, if you

would just pack them in a container."

"Would you like them in separate boxes?"

Stephen picks up his utensils. "Oh no, you can pack them both in the same container, no need to make more work for you."

I grin and remove the appetizers. "Great. And your glasses of William Hill will be right up. Enjoy your dinner family."

Graham signals me over to the bar.

"Hey, kid, these glasses of wine have been here for a while, hurry your ass up. I got a full bar here," he says.

I smirk. "Cool, your jets; I got it covered. Give me a break. I'm just getting out of the weeds."

"Hey, you little shit, just because you took Billie's job doesn't mean you can mouth off to me like that. Just get your drinks and move it along."

"I got it." I pick up the glasses and return to 17. They seem to be enjoying everything. There's no reason to interrupt. This is the perfect time to head to the POS and close out 15 and 13. When I get to the server station, Tina's occupying the computer. I pay her no mind and while I wait for her to leave, I count out the cash Greg and Georgia left for their tab. Holy shit! They left a hundred bucks on a $125 check. I should rub it in Tina's fat face but I'd rather just relish in the fact that I know I'm a better server than her, or at least I could be. With what the twins left for a tip; I can at least enjoy myself for one more night. This will be just fine. I'll get that ball off of Tracie when she gets here and the half-empty bottle I have left over from last week is going to pair well with the coke.

"Yo!" Tracie shouts as she approaches the server station.

With the cash tucked under my thumb I shake her hand, "I'm fifty bucks short do you mind?"

"Nah, it's cool with the money you'll be making here. I'm not worried about it."

"What's going on, Trace? How's Billie holding up? I tried calling and texting, but he won't respond. What's his fucking deal?"

"From what I heard, it sounded like he destroyed his room and I'm not going to lie, Mikey, it kinda looks like you replaced him. I'm just saying," she says and shrugs.

"You can't be fucking serious. To even think I had anything to do with him getting fired is fucking crazy."

"Calm down, and yeah, I know it's not your fault, believe me I know. I'm just telling you what everyone is saying."

"People are saying shit? What are they saying?"

"You know who stupid; Jackie and Tina." She turns away from the dining room camera and slips the coke into my apron. "But fuck what they think man. Just make money until you find another job if shit doesn't work out here, you know. Keep your options open. It's not your fault Billie got the can and it sucks you getting blamed for it. Just keep your head on a swivel. If things start to get a little hectic here, just look for another gig. You're a smart kid, Mikey. I mean, yeah, you're a nervous wreck at times but unlike me, you have your wits about you."

"Thanks, I guess."

"I told Cam I'd be right back so let me get outta here, maybe I'll see you later?"

"Given what's happened today, probably not."

"Yeah, I get it. But, if you change your mind and feel like having some company, call me; I'll come over after Cam falls asleep."

"Maybe, I'll let you know."

"For sure." We embrace each other. Giselle storms towards the server station staring Tracie down as she moves towards the exit.

"What the fuck was that?" She yells.

"Giselle, calm down, I have no clue what you're talking about."

"I saw that sloppy bitch put something in your apron."

"I don't know what the fuck you're talking about. Please enlighten me."

"You're so full of shit, Weathers, and you know it—you lied straight to my face. You said you hardly knew Tracie. Well from the looks of it, you guys seems real fucking tight." She pushes me into the POS and forces her hand down my apron and comes up with the bag of coke then throws it in my face. "And, to think I actually thought you were different from the rest of those fucking coke-heads. You're just another piece of shit like the rest of them, only difference is, you're Black. You're just another coke-head who knows how to play the part. Don't you ever fucking call or text me again, you fucking loser... Oh yeah, A.G. told me to tell you, you're cut after 17 leaves." She marches back to the hostess stand. I find the coke and place it back in my apron.

After Stephen and his family leave, I close out their table. They paid with a credit card and they left seventy-five bucks on a 150$ tab—more than generous. I would like to think they left that because of my service and not because I'm a person of color in a place full of whites. Or maybe they saw something in me that I don't. On this job, these people see me as a charity case. A lost cause. The only way I can cope is rushing to the bathroom stall again just to put coke up my nose and when the fleeting drip hits, it's how I deal. I guess the drugs helped me adjust since I left LBS. I haven't felt comfortable in my own skin for a long time.

Maybe that's why Billie always used to run to this stall every twenty minutes; he wasn't comfortable with who he was or where he was at in life, and maybe that's where his insecurity derives from. As different as some people may be, we're all the same when that casket drops or when those ashes burn. I'd rather not succumb to the idea that "we're all the same." The world has made it very apparent that I'm not. I know Martin had a dream but I wasn't in it.

As I break every pebble and refined every spec into powder; my hands begin to sweat. I spent too much time preparing the coke so I unravel a ten-dollar bill to rail off the toilet cover and run the residue across my gums. Fuck it, germs are everywhere. Even if my hygiene is better; at the end of day, I'm a coke-head just like Billie and whoever the fuck else. I check the mirror; my nose is clear. I wash and dry my hands. The drip takes a strong hold. My throat tightens up as I make my way into the kitchen to restock to-go plates and ramekins. It's the least I can do before I make my escape. A.G. burst through the doors with, "Hey, Mike."

I stop replenishing. "Yeah, what's up?"

"17 left a great comment about you. They said: *"This was the best service we've ever received in any restaurant we've been to. Michael was so knowledgeable and steadfast. He was truly a delight. But, not for the small talk, such a discrete server. Looking forward to our next time coming here. Second House has a superstar, and his name is Michael Weathers. :) Thanks again."* You know, Michael, since we've been open, we've never had a guest leave a comment like that. They really enjoyed themselves and you're the cause of that. You are. And, that only solidifies your purpose here, kid. Great job."

"You sure you didn't write that," I say and smirk.

He scowls. "Come on man, you can't be serious."

"Thanks, A.G. but I'm not too big on comments. It's cool, I guess. But at the end of day, I'm just doing my job, that's it."

"See, Mike, that's what I don't get about you. You're an exceptional waiter and you know that. I guess downplaying your abilities is how you operate and I don't have a problem with that. Shit, I wish Billie or Tina were more like you—even Jackie. But, one day you're going to realize who you are and be proud of it. Maybe one day you'll realize you're capable of more than what people expect of you, or what you expect from yourself. And only then will the limitations you set on yourself disappear."

"... that makes sense."

He chuckles. "That's for you to decide. After you finish up restocking you can clock out. You had a long week."

"Uh, Graham was going to show me how tip out the bar and bussers. I was going to stay for that."

"Nah, that's not important for now and there are no bussers here to tip out. Just come in early like you always do and get it down then. You've been through a lot and I need you at your best tomorrow. So, go home and get some rest and I'll see you tomorrow." A.G. pats my shoulder and disappears into the bar. I say my goodbyes to Jose. Tina and Jackie look away as I leave and Giselle buries her face as I move through the hostess stand and out the door. I take in the fresh air and the drip returns. As I pass through the trail, the trees never looked so quiet. I glance up at the Tracie and Billie's balcony and spit a mixture of saliva and coke into the river.

Once I make it across the street. The sharp pains of the night run through my heels and feet. My pace becomes slower, as I tread up the hill. After twenty steps, I reach the entrance to my apartment. The three flights of stairs are often unfriendly. I've grown to hate this place. It's the start of my misery and the end of it. Every day that I climb out of that low-sunken mattress, it's a daily reminder of the world I'm forced to sulk in. The hockey trophies that sit on my living-room mantel only remind me of how I didn't belong. What were my parents thinking? Hockey is no place for a person of color, why couldn't he have stuck me with basketball or football? Something where Blacks don't stick out like a sore thumb. It had to be me.

I remove the clutter from my coffee table and hike my left pants leg up, take the coke from my sock, plop down on the couch, and retrieve the bottle of Jameson from under it. The cap comes off with ease, and the first swig is harsh. I take another and another until I feel whatever it is I can. I pour the bag of blow onto the table and with the same ten-dollar bill I used in the stall along with the base of the bottle, I break it down.

When I lift the bill, it's refined. I remove my Wachovia bank card and divide what looks like about a gram and a half into six lines about the size of my index finger then roll up the bill. I sniff until I need air. I stop halfway through the fourth line before I take a minute and finish what's left. The rest of the pile sits idle while I chug the whiskey from the bottle. "Ahh, yup. There it is..." I say as the booze rushes into the drip and the feeling is tremendous.

Why can't this sense of courage always stay? Why must it drift like the summer breeze? Why can't it prolong its stay as if it were the winter chill? It's funny how drugs can't judge. I guess that's why people sniff coke, smoke weed, shoot heroin, and all that other bullshit. It's free from judgment. Yet there's no escape from the comedown, it's horrid and blank. As if you're staring into an abyss of endless thoughts and doubts.

"FUCK DRUGS! WHITE PEOPLE TOO! FUCKING CRACKERS!" I don't really know where that came from. Well, yeah, I do. "HA," I chuff. When I'm high my subconscious speaks louder than I can. I'm not as brave; I don't have a sense of courage or rage. If I did; I would've stood up to that cracker ass bitch Tammy back at LBS. I would've punched every offending pale kid in junior hockey, and stood up to their endless racist remarks. "...*Jiggaboo, porch monkey, Oreo, spook...*"

And that one summer at hockey camp, when Joey Leary would throw fifty-cent at me every Friday night and say, "There you go Weathers, you're in America now. Send that back to your family in Africa..." I should've shoved those quarters down his fucking throat. If I had any type of a spine, I would've spent more time around more Black kids in college, and I would've punched my old roommate, Colin in his shit for every time he cracked a Black joke. I would have slapped the hell out of him for every race-baiting comment he ever made, fucking pill-head. If he hasn't realized heroin is cheaper than Percocet then he's close to it. And, that fat fuck Billie. What a fucking degenerate. And to think I thought you were my friend. All you did was put coke up your nose and pretend you were Black whenever I was around. You wanted to be my pigment so bad...and you had the nerve to say you're "Blacker" than me. You're nothing but a thief and a coke head, I tried to help you—I fucking tried but no, you just had to stick your nose in the air and expected me to shuck and jive for you. You wanted me to be the perfect house nigga... "You know what, Bill?..." I wash the steady drip down with more Jameo. "You were fucking right... I'm just a fucking house monkey, only there to fit a quota." I dump the rest of the coke onto the table and bust it down. Fuck making lines; I'd rather sniff from the pile just like that fat fuck Billie.

After counting to ten, I stop railing. I didn't even make a dent in the pile. I light a smoke and ash on the floor. The dust on my hockey trophies glistens in the dim light. I have no idea why mom thought they would serve any purpose here. The only thing they do is remind me of how I was a Black kid playing a white man's sport. Everybody knows Black people don't belong on ice. Sometimes I wish my parents just didn't bother. Only if they knew the pain and torment it would cause. I can't blame them; they gave me a very privileged life but... at what cost?

Giselle made it very clear and strong that night we first hung out that maybe I'm not Black. Maybe, I've been forcing the issue my entire life. Between how I was raised and how the world views my existence, I'm white yet trapped in a Black person's body. Who the fuck am I kidding? I spent so much time trying not to become an Uncle Tom, that I became one. I'm a disgrace to my race. I don't deserve to be this shade of bronze. I'm an insult to my African heritage, and it's no secret. What the fuck did she say? 'Saving Face?' No... 'Waiting Face.' Unfortunately, I can't wait any longer.

Fuck it. I dead my cigarette on the coffee table and separate more coke into three bulky lines, they take the shape of three miniature mountains. I manage to get three-quarters of the first pile up my left nostril. This drip is the harshest I've ever felt. I'm enraged. I spark another smoke. The next taste of whiskey is welcoming and quenching. You know, when I first met Tracie, she taught me so much about the restaurant industry. From clearing plates to spirits, the temperatures on meats, anticipating guest orders, even my first taste of cocaine.

Now that I think about it after Dick closed the restaurant, she's hardly kept a decent bartending job. And that's when she first introduced me to Cam. I recall the kid's bubbly smile and high-pitch laugh when I asked about her age. I think she had just turned four then and she still spoke in toddler language. So adorable she was and still is. Cam couldn't pronounce 'Mike' so she called me 'Ike' for about a year. She asked about her father once, when I took her ice skating for the first time, and I didn't know what to say. I just said I can't wait to meet him. Shit, I wonder if he ever held Cam as an infant, fed her a bottle, or even changed her diaper? Tracie never talked about him and when I ever asked about where he was or who he even is, she would just shut it down.

All I know is she became a full-blown lesbian after Cam's fifth birthday. Whatever her child's father did to make her convert to the opposite sex must've been some pretty fucked up shit. But she's doing Cam no favors by letting some fucking degenerate fuck her for product and selling coke out of a shared apartment. Who's going to be there for Cam? And Tracie does a pretty bad job of that now. You become another version of your parents when it's all said done. I pray for that little girl. It is crazy; as much as someone says they never be like their parents, they turn out like them.

Tears trickle down and combine with the snot that's running onto my lip. I use my shirt to wipe it away. I clear my nose with a Kleenex that was stuck between the cushions. Never mind what it appears to be; I know it's smeared with coke particles and dried up boogers. It's as useful as I ever was—as I'll ever be. All I know is my nose is clear enough to snort more. I reach for the bill and stare at the blood specs that sit on the edge. I unravel it, rub the residue onto my gums, and lightly burn away the fluid. I twist it back and snort the leftover line and the one next to it. Wow, I was able to get that whole thing in one shot. Ha, I must be drunk. You know, it's too bad; I fucked up things with Giselle. She was the first Black girl I ever slept with. Shit, she's the first Black girl that showed any interest.

Should've just listened to her when she told me to stay away from the front of the house. Maybe I wouldn't feel so guilty about Billie getting fired. If I'd kept my distance, maybe Jackie wouldn't think it was my fault he got canned and maybe that would give her cause to see that Billie is a piece of shit, and she's not so great of an assistant manager by sleeping with an employee.

Oh well, she and Giselle can both go to hell... I guess A.G. is an alright guy, he just hired all the wrong people. I don't think I'm capable of showing any anger towards him; it's not his fault I'm Black. He was just trying to do his job when he gave me the ultimatum of quitting or signing that piece of shit contract. It shouldn't have been him to present all that bullshit to me. I take a swig. It should've been those spineless owners of that shithole. I take another swig. I never met them but we already have something in common—no backbone.

I rail half of the last line and light my second-to-last smoke. I reach for the empty notebook under the table and rummage through my bag for a pen. I retrieve a fountain pen. My favorite writing instrument—how fitting. I inhale half of the cigarette and put it out then I place the pad on my lap.

To Whom It May Concern:

I never did fit in. No matter if it was with white or Black people. I either sounded too white to be around Blacks, or it was deemed appropriate for whites to crack Black jokes around me because I didn't talk in Ebonics. Maybe those aren't justified causes to treat someone different but in this society, those things are justifications for why at an early age, I failed to find a demographic. It has plagued my entire adult life. Maybe, if I sagged my pants a little more, said 'nigga' in every other sentence, and wasn't passive whenever I heard a racist remark, I would be accepted by my own kind. Maybe if I was attracted to only white women and stayed at LBS, I could've avoided having an identity crisis. I guess that's what you call it when you don't know who you are, or where you belong. Unlike everything else in the world, I serve no purpose. I have no place in this society. Thanks, Tina—and especially you Officer LePore—for helping me realize my waste of existence. Mom and Dad, you did your best.

PRE-EPILOGUE

It's the twenty-eighth of April, Michael and his father have just finished towing his 2001 Honda Civic from an off ramp on I-95 to the Weathers' driveway. As Michael pays the tow driver, his mother emerges from the kitchen entrance with a towel rag she used to remove droplets of pasta sauce from the stovetop, while his father examines the car's engine. As the tow-truck turns onto the street, Michael waltzes over to his parents wearing a neglectful smirk which causes his Nancy to shake her head. "Thanks Pop," Michael says.

"For what?" he smirks. "Mikey, you know this engine is completely blown, why didn't take it to Phil's to get it checked. I know you saw the check engine blinking. It's probably been flashing for like a fucking month now."

"Uh-unh," Michael grins, "more like a month and half, Pop."

"Jesus fucking Christ, Michael, what the fuck? You move out and become too good to ask for help? Why didn't you come to me about this?"

"W-well, I figured since after what happened at LBS, I thought you guys needed a break from my bullshit."

"Bullshit!" his mother shouts.

"Nance, come on' don't start."

"No," she scolds, "bullshit, huh? So, tell me son, you think getting called a nigger and threatened at your place of business is bullshit?"

305

"Oh my God, Ma, can you not... Like damn, you act –"

"Act like what?" she yells. "Act like what? Like I care too much? Like I'm a Black person and it happened to me? Well guess fucking what? I'm not Black and didn't happened to me but it happened to my Babyboy," she cries. "So don't tell me it's bullshit, Michael Henry–don't you dare do that."

Hank finally turns away from the hood to embrace his sobbing wife. The regret of calling his dad when he pulled onto the off ramp is becoming heavier as Michael watches his mother weep. He feels responsible for what happened that faint evening in the xerox room but so do his parents. The wretchedness of guilt can't be placed but the shame is dispensed amongst them all.

"Look guys, I'm, sorry. I didn't mean to make it seem like you didn't or don't understand. It just...you know..." Michael sulks.

Hank pulls his son in for a fatherly embrace. He tugs on his son, "I see you got on the jersey I got you for Christmas."

"Hell yeah, we're about to clench the first place...you bet I got it on. Since the all-star game, the Rangers have been on a hot streak. Can't let up now."

"You got that right, Mikey. Hey why don't you wash up for dinner and put the game on. I'm going to tinker around this engine for a bit..."

"Cool. Ma, is the pasta ready?" Michael asks.

"Yeah, Hun, make you sure wash those hands before you go digging in my pot.""I'm twenty-six, Ma, you don't gotta tell me that."

She scoffs, "Yeah right, your father is fifty-six and I still catch him fixing his food before washing those paws of his." She taps her son with the dish rag. "Go on, dinner is ready, but you make sure to clean those hands, Michael Henry, or you'll be eating outside."

Michael rushes up the kitchen entrance as his parents watch the screen door slam.

"So…" Nancy starts.

"So, what Nance?" Hank questions.

"Well… your son is becoming more dismissive about coming to us defense ever since that bitch—"

"Nance," Hank scolds, "can we give it a rest already? The kid's been through enough already. What else do you want, huh?"

"I want him to come back home, Hank, that's what I want. He shouldn't be living on his own right now. And why does he want to go back to work so soon? He has a whole degree and he wants a job serving tables," she scoffs, "I feel like I'm losing my only child all over again." Hank embraces his wife tightly as she sulks in his chest.

"Nance, we raised a very resilient kid. He's been fighting ever since he came out of the womb. You gotta give our boy a chance to experience life for himself. If you think more therapy sessions are going to help…the boy's gotta feel… he's gotta grow a taste for life himself. And, unless he calls for us, that's the only time we are obliged to whatever he might need," hesays and lifts his wife's face. "Until then, Michael has to find, Michael."

She nods and wipes her tears.

Michael returns through screen door and calls out, "Pop!"

"Yeah, kiddo!" Hank yells.

"Come on, the game's about to start. And Ma, I can't find my Rangers bowl, where'd you put it?"

Nancy smiles, "You want me to come find it for you?"

"No, ma'am, just tell me where you might've put it."

"Try the Tupperware cabinet, Hun."

"Alright," Michael vanishes back inside.

"See," Hank grins, "he's got it."

"And, you got it," she smirks.

"And that's what?"

Nancy heaves the dishrag in his face and yells, "Dish duty!" As she bolts insides.

Hank can't help but to get his revenge. "Hey!" he shouts, "you got a head start—that's cheating."

EPILOGUE

Sunday, the 17th of May. Nancy and Hank Weathers mourn together in the hospital morgue. The air conditioning throughout the building is just as cold as their son's body. Michael's parents can hardly bare the glimpse through the heavy-plated window at his lifeless figure on a metal gurney. 5 am is when they got "The Call." The call all parents fear. When Hank and Nancy first arrived at the hospital, they were greeted by an officer in plain clothes before being directed to the lower level to identify their only child. When the coroner raises the blinds, Nancy finally catches her breath after ten minutes of hysterical wailing. Hank Weathers is steadily keeping his composer not just for himself but also for his wife. Nonetheless, tears still fill his bloodshot eyes. As water builds around his pupils, Hank is careful not to let them fall so he brushes them off before they trickle down.

Nancy can't bear to look through the glass, while her husband stares aimlessly through it. The officer and the coroner give them their space as the Weathers identify their son. They don't have to say one word to the coroner; their gasps and screams give "Michael H. Weathers" a positive I.D. The investigating officer shields Nancy and helps her out of the room. More tears of anguish swell up in Hank's eyes. This is by far the worst day of his life; the worst day of any parent's life.

The coroner steps forward and hesitates to place her hand on Hank's shoulder. "I'm sorry for your loss, Mr. Weathers. I can't imagine the pain you're feeling at this moment and I won't try. But, I have to ask you something? And it's a very unsettling question but I must ask to prevent other parents from experiencing what you are now." She clears her throat. "Did you know your son was suicidal or did he ever tell you or your wife about killing himself?"

Hank wipes his eyes once more and takes a deep breath. "Uh, no. Never. He dealt with some issues at his previous job and that caused him to quit, but he was seeking help for it. Or at least I thought he wa—" Hank finally breaks down and begins to weep. He slowly drops toward the floor and the coroner catches him and guides him more easily to his knees as he sobs.

The coroner is doing her best to console the heartbroken father. After twenty years of observing and investigating dead bodies, and she still isn't able to separate herself from these horrific moments; like the one she's in now. Luckily for her, she has no offspring of her own and she's pass the age of having a healthy birth; as far as having children, that ship has long sailed.

After a few moments pass, Hank finally pulls himself together. Just in the nick of time as he couldn't stomach to have his wife see him in such a manner. It's bad enough a total stranger had to witness him at his weakest but not the mother of his only child. He couldn't stand the thought. Hank dusts off his pants then uses the inside of his shirt to clean the snot under his nose. "I have Kleenex right over there Mr. Weathers."

"It's okay, but thanks. And just call me Hank. This situation doesn't call for formalities," he forces a chuckle.

She smiles. "Why thank you, Hank."

"You'll have to excuse me, given the events and all. What was your name again?"

"Laura. Laura McDowell. Director of Coroners. But you can call me Laura." For a brief second, they share a genuine smirk. The first responding officer approaches and follows Nancy back into the room. Hank is in awe that she can now bravely contain the hysteria even if it's just for a few minutes. He's amazed by his wife's composer. Nancy was never one for wearing makeup, yet was doing so now since they were attending a friend of the family's fiftieth wedding anniversary when they got the news. Here, her foundation is smudged and her eyeshadow runs down, turning her dried tears black. "Why? Why? Why?..." Nancy utters.

"I can't imagine the overwhelming grief running through you right now, Mrs. Weathers. But I must inform you your son had cocaine in his blood and an enormous alcohol level was detected as well. He was extremely intoxicated when he jumped into the river. Vaguely speaking now, these substances didn't cause his death, but drugs and alcohol combined can be used as a deadly cocktail to fuel someone's suicidal tendencies," the coroner explains.

"BUT HE STILL..." Nancy screams as she buries her face in Hank's chest.

"I'm sorry, Mr. Weathers—I mean Hank. I didn—"

Hank shakes his head. "It's okay, you're just doing your job. We had no idea Michael was experimenting with cocaine or anything that hard. I mean he smoked a little bit of pot but what twenty-five-year-old doesn't? Completely no idea my son was doing that. I'm in complete shock."

"Where did Michael work?" The investigating officer steps over and takes over the questions. "Wherever he was employed could shed some light on why he would take his life."

Hank guides Nancy into Laura's arms, as she fights with her tears again as the coroner carries her out.

"Uh hold on a sec, let me backtrack... Uh okay, he was working for an investment company for the latter half of two years until a pretty bad incident occurred between him and one of his colleagues, and to make matters worst, my son didn't want to address the situation to the higher-ups, so he just quit." He wipes the tears forming and takes in air to continue. "Uh okay, so then he got a job as a waiter near his apartment, I believe he had only a few days of training before he started taking tables. He wasn't there long. We're supposed to have dinner there tonight."

The officer nods then tucks his pen and pad back in his shirt pocket. "Well that would explain the cocaine in his system. Unfortunately, the restaurant industry has a major substance abuse problem, especially with coke. The long hours rushing around, the high demand to fit customer's needs; cocaine is used as the quickest 'pick me up.' If you know your son not to indulge in heavy drugs then that would mean someone had to introduce him to that lifestyle. Given that Michael could legally drink, and alcohol is typically used as a suppressant when consuming a lot of cocaine or benzos, which are mostly taken in pill form, it would explain the high level of it. But, when someone combines alcohol and cocaine especially dealing with what could have been anxiety and what seems to be situational depression, your son was bound to crack any moment. To be honest with you, Sir, his suicide note strongly showcases your son was or has been going through an identity crisis. When did you adopt Michael?"

Hank clears his throat as tears continue splash toward the tile floor. "We took him home at three weeks and signed the papers to make him ours at six weeks, Sir," he explained.

"Did he ever have contact with his birth parents?"

"No, they both overdosed a week after he was born," Hank replied.

"Ah, so your son was born with drugs in his system?"

Hank turns to Michael's corpse. "Yeah, crack-cocaine to be exact. When he came out of the womb, he barely weighed a pound."

"I'm glad that the universe brought you, your wife, and Michael together. You gave him a great life from the looks of it. I'm sorry to say this, but since both his parents were drug addicts, they passed that gene on to your son. I don't want to sound so morbid but, Mr. Weathers—I'm sorry Hank; Michael was doomed from the start especially being born with amphetamines in his system. Have you ever told him who his birth parents were?"

"No."

"I know this is hard Hank; I can't imagine your grief. Nothing I can say will bring back your son. I don't know if you noticed, at the same time it's nothing I choose to make victims aware of but I, myself, am biracial so concerning your son; I can see the correlation between the substance abuse and the identity crisis. I'm certainly not saying that's your fault. You were just protecting him as any good parent should. To be honest with you, I would've done the same... I have to ask you another question."

"Sure, Detective-what it is?"

"Given the fact you and your wife are white, did you ever try to incorporate Michael with more African-Americans whether they were kids or adults? As I was saying before, my father is Black and my mother is Jewish. My father was adamant I knew who I was growing up. So, was there some sort of community outlet Michael would go to, or a mentor of some sort that could help your son form some idea of who he was?"

"What do you mean being around other Black people? My son knew who he was," Hank shouts, "And we made sure of that!"

"I do not doubt that you and your wife provided a safe and privileged environment for your son to grow up in, but outside of that safety zone is a very cruel and unforgiving world. From the looks of it, you and your wife were unaware of the dangers that awaited your son outside of the home. I'm not saying you failed as parents but I would have to assume he was unprepared when he left the nest."

Hank turns away from his son. "What are trying to say then, Detective?"

"Well, for example, there's a difference between a Black barber and a white barber. When your son was a child and needed a haircut, which barber did you take him to?"

"My barber is white, and that's who I took him to. Bu-but what does that have to with my son lying on that gurney?"

"I can tell by the razor bumps on Michael's neck that the barber used a straight razor and most people of color.... well, at least your son and I should use buzzers as it prevents ingrown hairs and such like your son has. Not only that, being around other people who look like your son would've given him a sense of self-worth. He would've been more secure in his skin versus struggling with his identity. That's why I mentioned it-I believe your son was having an identity crisis."

"Identity crisis? What's that?"

"Twenty-five to thirty percent of people who commit suicide leave some sort of manifest or letter in most cases. Some notes may contain instructions with what to do with their remains, or meant to leave the survivors with some sense of guilt."

"So you're saying Michael left a note?"

The Detective clears his throat. "Yes, before I give it to you. I just want you to be aware of everything we've talked about. I don't think your son wanted you to have guilt or feel like this is any fault of yours or your wife's. There are some things he expresses about himself, about his place in the world, that I have become privy to after reading his last words. Still, nothing I say will prepare you for what you're about to read but I can say one more thing," he pauses, "Your son saw things for what they are and not how they should be. I'm not a psychologist Hank, but I think your son was suffering from Survivor's Guilt as well." He pulls out a clear evidence bag which contains the last thing Michael H. Weathers ever wrote. He hands it over to the grieving father.

As Hank reads his son's handwriting, teardrops rapidly hit the page. He hasn't cried this much since his first and only natural-born child died in the cradle at six days old. Nancy couldn't speak for three months afterward. He thought he would never see the day he would lose another son. At this moment, his heart has split in two and his mind has gained a metric ton in weight. His son's life was plagued with self-hate and anguish. Hank keeps his murderous rage contained as he passes the moist note back to the officer.

"Who is Officer LePore and why does the name sound so familiar? Hank questions.

"LePore used to be a hockey coach before he joined the force."

"My son had a lot of coaches, I can't recall this LePore being one, maybe at some point, but what is the relation between him and my son outside of hockey?"

"I was going to explain that after you and your wife have had some time to grieve but since you brought it up... LePore stopped and asked Michael for identification the night before last."

"Why?"

315

"Dispatch said, 'suspicious behavior'. He was spotted in the Lux Building Complex, two blocks from his apartment."

"What the fuck is so suspicious about my son being in his own neighborhood?" Hank shouts.

"I have my assumptions, but mainly because of your son's skin pigment. See, LePore has more citizen complaints than any other officer on the force. Most of the grievances against him come from Hispanics and Blacks. Complaints stating he used 'excessive force' when he detained or questioned someone. Now, I don't know LePore personally but I obtained this information from Internal Affairs as soon as Forensics gave me the note. I can't place blame on him just yet but I do believe he is responsible for the bruises on and around Michael's eye. Not to mention his contusion is no more than a day or two old. The timeline from when your son was stopped and now... I would say LePore gave your son that black-eye."

Hank charges for the exit. The Detective quickly rushes to the door to block his path.

"Detective, please get out of my way, I'm not going to hurt anyone, I promise. I just want to get some answers to why my son is—" Hank begins to weep as his legs give out from under him while his screams echo down the hall. Once Hank hits the floor tiles, he sobs in silence. Unfortunately for the Detective, he knows this situation all too well yet he's still overwhelmed with great compassion, not only for the weeping father, but the Weathers family as a whole. For the worse has yet come. The five stages of grief will be the most devastating process to endure. The officer paces the room as the minutes go by, allowing enough time for Michael's father to rise to his feet and collect himself. "I'm sorry if I startled you, I just... I just... thank you."

"For what?" The Detective asks.

"Everything... You never met my son but were able to relate to him in a way I never could and for that, I'm forever in your debt."

"I appreciate that, Hank, I really do. But you owe me nothing. Unfortunately, I'm just doing my job and I'm sorry that it's under these horrific circumstances that we have to meet. I didn't have to know you my entire life to get a sense that you are a good man. Truth be told, it doesn't matter one bit that you're a different color from your son. What does matter is, that you tried your best to give Michael the life he deserved. He came into your lives for a purpose, and vice versa. Now you have to try your hardest to understand what that purpose is, and it won't come from some vengeful payback. It has to come through an effort to understand who Michael was and what he wanted out of life. You owe it to him more than ever to understand what he was dealing with instead of coping using mindless violence. Adopting Michael gave you and your wife something to believe in, and now you must keep that faith alive."

"Thank you," Hank says.

"You don't have to thank me, it's what comes with basic decency. I have one more piece of information for you. I'm hoping it will offer some relief regarding your son being a possible victim of police brutality. LePore as of five minutes ago has been placed on administrative leave without pay. As of tomorrow, Internal Affairs is conducting a full-on investigation into your son's encounter with hi,, my captain just informed me through text. And, I just wanted you to leave here knowing that something is being done about the injustice your son experienced and hopefully we can stop this from happening again."

"Rest assured, that does bring some relief to know that asshole is not on the street doing the same thing he did to my poor son."

They shake hands and Hank begins to exit but turns with an afterthought. "I'm sorry Detective but do you have a card of some sort? That way I can keep in touch with about this LePore guy," Hank asks. The officer reaches for his wallet and removes his contact card.

"Here, you go. My cell is there too, just in case you need to talk to me about anything other than that bastard cop."

Hank studies the card. "I'm just now realizing I've been calling you 'detective' this whole time; I'm sorry about that. Well, once again, Officer Ragsdale, you've been an overwhelming help with all of this, thank you."

"You're welcome anytime. And, if you don't mind everyone at headquarters just calls me Mike."

The couple is asked to sign some lengthy paperwork, and afterward, they give their son their final goodbyes. The car ride home is a painful one where every five minutes, Nancy breaks into tears while her husband just drives in silence with one hand on the wheel and the other on her thigh. After all, what can he say against her grief, for he just lost his son too. The only thing reverberating in his mind is, "who the fuck is Tina?" The car stops at a red light and Hank pulls out his phone, finds the GPS app, and types in Second House. The directions read, "ten minutes away." Hank jumps on the highway and weaves through traffic as he rushes to the house he and Nancy bought three years after Michael graduated from high-school. They figured since he was beginning to grow into adulthood, it was time for a change.

Nancy always thought Michael fought too hard to showcase his independence. Whether it was refusing help on his homework or icing his bruises after hockey practice; the only thing running through her mind now is that her baby boy chose to suffer in silence rather than asking for help. She now wonders if he was, "ashamed" of the unconditional love she gave him day in and day out. But it's too late to ask her baby boy 'is everything okay?' or say, 'honey if you need anything, you know we're just one call away.' All she can do is mourn. Nancy always assumed her son hated when she called. She thought he considered it nagging but in all actuality, perhaps Michael didn't know how to ask for help. Especially considering they didn't have any answers because she and Hank aren't Black. How could they relate to his daily frustration, self-hate, and torment? They couldn't. But what their son didn't know; his parents loved him for who he was and not for what the world thought he should be.

There are no cries or sobs when they finally reach their driveway, just the afternoon sun glimmering through the tree branches and leaves that overlap into the neighbor's yard. Hank's parents live in Florida and Nancy's mother resides in a nursing home upstate. There's nothing for the grieving parents to expect to be waiting—not even pets—in that house. What waits for them in the two-story structure is the agony of family photos on the fridge, covering the fireplace mantle, and along the staircase wall that leads to their bedroom, and what was or could've been Michael's bedroom if he ever decides to move back in, which Nancy secretly hoped for, unfortunately; it will stay a useless guest-room. Sitting there and knowing what emptiness awaited them now, they each reminisce.

"You remember when we got him his first bike and it took him an entire month to try and get on it?" Hank says and smiles.

"How about how he face-planted soon as you let him go? My poor baby scraped half his face-off," she laughs.

"He didn't even realize his shoelace was caught in the bike chain so when he fell, the bike came down right on top of him."

"The fact he didn't even cry after eating the pavement was the scariest part. What six-year-old doesn't cry after a fall like that?"

"That was our Mikey. Tough as the ground he fell on that day."

"Almost too tough. He hated to show any kind of vulnerability. Remember how bad he cried when we first took him home? He cried so much; I don't think he had anything left that day when he fell. Sometimes I think he wanted to prove how strong he was to us."

Hank clenches her hand. "I don't know...something tells me he always felt it was a strain having us as his parents, you know. I feel like he didn't want us to have to deal with him showing emotion. Our boy took it upon himself to never show any feelings probably because he thought his adoption was hard enough for us."

"But we did everything to make him feel secure, what else could we have done, Hank? What else?"

He holds back his tears. "I don't know... I don't know..."

"We were good parents? Weren't we?"

"Yeah, we were. I mean we are, it's just... Look, Nancy, I need you to go into the house and sit tight for a while."

"Why, where are you going?"

"Just go in the house and sit tight, I'll be back."

Nancy becomes disgruntled. "What the hell do you mean sit tight, Hankery?" she shouts. "Our fucking son just killed himself and you want me to 'sit tight', you must be out of your freaking mind."

"I just wanna find out what his job environment was like and inform them that our son will no longer be of service to their establishment. I'm pretty sure Officer Ragsdale won't do it, so..."

"Hank, you're not in the military anymore. This isn't some covert mission. I've known you for thirty years; I've never seen you do anything for no apparent reason. There's not one reason why you should be leaving me here alone when my only son just died." Tears begin to form around her eyes and within a few seconds, she starts to openly weep. Hank feels her torment but his mind is already made up.

He embraces Nancy then clears the wetness from her cheeks. "Hey, you're right. What the hell was I thinking of going to his job for? I'm sorry …I just don't know how to react other than to find out what would lead our boy to kill himself. I apologize for being selfish. Come on, let's go inside and take a minute and try to relax and soak everything in, then we'll call my parents and your mom, and..."

Nancy grazes Hank's five o'clock shadow. "I know this is something in a million years we couldn't fathom. But, Michael is supposed to be burying us, it's not supposed to be the other way around. And I know your hurt because I feel it too. We just lost our son, which means we lost apart of ourselves. I can't go through this alone, you can't do that to our Michael. He wouldn't want to see us like this..." They embrace for a few minutes before they both exit - she leads the way down the cobblestone path that guides to the kitchen entrance. He waits until she is about ten paces ahead, then shouts, "Hey hon, I left my cell in the car."

She yells back, "Oh, well I'll meet you inside. I'll get a pot of tea going."

Unbeknownst to her, when Hank cut the engine, he didn't remove the key from the ignition. He watches the screen door slam behind her as he climbs back into the driver's seat. Tears of determination fall onto his lap as he turns the key. He throws the car into reverse and peels out of the driveway. A robotically feminine voice speaks from his cellphone saying, "You are twenty minutes away from your destination." Hank sobs as he speeds off following the route to Second House.

Oblivious to the length of time it takes to get there, before he knows it, Hank arrives at Main Street and finds parking right in front of the restaurant. He turns the engine off and yanks the e-break upward. He has never used the emergency brake for this car unless he was parked on a steep hill, but at this moment, he needs anything to release the tension before making an entrance.

He looks to the sun as it glimmers through clouds that take the shape of mountains protruding into the horizon. Without looking at the time, the former staff sergeant now knows it's a little past three o'clock.

Before getting out, Hank starts to reminisce back to the morning of Michael's first hockey practice, and how his son was so excited to be skating with other kids. Michael was a natural when it came to ice skating, and once his father put a hockey stick in his hand, he then became a fierce competitor. Michael always played as if there was something to prove. And, there was. Michael Weathers was Black in a white man's sport. No matter how good he was, he would never be good enough to be considered a "great" addition to the sport.

The car door slams as Hank marches inside. Barbecue spices and a spilled beer aroma creep into his nostrils. He stares at the hostess desk covered in yesterday's specials and dirty menus. He taps the service bell before he pokes his head into the dining room. "Be right there, Sir," Giselle shouts. He's taken aback at how beautiful she is. Giselle swings around the corridor and jumps behind the hostess stand. "Hello Sir, welcome to Second House. Do you have a reservation?" she inquires.

His palms begin to sweat, "Ah, no this is my first time here. Do you have a bar?"

"Of course we do, you're going to take this and the bar is to the right and Graham will be your bartender. Just go ahead and find an open seat."

"Thanks."

Giselle smiles, "No thank you, and welcome to Second House. Enjoy."

Before heading into the bar dining, Hank stops and turns. "Pardon me, Miss but I didn't get your name."

She blushes. "Oh, I'm sorry. I'm used to people just saying their reservation and walking into the bar or whatever...my name is Giselle."

"Well, I'm Hank, Giselle, and may I say you're more than just that hostess stand and for people who don't take the time to introduce themselves to you, they're probably blinded by how beautiful you are."

"Oh my goodness, you are too kind. It was a pleasure meeting you."

"No, the pleasure is all mine; until next time, I bid you adieu."

She pauses and stares.

"Did I say something wrong?" He asks.

"Uh-no, no, not at all. It's just someone I know says that, and I thought it was the cutest thing. Until I found out what a lying asshole he was. I'm sorry, I shouldn't be telling you all that. But, yeah I was taken aback for a second there when you said that," she laughs. "Yeah, that's all...sorry if I looked at you all crazy."

Hank smirks, "You're fine. As for that 'lying asshole' you just mentioned. If he was—I mean, if he or she is a good person and not to mention if this person didn't physically or emotionally cause you harm, you should find it in your heart to forgive them. I'm much older than you are so this next line I can say with confidence," he chuckles, "But in this life, you have to take your time with people, because you can't get either one back."

"I like that, maybe I'll take your advice."

"Maybe is good...it's that "no" that always gets in our way. But don't let me keep you. I'll wave before I leave," he says.

She smiles and starts to clean and prepare menus. Hank strolls into the bar and stares down Graham as he wipes down the counter-top. Hank doesn't take his eyes off him as he looks for a seat suitable for conversation and close to the exit in case he becomes violent. The feeling of calmness he had while talking to Giselle has washed away. The grieving father is growing more disgruntled with every second passing. He decides to make his presence known. "Excuse me!" Hank shouts.

"Oh hello, Sir," Graham laughs. "I wasn't paying attention, didn't hear you come in."

"The music is kind of loud so it's hard to hear anything, but don't worry the element of surprise runs in my family," Hank jokes casually. "But if you aren't too busy, I'll take a Hennessy on the rocks, make it a double, will you."

Graham smiles then hurries to make his drink. "Yeah, I'm sorry about that. Usually, there's nobody in here after our brunch rush, so I'm prepping the bar for the dinner crowd. My name is Graham and I'll be your server, would you like to see a food menu?"

Hank chugs his drink and pushes the empty in front of Graham. "No sir, but since I have your attention; I would like another drink."

Graham chuckles, "A double?"

"Please and the same glass."

"You got it," he smirks, "You sure know how throw it down." Graham chucks in fresh ice and fills the glass to the rim. "Have you been here before?"

Hank sips. "Never."

"Hmm, something about you seems familiar. You wouldn't have a brother by the name of Tom, would you?"

"No," Hank answers. Halfway through his second drink, he spots a short, stubby, blonde-haired woman bursting through the kitchen doors. She waddles to the end of the bar and greets Graham with a high-five. Although there are no other customers, with the country music blaring, Hank can't make out what they're saying.

Soon as he entered, his first intentional thought was to start asking questions immediately but after he saw Giselle's tender face, something about her presence made him want to take a seat and have a drink to calm his nerves. Yet while Graham and Tina continue their conversation, the tension he's feeling begins to grow. Hank starts to regret the decision to leave his wife and confront whoever is to blame for his son's death. An overwhelming cloud of grief begins to overcast his anger. The disgruntled father reaches for a cocktail napkin and places it on top of his drink. With a violent rage seeping through his body, he quietly gets up. "Your bathroom?"

"Straight back and take a right, just follow the sign," Tina answers.

"Thanks." He carefully paces to the restroom. Before he reaches the right he was instructed to take, he stops and turns, "Excuse me, Miss, what's your name? I know Graham's but I don't know yours."

She smiles. "It's Tina."

"Ah, Tina. What a nice name... and the bathroom is to my right?" She confirms with a simple head nod. When he reaches the entrance to the men's bathroom, something forces him to pause before entering, he zones out with a blank stare. When he finally comes too, he speeds right into the same stall his son would sneak off to and snort cocaine. He aimlessly paces around the 4x6 structure. He suddenly notices a white powdery substance on the top of the toilet tank. The sight alone, is the tipping point for him, he kicks the cover of the tank off and punches the stall door. He clenches his fist as sits on the toilet, engulfed in frustration and agony as tears begin to pour. He weeps in silence.

Soon after, Hank is all cried out, he exits the stall then washes his face. Still plagued with being in the place responsible for his son's death; he manages to administer a calm exterior. He tugs down on the paper dispenser and dries off. He takes three deep breaths before exiting the bathroom then makes his way back to the bar. Before taking his seat, he removes the napkin from the top of his glass.

"You were in there for a while, everything okay?" Graham questions.

"Yeah, I'm fine," Hank replies as he finishes the rest of his drink then signals for another.

Graham grabs the half-filled bottle then pours it over ice. "Not too many come in here asking for Hennessy this early. Special occasion?"

"It was my son's favorite drink."

"Oh really?" Graham asks, "How did that come about?"

"You ever watch the first Godfather?"

"Yeah, who hasn't?"

Hank chuckles. "Well the scene where Michael has to flee to Italy, there's a fifth of Hennessy on a nightstand and since my son's name was Michael. He thought it would be cool to have his first drink be what he saw in that scene."

"Hennessy!" Graham shouts. "Most of the people who come in here and order Hennessy are Black, it's funny, you know."

"What is?"

"We just hired someone named Michael and he loves Hennessy, and he's also Black. He'll be here in about an hour or so but he usually shows up thirty minutes early. I don't know anyone who would show up to work that fucking early, something is definitely wrong with that kid."

Hanks is taken aback by Graham's comment and he clinches his glass in restraint. "What do you mean there's 'something wrong with that kid?' You sound as if showing up early for work is a bad thing. Maybe he just likes to be punctual with his timing." His voice becomes higher in pitch. "Would you prefer my—I mean, this kid to constantly show up late?"

"Nah, I'm not saying anything bad about the gu—"

"You just said there's something wrong with that kid. You just fucking said that!" Hank shouts.

"Easy man, relax. It's not that serious. Do you know this kid or something? You're getting mighty defensive."

"N-no, not at all. I'm just saying there's nothing wrong with being early for work. Didn't mean to come off so abruptly. I did twenty years in the military, and if you weren't early to pretty much everything then you were considered late. Whoever that boy's parents were, they taught him well, and they should be proud." Hank chugs his drink halfway down, and as the liquor warms his chest, it settles his shaking left leg. He leans into the bar and whispers, "Hey, Graham."

"Another round?"

"Yeah sure why not, but ah…" Hank flashes a fifty-dollar bill then under his breath he mutters, "You know where I can score some blow?"

Graham stops polishing glasses and gives him a side-eye. "Oh, you party?"

"A little something…whenever I could find it. The guy I used to it get off is locked up. I and my wife have been going through some things as of late, that's why I'm here. I know all the good shit is always at the bars, so you think you could help me out? I'm just looking for a quick pick me up." Hank stares with desperation in his eyes.

"Sure, I think I could help you out." Graham waves down Tina as she passes from the dining room to the bar. He motions for her to meet him at the other end of the bar and there, he whispers something in her ear. Tina looks bewildered and then grins. She rushes over to Hank's barstool.

"Heard you looking for a quick pick me up?" She asks.

Hank gulps down the rest of his drink and smiles. "Ahh, yes, yes I am. Can you help me out?

"Yeah, I think can. Hold on, I gotta make a quick call."

"Alright." Hank signals Graham for a refill. Tina whips out her phone and after three rings she says, "Walk over." She ends the call and jams the phone in her back pocket then turns to Hank. "Hey, you feel like taking a stroll?" she questions.

"Yeah, we gotta go get it?"

"Yup, she's right there in the Lux Apartments, literally a two-minute walk. You up for it?" she laughs.

"I'll be quite fine, let's go!" He belches loudly then slams his half-filled glass on the bar counter. Graham and Tina both gawk and laugh.

"You better get there quick, Tina, and make it fast. This guy has only been here all of twenty minutes and already, he's on his last leg," Graham jokes.

"Hey, fuck you, buddy." Hank slaps his leg and laughs along. "I'm just kidding Graham Cracker, HA. Graham Cracker, I bet you get that all the time. I'm just messing around with you; you're a good guy," he hiccups, "and a great bart-barten-BAR KEEP!" Hank takes the rest of his Hennessy and throws it back till there is nothing left. The liquor burns as it travels from his esophagus to his liver. He staggers towards

Tina, then throws his arm around her. "Come on, Tina let's get to it."

She laughs. "Just wait one second there, let me clock-out." She unhooks herself from Hank's arm and marches around both the bar and Graham to punch out before she rushes back to Hank. "Alright, Mr. Drunky, try and hold it together."

Hank almost falls over his stool as he stumbles behind. He begins to realize he hasn't been this inebriated since Michael graduated from college. He took his son to his first strip club that night and got so intoxicated he threw up on the sidewalk right after exiting the club's doors. Michael hardly drank back then so it was safe for him to drive them home. Soon as they got into the car, Michael watched his father recline his seat back, and before he knew it; Hank was out like a light. All and all, Hank felt Michael knew the man who took a strung-out newborn home some twenty-odd years ago was happy and proud of what his son had accomplished.

Hank doesn't recall much from the night of Michael's commencement but what he does remember is his son's ear-to-ear smile. Michael never had to wear braces or a retainer. Unfortunately, Hank's own teeth grew in horribly crooked, and at the age of ten he was deemed "metal mouth" by his grade school peers on into his late teens. The month before he met Nancy, he was fortunate enough to have the braces taken out. He was always a little jealous of his son's perfect choppers, but all that meant was his biological parents had great smile-genes. But a great smile wasn't the only thing Michael inherited from his maternal parents which is one of the many reasons why Hank and Nancy Weathers wanted to give a premature drug-addicted infant love in the most unconditional and purest form.

As Hank and Tina make their way towards Tracie's apartment, fifty feet ahead, the local police have blocked off the area where his son's body was found.

Half of the walking path is covered with pedestrians who stand behind the fluorescent yellow police tape, and beside white signs in big bold black letters on both sides of the tape that that read,: 'Police Line: Do Not Cross.'

"What the fuck happened here?" Tina asks.

Hank struggles to keep his composure in order not to go into a state of hysteria again, and yet he looks as if he doesn't have the slightest clue of what is going on. Due to all the alcohol he's consumed, his words slur as he responds, "I heard something on the news; I think they said someone jumped off the bridge last night and they pulled a body out of the river."

"Did they say who?"

"They," he hiccups, "No, they didn't."

"Wow, that's some crazy ass shit. I hope it's nobody I know..." Tina notices a uniform police officer then decides to catch her attention. "Excuse me, officer lady!" She yells.

"I need you to take a few steps back, please, this is a crime scene," the policewoman instructs. "How can I help you, Ma'am?"

"I have a friend who lives in this building and there's no other way to get through. I was wondering would it be okay to walk through if we stay to the left of the police line and outta the way?"

"Sure, just make sure when you leave, you find me, or another officer and tell them where you're going."

"You got it, Ms. Officer, thank you so much," Tina replies.

In return, the policewoman nods signaling the two now have free passage. With Tina still leading the way, she abruptly turns and to her surprise, she bumps into Hank, who she didn't realize was following her so close. "Damn, man, can I have some space?" Tina scolds then shoves him to the left. "Excuse me, officer," she shouts at a plain-clothed male cop.

"Yes!" The officer yells.

"Sorry to bother you, but did you guys find out who jumped in the river?"

"All we know is that the person worked in the neighborhood and lived closed by. That's all I can confirm at the moment, please move along, Miss."

Hank and Tina continue to the front of the complex. Before they get closer to the entrance, she reaches around and whips out her cellphone and clicks 'recent call' then in the top column is Tracie's contact. Tina mashes on her name and stares at Hank. The call rings twice.

"Yo, hoe," Tracie answers.

Tina is in awe that she picked up the call so quickly. In her excitement, she gives Hank a silent, surprised gasp. "Where you at bitch? I'm outside."

"What did I tell you about bringing people to my house? I swear you want me to go to jail. How the fuck am I going to take care of Cam if she ends up in state custody and I'm locked up? You don't see all those fucking cops on the side of the building? Come the fuck on Tina, you must want me to get arrested."

Tina's tone lowers, "You can see me?"

Twenty yards from the entrance Tracie ends the call then screams, "Yo, what the fuck?"

Hank whispers, "Is that your friend?"

" Yeah - that's my main bitch, right there," Tina says under her breath.

"If that's your 'main bitch' then why is she walking over here like she's going to punch you square in the mouth?"

"I don't know, she's always like that. Trace stays mad about something—if it's not one thing it's another," Tina answers. With Tracie a few paces away from where they're standing, Tina becomes overwhelmed with suspicion. "But what I do know… is you've been asking way too many fucking questions." All of sudden, Tina turns and snatches at Hank's shirt. If this was the during the Cold War his initial reaction would've been to break her arm in two, instead, he just stands there with his hands in his pockets.

"What are you doing?" he smirks.

Tina releases her grasp, "Sorry, I had to see if you were wearing a wire, you never know who you're really dealing with."

Hank fixes his appearance, "You're right about that, you never know who you're dealing with. But, rest assured that I'm who you see in the flesh and nothing more."

As Tracie approaches, Hank can sense his presence is untrusted. He then realizes he's drunker than he intended to get. There's a piercing anxiousness that runs through his body as Tracie draws near.

Out of nowhere, a rush of nausea sets in, the liquor has finally cashed in.

Given the fact he only ate a few appetizers at the anniversary party, (Nancy got the call from Ragsdale right before the guests were served dinner), the last time he had something sustainable was yesterday's breakfast, which was a favorite of his and Michael's: Apple Jack's cereal.

Tracie scowls at the two. "Who the fuck is this?"

"Uh, uh this is…Je- Hank?" Tina guesses.

"Hello, Tracie and yes, my name is Hank, it's a pleasure to make your acquaintance."

"Wait... how the hell do you know my name?" She shakes her head at Tina. "Whatever... well Hank, I don't know you and Tina shouldn't have brought you here. Did you check him for wires at least?"

"I did."

"Jesus fucking Christ, Tina, I was just kidding. What the fuck is wrong with you? I'm sorry about that, Hank, but whatever you were looking for I don't have it. Sorry."

"Come on man, I'm no fucking cop." Hank whips out his wallet and pulls out his last twenty-dollar bill. "Look, I know it's not much but I'll give you an extra twenty just to get fifty worth, come on man I need this. I told my wife I wasn't going to go to the bar but I just lost my job. And, this shit is killing me. Even though I don't know you, I didn't mean to make you uneasy but I'm begging you, find it somewhere in your heart to help out a desperate man..."

Tracie ponders his desperation then ice-grills a disgraced Tina, "All right man." Then right out of Hank's hand, she snatches the cash. "You're going to have to do something for me if you want what you're looking for."

"Anything, whatever you want," Hank pleads.

"If you want what you came here for... you're going to have to do it in front of me."

The search for who is to blame behind his son's death has gone way over his head and not to mention he's never sniffed cocaine a day in his life, let alone seen it in person. Beads of sweat start to form on the back his neck and palms. He has no clue what he is about to embark on, yet he manages to crack a smile and say, "Sure, that's not a problem at all." He and Tina follow Tracie to the entrance door and watch as she punches in the code to enter the building.

With Tina leading the way into the elevator; Hank is ready to defecate his pants. His back is covered in perspiration by the time they reach the second floor. Hank begins to search his pockets for his phone but realizes he left it at the bar. So engulfed in his madness; he forgot about his wife. "She must be thinking the worst, I'm a piece of fucking shit," is the only thing on his mind as he steps onto the fourth-floor hallway. With every second passing, he begins to regret almost every decision he's ever made regarding his son's upbringing.

"You party often, Hank?" Tracie questions.

"Party?" Hank asks.

She presses her left nostril and makes a sniffing gesture. "Yeah like..."

"No, can't say that I do. To be honest with you, a coworker introduced me it to at an office party a while back. I had a little too much to drink, he took me to the bathroom and gave me a bump, and before I know it; I was sober as a bitch."

Tracie rummages through her purse for the keys. "That's believable."

Hank coughs up a nervous chuckle. "Why would you say that? I'm telling the truth of course."

"Yeah, I can figure that much. The only reason your story sticks is, one of my best friends works with that," she points at Tina, "numb-nut."

"Hey," Tina cries.

"Anyway, like I was saying," Tracie leads the way into the kitchen. "My close friend, who, I introduced to coke when we worked together a few years back just bought an eight-ball off me last night." She gasps. "Oh, that just reminded me to get the rest of that money off that son of a bitch." She reaches for her phone and starts to think "it could wait" then places it on the countertop. "You know, he's probably just walking into work, I'll call him after the dinner rush."

Hank is so intoxicated he can't pick up on one-word Tracie uttered. The only thing to catch his attention is the kitchen island. It's scattered with red solo cups, rusty razors blades, and tiny white dust particles that he assumes is coke residue and he couldn't be more right. He stands as the ladies take seats on the same side of the island. Hank is inwardly disgusted to think his son, a former hockey star and a college grad, actually considered Tracie's shared apartment suitable for his leisure.

He starts to think, how can a woman live like this?." He'd rather stand the entire time with his hands buried in pockets and so he does.

The thought of taking a sitting down position anywhere in the loft revolts him. "I know you don't usually fuck around like this, Hank, right?" Tracie asks.

"Correct," he replies.

"Yeah, so you don't fuck around like this but this shit right here is the best coke in town, it'll have you up like a motherfucker." She removes a little more than an eight ball from her purse and places it on the broken mirror. She then retrieves a baby feeding spoon from the dish tray to fish out three spoonfuls of cocaine.

Hank's heart begins to race, simultaneously his stomach starts to jump. He senses a troubling need to make a bowel movement, yet he appears unscathed. "So is that the fifty bag?" he asks.

"No, this is just for the community. You gotta try it before you buy remember?" Tracie refines the coke under Hank's twenty. Soon after she lifts the bill; she takes a debit card and scratches off the substance of the money onto the mirror. She then removes the leftover sprinkles with her pointer finger and rubs it between her gums. Hank can't help but stare at Tina and how she stands greedily gawking at Tracie as she separates the coke into three lines the width and length of an average pen.

Tina's face lights up as if she were a child waking up on Christmas Day. He wants nothing more than to take the jagged-edged part of the mirror and slit her throat to watch her blood seep into the cracks of the floor tiles. But for now, he can only imagine the act of piercing her carotid and wait.

"Damn bitch, hurry up, I gotta get back to work before A.G. notices I'm gone," Tina cries.

Tracie rolls her eyes. "Don't get your panties in a bunch. You know you're about to get high for free so I don't know what you're complaining about, you act like you put money in my hand for these lines. So for once just shut your mouth and wait your turn."

Tina waves her off and starts scrolling through her phone. With each passing second, Hank's bowels are becoming more and more unpleasant and difficult to ignore. Tracie rolls the twenty up and rails the smallest line. After the strip of coke disappears, she lightly places the bill on the glass and breathes through her nose as hard she can to capture the drip. As Tina reaches for the coke, Tracie swats her hand away.

"Damn Tina, you're that thirsty, shit, don't you have any decency? We have a guest in our presence." Tracie slides the mirror over and hands Hank the twenty. "Here you go. Be careful though, you might shit yourself, it's some really good shit," she snorts and laughs.

Without hesitation he places the bill under his right nostril then adjusts his body to be parallel to the mirror. Right before he gets ready; he pauses and questions why his only son would succumb to this type of living. Stricken with guilt and remorse, Hank contemplates snorting the coke. He glances at Tina, then at one of the razor blades. His eyes become blurred, as he flashes back to seeing Michael's lifeless body on that steel bed. With feverish haste, he inhales the entire line. The powder reaches the back of the throat which causes him to gag. The drip doesn't wait as it did for his son, it hits him instantly. He's puzzled by the rush and taste that sits in the back of his throat. His eyes widen and an ability to hyper-focus sets in as he starts to feel less impaired as he did when he first walked out of Second House. In order to protect his cover, Hank pretends he's only reacting to how "good" the coke is. He tilts his head back and snorts. "Wow, that's pretty. You weren't kidding, this stuff is top-notch."

Tracie smiles. "That's funny."

Hank sighs. "Don't tell me you think I'm lying again."

She takes the plate and passes it to Tina saying, "The friend I was talking about before we came in says, 'top-notch' so it's funny hearing someone else say it. Now, that I think about it... you sorta remind me of him."

"Oh yeah, THAT'S who you remind me of!" Tina yells, "That sooo fucking weird." Tina then snorts her line. "Yup, that's the one! I'm alive now. But yeah man, you totally remind me of this kid I work with. I mean, you're not Black so it's not by looks or anything, just the way you sound. I guess you guys have the same uhh, uhh..."

"Vernacular, you retard!" Tracie shouts.

"Yeah, whatever she said. But yeah, you remind me of that Black bastard for sure," Tina laughs.

"I'm sure he wasn't—I mean, I'm sure he's not that bad," Hank adds.

Tracie sets more powder on the mirror and begins to break it down. "He's not, she's exaggerating."

"Woah, you're talking about the same person that took Billie's job, right? He knew what he was doing soon as A.G. hired him."

"Nah, I don't think Mikey planned that at all, you don't know him like I do. He just rubs you the wrong way, you should really give the kid a break." Tracie rails another line and offers Hank one more. Now that he is feeling the sensation of his first cocaine high, he is reluctant to decline. He takes the mirror and bill and then snorts half of the biggest line. With the powder from the last line still trapped in his nose-hairs, the cocaine causes him to gag twice as hard. Soon after he catches his breath, a horrible rumble in his abdomen strikes. Hank has to pass wind but is fearful of doing so as it might immediately lead to more, based on his stomach's current signaling.

Hank throws the bill down and shoves the plate aside. "Do you have a bathroom I can use?"

"Yeah, it's right behind you," Tracie says. Hank clenches his buttocks and speeds into the bathroom, then as he shuts the door, Tracie yells, "Make sure you courtesy flush, can't have you stinking up my house!"

While Hank is relieving himself, the ladies fill their noses with more cocaine. A few minutes pass and Tina decides she's in dire need of a drink to take the numbing edge off. Before she can make her way over to the fridge, she's interrupted by Billie's entrance.

"Hey, Bill you look nice for once," Tina greets.

"Please, he just took a shower and put on a clean shirt," Tracie cracks.

Billie silently shovels through the kitchen and into the living room then unbuttons his dress shirt, "I start at that Irish pub tomorrow, you know, Mickey's..."

"Wow, that didn't take long. Way to go Bill!" Tina shouts. "We should celebrate."

"No the fuck we shouldn't," Tracie interjects. "He's still gotta cover

338

for this month's rent."

Billie throws his body onto the couch. "Sad to say it but she's right."

"Whatever man, you know none of this would be happening if it weren't for that uppity nigger," Tina states.

"Yeah, but—" Billie catches a whiff of Hank's feces as the odor creeps into the apartment. "What the fuck is that? Is somebody taking a shit?"

Tracie laughs. "That's a stray she brought from Second House," she says with a grimace. "And, yeah, he's in the bathroom taking a shit."

"What the fuck, Tina? We told you about bringing people here for that bullshit, stop looking for free shit!" Billie shouts.

Tina frowns. "You should be the one to talk. Mr. Sticky fingers."

"Ay, shut up, that wasn't called for. Yo Bill, you want a line?" Tracie offers. She then cuts up a sizable line and slides the mirror in front of Billie.

"Who is that guy Tina?" he asks.

"He's just a nice dude, he's going through some shit right now. He gave me a good vibe so I decided to help him out. Besides, Tracie always complaining about how she needs more money so I decided to help."

He rails his line as Hank exits the bathroom. Both men awkwardly stare at each other, and almost instantly they can sense some familiarity. Hank tosses the paper towel he used to dry his hands into a wicker basket right outside the restroom door and then attempts to break the excruciating silence by extending his hand in introduction, "Hello, my name is Hank. I'm assuming your name is Billie." He grins. Billie nods and remains unmoved by his presence but to be cordial; he shakes Hank's hand with a noticeable lack of firmness. Hank realizes right away he has worn out his welcome.

"Well Tracie, I think it's time I hit the road," Hank says.

"Ah, stay awhile, don't mind him. He's just mad he got fired," Tracie replies.

"Dude," Billie shouts, "What the fuck?"

Tina smirks, "Well, it's true, you did get fired."

"If you don't mind me asking what did you get fired for?" Hank asks.

"Well, basically calling who use to be my friend a nigger, because he was acting like one but at the same time I was just joking and it's not like I said it to his face. I was talking to a friend who actually got into it with the kid 'cause he spilled food all over him. But, before they got into it, I guess another customer overhead what I said and told my manager. Honestly," Billie shakes his head in disappointment, "I had it coming. I guess that was the tipping point."

"Oh, that's unfortunate you lost your job, but you can't blame my—I mean that person for what you did, that's unfair and it shows that you have poor accountability skills. I'm not judging you at all and I can't because I don't know you. I'm just stating the obvious; learn to own up to your mistakes."

Tracie snorts another line then shoves the mirror in front of Hank. When he declines, Billie is quick to take it. "Ah, I mean really I was just kidding when I called him that. I'm sure you can relate, Hank."

"No, no I can't"

Tina gasps. "Come on dude, you never even cracked a Black joke? There are tons of them. Here's one—"

"I'm sure it's funny, but I don't care to hear it or any of them for that matter, and all those kinds of jokes are usually told in poor taste. Especially from a person who is not a professional comedian. Are you a professional comedian?"

"No, she's definitely not," Tracie adds.

Hank smiles. "And I'm assuming you're not one either, Billie, so why would you even joke about that? Especially since it cost you your occupation."

Billie wipes his nose. "Like I said, we were friends before he took my job; I mean, before I lost my job. Look me and Mike always played around like that so I don't know what the big deal is. I don't know why he had to go and take my job. When in fact, I'm the one who got him the fucking job in the first place. Fucking backstabber. Should've stayed at fucking LBS like the Uncle Tom he is," Billie rants and rails another line.

Hank now sees the connection between his son's suicide and Second House. He shoves his hands back in his pockets, clenches his fist, then clears his throat. "Hey, Tracie you got that bag for me? I'm going to head out now."

"Sure, let me get a baggie and get it ready for you." She rises from her seat and walks over to the kitchen sink. To the left, there's a drawer where the cutlery is kept and under the silverware tray is where Tracie keeps her bags for packaging cocaine. She retrieves one, returns to her purse and fishes out a digital scale. She then carefully places it on the countertop, mashes the 'on' button, and from the bag filled with coke, she picks up a boulder shaped piece. Using her fingers, she breaks it in half and places the smaller half on the scale. The weight comes out to a .5 as Tracie cries out, "There's nobody who eyeballs coke better than me, fucking nobody!" She loops the bag into a knot then hands it over.

"Thank you for services Tracie; I have to get back to the bar and close my tab and convince my wife, I took a stroll on the beach or something," Hank says as he reaches for his phone and remembering it's not in any of his pockets, shrugs. "Well, I bid you all adieu."

Billie and Tina gasp, while Tracie just stares. Tina blurts out, "That's fucking crazy."

"What is?" Hank asks.

Tracie finishes railing a line. "Mike says that same thing every time he leaves, that's why she said that."

He starts for the exit. "You don't say?"

Billie takes the mirror from Tracie and snorts a line, "Yeah, it's pretty weird if you ask me."

"Yeah... I guess it is. Well, thanks again, Tracie. Billie, it was a pleasure, hope to see you soon. I would take your number down Tracie, but I seem to have misplaced my phone."

"Well, whenever you find it just get it from Tina. Matter of fact, don't you have to get back to work soon?" Tracie asks.

Tina jumps for her purse. "Oh shit, you're right. A.G.'s going to have a fit if sees I'm not there. Mind if I get another line for the road, Trace?"

"Sure mooch, anything thing for you, mooch" She laughs then cuts up another line. "You want one for the road Hank?"

He declines with a smirk. "Thanks but no thanks. I'm pretty high for the most part. And I'm almost certain my wife is having a nervous breakdown right about now. So, I'm going to head back to the restaurant and settle up." He showcases the baggie then flicks it. "But I got what I came for, so everything should be alright, thanks again."

Tina rails her line then jumps up and scurries pass Hank out the kitchen door. "Alright homies, see you after work," she yells as she darts down the hall.

"I guess that my cue...hope to see you guys soon. It's been a pleasure," Hank smiles as he closes the door behind him. His grin drops immediately. When Tina reaches the elevator. She immediately starts mashing the call button as if it'll make it arrive faster. He notices the elevator's indicator blinks "2."

He turns his steady trot into a light jog to catch up. As Hank approaches; he begins to imagine his large hands wrapped around her loose neck as her arms wail aimlessly around, which would cause her to feel, a slow and agonizing death. The effects from the cocaine fill his mind with rage and anxiousness, and he begins to think, "with my credentials and the fact that I just lost my son. The judge will grant me plenty of leniencies, maybe I'll do five to seven; I'll get out in three with good behavior. I could kill this fucking bitch right now and it'll totally be justified…"

As the elevator car makes its way up, Hank's murderous daydream becomes more brazen. He blurts out, "Maybe a bare-naked choke would do it."

"What?" Tina questions.

"Maybe artichokes," he says.

"Artichokes?"

"Yeah, I think that's what my wife told me to pick up before I left the house, it's so hard to remember anything, this stuff has me all over the place. Feels like this elevator is taking forever, doesn't it?"

Tina rolls her eyes then she rapidly presses the call button with, "Sure." The elevator indicator shows that the car has stopped on the third floor. Hank's intentions now, feel written in stone—as soon as they step foot on the elevator, he is going to end Tina's life by asphyxiating. Before doing so he will tell her who he is, who his son is, and the reason she is going to die a slow and painful death. As the car starts for their floor, Hank decides to stretch, then from left to right, quickly cracks his neck. Tina becomes impatient and starts to tap her foot until the elevator car finally arrives. Hank mentally prepares to end her life as the doors slide open.

Tina gasps loudly, "Oh my God, how are you, little bug?" She tightly embraces Tracie's daughter, Cam, who is accompanied by her grandmother.

Cam squirms. "I'm good Tina, but you're squeezing me too tight."

Tina releases her grasp and grips Cam's face. "I know I am sweetie but I'm trying to squeeze all the cuteness out of you." She grazes the child's puffy cheeks before she rises. "How are you, Lorna? It's good to see you."

The grandmother scoffs, "I would say the same for you but you know... you got a smoke on you? I left mine in the car."

Tina sighs. "Sure, you did." She reaches in her purse and comes up with a loose Marlboro Light.

Lorna lets go of her granddaughter's hand as she takes the cigarette then lights it. "Grandma, I don't think you can smoke in here," Cam states.

"I survived two heart surgeries, not to mention raising your carpet-licking mother who I stuck by and sent her money while she was in jail pregnant with you. I'm sorry Cammy, but Grandma is gonna smoke whenever and wherever she wants." She exhales a thick cloud of smoke into a ceiling vent. "And, ain't no one in or out of this building gonna tell me different." She turns to Hank. "Who the fuck are you?"

He smiles. "Just a man, trying to get home to his wife, Ma'am."

"If you're smart then you'll get there as fast as you can and stay there. Don't know what a nice-looking man like yourself is doing with a sack of nothing like her."

Tina frowns. "Lorna, I'm right here, you could at least wait till we get on the elevator to talk shit, geez."

"Why wait? You know me better than that by now, come on Cammy let's get you to your mother."

While Cam trails behind Lorna she yells out, "Tina?"

"Yeah, babe."

"Is Michael in the loft?"

"No, why?"

"'Cause I saw him jump into the river last night and wanted to surprise him and tell him that I saw hi—"

Tina's face turns white. "Wait, you saw who jump in the river last night, sweetie?"

"Michael, my mom's friend. And, yeah it was last night after I went to use the bathroom. I went on the balcony to get to some air and there he was standing over the rail."

"Are you sure it was him?" Tina asks.

Cam tugs on her arm-cast. "Positive. The street light shines very brightly on the path. I always wanted to know how the water felt. He's going to take me to the ice-rink today."

"Girl, be quiet you ain't see no one jump in anything. Don't pay her no mind, you know children are always telling their little made-up stories. And, she's been talking about that damn ice-rink all day, and personally, I can't wait, she's been working my last nerve. It'll be good for her to be around a decent person for once," Lorna says and pulls on her Granddaughter.

"Alright, say goodbye it's time to go inside, you'll see Michael later," Lorna says and puffs then ashes her cigarette directly on the floor. Cam waves the two off.

The timer to the elevator car beeps as the door creeps shut. Hank quickly reacts and catches it before it fully closes. Tina in disbelief of what she just heard, stands there, staring at the other end of the hallway as the door close.

"Excuse me, Tina don't you have to get to work?" He asks.

Tina shakes out of her doze. "Oh, oh, yeah." As she rejoins him inside the elevator, Hank is stricken with pity. She presses the button to the ground floor and he, intrigued by her silence, decides to inquire.

"So, that little girl knew your co-worker?"

"Yeah, he knew her since she was younger. He would watch her whenever her mom worked or whenever Lorna was too high to do anything," she replies.

"That little girl also said she saw him jump into the river. I mean, I know children have a knack for saying things but she isn't lying about what she saw. And, if tha—"

Tina snaps and shouts, "Shut the fuck up, just shut the fuck up. Please..."

Hank stares bewilder and yet, he's somewhat pleased to see her reaction, which makes the decision to not strangle her to death an easier option. He takes a step back for her to walk into the lobby then he makes his way off the elevator.

"Look, I'm sorry I just lost my shit, but I don't even fucking know you and I just found out through a fucking child that my co-worker may have just committed suicide." She pauses then collects herself and resumes. "I'm sorry, I just need a minute."

Amid Tina's hysteria, Hank notices she left her bag in the elevator, he clenches the bag of coke in his pocket and retrieves her bag before the door closes. Without Tina noticing, he slips the baggie between two tampons and her clutch. He then hands over the purse. "No need to apologize. What you just found out is a lot to process, but understand that you have to readjust and get back to the restaurant to inform your employer, that's if the police haven't already. There's nothing about standing in this lobby that will help."

Tina drags both palms down her face. "You're right, let's go." The path-walk is swarmed with more uniformed cops than before. Tina is reluctant to seek out the policewoman who gave them passage when first arriving at the complex. Hank trails behind as he contemplates whether to disclose his son's suicide note to the Second House management.

For now, he satisfies some of his grief by watching Tina sulk in misery as she staggers along. They continue outside of the police barricade and onto the one-way street that leads to the bus terminal. From there, they wait for oncoming traffic to pass to cross the street. In the front of Second House, right next to the patio stands A.G. with his phone pressed to his ear. Hank pretends to be a regular pedestrian as he strolls right past him toward the entrance.

A.G. shoves his cell in his front pocket and faces Tina. "Where'd you go?"

"I had to run over to Billie's really quick, I left my apron over there last night. And, I wanted to see how he was doing, you know... Sorry."

"How is he doing?" he asks.

She wipes her nose. "He's feeling better, I think. He's already found a job."

A.G.'s eyes widen. "Oh really?"

"Yup, right up the street from here, that Irish Pub."

"We'll see how long he lasts there. Billie's like a cat that's always falling off a couch, quick to land on his feet, yet quick to fall off the couch again."

"You got that right."

"You haven't heard from Michael, have you? He's forty minutes late and his phone is going straight to voicemail."

"I don't even have his number, that's funny cause he's usually early."

"Exactly, I hope he didn't quit."

Tina goes mute as she stares down Canal while three police cruisers with sirens blaring approach They come to an abrupt halt as the first car screeches in front of the restaurant. As the cops park their vehicles, here comes Tracie and her daughter, hand-in-hand nearly speed-walking towards them. A.G. becomes distraught as he sees the man who just walked past him consoling his weeping hostess near the entrance. A policeman opens the back passenger seat for Nancy who spots Hank and becomes instantly confused as to why some young woman is crying in her husband's arms. Hank lifts Giselle's face and clears her tears. "My son cared for you deeply. I think you helped him realize who he wanted to be. It's not your fault. Don't ever think that," he says.

"I didn't know, I didn't kn—" Giselle sobs.

"He didn't either."

Officer Ragsdale enters behind a bevy of police and approaches Hank. "Mr. Weathers, I told you I was handling it. But, I understand. I'm glad you managed to remain safe."

Hank removes himself from Giselle, pulls Ragsdale aside, and speaks in a voice too low for Giselle to hear. The officer nods and listens carefully. "Well, to be quite frank with you, you would have made one hell of a detective. Can you point to the woman now?" Ragsdale asks.

Hank clears his throat and replies, "The woman with the pink purse, talking to that tall gentlemen."

"Thank you." As Ragsdale approaches Tina, she becomes anxious and lights a cigarette.

"Excuse me, Officer, can I help you?" A.G. asks.

"Do you work here, Sir?" Ragsdale questions.

"I'm the General Manager."

"Okay, just the person I needed to speak to. I'm sorry to inform you but one of your employees, Michael H. Weathers, committed suicide last night by jumping into the river at the Lux Apartment pathway."

A.G. gasps. "Oh my god."

"Unfortunately, Sir, that's not all the bad news I have. The woman standing next to you, is her name Tina?"

"Ye-yes it."

Tina trembles as she tosses away her cigarette.

"Ma'am, it's been reported that you are carrying an illegal narcotic. I'm going to ask you to dump the contents of your purse onto the floor here. Will you do that for me please?"

Tina's eyes well up. "A.G. what is he saying? I have to do what?"

"Tina, everything will be fine, just take your purse and turn it upside down. That's all he asking."

She turns her purse to the ground as her concealer, clutch, and a few tampons fall onto the pavement. Officer Ragsdale spots the cocaine Hank slipped in as it lands in a sidewalk crevice. "Ma'am, I need you to put your hands behind your back, you're under arrest."

Tina begins to wail and plead with A.G. to get the officer not to cuff her. A.G. begs her to follow their orders. As the officer clamps the handcuffs, Cam begins to cry as she and her mother approached the detained waitress.

"Officer why are you cuffing her?" Tracie cries.

"This woman is being arrested for possession, please stand back."

Tina turns. "Officer wait, she's the one who sold it to me, please don't arrest me. I'm not from this country. I don't want to be deported."

"What, you fucking bitch!" Tracie shouts as she attempts to flee but not before a nearby uniformed officer tussles her to the ground, leaving her daughter distraught. Hank approaches as other officers help prepare both women for transport. Cam hysterical as Ragsdale tries to get her next of kin information.

"Cam?" Hank leans down and says.

She whimpers. "Who-are you?"

"I'm Michael's father."

She catches her breath. "You are?"